IN THE SHADOW OF THE PAST, A NEW GENERATION SEEK

Renno—Proud namesak[...] dian, he has served a[...] emissary for three pr[...] Now he faces the grea[...] the torch of his wisdom and leadership to future generations.

Little Hawk—A proud Seneca soldier like his father, Renno, he never runs from a fight. A graduate of West Point and a hero of the U.S. Marine Corps, he must now find the will, the resources, and the courage to survive and escape a harrowing fate . . . slavery at sea.

Gunner Griffiths—A British officer on the HMS *Cormorant,* he is a brutal taskmaster who exercises his authority with an iron hand and a cutting lash. He'll stop at nothing to crush the spirit of the one man who dares to defy him: Little Hawk.

Tecumseh—Creator of a great Indian union, he has vowed to win back by force the lands taken from his people. His power is his vision, and his purpose is war—in alliance with the British against the United States.

Ta-na—Renno's youngest son, he must choose between his new bride and the legacy of the White Indian. As his father once fought alongside George Washington, Ta-na's destiny may lie with the army of William Henry Harrison . . . in the war against Tecumseh.

The White Indian Series
Ask your bookseller for the books you have missed

The White Indian Series
Book XXV

WAR
CLOUDS

~~~~~~

Donald Clayton Porter

 Producers of **Children of the Lion,**
The Holts, and **The First Americans.**

Book Creations Inc., Canaan, NY • Lyle Kenyon Engel, Founder

BANTAM BOOKS
NEW YORK • TORONTO • LONDON • SYDNEY • AUCKLAND

WAR CLOUDS

A Bantam Book/ published by arrangement with Book Creations Inc.

Bantam edition / March 1994

Produced by Book Creations Inc.
Lyle Kenyon Engel, Founder

ISBN 0-553-56141-3

Published simultaneously in the United States and Canada

Bantam Books are published by Bantam Books, a division of Bantam
Doubleday Dell Publishing Group, Inc. Its trademark, consisting of the
words "Bantam Books" and the portrayal of a rooster, is Registered in
U.S. Patent and Trademark Office and in other countries. Marca
Registrada. Bantam Books, 1540 Broadway, New York, New York
10036.

PRINTED IN THE UNITED STATES OF AMERICA

OPM   0 9 8 7 6 5 4 3 2 1

WHITE INDIAN FAMILY TREE

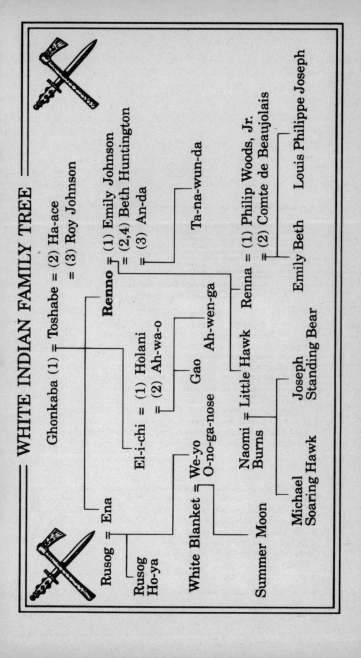

WAR
CLOUDS

Chapter One

On the fiftieth day the Prophet turned his gaunt face upward. He stood within a circle formed by a thousand warriors, who looked not to the sky but to him. He had removed the patch from his right eye, for exposure of the raw, empty socket made his appearance more terrifying.

The sky was cloudless. The day was a promise of the summer to come. As the appointed hour approached, sunlight flooded the landscape, causing a brightness that contrasted with the dark doubt that filled the Prophet's heart. At the prompting of his brother, Tecumseh, the Panther Passing Across, he had promised that he would darken the sun. He had said, "The Great Spirit will seize the sun and eat its light, leaving darkness to envelop the earth."

Nervously, the Prophet, who had changed his name to Tenskwatawa, looked around for his brother; but the Panther, Tecumseh, was nowhere in sight. Incertitude and fear clouded the Prophet's mind. At such times the spirit of his right eye sent sharp pains through his head, reviv-

1

ing memories of the day when, as a boy, he had looked into the sky and, by chance, a flint arrowhead pierced his eyeball. He vividly remembered the pain that was his when Tecumseh pulled the barbed head out, bringing with it blood, fluid, and the eyeball itself.

He remembered how the tribal oracle and medicine man had packed the empty eye socket with buzzard down to stanch the flow of liquids. Grim satisfaction came to him as he recalled the many times he had used his disability to create guilt in the hearts of his brothers—both the one who had shot the arrow and Tecumseh, who had done such a poor job of removing it.

As the sun crept toward its zenith, he could no longer drive from his mind the purpose of his vigil. He could not ignore the hundreds of pairs of eyes that held him in their grasp—waiting, waiting, waiting. Ah, how they would berate him if he failed.

Tenskwatawa's physical presence was commanding. He was a solidly built man, but slim of face. His knife-sharp features were dominated by a large, hooked nose and high, pointed bones over hollow cheeks. One of his ears was noticeably longer than the other. His rare smile was a crooked thing, a smirk that dropped one side of his mouth while raising the other.

There were times when his resentment overflowed, and he gave way to rage. Even now it bubbled just below the surface as he looked up at the sun—bright, hot, painful to his good eye—and remembered the panic he had felt as Tecumseh read a letter from the governor of what the Americans called Indiana Territory. The missive contained the challenge that had brought him to this meadow outside the village of Greenville, with the eyes of one thousand Indians watching him expectantly. He could almost hear the words.

"If God has really empowered him," William Henry Harrison had written in his challenge to the power of the Prophet, "He has doubtless authorized him to perform miracles so that he may be known and received as a prophet. If he is really a prophet, ask him to cause the sun to stand still or the moon to alter its course, the river to cease to flow, or the dead to rise from their graves. If he does these things, you may believe he has been sent from God."

The words put into Tenskwatawa's mouth by Tecumseh in rebuttal to Harrison's letter had been even more frightening to the Prophet.

"Harrison has said that if I am a prophet, I will cause the sun to stand still. Those are his words. Now listen: Fifty days from now the sky will be cloudless. When the sun reaches the middle of the sky, the Great Spirit will take it into his mouth and hide it. Darkness will come in the middle of the day, and the stars will glow above us. Birds will go to their roosts, and the little brothers of the night will waken to begin their hunt. Then, as the white chief Harrison has said, you will know that I speak for the god of the Shawnees, Moneto."

So it was that on the fiftieth day they waited. They waited in villages scattered throughout the lands north of the Ohio, for the Prophet spoke for Tecumseh; and those who supported the Panther Passing Across knew that Tecumseh's dream of uniting all tribes as one would fade if the prediction failed. Although there were many who stood with the man who preached the necessity of a Pan-Indian confederation against the encroachments of the white man, there were also many who knew the uselessness and pain of opposing the whites, who bred like rabbits.

At the appointed time the Great Spirit ate the sun.

At first it was only a small bite that was taken from the burning orb. A murmur of fear went through the thousand who watched at Greenville. The Prophet lifted his arms and chanted his praise to Moneto. Some who stared too long at the terror in the sky suffered partial blindness and would see the black shadow of the Prophet's miracle for the rest of their lives.

A laugh burst from Tenskwatawa's lips, a shrill cackle more suitable to an ancient crone than to a man. "Behold!" he shouted. "Behold the Great Spirit as he eats the sun! Behold how night comes at midday!"

*   *   *

Vincennes, capital of the Indiana Territory, sat on the edge of a broad prairie on the east bank of the Wabash River. By the Church of St. Francis Xavier were the ruins of an old fort that had been captured by Colonel George Rogers Clark during the War for Independence. Over four hundred homes, some of them made of neat, white-washed planks, swept away from the river in regular rows to outlying gardens of wheat, tobacco, corn, hemp, hops, and fruit trees. In the distance were the forest and mysterious, hundred-foot mounds, said to have been built by prehistoric Indians.

On a rise in the middle of a grove of walnut trees, the first brick mansion in the territory rose to a height of two and a half stories, topped by four large chimneys. Governor William Henry Harrison had traded four hundred acres of land, estimated to be worth a thousand dollars, for the brick alone. The house was called Grouseland. On the day in June when the Prophet stood under a cloudless sky in the center of a ring of one thousand warriors to witness a miracle, Governor Harrison was taking an early lunch with his family.

In its interior, Grouseland was luxurious and civilized. The walls of the large dining room were girded by wainscoting of polished black walnut. A hand-carved mantel graced a large fireplace. The woodwork of the sashes and doors was the work of craftsmen in Chillicothe and Pittsburgh. The glass of the windows had come all the way from England.

Grouseland matched any home in St. Louis for comfort and in living space for a growing family, but it was also built for war. The outside walls were eighteen inches of solid brick with slits for rifle ports. In the attic the windowsills had been built to act as solid and steady firing platforms for sharpshooters. The six-foot-high windows on the other floors were equipped with heavy shutters inside and out, and a stout room in the cellar served as a powder magazine.

To the north and west was the wilderness. Along the Ohio and westward, and even to the south in Kentucky, the old and bloody wars with the Ohio Indian tribes continued; and now two brothers, Tenskwatawa and Tecumseh, were complicating Harrison's efforts to pacify the Indians and keep the peace.

The Prophet and the Panther were Shawnee, members of a tribe that had no land of its own but acted as the Indian equivalent of Hessian mercenaries in exchange for hunting rights in the homelands of others. Only recently the Prophet had stirred new fears among the tribes by going on what had been, literally, a witch hunt. Harrison did not doubt for one minute that the Prophet's actions were undertaken at the behest of his brother Tecumseh.

It was no coincidence, in Harrison's opinion, that most of the so-called witches killed by Tenskwatawa were friendly to the United States. The Delaware chief Teteboxti, who had been among the first to sign Anthony Wayne's Treaty of Greenville, was the first to be condemned by the Prophet. Others were roasted slowly over coals for days until, in terminal agony, they confessed to carrying the paraphernalia of witchcraft—medicine bags and various charms and amulets.

It was Harrison's eldest son, William Henry, Jr., who first noticed the change in the light. He ran to a window and cried out, "Father, come quickly!"

The eclipse of the sun was just beginning. It took Harrison only a moment to realize what was causing the dark shadow to encroach on the sun.

"Anna, hurry," he said to his wife, "bring me the almanac."

It was there in black and white, but he had not noticed it in advance—the statement that a solar eclipse would begin on that June day exactly at noon.

"Tecumseh," Harrison whispered, realizing the ramifications.

"What, dear?" Anna Harrison asked.

"He knew," Harrison said. "He would have known, of course, and now there'll be hell to pay."

The darkness lasted for almost seven minutes, not counting the periods of dimness during the waxing and waning of the eclipse.

"Behold!" the Prophet shouted. "Did I not prophesy truly?"

Some ran into their cabins and hid, but that would not prevent the word from spreading from the great, freshwater lakes of the north down the Father of Waters to the salt sea of the south, from the Ohio to the Mississippi and beyond. The Prophet spoke true. With such enormous powers at his command, could the Prophet be wrong in promising that a united confederacy of the tribes could push the white man back across the Ohio? And the Prophet spoke for Tecumseh.

Tecumseh . . .

The name was whispered. It was shouted with defiance. It was spoken proudly by those who believed and snarled with disdain by those who felt that war against the United States was futile.

Tecumseh . . .

He was a warrior, not a chief. He was everywhere, phantomlike, coming and going with the wind but leaving behind him a dream, a vision of one Indian people. He painted a picture of a time when all tribes would be united to fight as one great, invincible army. He did not coax or beg. He explained. He spoke reason. He reminded them of a time when the first white men came as strangers offering help, asking only that the story of their god be heard. The first of them, men in flowing black robes or white collars, were followed by strong and curious men who wanted only to see what was beyond the next ridge and by sun-bronzed woodsmen with excellent gifts to be traded for the fur of animals. Soon there were fewer animals.

Then came men who squinted and lied and marked trees and rocks and recorded words and figures on paper. These men brought greater and more marvelous gifts to be traded for land. They wanted only a little, and there was so much of it, an endless wilderness stretching in all directions. These men brought their women and children and called the land, which belonged to all, their own. They felled the trees and burned the grasses and slashed the rich earth open with iron plows drawn by lowing oxen. And then the Indian could no longer hunt where he pleased.

They came crying "Peace, peace," those white men with their measuring instruments, with their axes and plows. But if the Indian objected to the presence of the intruders, there came men dressed all alike and carrying muskets with long knives mounted on the end.

"These men killed our fathers and took our women. They plowed the earth over the graves of our ancestors. They brought war, and with each little war came change, for when the fighting was over, with the white man again crying, 'Peace, peace,' the white man's boundary was ever closer to the setting sun."

Tecumseh's message was simple. "Only as one people can we turn aside the flood of white faces. It can be done. It must be done."

To ease the suspicions of Governor Harrison, and to give his growing following ample hunting ground for game, Tecumseh moved his people away from the village at Greenville. The site he chose was far from the Ohio and far from the whites. He built his town on high ground on the north bank of the Wabash two and a half miles below the point where a stream called the Tippecanoe entered. He sent messengers to Vincennes to assure Harrison that he had moved his village to ease the minds of the whites around Greenville and to be closer to Harrison so as to enjoy his protection.

William Henry Harrison received the message from Tecumseh with great formality. He hid his suspicions well when the spokesmen from the new Indian village near the mouth of the Tippecanoe said, "We want only to live in peace, to grow our corn and tend our women, children, and old ones."

Harrison did not ask the question that was in his mind: *And those who come from far away to listen to the words of the Prophet and to Tecumseh, are they talking of peace?*

"War will come, Anna," he told his wife. "The brothers will see to that."

Harrison had his orders, and he remembered them well. They had come originally from Thomas Jefferson. "Our system is to live in perpetual peace with the Indians," the President had written, "and to be just and liberal with them, and to protect them from wrongs at the hands of white men."

But there was more to the policy laid down by Jefferson. The Indians were to be encouraged to adopt the ways of the white man, to learn how to farm and spin and weave. After this was accomplished, Jefferson informed Harrison, "They will perceive how useless to them are their extensive forests and will be willing to pare them off from time to time in exchange for necessaries for their farms and families."

Yes, Harrison knew his mission. He had been with Mad Anthony Wayne when the lands north of the Ohio were opened to white settlement by the victory at Fallen Timbers, and he had learned the art of negotiation as he watched Wayne hammer out the Treaty of Greenville. His goal was the same as Jefferson's—to keep peaceful but relentless pressure on the Indians until the frontier of the United States lay along the Mississippi River.

And, as Jefferson himself had written, "Should any tribe be foolhardy enough to take up the hatchet at any time, the seizing of the whole country of that tribe and driving them across the Mississippi as the only condition of peace would be an example to others and a furtherance of our final consolidation."

There would be war. At the moment Harrison was not prepared for it, but soon he would be ready. It would be necessary to instill discipline into the militia and, he hoped, to have a strong force of regulars sent into the territory from the United States. He wished for just one sublegion of Wayne's American Legion, the force that had marched with fixed bayonets into Fallen Timbers. And he wished for information about the activity of Tecumseh and his brother.

As aide-de-camp to General Wayne, he had often benefited from the reports of two of the finest scouts he'd ever seen in action, two men whom he counted among his friends. He had seen them only once since Fallen Timbers, when they came through Indiana Territory on the trail of Aaron Burr's ill-fated and overrated army. Right now he needed men like those friends, men like crusty, old Roy Johnson and his son-by-marriage, the Seneca sachem Renno. With just two men such as they, he would not be blind to events being promulgated by the Shawnee brothers.

Thomas Jefferson was in the last year of his presidency. The word was that the next president would be another Virginian, little James Madison. Harrison had no direct knowledge of Madison's character or of his personality. Jefferson, he knew. He decided that if he was to get anything done regarding a buildup of federal troops in the territory, his best chance was with Jefferson. He took pen in hand and, at the end of his letter, added: "I wonder, Mr. President, if you know how to contact a man who has been of service to you in the past and to General Washington before you. If so, I would be grateful if you would forward the enclosed letter to the Seneca sachem called Renno, who was chief of scouts for General Anthony Wayne at the Fallen Timbers, or to Colonel Roy Johnson of the Tennessee Militia."

Thomas Jefferson was tired. He was sixty-five years old, and most of his adult life had been spent in service to his state, Virginia, or to his country. He longed for the peace and privacy of the home he had designed for himself and his family, of which only his daughter was left. He yearned for the comfort of the house he called Monticello even more desperately when a bad tooth caused a jaw infection that put him through a month of horrendous pain. He could not find the motivation to, as he expressed it to James Madison, "clean out the Augean stable every night, only to find it filled again in the morning."

There was a dismaying sameness to the job of being president. From the time of his first inauguration, the New England Federalists had done everything within their power to make his task more difficult. Now, once again, New England hotheads were threatening to separate the seaboard states from the Union.

"James," Jefferson said to Madison, the man he had chosen to be his successor, "I am beginning to think of the Embargo Act by its popular nickname."

"The Dambargo," Madison said, nodding. "You've heard, I believe, the verse that is currently making the rounds."

Jefferson's jaw was swollen. He smelled of oil of wintergreen and cloves. He shook his head in negation and winced at the pain.

Madison recited:

> "Our ships all in motion,
> Once whiten'd the ocean;
> They sailed and returned
> With a cargo.

> "Now doomed to decay,
> They are fallen a prey,
> To Jefferson, worms, and embargo."

Jefferson was moodily silent.

"The harbors of New England are forests of idle masts," Madison said. "There are soup kitchens for the unemployed. It is estimated that a full thousand sailors from New York alone have gone to Halifax, where the British have given them employment."

Jefferson frowned bitterly. "They go to those who fired three broadsides from point-blank range into an unprepared American vessel, to the same nation that halts our ships on the high seas and takes our citizens into virtual slavery."

"There are those, Mr. President, who say that there will be a rebellion against the embargo in Congress when it reconvenes."

"But we are hurting our enemy, James," Jefferson said. "The mills in England are idle for lack of American cotton."

"And seventy thousand barrels of flour are souring on

the docks in Philadelphia," Madison countered. "Our people in Pennsylvania say they will vote Federalist in the coming elections. John Randolph—"

Jefferson grimaced at the mention of his old political critic.

"—says the embargo is like cutting off one's toes to cure one's corns, and I'm sure you've read the Federalist statements saying that you're waging war against your own countrymen."

Jefferson waved one hand to show his contempt for Randolph's opinion.

"Smuggling has become a way of life," Madison said. "Bands of men ply the Great Lakes on heavily laden rafts. They are so well armed that they simply defy federal agents who attempt to stop them."

"Are you advocating that I expose myself to charges of inconsistency and disregard of the national honor by backing down?" Jefferson asked.

Madison shrugged. He was a small and rather ugly man, but there was a warmth in him that endeared him to Jefferson. "Just being the devil's advocate, Mr. President."

"I pray, James, that I have not left you with a war after I go home to Virginia."

Madison chuckled. "I have not been elected yet."

"You will be, and it will be up to you to decide whether or not to continue to punish England—"

"And our own people."

"—by enforcing the embargo. May God help you."

"It is my opinion, Mr. President, that conflict is inevitable. England is in dire straits because of the long war with France. She's lashing out in all directions. She condemns us as Yankee dollar grubbers because our merchantmen pay higher wages than the Royal Navy and, thus, tempt men to desert to sign on with an American ship. They say that while England is forced to make war, the Yankees make money. But they will not try to reform their navy so that their ships are no longer floating hells. They will continue to compensate for a shortage of men by pressing American seamen into service by force, for they know that their navy is all that is keeping England alive against Napoleon."

"Well, all such problems and the splendid misery of the Executive Mansion will be yours in a few months, Mr. Madison."

"You're determined to keep the embargo in effect, then?"

"Until, my friend, I am officially freed from the presidential penitentiary," Jefferson replied. "Then the decision will be yours."

"And the war that will surely result will be mine," Madison said.

"You'll have to build a navy, James," Jefferson warned, "but there will be compensations. The British merchant marine will make good pickings for American privateers. And have you considered what a rich prize Canada will make?"

"I have considered that it required the help of France and other friends to enable us to defeat England in the fight for independence."

"But we're a united and much stronger nation now," Jefferson pointed out. "England has been weakened by years of war. We have extended our boundaries to the Pacific in the west. Extending them northward to encompass all of Canada will be a frontiersman's frolic, a mere matter of giving the order to march."

"Henry Clay agrees with you," Madison said gloomily. "He says he can take Canada with Kentucky militiamen, but I seem to recall that Kentucky militiamen have not been able to subdue the Ohio tribes, who continue to fight us even without the active participation of the British forces in Canada. What will be the outcome if British regulars join the Indians?"

Jefferson rubbed his aching jaw and was a long time in answering. "James," he said mournfully, "we'll have to fight a redcoat army sooner or later. I firmly believe that sooner would be better if that fight can be confined to the western frontier. Our population is spread thinly in the west, but that area is more ready for war than any other section of the country. We have the forces in place to meet any British belligerence along the frontier. In the Indiana Territory, Harrison is training a respectable little force, and if the British decided to come down the Mississippi, we have Meriwether Lewis in place as governor of the Louisiana Territory. He's a good man, Lewis is, and he's building a militia that could stand against any Indian attack or, for that matter, any combined force of Indians and Canadian British."

Madison nodded. He, too, had a great deal of respect for Meriwether Lewis, although he had not been as closely associated with Lewis as had Jefferson.

"I will not, of course, try to set policy for you when you occupy this office," Jefferson said, "but I do hope that you will retain Meriwether as governor. No one knows the lands west of the Mississippi as he does."

"I don't doubt Lewis's ability as a leader in the field," Madison said. "I understand, however, that there have been some questions about his skill in administering the affairs of the territorial government."

"Just give him a little time, James," Jefferson said. "He's been in the office only a few months."

Almost halfway across the continent the subject of the discussion between a president and a president-to-be had some questions of his own . . . not about his adequacy as an administrator but about his own sanity.

"William," Meriwether Lewis said to his longtime friend and erstwhile traveling companion, Captain William Clark, "why didn't you tell me that it would be crazy of me to take this blasted job?"

The two men who had been the first whites to travel from the Mississippi to the point where the Columbia River entered the Pacific Ocean were sitting in the governor's office in St. Louis. It was raining. Clark's boots were muddy, and his uniform was damp.

"Would you have listened?" Clark asked with a grin.

"Probably not," Lewis admitted. "It's a mare's nest. I'm supposed to govern an area whose dimensions are not known to within a couple of thousand square miles, an area with remnants of Spanish and French influence, with a score of Indian tribes, most of them potentially hostile, and with General James Wilkinson competing for authority from New Orleans. That's not to mention the petty jealousies and politics of half a dozen men who think that they are better qualified than I to sit in this chair." He grinned again. "At least two or three of whom would gladly put a knife into my back literally, as opposed to their figurative everyday efforts."

"Not quite as simple and peaceful as it was in old days, huh?" Clark asked.

"I'd rather fight a grizzly than try to get promised appropriations out of the bureaucrats in Washington," Lewis said. "There are times when I go into my own pocket to finance actions that simply cannot wait, and all I can do is send in a voucher claim and pray to God that Washington repays me before my creditors eat me."

"They can kill you, but they can't eat you," Clark said. "Cannibalism is against the law."

Lewis laughed in spite of himself. "Is that supposed to make me feel better?"

"Just trying to cheer you up," Clark said dryly. "What are friends for?"

"I'm really glad you're here, William," Lewis said seriously. "I hope you don't mind if every now and then I try to unburden myself at your expense."

"Not at all," Clark said. "My shoulders have always been broader than my mind."

The rain had stopped. Clark rose and said, "I reckon I'd better go whilst I can without having to swim."

Alone in the governor's office, Meriwether Lewis leaned back in his chair with his hand behind his head and watched the rain begin again. It was a long time before he turned his attention to the stack of papers on his desk. He sighed and began to read, but he couldn't concentrate. For the second time Washington had refused to reimburse him for money he had spent in an effort to put the territorial records in order and bring them up-to-date, and he had yet to hear from the East regarding other expenditures out of his own pocket. Meantime, he had notes due on investment property, and even his own personal finances were in questionable condition.

The *Comtesse Renna* had the sleek, sharp lines of a Baltimore clipper. Her cargo area was not as large as, for example, the square-rigged *Beth Huntington,* the flagship of the merchant fleet owned primarily by the flame-haired woman for whom the latter ship was named; but she was swift and maneuverable, a good ship to run the British blockade of the southern American ports.

The *Comtesse Renna* approached her home port in North Carolina from the southeast, having skirted southward of Bermuda to fly before the prevailing winds toward that large indentation in the shoreline below Cape Fear called Long Bay.

The owner and her family walked the well-joined oaken decks as the clipper eased around the long extension of shoals below the bald head of Cape Fear and into the mouth of the river.

There was a pleasant air of expectation aboard the ship as she maneuvered her way up the estuary, and no one was more pleased to be home than Renno, patriarch of the family that was traveling, to his great pleasure and satisfaction, aboard the *Renna.* He was dressed for fashion, not comfort, in tight breeches, a ruffled shirt, and a greatcoat tailored in London. He stood beside his wife, the flame-haired Beth, with his arm around her shoulders.

Beth, too, was bundled against the chill. Her cheeks were flushed. Her green eyes flashed with excitement, but her smile faded as the ship neared the port of Wilmington.

The broad, dark river was full of ships, but it was immediately evident that the vessels were laid up. Decks were empty, hatches battened down, and no one moved on board the score of vessels at anchor or at dock. On the wharfs there were no boxes, no bales of cotton, no casks and barrels waiting for shipment to the ports of Europe. On the waterfront the countinghouses were boarded up, the warehouses closed.

Adan Bartolome, captain of the *Renna* and minority

partner in the Huntington Shipping Company, came to
join Renno and Beth at the rail, leaving his first mate to
maneuver the ship toward the Huntington wharfs.

"The politicians in Washington and London play a
madman's game," Adan said, "to see who must yield."

Renna, daughter of Renno, the pale-haired beauty
for whom the ship was named, shook her head. She could
not help but feel a sadness in seeing the tall ships idle. It
seemed logical for the United States and England to com-
bine forces against the man who had conquered most of
Europe; but she suffered from divided loyalties. American
by birth, she was French by marriage, although her husband, the comte de Beaujolais, had been reported dead in
Portugal.

"Napoleon will never yield," Renna said.

"It is not Napoleon who stops our ships at sea and
kidnaps American citizens to man his own vessels," Adan
said.

"I assure you," Renna said, "that is true only because
he does not have the navy to do it."

"You may be right, Renna," said her brother, Little
Hawk. "I would guess that Napoleon welcomed the embargo as a blockade on the British Isles, something he
himself has not the power to impose."

"I had a brush with some of Napoleon's ships in the
Bay of Biscay," Adan said. "Had we not been successful in
eluding them, the *Renna* would have been seized glee-
fully by the French on the grounds that under the terms of
the Embargo Act we should have been tied up in our
home port."

"It looks as if we'll all have a little vacation," Beth
said.

Naomi, Little Hawk's wife, was admiring the stately
homes on the bluff overlooking Cape Fear. "Look, Beth,"
she said, "there's your house."

"It needs a new coat of paint," Beth said.

"You'll have plenty of willing hands eager to earn a
wage," Adan said. "I spent a few sleepless hours the other
night adding up the number of people whose living depends on sailing orders for Huntington ships. There are at

least two hundred individuals, counting women and children. There'll be men who will be willing to work, even if it means climbing scaffolding to paint the eaves of your house instead of scaling the rigging of a ship at sea."

Renno was silent as the *Renna* edged toward a mooring at dockside. The port of Wilmington had changed since he first saw it, but on the west bank of the river the forests still grew tall and dark. Unlike the others, he was not looking at the deserted docks or the almost empty streets behind the waterfront. He was facing westward, and it seemed that he could feel the distances. The mountains were there, snowbound at this time of the year, wild and empty save for scattered log cabins of the Cherokee and the interloping white settlers.

And beyond the mountains were home and family, his mother and the man who had been his father-by-marriage twice, once as the father of his first wife and again when Roy Johnson married Toshabe, his mother. His brother, the shaman El-i-chi, was on Renno's mind as he looked into the westward distances, into a sky beginning to flare red with the lowering sun. There, too, far to the west, was his fine young son, Ta-na-wun-da, product of the womb of An-da, dead now for so many years.

He was in a melancholy mood when he felt a small jolt as the ship's oaken hull came to rest against the hemp bumpers of the wharf, and that was, he knew, a very unIndian attitude.

More than once in the past months he had been riven with conflicting feelings. The Indian in him, the blood of his mother, remembered the feeling of rightness that came to him whenever he ran free in the great wilderness that belonged to all men of red skin. In that he was Seneca, and that half of him ached for the rolling, wooded hills of the Cherokee Nation and for places far removed from white civilization. But he was his father's son, too, and the blood of the white Indian blended with that of his Indian ancestors and allowed him to feel at ease in the proper English dress he wore as he helped Beth up onto the wharf.

There was work to be done by the owner of the ship

and by her people, for the cargo that the *Comtesse Renna* had brought from England was all the more valuable because of the mandated suspension of trade with the British Isles. Renno accompanied Little Hawk, Naomi, Renna, and his four grandchildren—three of them babes in arms, the other a pretty little girl named Emily Elizabeth, who looked very much like her mother—to the Huntington house on the bluff. The two women set about feeding the younger ones and preparing them for bed. Emily Elizabeth chose to stay with her grandfather. She was just past two years old. She spoke French with a charming lisp and English with some confusion. She sat on Renno's knee and watched the sunset beyond the river, pointing at the sun-reddened clouds.

"Pwetty," she said. "Like Maman."

"Yes," Renno said.

"And Papa."

"And your papa," Renno said. She was too young to understand that she would never see her father again, too innocent to grasp the finality of death.

She was so like Renna at two, a sturdy child, well formed, with the pale hair of her grandmother, flashing blue eyes, a ready smile. He saw not only Renna in her, but sweet Emily, the love of his youth, the mother of his first son . . . and again he was swept away on the wings of melancholy.

While Emily Elizabeth chattered and clung to him as the night shadows replaced the red glow of sunset, he reviewed—not for the first time—the decision that had sent him to England and to Spain and Portugal. And not for the first time he questioned his wisdom in stepping down as sachem of his tribe.

True, there were many who disagreed with him in his belief that the future of all Indians, not just the small clan of Seneca living in the Cherokee Nation, was with the United States; but, they wanted to know, was that sufficient reason to abandon his people?

Well, he had done so. That part of his life had ended, and there were times when he welcomed the freedom from the responsibility he had passed along to El-i-chi.

He looked up as Little Hawk entered the room. His son wore the dress of a ship's officer and wore it very well. He was tall and straight, and his bronzed face was a pleasant one. His hair was sun bleached from the voyage.

"It's nice to have something solid underfoot," Little Hawk said.

"I agree. Are the little ones safely abed?"

Hawk nodded as he took a chair facing his father. Darkness obscured the far shore, although the sky was still pink with the residue of the departed sun.

"You keep looking toward the west," Little Hawk said.

"So," Renno said, which was his way of being noncommittal.

"It will be good to see Grandmother and Roy," Little Hawk said.

"Very good."

"And, of course, Aunt Ena, Rusog, and the boys."

"And your brother."

Little Hawk sighed. "I know. Sometimes I forget. They're so close, my brother and my cousin." He was speaking of Ta-na and El-i-chi's son, Gao.

Renno felt quick guilt, for he, too, often found himself thinking of Ta-na as brother to Gao.

"Will you be going home?" Little Hawk asked.

"Beth has problems here," Renno said. "And you?"

Little Hawk didn't answer for a long time, and when he did, it was a question. "How have you been able to move back and forth between two worlds so successfully for all these years?"

Renno smiled ruefully. "I'm not so sure, Os-sweh-ga-da-ah Ne-wa-ah, that I have done so successfully."

"You're at ease here in this house. You were at home in one of the great manors of England. I lack your ability to adapt. Sometimes I find myself wondering where I am and who I am. I wake from a dream of hearing an owl call, and I think for a moment that I'm back in the village in the longhouse and that when I come fully awake I'll walk across the commons and have breakfast with my grandmother. Or I'll dream of breathing deeply of air that has not been fouled with the chimney smokes of a city. Then, when I am fully conscious and find myself in a town, I feel as if I've lost something."

"So," Renno said.

"I've been thinking a lot lately of my cousins, Ho-ya and We-yo, and the choice they made. I envy them, at times. I remember how it was when I was alone in the northwest, so far from home, and how wide and untamed the land was as we journeyed eastward. The mountains and the plains and the rivers . . ." He brushed back his blond hair and grinned. "And yet I can't quite reconcile myself to taking Naomi and the twins and striking out into the wilderness to live in a lean-to, with nothing to eat except what I can shoot or dig out of uncultivated ground."

"When I was a child," Renno said, "I listened to very old men speak of a time before the Europeans came, or, at worst, when the white men were pent up in small settlements along the coast. The land was so fruitful that living was easy. There were buffalo in the forests, and a boy could feed his entire family by throwing rocks when the great flocks of passenger pigeons came. If I could choose, I would live then, in the days of the great peace established by Degandawida and his disciple, Hiawatha. I think a man's duty would have been clear then, regardless of his blood—to hunt and feed his family, to uphold the honor of the clan and the tribe and the Iroquois League."

"It hasn't been easy for you, has it?" Little Hawk asked.

Renno did not have to ask his son what he meant. He shook his head. "No, it hasn't been easy."

"Perhaps they'll listen to you now," Little Hawk said, speaking of the people of their tribe. He sighed. "If they could only see what *we* have seen. If they could see the great ships and the cities, if they could only realize that it is impossible to stem the westward flow of the white man's land hunger. I have heard you say it many times: Kill all of the white men west of the mountains, then kill all who come for the next ten years, and they will still come. They will come in their thousands, with their guns and their cannon and their plows."

"But what if there had been a Tecumseh to teach unity when the first ship landed?" Renno mused. "If Indians had met the Europeans on the beach with war club and ax?"

"The Spaniards would have moved up from the south," Little Hawk said. "If we had killed them as they landed, others would have come, and in greater numbers. The result would have been the same or . . ." He watched the last red glow fade in the west. "Or by fighting from the beginning, by forcing the Europeans to send great armies to seize their footholds on the shores of America, the extermination of all Indians might very well have been accelerated. The Choctaw learned quite early that flint arrows and stone axes did not stand against mounted men in metal breastplates and armed with muskets. Even if, by some miracle, all tribes could have been unified, the Indian still could not have mustered enough strength to face European cavalry and cannon."

"Still, one wonders," Renno said.

"I'm hungwy," Emily Elizabeth said, waking from a brief nap on her grandfather's shoulder.

"Here is a person of intelligence," Little Hawk said. He tickled the little girl under the chin. "You're a smart one, Emily Elizabeth."

"And hungwy," she said.

"Run along and find Aunt Naomi," Little Hawk said, "and tell her we're all hungry."

The child climbed down and ran toward the stairs.

"In answer to your question," Little Hawk said, "I think what I will do depends on you and Beth. Sooner or later I'm going to have to report back to Washington, but I don't want to leave Naomi and the boys alone. If you and Beth go back home, then I think we'll go with you. If you stay here—"

"Your duty, then, lies with the United States?"

"So you have taught me."

"May the Master of Life forgive me," Renno said. "You have done right. Never have I enjoyed myself more than when President Jefferson sent me west, to find Meriwether Lewis's expedition and accompany him back to civilization."

Renno nodded his thanks. He grinned. "Maybe President Jefferson would give me a commission in the marines."

"I'm sure he would if you asked."

"And whom would I fight?" Renno asked.

"John Bull, surely," Hawk said.

"A worthy opponent," Renno said, "but I have fought the British before."

"I pray that good sense will prevail on both sides," Little Hawk said.

"After Beth gets her affairs straightened out here, we'll go west," Renno said, making the decision even as he spoke. In so doing he felt an easing of the doubt that had been plaguing him for months.

Beth allowed Adan to help her into a carriage. She didn't speak until Adan had boarded, clucked the horses into motion, and the vehicle was clattering down a brick street. She looked back just once to see three cotton-headed children playing in the bare front yard of a small, unpainted shack. Inside, the modest house was neat and clean. It belonged to a seaman who had been sailing on Huntington ships since Beth's first purchase of a vessel.

"What we'll have to do," she said at last, "is to continue their pay."

Adan looked at her with raised eyebrows. "That will be very expensive."

"We have no choice," she said.

Adan had seldom been in disagreement with Beth Huntington, but he had been plowing most of his wages and all of his bonuses into buying a share of the Huntington Shipping Company. Beth's decision to continue to pay workers who were idled by Mr. Jefferson's Dambargo was, Adan felt, a prime example of female illogic.

"Beth," he said, "with due respect, I would like to remind you that you've been pretty much the absentee owner, that most of the business decisions have been left to me for a number of years."

She put her hand on his arm, and her touch burned through his clothing.

"This is not a business decision," she said. "It is a matter of the heart, and of right and wrong."

"I'm not sure—"

"Dear Adan," she said, "I am grateful to you for your loyalty in the past, and I do respect your opinions. But I feel strongly about this. We can't allow our people to go hungry, to lose what little they've been able to accumulate, to suffer simply because of the politics of great nations."

Frustration caused Adan's swarthy face to flush darker. He could not help but admire Beth for her compassion, but his business sense was shocked into numbness when he added up what it would cost the company to keep its employees on full pay until someone decided either to go to war or end the embargo.

"You won't fight me on this, will you?" Beth asked, smiling up into his face.

His anger and frustration were leavened by the love he had felt for this flame-haired woman from the first time he saw her. "There is an alternative," he suggested.

"Oh, no," she said quickly. "I know that you and all the other seamen have little patience with a law that not only punishes American workers but, I believe, strains the very fabric of the Constitution. But no Huntington ship will be involved in smuggling."

"As Renno says," Adan said with a grin, "so."

The noncommittal *so*. It rankled Adan that thousands of bales of cotton were lying in storage in the exchange on the waterfront and in sheds at several plantations along Cape Fear. The idle textile mills of England would turn that cotton into gold for the man who had the steel in his bones to get it there.

Chapter Two

The Wilmington Customshouse was not nearly as grand as its counterparts on Chesapeake Bay and in the large cities of the Northeast, although in normal times Wilmington shipped thousands of tons of cotton and naval stores to English factories and shipyards and enjoyed a lively trade with the islands. New Englanders thought their ports were the heart of American commerce, and citizens of Washington and Virginia considered Chesapeake Bay to be of prime importance. Both regions' residents looked on Wilmington as a minor port in a small town in a backward farming state.

The customshouse sat on the east side of Water Street. From its windows the federal appointee in charge could look out over the river to see the vessels idled by Mr. Jefferson's embargo. It was not considered necessary by those who directed the expenditure of federal funds to have a vessel from the Revenue Marine Service on full-time duty along Cape Fear, but now and again, at unannounced times, a revenue cutter would venture up from Charleston to show the flag.

Between visits from the tax arm of the federal fleet, the presence of the central government in the port of Wilmington was represented by a distinctively contoured thirty-foot ketch moored in front of the customshouse. The ketch provided a means for the customs collector to board any ship entering or leaving the port. To help the customs collector enforce the embargo, a federal marshal had been sent to Wilmington to make certain that any ship leaving the port had papers binding it to coastwise trade.

Circumventing the Dambargo seemed, on the surface of it, to be a simple task. Hypothetically a skipper could merely sign papers swearing that his ship was bound for a United States port. Once clear of Cape Fear and the possibility of having its sails sighted by the revenuers, the ship could set her course eastward. Two factors belied the apparent simplicity of such a scheme. First, there wasn't much coastwise trade. There was only a small demand for southern cotton to be used in the textile mills in the north. The bulk of that crop had always been destined for England. This lack of cargo opportunity between U.S. ports made it difficult to thwart the embargo, for not even a federal employee such as the customs collector or the federal marshal would readily accept that yet another load of cotton was headed for Boston Harbor. Secondly, even if the authorities could be convinced that the ship's cargo was intended for a port in the United States, documentary proof of delivery of that cargo was required in order for the ship to reenter its home port without penalty.

When Beth directed payment of wages to warehouse workers and sailors who were sitting idle on the hill with no immediate prospects of earning their pay in a way that would be profitable to Huntington Shipping, Adan envisioned a steady and continuing drain on the company's reserves. His first reaction was to question his common sense. He had ventured into the area of entrepreneurship twice in his life, once as a pirate and now as a minority partner in Beth Huntington's shipping business. His second venture, though legitimate, seemed doomed to be as financially unrewarding as his first. His next thought was to prevent the loss of his investment by means of an action that was not quite as seriously illegal as piracy. A pirate could be hanged. A smuggler disobeying an unpopular law would not be treated so unkindly if caught. Besides, he told himself, civil disobedience of the embargo was unofficial public policy.

With great caution Adan went about his preparations. On the pretext of calling on a buxom young widow who lived in a small village near the mouth of the river, he sailed a small ketch by cover of darkness to the loading piers of three different plantations on the western bank. He found the proprietors of the large agricultural businesses to be as willing as he to circumvent the Dambargo. He arranged to have half a dozen owners deliver their baled cotton to an isolated spot, the site of Old Brunswick Town, the colonial settlement that had been burned by the British at the beginning of the War for Independence. There were no docks at the location, since they, too, had been destroyed by the British forces. The cotton would have to be loaded by launch. Because no one in his right mind would attempt such a difficult job, the sheer unlikelihood of it would prevent either the customs people or the federal marshal from suspecting that a sizable and valuable cargo was being smuggled out of Cape Fear.

Beth's house on Front Street was a structure of two and a half stories. The kitchen and servants' quarters occupied the English basement. The first floor housed a formal dining room, butler's pantry, parlor, comfortable workroom-office equipped with both a desk for Beth's paperwork and a sewing table, and a large room with a fireplace and windows overlooking the back garden and the river at the rear. On the second floor were four large bedrooms and a roomy bath-dressing room. Colonnaded porches ran the length of the rear of the house on both floors. It was a spacious home, and to a man who had spent his youth in a Seneca longhouse, it seemed adequate for the three families in residence. In fact, the house on Front Street was peaceful and quiet when compared to a longhouse in winter with as many as a score of people, adults and children alike, plus a dog or two, sharing space.

Renno, however, had not lived the semicommunal life of the old-fashioned longhouse since he was a child. He had spent many nights in the open with nothing more than one skin for covering. Before his marriage to Beth, in Rusog's village in the Cherokee Nation—his home since his father led a small segment of the Seneca tribe far to the south of the ancestral lands—he had lived in his own house with the pale-haired Emily, the mother of his firstborn son and Renna.

There were times, then, when Renno found Beth's house to be a bit crowded and noisy, but the pleasure of having almost all of his family together compensated for any momentary irritation. He was content—at least for a time—to observe his daughter and his new daughter-in-law in their roles as mothers, to take his granddaughter, Emily Elizabeth, for long walks, and to sit around the grand table for the evening meal in conversation with those who were nearest and dearest to him. He made no protest when Beth called in a tailor and ordered suits not only for him but for Little Hawk, too.

Renno thought often of his brother, El-i-chi, and of the other members of his extended family; but the events that had occurred in the adjoining Cherokee-Seneca villages before he left for England had left a hole in his heart, a malaise that precluded any decisive action on his part. He would, of course, go home to see brother, mother, son, and sister, but there seemed to be no urgency to it.

He listened with concern as Beth spoke of her problems with the business and of her commitment to care for her employees in times of trouble, but he took only a mild interest in news of national affairs beyond thinking that President Jefferson was wrong in continuing the embargo, because it was hurting the Americans more than the English. When he was forced by lurid accounts in the newspaper to think about the state of the nation, it was with some concern for the future of Beth's interests in Wilmington. If war should come, coastal North Carolina could well be, once again, a battlefield. Only a few blocks away stood the house that had served as headquarters for General Cornwallis while the British occupied Wilmington during the War for American Independence. If a new British commander decided that the back door to Washington and the populous cities of the Northeast opened south of Chesapeake Bay, Wilmington could very well be overrun again. He determined that if war came, he would take his family to Huntington Castle, the home that Beth had built near Rusog's town in the Cherokee Nation. Rusog was solid-minded enough to keep his Cherokee neutral in any war between the United States and England.

Beth had assigned Little Hawk and Naomi to a bedroom overlooking Front Street. Next door an improvised nursery was presided over by a motherly black woman who had moved a cot into the room to be near her four charges around the clock.

Naomi's twin boys had names now—two each, as a matter of fact. Big Boy, firstborn, had been christened Michael by a wordy Episcopalian minister. Little Boy was called Joseph. So each infant had a solid biblical name to be used in the white world; but in another, more private ceremony, with their grandfather presiding in the absence of a shaman, the twins were given polysyllabic names in the Seneca tongue to go with the small amount of Indian blood that coursed through their veins.

Little Hawk and Renno, if they had been asked, would have said that the twins were Seneca. In actuality, the Seneca blood was mixed with the English blood of the Harpers and the Johnsons; with the Erie and French blood of their paternal great-grandmother, Toshabe; and with Biloxi blood from their great-great-grandmother Ahwen-ga: but there was Seneca in them, and there was Seneca in the hearts of both their father and their grandfather. Thus they were Michael Soaring Hawk and Joseph Standing Bear Harper.

Naomi was pleased when Little Hawk decided to

stay in Wilmington with Renno and Beth. She was a dutiful wife, and she would go where her husband beckoned; but she found living in Beth's fine house to be quite pleasant, as were wearing beautiful gowns sewn in Beth's workroom by a talented black seamstress and riding out in Beth's carriage on fine days with the twins in their little carry beds. Naomi, the daughter of pioneers, product of a two-room log cabin on the Tennessee frontier, wanted her sons to have good lives. She liked the way Renno made himself at home in the white man's world. She wanted her sons to be as self-confident and dignified as their grandfather.

Little Hawk was devoted to his wife, and he doted on his twin boys; but he was young, in his midtwenties, and he was more aware of the flow of events that seemed to be sweeping the United States toward war with England. He had only to look at the forest of bare masts at their moorings to realize the seriousness of the situation. Although he had resigned the military commission given to him personally by Thomas Jefferson after his stay at West Point, he felt that he owed a duty to Mr. Jefferson and the United States. When the time came, he would return to that duty.

In the meantime it was good to be with the family. Renna's grief over the news that her husband had been killed in Portugal had run its course, at least as far as her demeanor before the family was concerned. It was good to watch his sister and his wife tend to their infants, good to hold his own sons and his nephew, Louis, in his arms. It was also good, now and then, to leave the infant-scented, woman-crowded house to venture out across the river. More than once he hunted there with his father, but more often he went alone. Great stretches of the former wilderness near the river had been turned into giant fields of indigo and cotton. In low areas there were extensive rice paddies, but there were still areas of forest, some of it second growth, where a man could stalk a deer and venture home with fresh venison for the table.

It was some weeks before the long periods of inactivity that were part and parcel of life for an unemployed man in a town began to weigh heavily on Little Hawk. As the days passed he became more and more restless. He spent time talking with Adan at the Huntington docks, but Adan had other things on his mind, namely—according to the handsome Spaniard—a certain young widow in the village of Smithville.

"If you don't mind," Little Hawk said one day while Adan was preparing to set out downriver once more in his little ketch, "I'll ride along with you."

Adan pursed his lips thoughtfully. "I would love to have your company," he said, "but there would be nothing for you to do in Smithville."

"I wouldn't want to interfere with your courting," Little Hawk said. "I'll take a look at the town and then explore the countryside a bit."

"In the dark?" Adan asked.

"I guess it's a bad idea," Little Hawk said, because it was obvious that Adan did not want him along.

For several days Adan left the Wilmington docks late in the afternoon. It was over twenty miles by water to the village near the mouth of the river. Little Hawk had the use of a small boat. He had learned to handle it well. He had sailed downriver a few miles, and he knew that the trip to Smithville was not one to be undertaken lightly. He doubted that Adan was going all the way to Smithville, but he kept his suspicions to himself. He feared that the handsome Adan had made a conquest closer to home and that the fair lady's marital status demanded secrecy.

When crewmen boarded the largest of Beth's ships, the *Beth Huntington,* and began to prepare her for the sea, Little Hawk sought out Adan.

"I've managed to get an order for naval stores from a New Orleans shipyard," Adan explained. "We'll be observing the terms of the embargo, calling only at an American port."

Barrels of pitch were loaded into the ship's hold. Rough-sawn timbers were carried aboard, and huge, long pine logs suitable for masts were lashed to her deck. Little Hawk watched the work for lack of something more exciting to do.

"She's not nearly fully loaded," he remarked to Adan as the crew made ready to take the *Beth Huntington* to sea.

"I'm afraid it's a rather small order," Adan said, "but we'll show a profit. We'll bring back cowhides and ship them to the leather makers in the north."

"Why not take a smaller ship?" Little Hawk asked.

"We'll fill her holds with hides for the trip back," Adan explained.

A bond was posted with the customs collector. The ship was eased into the current, and men scurried into the rigging to set sails.

All the family had come out to watch the ship sail. They stood together on the dock and waved to Adan.

"A beautiful sight," Naomi said to Little Hawk. "You'd like to be going with her, wouldn't you?"

"I've had enough of the sea for a while," he said, taking her hand.

Renno was thinking that perhaps he had erred in not being aboard the *Beth Huntington* with his family. From New Orleans it was a fairly easy trip up the Mississippi by boat to Natchez and over the trace that led into Cherokee country.

It was two days later that Little Hawk walked alone down Water Street to the docks to check on his boat. It had rained, and she needed bailing. He was almost finished with the job when he looked up to see a familiar sight, Adan's little ketch under sail, coming up the river. He finished removing the rainwater as the ketch turned toward the docks and landed not at the Huntington pier but at the far end. Dusk was coming as Little Hawk walked along the pier, his moccasins making his progress soundless. A man, his back turned, was bent over and tying the ketch as Little Hawk approached. When the fellow straightened, Little Hawk looked into the face of a distant cousin, Nathan Ridley's son, James.

"Hawk," James said in surprise.

"Jump ship, James?" Little Hawk asked.

Ridley seemed at a loss for words. He was a compactly built young man of just twenty-one years. He wore his hair seaman's style, long, and clubbed at the nape. He cleared his throat. "Well, Hawk," he said, "we found out that some of our freshwater casks had been contaminated, so we're tied up downriver and taking on more."

Little Hawk nodded.

"I took advantage of the delay to come up and spend an hour or so with my wife."

James was newly married. Little Hawk smiled. It was a logical explanation for why the *Beth Huntington*'s first mate was in Wilmington two days after the ship had sailed for New Orleans.

"How far downriver is the ship?" Little Hawk asked.

"A few miles. We'll probably be sailing tomorrow."

"Well, James, I'm sure you're eager to get home to your wife."

Ridley grinned sheepishly. "Yes. I'll see you when we get back from New Orleans, Hawk."

It was a natural thing for Little Hawk to relate his news about the ship at dinner that evening. He told his family how he'd encountered James Ridley and about Ridley's explanation for his presence in Wilmington.

Beth put down her knife and fork and looked puzzled. "There's no place to take on large quantities of water this side of Smithville," she said.

"They could be getting it from the wells of one of the plantations," Little Hawk ventured.

The color rose in Beth's face. "I don't like this. I had a suspicion that scalawag was up to something."

"Such as?" Renno asked.

"I don't know," she said.

"I had asked him why he wanted to take the *Beth Huntington* when the cargo he carried wouldn't have filled the holds of a smaller ship, such as the *Renna*," Little Hawk added.

Renno thought for a moment. "The *Beth* carries more sail. Perhaps he wants her speed in the event he encounters any of His Majesty's finest."

"He's up to something," Beth said. "We posted a

large bond. If he breaks that bond and we lose the money, it will hurt the business—not to mention the fact that if he defies the embargo, the ship could be confiscated."

"What could he have in mind?" Renna asked.

"I'm afraid to say," Beth said, "but my guess is that his first destination will not be New Orleans."

"Would you like me to find out?" Little Hawk asked.

"I would be grateful," Beth said. "Tell him for me that if he loses my ship, I will personally—" She shook her head without going into detail about her sanguine intentions for Adan.

At the docks Little Hawk checked the mooring at the far end to find that Adan's little ketch was still in its place. He hurried to his own boat. There was little wind, but the tide was falling, adding to the power of the flow of the river. The going was slow, but the night was beautiful, with a navy sky of many stars and a half-moon that reflected off the dark surface of the river.

It was past midnight before Little Hawk noticed moving points of light on the western bank of the river. He steered the boat toward the lights and soon saw the shadowy bulk of the *Beth Huntington* lying near the shore. He landed his skiff a hundred yards north of the ship and made his way quietly through dense woodlands. He knew the site; he had visited the location of the old colonial town with the family on a picnic outing. As he drew near he heard voices and saw movement in the light of lanterns.

Black slaves were loading bales of cotton onto a small barge at the water's edge. In the lantern light on the *Beth*'s deck he could see other men lowering the bales into the ship's hold. He heard Adan's voice and spotted the captain standing beside the barge. Little Hawk stepped out from his cover and walked without notice to stand behind Adan.

"What I want to know," Adan was saying with some heat, "is just where in hell is James Ridley?"

"I imagine that he's in the arms of his wife at this moment," Hawk said.

Adan turned quickly. *"Madre de Dios,"* he said. "What are you doing here?"

"I'm here to find out what you're doing here," Little Hawk said.

"That young fool went into town, didn't he?" Adan demanded.

"I saw him by accident," Little Hawk said. "I'm sure he'll be careful. You're not planning on going to New Orleans, I take it."

Adan lifted his hat, then ran his hand through his hair. He laughed. "Of course we are going to New Orleans, but only after we pay a quick visit to a friendly port in the Bahamas."

"Beth suspected as much, I think."

"She knows?" Adan asked.

"I mentioned that I saw James, and I told her what he told me, that the *Beth* was moored downriver taking on fresh water."

"And for good measure did you then tell as much to the federal marshal and the collector of customs?"

"Adan, as I understand it, if you're caught you risk losing the bond that the company put up as well as the ship," Little Hawk said.

"We will not be caught," Adan said. "We will sail to the Bahamas and sell the cotton to a broker who will then ship it to England in a British bottom. Meanwhile we will sail with our small cargo of ship's stores on to New Orleans, where we will obtain the proper documentary proof that our voyage was completed as bonded."

"Cap'n Adan," someone called. "This is the last of it."

Two more bales of cotton were placed on the barge.

"All right," Adan said, "that's it, gentlemen. My men can handle it from here. I suggest that you take your laborers and fade away softly into the night."

"Good luck, Cap'n," the man said.

"If God is with us, you will have your compensation when we return from New Orleans," Adan said.

"Just don't let any English bastards catch you," the man said.

"You might as well come aboard while we're finishing the loading," Adan said to Little Hawk. "Where's your boat?"

"A hundred yards up the river."

"Did Master James give you any inkling of when he might deign to return to his post?"

"None," Little Hawk said.

He stepped onto the barge and sat down on a bale of cotton while men poled the load away from the muddy bank. When the barge banged against the side of the *Beth*, he clambered up a rope ladder behind Adan and stood aside to watch the bales being hoisted aboard with a davit, then lowered into the hold.

"Something's coming, Cap'n," a man called out.

Adan went to the stern of the ship and watched his ketch emerge from the darkness. He was silent until James Ridley was aboard. "I could have you flogged," he said.

"I'd appreciate it if you wouldn't," James said.

"You jeopardized the ship and its cargo."

"Not really," James said. "No one saw me."

"Hello, James," Little Hawk said.

"Damn, Hawk," James said.

"No one saw you?" Adan challenged.

"No one but Hawk."

"Who told his entire family," Adan said.

"You didn't," James said, looking at Little Hawk with entreaty on his face.

"Saw no reason not to," Little Hawk said, shrugging.

The last of the bales was on the davit and being swung upward and over the rail.

"Cap'n, lights coming from upriver," someone called out.

"Oh, hell," James Ridley said.

"So no one but Hawk saw you?" Adan asked.

The heavy bale of cotton was swinging slowly toward the open hatch leading down into the hold.

"Captain, I ran into the marshal on the way back to the ketch," James said weakly. "I thought he believed me when I told him that we were just taking on water down here."

"Cap'n, that's the customs boat coming down the river," the lookout cried.

"All hands," Adan said. "Stand by to get under way. Dump that bale of cotton! Move!"

The men operating the davit worked at cross purposes, one of them trying to reverse the direction of motion to dump the bale overboard, the others intent on dropping the bale into the hold as the quickest way to get rid of it. Men scampered into the rigging. Others were turning the capstan to drag in the anchor. Sails began to unfurl even before the anchor was freed. The ship lurched as a breeze caught canvas and billowed. The cable holding up the last bale of cotton, strained by a hard night's work, parted, letting the bale fall and smash against the canted cover of the hatch. The hatch cover broke into a dozen pieces. One heavy chunk of wood whirled through the air and forcibly struck Little Hawk on the back of the head. He fell limply.

"See to him, James," Adan ordered. He then turned his attention to getting the ship under way. Dawn was coming. There was already light in the east, and with it came a breeze that became a wind from the northeast, just the air needed to send the *Beth Huntington* fleeing down the tide toward the mouth of the river.

"How is Hawk?" Adan asked, after he had the *Beth* moving well.

"He's breathing," James said. "He's had one helluva lick on the back of his head."

"Get the ship's doctor up here," Adan said. "On second thought, take Hawk to my cabin and have the doc look at him there."

"Captain, he's not going to be happy when he wakes up at sea. Your ketch is trailing behind us. We could put him off—"

"We can't do that, not knowing how badly he's hurt," Adan said. "Cut the ketch loose."

"But his folks won't know what has happened to him."

"Madre de Dios," Adan said. He could not leave his friends to wonder what had become of the Hawk. "Jake

Stone sprained his ankle during the loading. Put him on the sloop and tell him to get word to Beth that the Hawk is with us, hurt a little bit so that we couldn't send him back but all right."

"Aye, sir."

"And James?"

"Yes, sir?"

"If my little ketch is seized and lost, it's going to come out of your share of this voyage. Do you understand?"

"I understand."

"Move, then."

Ridley obeyed his orders. Soon Little Hawk was in the captain's cabin with the ship's doctor in attendance. Jake Stone was helped down into the ketch, and it was cast off. Stone raised a sail and took the little vessel toward the shallows along the eastern bank. Behind them the lights of the pursuing vessel became dimmer.

As the sun rose, the *Beth Huntington*'s bow began to lift and fall to a gentle swell on the river bar, and then she was in the open sea, making southeastward to round the Frying Pan into the broad Atlantic. The northeast wind held, and Adan ordered all sails set. The *Beth* pounded southeastward with a bone in her teeth.

Little Hawk's head was trying to become independent and fly away like a bird. At first when he opened his eyes, he saw two of everything and could make sense of nothing. He sank back with a groan and waited. The world was moving up and down under him. He opened his eyes again and saw a chart table, a captain's chest, a swaying ship's lantern. Light came through a salt-caked porthole, and he realized that he was at sea, that it was not the world that was unsteady but the waters of the ocean. He sat up with an effort, held his head in both hands, and explored the knot above the nape of his neck. He took deep breaths, and the pain in his head eased enough for him to venture out to the deck.

The ship's sails thundered in a brisk wind. Salt spray

cooled him and completed his recovery. He looked around to see nothing but ocean wastes on all sides.

Adan was standing beside the steersman. When he saw Little Hawk, he grinned. "How's the head?"

"Still there, just barely," Little Hawk said. "What happened?"

Adan told him. Little Hawk rubbed his head thoughtfully. "I don't suppose there's any turning back."

"Not unless you want Beth to lose a ship," Adan said.

"I see. So I'm going to the Bahamas."

"I'm sorry, Hawk."

"Not your fault, I guess." He rubbed the sore spot on his head and frowned. "Of course, if you had not decided to beat the embargo—"

"Or if you hadn't been so curious," Adan said.

"Maybe I can find passage home from the islands."

"Not likely, not with the embargo. Unless there happens to be a British man-of-war planning to put into one of the American ports on the Chesapeake."

"My God," Little Hawk said suddenly. "Naomi won't know what has happened to me."

"We left a man behind," Adan said. "He'll get word to her."

"Well, that's some consolation," Little Hawk said. "Obviously you outran the marshal."

"If it was he," Adan said. "It looked like the customs boat, but it could have been a fisherman on his way to work. We couldn't stay to see." He put his hand on Little Hawk's shoulder. "Cheer up, Hawk. We'll see New Orleans together and be back home in a couple of months."

"Shoals to port, Cap'n," the steersman said.

A hundred yards away from the ship waves setting from two different directions met over a shallow bar, crashed, and sent white spume thirty feet into the air.

"Take a look, Hawk," Adan said. "It's underwater, but that bar is land's end, the last part of America we'll see until we sail back from the islands into the Florida straits."

Little Hawk nodded. The situation was not to his

liking, but it was of his own making. He had no choice but to accept it.

There are those who say that chance rather than divine predestination rules the lives of men. Adan would venture no opinion as to why, when first light came, the sails of a British man-of-war were directly ahead of the *Beth Huntington*. The ocean is large, and it would seem that the odds against two ships coming into such close proximity would be astronomical; but to old hands aboard the *Beth*, the meeting was inevitable. The *Beth* was on course for Nassau in the Bahamas. HMS *Cormorant* had sailed from Nassau bound for patrol duty off the coast of North Carolina and Virginia. The old-timers said that ships at sea have an attraction for one another. Collisions were not unknown, and almost every man had witnessed a brush with disaster when two ships alone in vast areas of water bore down on each other in poor visibility.

It did not matter whether it was chance or destiny at work when the lookout called, "Sail on the port quarter."

The situation was serious. Adan was called immediately. He put his glass on the sails and saw the bulk of a cruiser below them. He knew her class. She was fast—too fast and too close.

"Steersman, take her hard starboard and directly down the wind," Adan ordered.

The *Beth* heeled, then leaped forward as the full force of the wind cupped her sails. For long minutes the British cruiser diminished in apparent size. By midmorning, however, it was near enough so that Adan could make out her flag and the name painted on her bow.

"She'll be within range of her guns in another hour," Adan told Little Hawk.

"We're not at war," Little Hawk said grimly.

"*They* are," Adan said. "They're desperately short of men for their hell ships. They'll have a few of our crew before they're satisfied."

"It's too bad that certain men in Washington can't be aboard at a time like this," Little Hawk said.

Adan laughed bitterly. "Most of them would be rejected by a British press gang."

"But they'd know how it feels to be aboard an unarmed merchantman while being pursued by a man-of-war."

A puff of smoke emanated from the *Cormorant*. Seconds later a ball splashed into the sea thirty yards off the *Beth*'s stern.

"I underestimated," Adan said. "They're in range now."

"That's it, then?" Little Hawk asked.

"No choice," Adan said. He gave orders. Grim-faced sailors obeyed. *Beth*'s sails were furled. She lost headway and rocked slowly in the swell as longboats were lowered from the *Cormorant*.

"No resistance, men," Adan ordered. "We have no British deserters aboard. Maybe this lot will listen to reason."

Minutes later armed British marines swarmed up onto the deck of the *Beth*. They lined the rails all around, muskets at the ready. A last boat thudded against the side of the *Beth*, and two men from it climbed aboard. The first man over the rail wore the uniform of a ship's officer. He straightened his tunic and looked around disdainfully before approaching Adan.

"You are captain of this ship?" The ensign's voice was high-pitched.

"I am, sir," Adan said. "And I register a protest in the strongest terms against your interference with freedom of passage on the high seas."

"Noted," the ensign said. "I am Ensign Drake Mumsley, of His Majesty's Ship *Cormorant*. We have boarded you to look for deserters from His Majesty's Navy."

"We are all American citizens here," Adan said.

Mumsley sneered, but the expression seemed to be that of a spoiled child. His pouting mouth and his weak gray eyes did not lend themselves to severity. He was too young to be stern, too slender to be imposing.

"Of course," Mumsley said. "But you don't mind if

we check, do you? You fellows have a habit of issuing false citizenship papers to our seamen."

"I mind very much," Adan said, "and there are no false papers aboard this ship. We sail from Wilmington, North Carolina, and I know personally every man on board this ship. They've all lived in Wilmington for years, some of them born there."

"Tells a fine tale, don't he, sir?" asked the bosun from behind Mumsley's shoulder.

"Indeed, Mr. Griffiths," Mumsley said. "Gentlemen, may I introduce Bosun Gunner Griffiths, who will seek out the deserters among you."

Griffiths laughed. He was a robust Welshman, a dark, hairy man, with great tufts of black on his exposed wrists and pushing up out of the neck of his tunic. His craggy face showed the darkness of a heavy beard. He was small of eye. He moved forward and had to look up to stare into Adan's eyes.

"We'll take it for given, Cap'n, that you're a money-grubbing Yankee."

"Thank you very much," Adan said as his eyes narrowed.

"But this un," Griffiths said, moving to stand in front of James Ridley. "Now he looks likely. Your papers, man."

"I am a ship's officer," James said with indignation.

"Officer or not, you look English to me," Griffiths said. "Once an Englishman, always an Englishman, eh, sir?" He winked at Mumsley, who nodded imperiously. Moving with catlike quickness, he bent James's arm behind his back and jerked him away from Adan's side.

Adan's face showed his anger. He stepped forward. "You shall not have my first mate!" he bellowed. His hand was on the hilt of his saber.

Mumsley nodded to Griffiths. The bosun, with surprising swiftness, smashed the butt of his musket into Adan's head. Adan fell lifelessly.

Little Hawk's reaction was instinctive. He had been standing at Adan's left. When the solidly built Britisher decked Adan with his rifle butt, Hawk sent one well-placed blow to Griffiths' chin. The bosun sprawled across the deck but was up quickly, almost before Little Hawk could draw his marine saber. A dozen muskets centered on his chest, and he heard the click of the cocking actions.

Griffiths held up his hand. "Hold your fire," he ordered. "This 'un's mine." Little Hawk was disarmed. The bosun glared at him, then moved away, pointing to the strongest and fittest of the *Beth Huntington*'s men. As the men were selected, armed marines escorted them to the waiting longboats.

Adan stirred and sat up with a groan. He was helpless as the marines forced James Ridley and Little Hawk to climb down into the longboats with the other impressed sailors. He raged inwardly as the boats pulled away toward the waiting *Cormorant*, but there was nothing he could do. He had no guns to fight the man-of-war. He, like the nation itself, was hostage to the power of the Royal Navy. And, to make matters worse, he would have to continue his voyage as planned, lest Huntington Shipping lose the *Beth Huntington*. If she went back to Wilmington with cotton aboard, his plan to defy the embargo would be exposed, and she would be impounded by her own countrymen. The loss of the ship and the forfeiture of the bond that had been posted would bring the company to ruin.

Adan was forced to wait until he moored his ship dockside at Nassau to arrange to have another ship, which was also evading the embargo, take a letter back to the United States for delivery to the Huntington Shipping Company. He set sail for New Orleans to complete the voyage for which he was bonded. A pleasing amount of cash was locked in the ship's strongbox, but it did little to assuage the heaviness in Adan's heart. He grieved for the good men of his crew who had been impressed by the British, and he was in despair about James Ridley and Little Hawk. After a seaman told him that Little Hawk had struck the broad-chested bosun while Adan was unconscious, he became even more concerned.

Chapter Three

The election of James Madison as fourth president of the United States went almost unnoticed in the house on Front Street in Wilmington. Each of the adults in residence was consumed by more immediate, more personal concerns, one of which was shared. Although Jake Stone, the seaman from the *Beth Huntington,* had brought word of Little Hawk's enforced voyage on the day following the departure of the *Beth,* there was still the question of the seriousness of his injury.

In the weeks that followed, Beth tried to stanch her growing anger at Adan for taking what she thought was a reckless and needless risk; but that same anger was fed by the inadvertent involvement of her stepson in Adan's smuggling venture.

Naomi put on a good front, but when she was alone, she wept quietly into her pillow. She could only pray that the man she loved had recovered from his injury and that the *Beth,* good ship that she was, would bring him home safely. In the meantime there were winter clothes to sew for the twins and long, sisterly talks with Renna, who had recently lost her second husband and, thus, knew how to lift Naomi's spirits by reminding her subtly that, as the son of the white Indian, Little Hawk was indestructible.

The weeks passed until the arrival of Adan's letter from Nassau. The missive came up the river on a coastal trader running down from Baltimore and was delivered to the office of the Huntington Shipping Company. Beth was alone in the office, catching up on some paperwork. Tears of anger and concern quickly filled her eyes when she read Adan's brief account of the impressment of Little Hawk, James Ridley, and half a dozen of the *Beth Huntington's* seamen into the British navy. She was furious with Adan, and thoughts of severe punishment filled her head. But then she realized that no punitive action she could take would make him feel any worse than the self-recrimination he was no doubt already suffering. She went to the door, called a young black boy, and gave him a coin and instructions to find both Mr. Harper and Mr. Nathan Ridley and bring them to the office immediately.

"Ah, no, no," Renno whispered as he read the letter. He had heard from seamen about conditions aboard a ship of the Royal Navy. Although he tried to deny the thought, there was a possibility that his son was dead, for a man of Little Hawk's dignity and pride would find it difficult to accept the cruel, needlessly harsh discipline on a Royal Navy ship of the line. He whispered a prayer to the Master of Life for his son's well-being.

Nathan Ridley arrived in Beth's office five minutes later than Renno. When Nathan read the letter, his face went pale, then flushed fiery red. "They will have their war, the bloody bastards," he snarled. Then he shook his head. "Forgive me, Beth, for my language."

"There is nothing to forgive," she said.

"How much longer must we bear these outrages?" Nathan asked, his voice shaking with fury. "We've had enough talk among the diplomats. It's time now for action."

Renno said, "I would prefer to let my blade do the talking for me. Tell me a way that we can track down the

Cormorant and engage her in a fair fight, and I'm your man."

"It would take a man-of-war to do that," Nathan said.

"There *is* a time for talk," Beth told them. "I suggest that both of you come with me to Washington."

"To talk?" Nathan asked disdainfully.

Renno quickly saw the wisdom of Beth's suggestion. "Thomas Jefferson is still president. I have done favors for him. Now it's time for me to ask a favor in return."

"But Jefferson's been reluctant to spend public money building a navy," Nathan said bitterly.

"Deftly applied diplomatic pressure just might accomplish our purpose more quickly than a navy," Beth explained. "I'm willing to let future events settle the big differences between the United States and England. Right now I want James and Little Hawk and our seamen released and returned to this country."

"If you don't mind," Nathan said, "I'll let you handle the talking in Washington."

Renno nodded. James's wife would be distraught when she heard that James had been impressed. She was all alone, except for the Ridley family. All of her folks were gone, and she was expecting her first child.

"I think I'd be more needed here than tagging along with you," Nathan added. "You're the one who knows Jefferson, Renno, and I warrant that if you give Miss Beth a shot at the British representatives in Washington, she can charm them into doing anything she wants."

The news of the seizure of members of the *Beth Huntington*'s crew spread rapidly through the city. The customs collector was almost as incensed as Nathan Ridley and every bit as ready to go to war. To show his sympathy he rushed through a document to allow the *Comtesse Renna* to sail to Annapolis, the nearest port to Washington. *Renna* hugged the coastline, venturing into the open sea only to round Diamond Shoals, and with brisk, chill winds giving her wings, she arrived at her destination in near record time.

*   *   *

Thomas Jefferson's health had improved, but not his disposition. The Electoral College had made it official that James Madison was to be the next president. Meanwhile, the final days of Jefferson's term dragged on. Congress was back in session and was intent, it seemed, on humiliating the man with whom it had worked so well for almost eight years. John Quincy Adams stated publicly that Mr. Jefferson's personal influence with Congress was at an end. The Senate rejected presidential appointments and threatened to take actions that, Jefferson feared, would lead to war.

When word came to Jefferson that the Seneca sachem Renno was in the reception area of the White House, he seized upon the opportunity to see an old friend and put aside, at least temporarily, both his resentments about Congress and his longing to be back home in Monticello.

The President greeted Renno warmly and bowed his admiration to the beauty of flame-haired Beth. He personally escorted them to a sitting room in the living quarters of the Executive Mansion.

Beth had been a guest at the court of England's king, had walked the halls of palaces, and had dined on plates of gold in the presence of Europe's elite. The grand old manors of the British nobility had not impressed her, but there was something in the relatively unadorned simplicity of the residence of the President and in the quiet dignity of the man himself that gave her a feeling that she was in the presence of history. The President's mansion, standing alone in open fields with struggling gardens just taking shape, seemed to be a symbol of the newfound strength of her adopted country. Jefferson—tall, dignified, considerate—was to her an example of the type of man who defined a new personal freedom for all.

She listened patiently and with interest as her husband and Thomas Jefferson exchanged reminiscences. A servant brought tea, an imported English brew that sat well on the tongue.

"It's interesting that you're recently returned from England," Jefferson said. He smiled at Beth. "How would

you, an Englishwoman, assess the mood of your countrymen regarding the possibility of another war between
us?"

"My *former* countrymen, Mr. President," Beth said
with a smile.

"Ah, I stand corrected," Jefferson said.

"If it were to be decided by the people I know,"
Beth said, "such as my brother, Lord Beaumont, there
would be nothing but amity between us. The problem
comes, I fear, from the desperation felt by those in the
British government. The war with France has been going
on for far too long. I believe the recent setbacks in Spain
will cause the government to look elsewhere for the pres-
tige and satisfaction of victory."

"In the Atlantic, against unarmed American ships,"
Jefferson said.

"Which, if you don't mind, Mr. President," Renno
said, "brings to mind the purpose of our visit."

Jefferson listened grimly as Renno spoke of the impressment of his son and the others. It was obvious that
the President's anger was growing before he burst out,
"They go too far when they seize our ship's officers and
innocent passengers, especially if that passenger happens
to be a personal friend of mine and one of the first gradu-
ates of my military academy." He rose and walked swiftly
to the door, summoned a servant, and gave an order.
Within minutes James Madison came into the room.

In contrast to the tall dignity of Thomas Jefferson,
the President-elect seemed stunted and almost dowdy.
He was not an attractive man. His skin had the texture of
old parchment. His hair was swept back from his forehead
to expose a prominent brow. He bowed low upon being
introduced to Beth but did not look her in the eyes.

At Jefferson's request Renno repeated his account.
Madison nodded. "I assume, Mr. President, that you want
me to make a strong protest immediately."

"I want you to burn the ears of the British minister. I
want a ship dispatched to England within the next forty-
eight hours to carry an official protest couched in the
strongest words that includes a demand for the return of

the son of a prominent North Carolina family, an officer in the United States Marine Corps, and the other seamen taken from Mrs. Harper's ship."

"It will be done immediately," Madison said. He bowed to Beth once more. "I'm sorry, Mrs. Harper, that we meet under such troubling circumstances. If you're staying in Washington for any length of time, my wife would be delighted to receive you."

"Thank you, sir," Beth said.

Renno remained standing.

"Sit, sit," Jefferson said.

"I know that you're a busy man, Mr. President. We won't take any more of your time."

Jefferson laughed. "Mr. Madison is the busy man now. I have already started an extended holiday away from the halls of power that will last, I pray, the rest of my life."

Renno lifted the tails of his coat and sat.

"I am reminded that I had a letter for you from Governor Harrison not too long ago," Jefferson said. "It was addressed to either you or Roy Johnson. I forwarded it to Knoxville."

"Do you know its contents?" Renno asked.

Jefferson chuckled. "It was not sealed too tightly, after all. It seems that Governor Harrison is in need of the services of the two master scouts who were with General Wayne at Fallen Timbers."

Renno shook his head with a laugh. "I fear that he's several years too late. Neither of us is as young as we were at Fallen Timbers." He lifted one hand. "Of course, I can speak only for myself. That old war-horse I call Father might be on his way even now to answer the call."

"That would be like him," Beth agreed.

"You mentioned being in Portugal," Jefferson said. "I'm intrigued."

Renno smiled. "I think you might have some Indian blood, Mr. President, since you like so well the telling of a rousing story."

"Perhaps I would be the better for it," Jefferson said.

The talk went on for a long time. Jefferson asked

questions about the English presence that Renno had seen in Portugal. He listened with interest as Renno spoke of General Sir Arthur Wellesley and his victory over the Frenchman Junot at Vimeiro before Lisbon.

"This Wellesley," Jefferson said, "sounds impressive."

"A good man," Renno said. "A strategist and a disciplinarian with the proper regard for the well-being of his troops. He would have destroyed the French army on the Iberian Peninsula had he not been ordered by his superior to break off the pursuit."

"Could that have had a bearing on why he threw up his command and returned to England?" Jefferson asked.

"From what I observed of his character, yes," Renno said.

"Well, the British have not always been brilliant in their selection of their top commanders," Jefferson said. "It makes one wonder. The son of a Corsican lawyer has brought Europe to her knees and threatens the existence of the British, yet they continue to choose their field commanders on the basis of their status at birth."

"One must admit, Mr. President," Beth said, "that the English always muddle through. Each crisis seems to create its own savior."

"If so," Jefferson said, "isn't it time for the man of the hour to make himself known?" He chuckled. "I wonder if our own crisis will create a leader to see us through." He did not wait for a response. "Perhaps it has. Perhaps my friend James Madison is the answer to this country's need."

A clock sounded the hour. Jefferson rose. "What remains of my duty calls," he said. "May I expect both of you at dinner?"

"With pleasure," Beth said.

"It will not be just a social occasion," Jefferson said. "I'll see to it that the British minister is present so you can speak with him yourself."

It was not a large dinner party. The guests, aside from Renno, Beth, the Madisons, and Anthony Merry, the official representative of Great Britain in Washington, were members of Jefferson's cabinet or the Congress. The woman who would next occupy the White House, James Madison's wife, Dolley, was acting as hostess for the outgoing president, who was a widower. She was a tall and handsome woman with a dignified bearing. She wore a striking gray silk gown that showed an expanse of snowy bosom. Her smile was charming, and her friendliness seemed genuine to Beth.

"James has told me, Mrs. Harper," Dolley Madison said, "that he invited you to call on us. After meeting you, I can understand why. James is an admirer of beauty."

"You are the greatest proof of that statement," Beth said.

Dolley beamed. "I knew I was going to like you the minute I saw you. You will come, won't you?"

"Of course," Beth said.

"At Mr. Jefferson's suggestion, I've seated you next to the British minister," Dolley said. She winked. "Give him Old Ned and add some for me."

Anthony Merry was relieved to find that he was seated next to a beautiful woman rather than the sour little secretary of state, who had been persistent in his repeated protests regarding British policy.

"You're English," he said with delight when he heard Beth's accent.

"Sometimes to my shame," Beth said, thus setting the tone of the conversation and putting Merry on the defense.

"My dear lady," Merry sputtered, at a loss for words.

"When my countrymen drag American citizens off their ships, when they extend their barbaric practice of forced labor to American ships' officers and to my stepson, then I must feel shame."

"Ah," Merry said, nodding. "So that's who you are, madam." He smiled ruefully. "And I thought I was being given a pleasant respite from the affairs of state."

Beth touched Merry's hand. "Poor man," she said. "Please understand my concern."

"I do, madam," Merry replied. "And I regret the

worry that has been given you. Because you are English, I think you know that certain of our countrymen are sometimes given to excess. There's a saying in this country that applies to many of the men who man our ships of war: We're scraping the bottom of the barrel. A true English gentleman of the sort with which we used to staff our ships would never have committed such an act." He sighed. "Unless you have lived in England in recent years, it is difficult to understand the situation. This war is a continuing hemorrhage that is bleeding the nation of its achievers. Unfortunately the first to go in war are the brave ones, the most worthy of our young men."

"I understand, but that doesn't remedy the situation regarding my stepson and my crewmen, does it?" Beth asked sadly.

Merry rolled his eyes. "What offense have I committed against God that this should happen to the son of a beautiful Englishwoman and one of President Jefferson's favorite officers?" he asked plaintively. "I assure you that I have already taken action. Messages are, even now, on the way to London." He smiled. "You'll be reunited with your stepson as quickly as possible."

Later, when she had a chance to talk with Renno alone, Beth recounted her conversation with the British minister.

"Messages were sent today to the Admiralty," Beth said.

"And they will take weeks to reach London," Renno said. "Months before the Admiralty can relay orders to the *Cormorant*, if she's still cruising American waters."

"I know. . . ."

Renno shook his head. "We've done all we can."

"Yes. I tell myself that I mustn't worry."

Renno took her hand and squeezed it. "Do you remember when we were alone, just the two of us, making our way southward from Canada?"

"With great nostalgia," she said, smiling.

"Things seemed so simple and straightforward then."

She leaned to kiss him on the cheek. "You're ready to go home, aren't you?"

He smiled. "It would be a lie if I said no."

"Then we should go. Our presence here or in Wilmington won't hasten Little Hawk's return," she said.

"No, but we'll know about it sooner." He shrugged. "There will be time to go home after Little Hawk returns and your business is on solid ground again."

"Thank you," she said sincerely.

The F Street home of the President-elect and his comely wife was a lively place under siege by office seekers, members of Congress who wanted to establish good relations with the next man in the Executive Mansion, friends, acquaintances who wanted to become friends, and others who merely wanted to speak with and shake the hand of the next president.

Renno and Beth were the guests of honor at a small dinner party. Dolley was a woman who loved to entertain, and she was in her element presiding over dinner. The wine was not as expensive as that served at Mr. Jefferson's table; but it was adequate, and the conversation was animated and pleasant.

James Madison seemed to glow in the reflection of his wife's charm. They worked well together to make their guests feel welcome. Madison refrained from talking politics or policy at the table and discouraged any attempt to do so. It was afterward that he sought out Renno.

"I am aware of your past service both to Mr. Jefferson and General Washington," he said.

"It was my privilege," Renno replied.

"It is a pleasure to know that the country has such friends as you among the Indian nations," Madison went on. "I hope that I can count on that relationship to continue when I am president."

"Of course," Renno said, "although I must admit that there are times when friendship is strained."

"We are an expanding nation," Madison said. "A rose is either growing or it is dying."

"As the tribes are dying in the northwest?" Renno

asked. He held up a hand to silence Madison. "I have long since accepted the inevitability of white expansion, but you must remember, Mr. Madison, that not all Indians have seen your cities with their teeming millions. Only a very few of them can comprehend the irresistible force of the expanding population in the United States and that which underlies all like a volcano ready to erupt. I speak of the masses of Europe."

Madison reflected on what Renno had said. "That is a very astute observation. I agree that there will be the pressure of immigration after this war between England and Napoleon is over. As for those Indians who do not understand the tide of history, the Shawnee Tecumseh comes to mind."

"Yes. There are others, of course, but perhaps not with Tecumseh's gift of eloquence."

"Will he unite all tribes?"

"No, not all. Perhaps enough to be troublesome."

"That's reassuring. Governor Harrison thinks that Tecumseh poses a threat. He keeps asking for federal troops in Indiana Territory."

"They may be needed."

Madison looked surprised. "Surely Tecumseh won't be able to amass a force as great as that which fought at Fallen Timbers."

"That remains to be seen," Renno told him. "It's been a few years since I was in the Ohio country, but the way our mutual friend the governor keeps gobbling up Indian lands is surely alienating more and more tribes."

"In the end," Madison said, "it will all depend on the British. The Indians are no real threat without British arms. Even with British guns they can be handled by militia and the regulars that are at Harrison's command—unless redcoats from Canada join them."

"Do you think that might happen?" Renno asked.

"Only God and those who formulate British policy know for sure," Madison said. "I fear the worst. It's no secret that the British would like nothing better than to avenge their defeat or, at worst, to have a hostile Indian nation on our western frontier."

Renno was silent.

"By the way," Madison said, "Meriwether Lewis is sending a delegation of chiefs from the Missouri country to talk with the 'great white father' in Washington. Mr. Jefferson has designated me to meet with the Indian representatives. They're due here within a few days. In addition to Lewis's Sauk, Sioux, and Osage, there will be Creek and Cherokee representatives from your part of the country. I'd appreciate it if you stood with me. I'm sure that your insight into the Indian perspective will be valuable."

"At your service," Renno said.

Dolley Madison came up behind James and said, "I hate to interrupt, but I'd appreciate your mixing with the other guests for a while. You can tell each other war stories some other time."

Madison laughed. "You're right, my dear," he said. "We will join the ladies immediately."

The party had been moved to a large drawing room. A string quartet provided soft music. Renno took a seat next to Beth, and the Madisons sat with them.

"I'm going to miss this house," Madison confided. "I find it difficult to think of the President's mansion as a home."

"We'll make it a home," Dolley said.

"If anyone can, it is you," Madison said fondly.

"We were talking about your guest who will be arriving tomorrow," Dolley said.

"Ah," Madison said. "Bey Sidi Suliman Mellimelli."

"Himself," Dolley said.

"The bey is the new ambassador from Tunis," Madison said.

"I'm dying to see if he's brought his harem," Dolley said, to a chorus of giggles from the ladies. "Beth, you and Renno must come with us to greet His Excellency. I'm sure it will be very, ah, interesting. You will, won't you?"

Beth looked at Renno, who nodded.

The Madison party, including Renno and Beth, traveled by official carriage to Annapolis to greet the new ambassador from Tunis. The arrival was greeted by a cannonade fired by a U.S. frigate. It took some time for the Tunisian ship to be moored at dockside. After the gangplank was securely in position, men in baggy pantaloons ran across to form a corridor for the emergence of a score of handsome, spirited, thin-legged Arabian horses.

"Magnificent," Dolley said.

"The ambassador should be as handsome," Beth agreed.

Sidi Suliman Mellimelli, a mature man of fifty years, was not quite as trim as an Arabian stallion, but he was impressive. He was huge, with a bulk that Renno estimated at nearly three hundred pounds. He was dark complected, almost as dark as the Negro slaves working on the docks. His massive head was topped by a wound turban studded with one great diamond at the front.

"Well, ladies," Madison said, "it is time for the secretary of state to go into action."

The little man approached the Tunisian and was introduced by a State Department interpreter. Mellimelli bent, threw his massive arms around Madison, and kissed him on both cheeks.

"I have brought gifts," Mellimelli said through the interpreter. He waved pudgy hands at the group of Arabian horses. "The choicest among them is for the President." He stopped talking and frowned. "But who is President? Mr. Jefferson is President, but you, Mr. Madison, are also President."

"A temporary situation," Madison said. "I will be happy, sir, to accept your gift on behalf of Mr. Jefferson and the nation, since, in fact, any gift to the president is a gift to the country as a whole."

"I did not bring my horses to be ridden by everyone in your country," Mellimelli protested.

"I understand," Madison said. "Trust me, Mr. Ambassador, to take care of the matter."

"I want the president of the Congress to have a horse as well," Mellimelli said. "And I have wonderful gifts for the ladies." He bowed his massive bulk toward Dolley and Beth. "Who are, as I was told, indeed lovely."

Both of the ladies inclined a well-coiffed head in acknowledgment. A marine escort saw Mellimelli to a government carriage. Madison rode with him, leaving the white Indian, Beth, and Dolley to follow.

Madison joined Renno and the ladies hours later at the house on F Street. He was smiling with amusement when he entered.

"I take it, my dear, that you have gotten the ambassador settled in," Dolley said.

"I have," Madison said, "but not without certain misunderstandings. It seems that our department of protocol has fallen down on the job concerning the customs of Tunis."

"I hope you didn't insult the bey," Dolley said, her eyes twinkling. "If he sat on you, James—"

"No, no," Madison said. "I was enlightened by a member of his entourage. According to Tunisian protocol the host nation is required to bear the expenses of the bey's visit. I don't relish explaining this to the secretary of the treasury."

"I should think not," Dolley said with a laugh.

"You might be intrigued by some of the listed expense items," Madison said. His voice was dry, but mischief tugged at the corner of his mouth. "Lodgings and food, of course, but one of the items that I will have to enter into the State Department's books will, perhaps, be called 'appropriations to foreign intercourse,' namely payment to a number of, er, ladies to act as concubines for our visitors."

Dolley put her hand to her mouth and stifled a laugh. "My dear, what a price you pay for service to your country."

"One of the ladies is listed as Georgia, a Greek," Madison said with a small smile. "I was, I admit, intrigued."

"Oh? Did you meet her?" Dolley asked with interest.

"I was so eager to get back to you and our guests, my dear, that I allowed that pleasure to elude me," Madison said.

Dolley rolled her eyes. "Ah, the sacrifices you make for your family."

Madison smiled broadly. "It will interest you to know, my dear Dolley, that it is also the custom to invite the ambassador to one's home."

"Oh, dear," Dolley said. "I'll have to search out a chair strong enough—" She recovered quickly. "But if you must, you must."

The representatives of the various Indian tribes who arrived in Washington in a group had the same legal status as the ambassador from Tunis. They, like Mellimelli, represented sovereign nations. Solemn treaties recognized the territorial integrity of the tribes. So it was that James and Dolley Madison decided to have done with diplomatic obligations in one evening by entertaining several "ambassadors" at the house on F Street. Dolley had decided to make the dinner informal. It was served buffet style, with tables and sideboards laden with food in both the dining room and a large parlor.

At first there was a certain stiffness about the gathering. The bey from Tunis and his entourage were dressed in their richest robes. The Indians sported a variety of finery ranging from bleached buckskins to a splendid assortment of military and frock coats mixed with colorful shirts and striped trousers.

Renno circulated among the Indians. When he addressed the Creek and Cherokee chiefs in their own language, they began to relax. Indeed, his name was known to them.

The western Indians—Sauk, Sioux, and Osage—communicated with more difficulty in a mixture of frontier French, broken English, and sign language. When the Tunisian showed an interest in the Indians, there ensued a scene that might have been witnessed in ages past at the tower of Babel; but the mood was genial, and the curiosity was mutual. The bey joined the Indians in feasting, and there was no visible difference in table manners as Arab and Indian alike used fingers and hands instead of the flatware set out on the tables.

By the time the house servants began to replace the ravaged platters with a fine selection of cakes, punch, and ice cream, the wine that had been served with the food was gone, and the guests were looking around in vain for more. They settled for a concerted attack on the desserts.

Mellimelli, through his interpreter and Renno, was questioning the Cherokee representative about Indian women. The Cherokee was a young man, robust in build, a proud representative of the "real people."

"It is known," he said, "that Cherokee women are the handsomest women on earth."

This statement, when it was understood by all of the gathering, brought forth a burst of protest from Creek, Sioux, and Sauk. Only the Osage nodded his head in agreement.

Renno had singled out the Osage, a strong young war chief named Young Elk, as a man of worth. He had had the opportunity to engage in conversation with the Osage and had learned that Young Elk's village was to the north of the Quapaw lands along the Arkansas, beyond the mountains.

"The women of the Osage are strong and as beautiful as the fresh green of spring," Young Elk said, "but I will agree with my brother that Cherokee women are handsome. Indeed, my wife is Cherokee."

"That is of great interest to me," Renno said in French, but before he could continue, Sidi Suliman Mellimelli let out a bass roar and pointed to the Madisons' black cook, who had come into the room carrying a fresh tray of cakes.

"Now *that* is a woman!" Mellimelli bellowed.

The cook's bulk matched that of Mellimelli. She was bosomy, to say the least. Mellimelli waddled toward her, threw his arms around her, and gave her an expressive hug.

"She reminds me of my most expensive wife," he told the bemused gathering. "She is, indeed, a load for a camel."

When Renno explained to the puzzled cook what the

Tunisian had said, she laughed loudly. "Ain't gonna find me up on no camel, Mr. Renno," she said.

"American women," Mellimelli shouted, intent on pursuing his favorite subject, "look like angels, as you can see." He waved a fat, bejeweled hand toward Beth and Dolley. "But in all due respect, there is something lacking. Now *that* woman—" He pointed toward the door that had swallowed the black cook.

"There is nothing lacking in Indian women," said the Creek.

"Are you insulted?" Dolley whispered to Beth.

"Mortified," Beth said, laughing like a schoolgirl.

"I'd like to see his most expensive wife," Dolley said.

"It cannot be denied," Mellimelli said, "that Allah gave Arab women the first place in beauty in all the world."

"Who is this Allah?" the Cherokee wanted to know, and thus the subject of conversation—ponderous, slow, often not fully understood—moved away from female pulchritude to religion, which led Mellimelli to quite undiplomatic utterances. After he understood that each of the Indians was advancing his own interpretation of God, he sputtered in shock at the heresy.

"You are all heathens and heretics!" he bellowed.

"I don't think I'll translate that exactly," Renno told Mellimelli's interpreter.

"Tell them that they are all learned gentlemen," the interpreter suggested.

"The bey states," Renno told the Indians in various ways, "that God is God, regardless of the name one gives Him."

A massacre on F Street having been averted, Dolley told the servants to clear the remainder of the cakes, punch, and ice cream, thus making it obvious to her guests, Arab and Indian alike, that the party was over.

Renno sought out the Osage, Young Elk, who was slightly tipsy from the wine and the punch. "If I may ask, brother, how did you come to take a Cherokee wife?"

"Through the kindness of the spirits," Young Elk said. "She came to me with her brother and others whom we allowed to settle in the mountains south of the buffalo plains."

"Was there in the group a warrior called Ho-ya?"

Young Elk's eyes widened in pleasure. "Indeed, for he is my brother-by-marriage."

"Then your wife is We-yo?"

"It is true."

"She is the daughter of my sister," Renno said.

"The world is small," said Young Elk. He extended his arm to be taken by Renno. "I greet you, brother."

"They are well, my niece and my nephew?"

"They are well. It pleases me to say that We-yo is my only wife."

"I am pleased as well. It was good of the Osage to give land to those who fled from the pressure of the white man."

"Does not the land belong to all?"

"It should," Renno said. "I ask your permission, my brother, to visit in your land one day."

"I personally will make you welcome."

"My niece has a daughter," Renno said.

"She is now my daughter, the little Summer Moon, and the boy Jani, adopted by my wife, is also mine." He grinned widely. "So there are Cherokee and Seneca in my house, and by the time I return there will be one who is Osage."

"We-yo is with child, then?"

Young Elk nodded.

James Madison had been busy seeing to the departure of the Tunisian entourage. The rooms were much quieter now, for most of the guests had departed. Madison came to stand beside Renno.

"I apologize, Young Elk, for neglecting you," Madison said. "I want very much to talk with you."

"That is why I have come," Young Elk said.

"I suppose," Madison said, "that my first question of you would be regarding your attitude toward Tecumseh and his attempts to form an Indian confederation. How do the Osage feel about him?"

"The Shawnee have no land," Young Elk said. "They

are whores who fight the battles of others in exchange for
permission to hunt the lands of others. We do not need
the help of whores or the dogs who lick their heels to
protect our own."

Madison nodded gravely. "Then I take it that it isn't
likely that the Osage will join with the tribes of the
Ohio?"

"Never," said Young Elk, "for there is too much bad
blood between us."

"There you have it, Mr. Madison," Renno said after
Young Elk had taken his leave with the others. "The Indian is often his own worst enemy. He fights his brother
instead of the real enemy."

"Who is—?" Madison asked.

Renno smiled but did not answer.

Alone with Beth in a guest room at Mr. Jefferson's
Executive Mansion, Renno told her of the coincidence of
We-yo's husband being one of the visiting Indian delega-
tion.

"She is such a lovely girl," Beth said. "I pray that he
is a good husband, that he is kind to her."

"Yes," Renno said, but his heart was heavy. Not even
to the woman who was closest to him in the world could
he express his sadness. He had fought and struggled to
make life better for his own clan and for the people of his
brother-by-marriage. Renno took it as a personal failure
that his niece was now living in an Osage hut on the edge
of the plains . . . living, he imagined, as Indian women
had lived in the days before the coming of the Europeans.
Life was hard enough in Rusog's town, where well-built
log cabins kept out the cold of winter, where rooms were
lighted with oil lamps, and where women had metal cooking pots and garden tools to do their traditional work.

Ah, well, he thought. Rightly or wrongly Ho-ya and
We-yo had chosen to return to the old ways. Such ratio-
nalization did not ease his feeling of guilt. If he had been
at home with his own people, perhaps he could have in-
fluenced his nephew to reconsider his decision to seek a
place in the western wilderness.

Chapter Four

"Mr. Harper, please," Dolley Madison said, "you *must* stay through the inauguration."

Renno genuinely liked the President-elect's wife, and, although the pressure of his duties kept James Madison preoccupied, the white Indian had nothing but respect for the little man who would lead the United States for the next four years. At Dolley's insistence Beth and he had spent the last two days and nights as guests in the house on F Street.

"I fear, Mrs. Madison," Renno said, "that you are directing your appeal to the wrong person."

Beth, dressed in a white gown that showed her long, graceful neck and English porcelain skin to good advantage, took the woman's hand and said, "I would love to, Dolley, really I would. But there's a rumor going around in Congress that the embargo will be lifted soon. When that happens I *must* be in Wilmington so that I can start the revival of my business as swiftly as possible."

Dolley Madison, too, was dressed in white finery, for guests, including the President, would be arriving soon. The gown she had chosen deemphasized her plumpness. She favored gowns that showed a wide expanse of bosom. She was quite regal, with her hair turned in curls that dangled in front of her ears and clung to her smooth forehead. She stood with her head held high, always looking as if she were smiling inwardly.

At that moment James Madison came into the room.

"Ah, here's my darling little husband," Dolley said.

Madison stood a full head shorter than his wife. Unlike Dolley he did not smile easily, but there was an aura of ease and dignity about him.

"James, might the embargo be lifted before Inauguration Day?" Dolley asked. "Beth needs to be in Wilmington when you men repeal that hateful act, and I do so want her to be here for the great events."

"My dear," Madison said, "I cannot predict with any reliable degree of accuracy the actions of others."

"Really, James," Dolley said, "we know that you're doing your own work and Mr. Jefferson's, too."

"Although the President has turned certain matters over to my keeping," Madison said, "they do not include the embargo. That is the one issue on which he stands firm. He feels that to repeal the act now would be backing down before the enmity of France and England." He shook his head. "I suspect that Congress will consider the problem early in the new year, but whenever Congress is involved, the mills grind slowly."

There was a stir at the front of the house. Thomas Jefferson, tall, gentlemanly, smiling, came into the room. At his heels was the servant responsible for announcing guests.

"Mr. President," Dolley said, beaming as she rushed forward to take Jefferson's hands. "You deprive my man of the pleasure of telling us of your arrival."

"If it means so much, Mrs. Madison, I'll go out and come back in again later," Jefferson said.

Dolley laughed with delight and dismissed the butler with a wave of her hand. "I'm glad you're early, Mr. President. Perhaps you can persuade the Harpers to stay through January and the inaugural events."

"You're welcome to stay in the Executive Mansion until the fourth of March," Jefferson said.

"It's not a matter of accommodations," Dolley said. "Beth wants to be in North Carolina when the embargo's lifted."

Jefferson's face darkened. "Oh? It's to be lifted, then?"

Madison gave Dolley a warning look. She did not notice. "You can tell us when, can't you, sir?" she asked charmingly.

Jefferson smiled. "I cannot, Mrs. Madison."

"There are other considerations," Renno said. "As a fond grandfather, I'm eager to see my little brood. I have a daughter, daughter-by-marriage, and four grandchildren in Wilmington."

"Oh, dear," Dolley said. She brightened. "Well, there's time. Perhaps I can change your minds."

"We have just enough time to get to Wilmington for Christmas with my family," Renno said.

The liveried butler reappeared in the doorway. "Guests are arriving, Mrs. Madison."

Dolley took Beth by the hand and led her off to greet the newcomers.

"I came early, Renno," Jefferson said, "in hope of having a word with you."

"You'll excuse me," Madison said diplomatically.

"No, James, you should hear this," Jefferson said.

"Very well," Madison said.

"Will you be going back to the western frontier anytime soon?" Jefferson asked Renno.

Renno smiled. "Because of my wife's business interests, my decision about going home depends largely on the embargo, sir."

"The Dambargo," Jefferson said bitterly.

"Beth is concerned for the people who depend on Huntington Shipping for their livelihood," Renno said. He raised one hand in a conciliatory gesture. "I'm not lobbying, Mr. Jefferson, but if the embargo isn't lifted

soon, there will be no Huntington Shipping Company.
Beth is continuing to pay wages to the idle dockworkers
and the seamen."

"Admirable," Madison said.

Jefferson seemed to be lost in gloom.

"To answer your question," Renno said, "I won't be
going home until the business is back on its feet. My
guess now is that I'll go back west with my family shortly
after Beth's ships leave Cape Fear with cargoes for England."

Jefferson nodded. "I think that Mr. Madison might
be able to tell you more than I about when the embargo
will be lifted."

Renno took that to mean that Jefferson would leave
the Embargo Act in effect for the remainder of his term,
which would end March 4, 1809. He nodded.

"When you go west," Jefferson said, "could I possibly persuade you to visit an old friend of ours in St.
Louis?"

"Meriwether Lewis?" Renno asked.

"The same," Jefferson said. "I've had a most curious
letter from him. He's doing a wonderful job as governor of
the Louisiana Territory, you know."

"No one deserved the position more," Renno said.

"Exactly," Jefferson said. "In his letter he says that
he has come into possession of some interesting but
rather disturbing information. Apparently he considers it
too sensitive to entrust to the mails." He looked into
Renno's eyes. "I know that you've been asked before to
leave your family and undertake a long, difficult journey.
Perhaps you will not be grateful that one of my last acts as
president is to ask you to assume one more task."

Renno nodded. "You honor me, as always, Mr. President."

"Good, good," Jefferson said, and visibly relaxed. "I
thought of you, Sachem, because Meriwether knows that
he can trust you. And, I warrant, he'll be pleased to see
you. After you have consulted with him, use your own
judgment with regard to how to proceed. If you consider

his information to be of vital importance, I would be grateful if you would deliver it in person to Mr. Madison."

"I, too, will be grateful," Madison said.

"I have been honored to serve three presidents before you, Mr. Madison," Renno said. "It will be my pleasure to report to you." He smiled. "So long as I am invited to one of your wife's excellent dinners."

"It is you who do me honor," Madison responded. A smile threatened to crack the wizened parchment of his face. "Dolley does set a good table, doesn't she?"

For the first time in his young life Ta-na-wun-da, youngest son of the white Indian by the beautiful Seneca maiden An-da, was having difficulty completing a hunt. The pair of deer that his cousin Gao and he had been following had separated to travel along two game trails. Gao had taken the left track, Ta-na the right. It had been an hour since Ta-na was able to hear Gao's call, the mournful coo of a dove.

Ta-na was his father's son. He was just sixteen, but he had grown to be taller than both his father and his uncle El-i-chi. His Seneca mother had been killed when he was but a babe in arms, and he had shared, with Gao, the ample bosom of his aunt Ah-wa-o, then had spent most of his sixteen years in the house of his uncle and aunt, calling them Father and Mother and calling Gao his brother.

The entire family of the white Indian called itself Seneca. Oddly enough, Ta-na was more worthy of that title than any of his relatives, even his father and his uncle El-i-chi, for he had the blood of his mother, a full-blood Seneca, in addition to that of his father, which was mixed. The three quarters of his blood that was Indian, half of it Seneca, gave Ta-na's skin a coppery sheen that was lightened by the quarter mixture of white blood. His hair was that of his mother—a heavy, black mane clubbed at the nape of his neck with a leather thong. His brown eyes were his mother's as well; but his nose, his cheekbones, his chin were taken from his Harper antecedents, so that his grandmother Toshabe often said that he was his great-grandfather Ja-gonh, disguised as a Seneca. Since Ja-gonh

had been of white blood—blue-eyed, blond of hair—
Ta-na had mixed emotions about the comparison. He believed there was merit in both the opinions of his birth
father, Renno, and in those of young men such as his
cousin Ho-ya. In direct contradiction to Renno's belief
that survival for all Indians depended on merging their
way of life with the whites of the United States, Ho-ya
had led a group of young Seneca and Cherokee across the
Mississippi to lands not yet targeted for white expansion.

In the rolling, wooded Cherokee hunting grounds
south of the Tennessee River, Ta-na was not thinking
about his background or his looks or the weighty questions posed by the future. He was concentrating on something of more immediate import, adding fresh meat to the
larder. His every sense was alert to the sounds, smells,
and signs of the forest. Gao and he had been on the hunt
for three full days without success, and the spoor he was
following was, he guessed, half a day old. Never had hunting been so poor. He had heard others complain about the
scarcity of game, but neither Gao nor he had experienced
it firsthand.

He stooped to push his way through a deer trail
arched over with brush and emerged on the sandy bank of
a small creek. His heart pounded with excitement, for the
old tracks were joined by fresh sign. He heard the soft
cooing of a dove from across the stream. He answered
with the call of a quail. The signal from Gao was repeated
four times quickly—an alert. He concealed himself behind a deadfall and peered out through a canopy of leaf-
less brush. He heard a twig snap in the bushes on the
other side of the stream and readied his rifle. A young
buck with yearling antlers pushed his way cautiously
through the brush to the edge of the stream, looked behind him warily, then bent to drink.

"Brother," Ta-na whispered, "I praise you for your
strength and your beauty, and I thank you for giving yourself that we might eat."

The deer leaped as the heavy-caliber ball smashed
into his heart but went limp at the height of his vault and
crumpled to the sand. Ta-na hooted like an owl and ran

across the creek to slit the animal's throat. Gao came crashing through the brush to help him lash the buck's rear legs and hoist the carcass to hang from a limb so that the blood could drain, thus removing some of the strong taste from the meat.

Working together the cousins fashioned a travois of thin saplings and brush and, with the deer loaded onto the makeshift sled, started for the village. It was hard work. By midday the sky had changed from winter blue to the gray of dark, threatening clouds. The last few miles were endured in a cold, misty rain that began to freeze with the coming of evening, so that as they reached the outskirts of Rusog's village at dusk, crystals of ice gleamed on the ends of the hairs of the deer's pelt.

El-i-chi stood in the doorway of his longhouse, a buffalo cape around his shoulders, and watched his boys at work. They looked more like brothers than cousins, but then Renno and he were cut from the same mold, so it wasn't too odd that the features of the boys were much the same, the identical chiseled nose, the strong chin, the un-Indian cheekbones. El-i-chi considered Ta-na to be as much his son as his own blood, Gao.

The boys quickly and skillfully completed the task of skinning and butchering the buck. Three families shared the meat. Gao took a portion of the kill to his aunt Ena's log cabin, and Ta-na took meat to his grandmother Toshabe. Ah-wa-o salted down a large cut from the deer's haunch to be braised slowly. The rest was hung high to season in the smoke from the fire that burned in the center of the room.

Ta-na washed away the blood of the kill, rolled down his buckskin sleeves, then squatted with his hands extended beside the fire.

"You hunted far," El-i-chi said.

"There are no deer near the river," Ta-na told him.

"I thought we were going to have to travel all the way into the lands of the Creek to find this one deer," Gao said. "Uncle Rusog's hunters were ranging far to the west."

"Are we too many?" Ta-na asked. "The old ones say that what remains of the Cherokee lands is but a small portion of what it once was. Will more of us have to do what Ho-ya and We-yo did, leave our homes to find new lands where there are no whites?"

"Maybe you'll have to learn to cultivate the soil," Ah-wa-o suggested as Ta-na lifted a pot of corn and dried squash from the cook fire.

"You sound like Uncle Renno," Gao said. "There will always be game. It's just a bad year."

"I am concerned," Ta-na said seriously, "since in the near future I might have to hunt for a family of my own."

"So," El-i-chi said, casting a look at Ah-wa-o. She had been expecting something along the lines of Ta-na's statement. For quite some time now Ta-na had been calling on a pretty half-Seneca, half-Cherokee maiden named Head-in-the-cloud. There had been some tension between the brothers because, for a while, Gao also seemed to have a fancy for the beautiful Cloud; but it seemed to Ah-wa-o that the girl had decided not to risk losing both Ta-na and Gao just for the fun of leading the two of them on a merry chase. As descendants of the white Indian, either boy was a good catch.

"I take it, Ta-na, that you are contemplating a serious step," Ah-wa-o said.

Ta-na nodded, his face impassive. He had learned the art of concealing his emotions from his two fathers.

"I'm hungry," Gao said.

"I have spoken with Cloud's parents," Ta-na announced. "I told them that the home I would give their daughter would be my father Renno's longhouse. Was I wrong in assuming that I have that right?"

"By Seneca custom, a husband joins the family of his wife," El-i-chi said.

"That is not the only custom that is changing," Ah-wa-o said with disapproval.

"I'm sure that Renno would be happy to have you use the house," El-i-chi said. "And have you decided when to take this step?"

"When my father El-i-chi says that *orenda* is favorable," Ta-na answered.

El-i-chi remained silent. Ah-wa-o took down ceramic bowls. Two-and-a-half-year-old Ah-wen-ga, the child named for El-i-chi and Renno's grandmother, helped her mother by handing the steaming bowls to her father and two brothers. El-i-chi served himself from the steaming pot, sat, and began to eat slowly. He had to blow on each spoonful.

It was a while before Ta-na spoke again, this time in Seneca. English was usually spoken in the longhouse, but when matters of import were being discussed, it seemed natural to all of them to fall back into the old language.

"My father El-i-chi makes no comment," Ta-na said.

"Has there been a question?" El-i-chi asked, looking up.

"Not directly," Ta-na said. "I now appeal to you not only as my father but as my shaman to offer your opinion as to the signs and omens pertaining to my early marriage."

"Since you have made a direct appeal, I will give you my answer," El-i-chi said. "It is my opinion that an event as important as marriage should be postponed until your father is here."

Ta-na chewed and swallowed before he spoke. "My father Renno does not coil the events of his life around *me*," he pointed out.

"Nevertheless," El-i-chi said, "for such a significant event, he should be present."

"With respect, Father El-i-chi, how long would you have me wait?" Ta-na asked. "Shall I wait until after the white man's holidays? Shall I wait for the time of the new beginning to see if my father Renno returns to his people? Shall I wait until it is time for the planting of the corn or until the great bear in the sky tips his color pot and adds flame to the leaves of the trees?"

El-i-chi ate in silence for long moments. It was true that it was impossible to predict Renno's return. His brother was more at home in the world of the white man than he himself could ever be, and Renno had left the village with a great wound in his heart, branded there by the seeming indifference of their people to his advice.

"You are convinced that marriage to Head-in-the-cloud is something you must do?" El-i-chi asked.

"If my father has an objection, perhaps it is time to voice it now," Ta-na said.

"I have no objection to the girl. She is of good family. That she is half-Cherokee is not to be held against her, since, as my brother has pointed out, the gradual absorption of our clan into the tribe of my sister's husband is inevitable. I could, however, point out that you are but sixteen. I would hope that in waiting for Renno to return, you would add one year to that age."

"Father El-i-chi," Ta-na said, frowning, "I have never disputed your wisdom."

"Until now." El-i-chi chuckled, remembering when he was not much older than Ta-na and madly in love with a half-wild Chickasaw girl named Holani. With an inward flush he regretted the cooling of the passion that had burned in him then. When he had fallen in love with Ah-wa-o, the flames had burned brightly once again. "Orenda is favorable for love at the time chosen by the lovers," he said. "If it is your wish, I will arrange the ceremony in cooperation with Cloud and her family."

"I will be forever grateful," Ta-na said.

Gao was pleased that the Seneca wedding ceremony was not lengthy, even when El-i-chi used the occasion to supplement his blessing and the good wishes of the tribe with advice for the young newlyweds. The weather was kind, a faultless day of hard, brittle, early winter light and mild temperatures. Head-in-the-cloud was exquisite in bleached buckskin. Her accessories were a mixture of Seneca and Cherokee handiwork.

Gao told himself that he should be happy for his brother, but in spite of his goodwill he could not be sincere in enjoyment of the day. There were two reasons for his melancholy. First, he felt a sense of loss. Reason told him that Ta-na would still be his brother and his friend, but things would not be the same. They had been inseparable from infancy. Ta-na's marriage would bring change. Secondly, although he was too loyal to his brother to admit it openly, Gao had been in love with the beautiful Cloud from the time he first began to take notice of the young girls in Rusog's settlement and the Seneca village adjoining it.

When the ceremony was done, the manitous praised, the parents of the bride congratulated—when bride and groom ran away hand in hand to privacy in Renno's long-house, across the commons from the cabin occupied by Roy Johnson and Toshabe—Gao sought the solitude of the forest. In one way he was more like his uncle Renno than his father: He was a runner. He set out swiftly, chasing his own shadow cast by the brittle winter sun, and he did not slow his pace until his lungs were on fire and his legs were wobbly.

A family of squirrels had made nests in the thatch of Renno's longhouse. The structure had been long in disuse, and cold tendrils of the coming evening found their way through chinks in the wall as Ta-na started a fire.

"It's too big," Cloud said. "I feel lost, it is so big."

"You'll get used to it," Ta-na said.

"It's not as cozy as a log cabin," Cloud said.

"If a log cabin is what you want," Ta-na said, smiling up at her, "I'll build you one."

"I'm cold," she said.

Toshabe, Ena, and the women of Cloud's family had supplied enough food for half a dozen newly married couples, enough for them to eat well for days. Ta-na lifted the lid on one of Toshabe's cook pots and sniffed venison stew still warm from his grandmother's fire.

"Are you hungry?" he asked.

Cloud took up a blanket and wrapped it around her shoulders. "We will freeze in this huge place," she whined in a little girl's voice.

Ta-na did his best to keep her warm. He succeeded, at least temporarily, for his blood was hot enough to heat hers. Actually, little effort was required on his part, for she, too, was at an age when desire can be all-consuming.

Neither Ta-na nor Cloud felt the chill breath of the night, not even when they let the fire burn low and a rising wind whistled around the longhouse, to disturb the squirrels nesting in the thatch so that they made rustling, rattling noises.

"Gao!" Ta-na beamed with surprise and pleasure when he opened the door to his brother's knock.

"You're both still alive, then," Gao said dryly.

"Come in, Gao," Cloud said without enthusiasm.

A fire was burning warmly. The heat was making the squirrels active. It sounded as if they were rolling stored nuts together. Ta-na looked smug and sassy. Cloud had let her hair fall and had not bothered to brush out the tangles. There were dark smudges under her eyes. Her deerskin gown was soiled and wrinkled.

"I'm glad to know someone else is alive," she said bitterly.

"I hate to disturb you," Gao said, "but Grandmother Toshabe is ill, and there is no meat in the house."

"You're not going to run off into the woods and leave me alone in this shack," Cloud said. Her voice had a sharp edge.

"We have to eat," Ta-na said.

"I've seen how you eat," she said. She held both hands in front of her mouth and made noises like a pig rooting. "Why doesn't her husband find her some food?"

"Grandfather Roy wants to stay with Grandmother," Gao explained.

"I do have my duty," Ta-na said pleadingly, putting his hand under Cloud's chin.

She slapped his hand away and turned her back to him. There was an embarrassed silence in the longhouse while Ta-na prepared himself for the hunt. Before the boys left, Gao helped Ta-na carry in wood so that Cloud could keep the fire going. The weather was cold.

"I may not be here when you come back," Cloud threatened.

"If you want to visit your family, that would be

good," Ta-na said. "Unless the manitous are with us and bring us luck, we may be gone overnight."

"If you expect me to sleep alone in this cave—" she said.

From the roof a shower of broken nutshells rained down onto Cloud's head. She brushed at her hair frantically and burst into tears.

Ta-na cast a quick glance at Gao, who nodded imperceptibly and went outside. Ta-na tried to comfort his wife, but she would have none of it.

"You are a savage," she sobbed, "with animals in your house."

"Do you want me to run them out in the dead of winter? They would not survive."

"I don't care. Take them into your bed if you want to, for I won't be here."

"You're being childish," he said with some irritation.

She lashed out at him, and her palm made a ringing sound when it connected with his cheek. Anger flooded through him. He stalked out of the house.

Gao respected Ta-na's silence until they were well away from the village, traveling southward along the side of a ridge.

"She is young, Brother," Gao said.

Ta-na grunted.

"She was the youngest and prettiest of a large family," Gao continued. "She is accustomed to having attention."

"Which I have given her," Ta-na said. "To the exclusion of all else in my life."

"Be patient with her, Brother," Gao said. There was envy in his heart, and he believed that if he were in Ta-na's bed, he could do a better job of making Cloud understand.

"Ho," Ta-na said, coming to a halt. Fresh sign leading eastward crossed their path. "The spirits are kind."

"Indeed," Gao said. "You will be back by your own fire this very night."

They tracked the deer for a mile and found the spot where another hunter had made his kill.

"I thought it was too good to be true," Ta-na said.

They turned their faces southward, and just like other hunts that winter, it was a long and difficult search before they could start back toward the village with a large buck on a travois.

Ta-na's longhouse was empty. The ashes of the fire were cold. Ta-na helped Gao finish the skinning and distribution of their kill before he went across the open fields to Rusog's town and the log cabin of Cloud's parents.

Cloud's mother greeted him coldly. "I see that my son-by-marriage has brought nothing from his hunt."

It was not the first time that his mother-by-marriage had spoken to him in a less-than-kindly fashion. He was cold and tired. He was disappointed that Cloud had not been at home awaiting him, with a warm fire going, with food in the pots. He spoke before he considered his words.

"I did not guess," he said, "that the men of my family-by-marriage were such poor hunters that they need my help."

"If you have come to eat, you're too late," Cloud's mother said.

"I have come for my wife," he told her.

Cloud was sullen as they walked home. He had started a fire, so the longhouse was warm. He spoke pleasantly of the hunt and described the difficulty in finding game. She wrapped herself in a blanket and huddled down by the fire.

"You've eaten?" he asked.

She nodded.

He had not. There was meat, but it was raw. He chewed on a piece of jerky. Cloud went to the bed without a word. He joined her there, put his arms around her, and cupped her warm, soft rump against his belly. He had been away from her for two days and a night.

"Ah, I missed you so," he whispered.

"No," she said. She was surprisingly strong.

"Cloud?" he questioned, after she violently thrust him away from her.

"You chased me shamelessly," she hissed at him. "You promised me such wonderful things. You told me you loved me for myself, and all the while all you wanted was this." She seized his manhood and squeezed painfully. "You got what you wanted, and now you have no time for me. You leave me on my own for days. You shame me by forcing me to seek the company of my family."

"Either we hunt or be forced to eat boiled corn all winter," he said, and frustration added an edge of anger to his voice.

"You would rather be with Gao and your family than with me," she said. "You are rude to my family."

"I will not leave you again," he said. "Except when it is my turn to hunt. I will hunt alone, if that will make you feel better." He knew that in making that statement he was punishing himself and Gao more than Cloud; but he was angry, and he was sixteen years old, with the girl he loved so close to him that he could feel her body heat. He reached for her. She slapped his hands. He turned his back to her and, with youthful need and passion fueling his anger, lay awake until she had settled down on her side of the bed and was breathing deeply and evenly.

He turned, put his hand on her shoulder, shook her. She whimpered. "How can you just go to sleep when I am in a turmoil?" he demanded.

"I'm tired, Ta-na," she said crossly. "If you must have me, do it and get it over with."

He took her quickly but without joy.

In the days to come Ta-na hunted alone within one day's march of the village and returned after dark with nothing more than squirrels. When Gao questioned him, he was evasive, so Gao got the impression that he was not welcome in Ta-na's house. Gao tried not to feel hurt, but not even a brother can withstand continual rejection without it taking its toll. The lifelong closeness between the sons of the former sachem and the shaman of the Seneca clan was suspended with hurt on one side and a growing frustration on the other, brought on by the demands of a spoiled sixteen-year-old girl who had not been ready for marriage, after all.

In the longhouse across the commons from the scene of Ta-na's marital trials, Roy Johnson was a worried man. For months now a change had been occurring in Toshabe. From being a plump and healthy woman in her sixties she had changed gradually to become thin and haggard. She was still the best cook in the country, but she could not partake of her own culinary efforts with any consistency. More often than not she vomited up what she had managed to eat.

Ena and Ah-wa-o helped Toshabe cut down her clothes so that they fit her shrinking form. Toshabe kept up a good front and never complained, but when she began to moan at night with pains in her stomach, El-i-chi took Roy aside and said, "It is time to send a letter to Renno."

"I hate to admit it," Roy said, "but you're right."

So it was that two letters crossed in Knoxville. One went east toward the North Carolina coast with a message for a son a long way from home; the other came down from Washington, through the Cumberland Gap.

Without stating it directly in his letter to Renno, Roy included enough information to make the white Indian understand the seriousness of Toshabe's ailment. He said that Toshabe was showing all the symptoms of the lingering disease, that a mass could be felt in her stomach. He said just enough to let Renno know that if he wanted to see his mother alive, he would have to travel swiftly.

The incoming letter was addressed to either Renno Harper or Colonel Roy Johnson. It was the latter who opened it. He showed it to El-i-chi.

"Sounds tempting, don't it?" Roy asked. "Sounds like Harrison's got himself a real situation up there."

El-i-chi was saddened. There had been a time, and it seemed only yesterday, when a summons from the President would have brought quick action. Such a call from George Washington, Thomas Jefferson, or even John Adams would have sent Seneca men toward the north almost immediately.

"I reckon General Harrison will have to make do without us," Roy said. Roy had lost one wife. In some way, he couldn't remember how, he had survived, but he'd been younger then. To think of continuing his life without the second woman he had come to love was painful.

"Unless *you* want to go in our stead," Roy said.

"I do not intend to sound critical of my brother," El-i-chi said, "but unlike him, I will not abandon my duty to my people at the call of the United States."

When Gao was told of the letter from Washington, he asked to read it. His reaction was quick and decisive. He had lost a brother, and the girl he loved was becoming an unhappy, harping, unpleasant shrew. His father, his aunt Ena, and his uncle Renno had served with and fought for the forces of the United States. Following in their footsteps seemed to be the obvious and natural thing to do.

Chapter Five

Little Hawk awoke with the stench of damp, unwashed clothing and sweaty bodies in his nostrils. There was movement around him. A hand touched his shoulder, and a voice said, "Rouse yourself, mate."

He rolled out of his hammock, landed on his feet, and began to pull on tunic and trousers. The man who had wakened him was already stowing his hammock.

"Do it this way, you see," the seaman said.

Little Hawk had been separated from James Ridley in being assigned to quarters and was on the starboard watch. James and all but two of the seamen from the *Beth Huntington* had been assigned to the port watch.

"You ain't no navy," the seaman said, "air you?"

"No," Little Hawk said, trying to stow his hammock as neatly as the seaman's.

"'ere, let me." The seaman took the hammock and rolled it quickly. "You'll catch on."

"Thank you."

"We'd best get on deck." He looked briefly into Little Hawk's eyes, then his gaze shifted away. "I'm 'ensley."

"Ainsley?"

" 'ensley."

"Hensley."

"That's wot I said."

"I'm Harper."

" 'arper. Wot you do, see, is you don't look 'em in the eyes. They takes that as defiance. You obeys orders, and you keeps your feelings to yourself. 'Specially when the gunner says 'jump,' you don't even wait to ask how high. You jumps."

In a mass, the starboard watch rushed out onto the open deck and into a ragged formation. Gunner Griffiths stalked up and down before the ranks. He halted in front of Little Hawk, who was standing beside the shorter Hensley.

"And a good morning to you, sir," Griffiths said with a wide grin. "I trust you slept well."

"Sir!" Little Hawk barked.

"If not," Griffiths said, "we'll see to it that you sleep well tonight."

Little Hawk had decided to draw on his experience at West Point, when, as now, he had been in a position where those in command had full rein to use their power unjustly. He had learned there that it is wise not to fight against authority and harsh discipline when there is no hope of winning. He knew that he would be a target for Gunner Griffiths. Aboard the *Beth* he had felt the jar of the contact of his fist with Griffiths' chin all the way up into his shoulder. The bosun would not soon forget the force of the blow.

Little Hawk spent the day slopping out the bilges. He worked in cramped, filthy spaces and was soaked to the skin with the putrid accumulation in the lower spaces of the ship. Griffiths checked on him at irregularly spaced intervals, always to find Little Hawk working.

It was dark when the bosun relieved him and sent him off to quarters. Tired as he was, and a bit nauseated from inhaling the stench of the bilges all day, Little Hawk took time to wash his clothing in salt water and to hang it up to dry after he had eaten his evening meal of rancid salt pork and wormy hardtack.

On the third day of impressment, the wisdom of Little Hawk's decision to cooperate fully was made clear by an example of the harsh and pitiless policy aboard a British hell ship. A sailor had stolen an extra ration of biscuit. His punishment was twenty lashes. He was tied to the mainmast with his hands raised over his head. His jumper was stripped away, exposing the white, tender skin of his back. Gunner Griffiths wielded the lash, and he gave the impression that he savored every blow. He took his time, waiting for a count of ten between each stinging, hissing fall of the cat-o'-nine-tails.

It was evident to Little Hawk that Griffiths wanted to see him lashed to the mast with his back exposed. The bosun took every opportunity to demean him with words and by assigning him the most taxing duties. He spent more than two weeks in the bilges, and after he was finished with that odious task, he spent days on his hands and knees scrubbing the deck.

"Well, pussy," Griffiths said at the end of a long day of labor that left Little Hawk's back aching, "not a spark of fight left in you, eh?"

"Sir!" Little Hawk said.

"And I thought there'd be a bit of spirit in such a handsome lad," the bosun gloated. "You must take your character from your mother, who was probably a whore on the streets of one of those villages you Yankees call cities."

"Sir," Little Hawk said, standing at attention.

"Had some military training, have we?"

"Sir."

"Not navy," Griffiths said. He leaned close. "Say nothing but 'sir' to me once more, boy, and I'll have your hide for breakfast."

"United States Marines, sir," Little Hawk said.

"Ah. Were you a good marine?"

"Yes, sir."

"I'll bet you were," Griffiths said. "Well, to show you

what I think of the United States Marines, my boy, I'm going to make you officer's orderly."

"Thank you, sir," Little Hawk said.

Griffiths laughed. Later, when he saw Little Hawk carrying the night jars from officers' quarters to pour overboard, he laughed again. "Still thanking me, boy?"

"Sir!"

Cold hate gleamed in the gunner's eyes. He lowered his voice. "Thank your God, you Yankee son-of-a-whore, that we're fair aboard this ship. You've managed to stay on the side of the angels so far, but you'll slip, boy. You'll forget yourself, and when you do—" He showed his teeth in a mirthless grin. "When you do . . ."

"You're showing more good sense than I ever thought you would," Hensley told Little Hawk as they rinsed out their clothing to hang up to dry. "But never you doubt that the gunner has it in for you. He'll catch you out sooner or later. You'll find that a lashing don't hurt nearly as bad as it looks like it does. You feels the first few, but then you get like a squirrel caught in a trap. You sort of funks it and don't feel nothing until you wakes up."

Fury surged up in Hawk, but he contained it. His teeth ground together as he promised himself that one day Griffiths would pay for having put him in a condition not far removed from slavery.

James Ridley did not have the benefit of Little Hawk's experience and common sense. James was just as much English as any man on board the ship, so he was naturally endowed with that quality of assurance that can be interpreted as arrogance. In addition, he was a native-born citizen of a sovereign nation, so the pride of being an American was added to his Anglo-Saxon cockiness. He knew, with a full measure of indignation, that his impressment was illegal. He was the product of a prominent family and had lived in comfort all of his life. He had never worked before the mast but had begun his maritime service as an officer. Not only did he build a caldron of simmering resentment at his own condition, he could not help but chafe at the treatment meted out to the common seamen aboard the *Cormorant*. The food was sickening. The men slept in a stinking hold with dozens of their unwashed fellows. They were always damp, always tired.

To add to the indignity of his captivity, James was isolated from the only man aboard whom he could consider to be a friend. He had been able to see Little Hawk only once during the first few weeks, and then only briefly. And he was infuriated to be separated from his young wife, from the savoring of their first months of married life and the child she would soon bear him.

There was a sameness to the days. The weather was calm, the temperature in the southern waters moderate. The *Cormorant* cruised back and forth across the shipping lanes leading to North and South Carolina ports. James told the men with whom he served that Mr. Jefferson's embargo must be working well, because no American ships were sighted.

The wind picked up in the middle of the port watch just before dawn, and men were ordered into the rigging to trim sail. James was aware that the noncommissioned officers drove the men hard, but he had not seen evidence of deadly cruelty and indifference until, at the beginning of a storm in the dim light of dawn, a man weakened by fever was forced to join his mates aloft.

James was not a total stranger to the rigging. He had picked up good, solid experience in the previous weeks, but he was still a bit tentative in his movements. To that date his occasional hesitation aloft had earned him nothing more than curses.

He was perched astride a spar and hauling in lines when the sick man, working beside him, lost his hold and fell thirty feet to the hard oak deck. The sound of his head breaking was clearly audible over the howl of the rising wind. James threw his arms around the spar and held on for dear life until he heard a yell from below.

"Ridley, move your arse or 'ave it stripped."

When he was once more on deck, he approached the bosun in charge of the port watch. "Sir," he said, "I request permission to speak with the captain."

"You what?" the bosun asked incredulously.

"Permission to speak with the captain, sir."

"Bloody 'ell."

"I think, sir, if you check regulations, that any man has a right to request a hearing before the captain," James said.

"Bloody 'ell," the bosun repeated. It was near change of watch. He saw Gunner Griffiths coming out of his quarters and called him over.

"The young gentleman 'ere requests to see the captain."

Griffiths looked at James with malice. "Were I you, I'd take back that request."

"I'm sorry, sir," James said, "but I feel that it is my duty to speak up."

"'ow about that?" the port-watch bosun asked with a chuckle.

"Go to your quarters," Griffiths ordered.

James started to protest, but the look in Griffiths' eyes urged him to caution. He was half asleep when a man shook him and told him to get dressed and report to the captain.

Captain Jonathan Bowen of HMS *Cormorant* was not the only officer in the British navy whose rank had been earned not by proven ability to command men, not by his knowledge of the sea, but by the name that had been given to him at birth. He was serving in the Royal Navy because being at sea seemed preferable to living with horses in the cavalry or risking one's life marching in the mud with the infantry. As the second son of a minor peer whose fortune was not large enough to allow generosity for siblings other than the firstborn son and heir, Bowen's choices had been limited.

After months at sea, however, the captain was not sure he'd made the correct decision in choosing the tailored and brass-rich uniform of His Majesty's Navy. There were many times—such as at the height of a minor storm—when he would rather have been anywhere than on board the *Cormorant*. Given his preference, he would have been in London with his artist and poet friends. He was much too sensitive, much too genteel to spend vital segments of his prime years on a tossing, stinking ship of the line on blockade duty off the coast of North America.

Bowen had learned during his months as commanding officer that things went smoothly and fewer demands were made on him when he left the running of the ship to the men who knew ships best, the noncommissioned officers. Although Gunner Griffiths' coarseness made him shudder, he admired the gunner's ability to keep the hapless crew in its place and to do whatever needed to be done with sails, cannon, and whatever. He himself was totally disinterested in the day-to-day details of ship keeping. He was content to spend his time in his cabin with his books, some of them in French and German, for even the officers were, he felt, beneath him. The best of them, in his opinion, was young Drake Mumsley, who was, at least, from a good family; but Drake was so shallow.

Bowen was reading a book in French when he heard a knock on his door.

"Come," he said.

Gunner Griffiths saluted. Bowen lifted one lax hand in acknowledgment.

"Cap'n, one of the new recruits has made a formal request for a hearing," Griffiths said.

"Oh, twit," Bowen said. "Handle it, Gunner, will you?"

"The regs say he's got the right, Cap'n."

"Bloody—" He paused, wiped his mouth. Living in such close proximity with coarse men had him speaking like one of them. "Must I?"

"Well, sir, no, you don't. Give me the word, and I'll toss his arse overboard," Griffiths said.

Bowen winced. "Very well," he said, pouting his lips. "Show him in."

He put a marker in the book he'd been reading, then placed it carefully on his desk. On the spine of the book the title was drawn in gold: *Les Crimes de L'Amour*. Next to the novels of the exquisitely sensitive German Sacher-Masoch, *Crimes* was his favorite reading.

When Bowen looked up he saw a man who resembled his own image. He saw a handsome face; soft, sandy hair; a proud, straight nose; a squarish, expressive mouth; gray eyes that seemed to be looking into a dreamy distance. He stiffened. A mere sailor had no right to look so much like his captain.

"Captain Bowen," James Ridley said, "if I may speak, sir."

"Yes, yes, go ahead," Bowen said impatiently.

"A man died on my watch just now," Ridley said. "He died needlessly. He was ill with the fever, Captain, so weak that he could hardly stand, and he was forced to go aloft."

"Is this true, Mr. Griffiths?" Bowen asked laconically.

"A seaman named Hull missed his footing and fell," Griffiths said.

"Sir," James protested, "he should not have been forced to work in his condition."

"Mr. Griffiths," Bowen asked, "are you in the habit of taking advice on how to run my ship from common seamen?"

Griffiths wet his lips with his tongue.

"Captain, I must insist that some—"

His next words were cut off as Griffiths seized him by the collar and yanked him backward. "Sorry to have bothered you, sir," the gunner said.

Bowen waved his hand and reached for his book. When he was interrupted he had just been reading a particularly interesting segment about the joy of giving pain.

"Captain Bowen!" James yelled. "I protest your indifference! I protest—" He grunted as Griffiths drove a belaying pin hard into his back just above his left kidney.

"Let him speak," Bowen said. "Just what is it you protest?"

James was white in the face, bent with his pain. "I protest that I am a natural-born American citizen, an officer in the United States Merchant Marines, and that I have been pressed illegally."

"Dear, dear," Bowen said. "Have you heard claims like that before, Mr. Griffiths?"

"I have, sir," Gunner said.

"Take him away."

"Yes, sir."

"You coldhearted Limey bastard," James said.

"And have him flogged to sanitize his nasty tongue," Bowen said, as if he were asking for a cup of tea.

"You monster!" James cried as Griffiths punched him in the kidney again with the tip of the belaying pin. "You motherless son-of-a-"

"I was thinking twenty lashes," Bowen said as Griffiths dragged James out of the cabin. "But I do believe he's earned thirty, don't you?"

"Thirty it is," Griffiths said.

"Send for me before you begin," Bowen said.

All hands were turned out to witness the punishment. The storm had abated as quickly as it arose, and the ship was loping along easily, running with a moderate wind over smooth-backed swells, with a half suit of canvas on her poles. James was tied to the mainmast, bare to the waist, his arms raised high over his head. Jonathan Bowen stood on the upper-deck level. He held a white handkerchief to his lips as the first blow of the lash raised a welt on Ridley's white skin. After a count of ten, the cat fell again, and this time blood sprang up.

Little Hawk stood stiffly at attention. For a while he was unable to take his eyes off the rise and fall of the lash. He could almost feel the bite of the cat as it curled around Ridley's ribs and lifted little tufts of flesh. Blood sprang up in the tracks of the lash.

Fifteen . . . twenty . . .

Little Hawk was holding his breath. At twenty he exhaled, for he thought that it would be over; but the count went on. Twenty-two, twenty-three, twenty-four . . . Ridley's head fell to one side and wobbled loosely on his neck. He would not feel the remaining blows. Little Hawk lifted his eyes to the face of the man he'd seen only two or three times since his arrival on

board the *Cormorant*. He saw a fevered intensity in
Bowen's gray eyes, saw the captain lick his lips and
breathe with his mouth open as he obviously enjoyed the
brutalization of a man who was Little Hawk's relative and
friend.

At the count of thirty Griffiths folded his lash and
turned to let his cold eyes play over the faces of the crew.
It was as if he were saying, "There it is, lads. If you want
some of that, all you have to do is ask." He let his eyes
linger on Little Hawk for long seconds.

Little Hawk waited until Griffiths had moved off. He
stepped forward and said to the port-watch bosun, "Permission to cut him down, sir?"

"Go ahead," the bosun said. "Wash out them cuts,
and I'll give you some rum to pour on 'em. And you'd
better bloody well use it that way and not drink it."

"Aye, sir," Little Hawk said.

He cut the ropes holding James's hands and caught
the limp, unconscious body. He cleansed the cuts himself.
James did not wake, not even when fiery rum was poured
into the gashes. Little Hawk stayed with his cousin. None
of the officers or noncommissioned officers bothered him.

James moaned as he opened his eyes. He jerked his
head and tried to push himself up. Little Hawk put his
hands on James's shoulders and gently held him down.
"Easy," he said. "Take it easy."

"Hawk?"

"I'm here."

"What they did to me."

"Yes."

"No right."

"I know."

"I'm going to kill them."

"Yes. I don't blame you."

"I will."

"Yes."

James tried to roll over.

"You'd better stay on your stomach," Little Hawk
said.

"Is it bad?"

"It's pretty bad."

It was not pain that caused James to begin weeping. Little Hawk understood. What James was feeling was total degradation, helpless shame, and most of all a frustrated desire for vengeance.

Little Hawk was not one to speak prematurely of his plans, not even to James, but as he sponged away fresh blood and white, clear fluid from James's wounds he vowed that when collection day came, Jonathan Bowen would pay along with Gunner Griffiths for the outrage that they had perpetrated on James.

For some time he had been secretly assessing the men around him. He considered Hensley to be a friend and a brave man. There had to be others who could be counted on in a crisis, but he had to be very careful with his choices. It was evident that a general mutiny would be impossible. The officers and their toadies had tight control of the ship, and only they had access to arms. His best chance to escape bondage was to do so stealthily with a small, determined group, all of whom would be willing to continue to suffer the indignities and harsh conditions until the exact moment of opportunity arose. He could not place James Ridley in that category, for James would be too emotional after his beating; but James would be with him when he left the *Cormorant*. There was no question that if he escaped, he would never leave his cousin in the grasp of men such as Bowen and Griffiths.

Ta-na had just finished an unsatisfactory evening meal. Cooking was not one of Head-in-the-cloud's noteworthy talents. She knew the basics of the art, but she had never been asked by her mother to practice them at home. Her contention was that if Ta-na wanted hot meals, he could take them—with her, of course—with either his grandmother or her mother. Since Toshabe was ailing and his mother-by-marriage had a tongue sharper than the well-honed edge of a tomahawk, their relationship sometimes became strained at mealtime.

That night Cloud had grudgingly half-cooked a roast of venison, leaving the meat bloody inside and charred on the outside. Her efforts with a corn and dried-pepper stew were no more successful.

Ta-na was relieved when he heard Gao calling his name from outside. He put down his bowl and opened the door.

"I need to talk with you," Gao said.

"Come in."

"Alone," Gao said.

"Don't mind me," Cloud said hatefully. "I'll just wait in the woods until you two great warriors have finished your highly important counsel."

"Walk with me," Gao said.

"I have no intention of spending the evening alone in this drafty, wooden cave," Cloud said.

"I won't keep him long," Gao promised. The furtive look of frustration that he saw in Ta-na's face caused his heart to hurt. He wondered what had gone wrong. He was surprised. Because he had long fancied himself to be in love with Cloud, it had been tempting at first to think that Ta-na was being cruel or thoughtless. In recent weeks Gao had begun to change his mind, for the beautiful Cloud had developed shrewish ways with a sureness and rapidity that made him wonder if she had inherited them from her mother.

"I don't care if you stay gone all night," Cloud said contradictorily.

On the previous day rain had marched across the Cherokee Nation, moving toward the east. Behind it had come icy-fresh air that smelled so cleanly and tangily of winter that many warriors of both villages had been moved to mount a hunt in order to savor the crisp, diamond-bright days. It was still and cold when Gao and Ta-na walked out of the village and down toward the swimming creek. Their exhalations formed white clouds in front of them. Two summer pups, rangy and frisky, yapped circles around them. A full moon painted silver-pearl beauty and cast shadows as they walked.

Gao halted in the middle of a frost-browned field of grass and looked up at the disk of the moon. He took Ta-na's arm in the warrior's clasp. "A word between brothers," he said, meaning that what he was about to say was for Ta-na's ears alone.

"So," Ta-na said, in unconscious imitation of Renno.

"You read the letter from General William Henry Harrison asking Uncle Renno and Grandfather Roy to scout for him."

Ta-na grunted acknowledgment.

"Because Uncle Renno is not here and Grandfather Roy must stay with our grandmother, I am going."

Ta-na's heart leaped, and for a moment he envisioned the two of them running together, just as in the past their fathers had worked as a pair. The feeling of excitement faded quickly, however. He thought of Cloud. He had family responsibilities now. As yet Cloud's stomach had not begun to expand, but one never knew when the manitous were going to bless their frequent joining with fruit in the form of a child. The almost nightly coming together was one of the few things in which they found some agreement.

"You heard?" Gao asked.

"Yes." He was silent for a long time before saying, "You have not spoken with Father El-i-chi and Mother Ah-wa-o."

"No. My father would understand. Mother?" He shrugged. "She would try to talk me out of it. I think it will be less painful for her if I leave quietly."

"Ah," Ta-na said, "making it my task to tell them where you have gone."

"That is my request to you, that you give them the information after I am safely away."

"Uncle Rusog and Aunt Ena went after Ho-ya and We-yo after they left without saying good-bye."

"That was different," Gao said. "They did not approve of We-yo's alliance with a Mingo."

"Our father and mother will not approve of your leaving without consulting them."

"I'm seventeen years old," Gao said. He was a few months older than Ta-na, although, from their looks, they could have been twins.

"You are determined, then?" Ta-na asked.

"I have prayed to the manitous."

Ta-na's heart skipped. Both his uncle and his father, Renno, talked with the spirits. He himself had tried, but talk as he would, he had never been honored with an answer.

"Was there—" He could not ask the question.

"A sign? A reply?" Gao shook his head in negation. "But in my heart I feel that it is right."

"You will be traveling alone."

"Yes. I have studied the maps in Grandfather Roy's trunk. I will travel slightly to the west of north to the Ohio and then follow the Wabash to General Harrison's town."

Ta-na chuckled. "And when you reach a river, how will you know whether it is the Ohio or the Tennessee or even the Mississippi?"

"I suppose if I have any doubt, I can ask the nearest white man."

"And lose your scalp to some wild Kentuckian?" Ta-na asked. "You have heard Grandfather Roy read from the newspapers that the Ohio Indians are still raiding into Kentucky. It's my guess that a settler won't stop to ask if you're friend or foe before shooting you."

"Perhaps, since you are so fearful for my safety, you'd better come with me. General Harrison requested both Uncle Renno and Grandfather Roy—two scouts."

"Would—" He paused on the verge of adding, "—that I could." Instead he amended it to, "Would *you* leave if you were married to Cloud?"

"No," Gao said. "In truth, I would not."

"When will you go?"

"Tonight. I have my travel pack hidden down by the creek."

A feeling of devastation emptied Ta-na of emotion. He clasped Gao's arm. "May the manitous go with you."

"Wait as long as you can before telling them," Gao said.

"Yes."

"Now you'd better get back to Cloud. She hates to be alone."

"I will pray nightly to the Master of Life to guide your footsteps," Ta-na said.

Gao did not look back. He walked with his back straight, his arms swinging. Ta-na allowed him to disappear into the trees before he ran forward and concealed himself to approach the creek in silence. He saw Gao take his gear from the hollow of a great oak tree, watched as he strapped on his backpack, slung bow and quiver, seated his tomahawk at his sash and, rifle in hand, marched away through the silvered swatches of moonlight and the dark of shadows to fade into the night.

Ta-na made his way back to the village slowly. His heart was heavy with sadness for himself and with fear for his brother. There was also the burden of having to tell El-i-chi and Ah-wa-o. He did not notice a curious, dark mound outside the door of the longhouse until his hand was on the door. He looked down, saw his winter furs, weapons, and sleep skins. He opened the door and stomped in, for the presence of his possessions outside the door was a definite message taken from Cherokee tradition.

"Cloud," he called. He was going to tell her that she could not expel him from the house that was owned by his father, but he did not have the opportunity. The longhouse was empty. She had moved swiftly, for he had not been gone more than half an hour at most. Her own things were missing. The fire was nothing more than embers.

For a few moments he was angry. Life with Head-in-the-cloud had become progressively more difficult. Nothing he did or said seemed to please her, and now this. She had chosen the way of her Cherokee father to tell him that she wanted no more of him, for a Cherokee woman could end a marriage by doing just what Cloud had done—by piling her husband's possessions outside the door.

His anger passed with a swiftness that left him numb. A sharp laugh escaped him. She had not intended to throw him out of his father's house. She hated the longhouse, wanted no more of it. It was only the symbolism, the traditional message that was given by the mute heap of his things on the earth beside the front door that she had intended.

Ta-na laughed louder. He would miss her soft, female body in his bed—or at least his sixteen-year-old glands would miss her—but he felt only relief as he stood by the dying fire in the empty longhouse. He burst into action, leaping through the door into the crystal night to run as he had never run before out of the village, across the brown fields to the creek. He leaped the stream, ran up the slight rise, and found the trail that Gao had taken. His heart was beating hard, but it was singing.

He smelled Gao's campfire before he saw it, approached it only after calling out with the coo of a dove until he got an answer, the assembly call of a scattered covey of quail. Gao was standing behind a tree in the shadows when he entered the clearing and stood beside the small fire.

"I thought I told you good-bye at the creek," Gao said, stepping out, leaning his rifle against the tree.

"Someone else told me good-bye tonight," Ta-na said.

"Ah."

"All of my things were stacked outside the door when I got back to the longhouse."

"Ah."

"Can't you say anything but 'ah'?"

Gao could not understand his own feelings. There was anger at Ta-na, for Ta-na had possessed that which Gao had wanted very much, and now his brother seemed indecently happy that Cloud was no longer his. But there was relief, too, for now he knew that Ta-na would travel north with him. There could be no other reason why his brother had run through the moonlit night to catch him.

"But perhaps you would prefer to travel alone," Ta-na said sullenly.

Gao's rush caught Ta-na by surprise, threw him off his feet so that he landed on his back with Gao on top of him. He tried to flip his brother off, but Gao had a hold that could not be broken.

"I'll show you who wants to travel alone," Gao said

playfully. He freed one hand and rubbed his knuckles roughly over Ta-na's scalp. Ta-na broke the hold of the other arm and gained the advantage, rolling Gao onto his back. Gao started laughing. Ta-na roughed up his brother's scalp and began laughing with him.

"Then the great love affair is ended, and you are human again," Gao said.

"I will try to be," Ta-na said, gasping, as Gao jammed a knee into his stomach and flipped him.

They rolled on the leafy floor of the forest, laughing, landing blows that, if struck in anger, would have been painful. At last they sat side by side, puffing hard.

"But you didn't bring your kit," Gao said.

"Gao, I will not run away in the night and leave our father and mother to worry," Ta-na said.

"That has concerned me ever since I left," Gao confessed. He rose and began to gather his pack. "We will sleep in the house of a friend of mine only recently returned to bachelor status," he said, "and speak with Mother and Father tomorrow."

It was as Gao had predicted. El-i-chi's immediate objections were reasoned away by Gao's eloquence and by Ta-na's sincerity.

Ah-wa-o said, "The only reason you want to go, Ta-na, is because you're upset that Cloud has gone home. Give her time. My guess is that she will come back."

Ta-na laughed. "*That* is the real reason I want to go, Mother Ah-wa-o, for fear that she *will* come back."

"You're horrid," Ah-wa-o said. "A typical man." But she was smiling. With a knowing look at El-i-chi she reminded him of her misgivings about the marriage even before it was consummated.

"When I first went to war I was younger than these two bear cubs," El-i-chi said.

"You were with your own people," Ah-wa-o said.

"I will be with my brother," Gao said.

"And I with mine," said Ta-na.

"This is not your fight," Ah-wa-o pointed out.

"Father Renno would say differently," Ta-na said.

"I will say no wrong against Renno," Ah-wa-o said, "but that does not mean that I always have to agree with him."

"Are we to change the tradition established by our forefathers of fighting on the side of the United States?" Gao asked.

"You are not bound by that tradition," El-i-chi said, "but I am pleased that you want to honor it. It is that, isn't it, and not just a desire to see new places and have an adventure or two?"

"In truth, Father," Gao confessed, "it is some of both."

El-i-chi laughed. He rose and put his arms around his two sons. "I pray that we have taught you well. You know to keep your blades sharp, your powder dry, your arrows straight. You know that you should never start or enter into a fight that you have no hope of winning. Pray to the manitous, and they will be at your side in battle, but remember that the best of all battles is the battle that is avoided. As scouts it will be your duty to seek out those whom your commander designates as his enemies, to report back to him. It is not your duty to kill, but kill if you must to preserve your own life. It is a sadness for Indian to kill Indian, but it will be so until good sense and practicality overcome the hate that has been built up among various tribes since the beginning of time. Serve the United States, and we will be proud of you. Do your job and avoid becoming involved too deeply, lest you get caught in the middle between the greed of the white man and the love of the Indian for the land."

"I hear," Ta-na said.

"And I," said Gao.

"Pay heed to your father's statement that it is not your duty to fight the white man's battles," Ah-wa-o said.

"We will," Gao promised.

"Now I will prepare food for the first stage of your journey," Ah-wa-o said.

Renno's little clan arrived in Wilmington in plenty of time to have Christmas dinner at the Ridley house. Before leaving Washington, Beth had promised Dolley Madison to return for the inauguration and attendant festivities if at all possible. It was a pleasant occasion marred only by two empty chairs left vacant to honor those who were missing, James Ridley and Little Hawk.

Gifts were exchanged and carols sung. The men walked in the garden to smoke cigars, and the women gathered to talk of babies and men and other topics dear to females of all ages. Those who had the appetite sat down again at the table to eat leftovers for an evening meal. Renno and Beth walked home under a glory of stars. Renna, Naomi, the children, and their black nanny took Beth's carriage. It was during the walk that Renno felt a surge of dread. It welled up inside him, causing him to look quickly over his shoulder. He shivered.

"Cold?" Beth asked.

"A goose just walked over my grave," Renno said.

"That's a horrid Americanism," Beth said.

"But expressive." Anxiety nagged at him, causing an uneasy feeling in the pit of his stomach.

"It makes no sense," Beth said. "Is this some future goose walking over a future grave?"

"It makes about as much sense as when an English person uses 'going spare' for losing one's head."

"Expressive, though," Beth said, taking his arm. "Tell me what's troubling you."

"Nothing. A feeling."

She shuddered. "I don't like it when you get bad premonitions."

"It's nothing. It will pass."

But it didn't pass. The dread came back full force upon the arrival of Roy's letter expressing his deep concern for Toshabe's health.

"We'll go, of course," Beth said.

"Not we," Renno told her as he took her in his arms. "I'll go alone. There will be deep snows in the mountains. You and I could make it, but I had planned for all of us to go together. It would not be advisable to take the girls and the children in winter. Then, too, your problems continue here, and you should stay to see them resolved. I'll travel hard and fast, and I'll come back for all of you in the spring."

She knew that his decision was a wise one. He could always be depended upon to choose the right course of action, but the thought of being separated from him again brought tears to her eyes. Also, she had grown to care for Toshabe and would have liked to say her last good-bye, should it come to that, and offer what comfort she could to Roy. She shivered as he held her and thought of the odd saying he had used as they walked home from Nathan Ridley's house on Christmas.

"What is so terrible about a goose walking over a grave?" she asked him, voicing the rather silly question as a distraction to keep from weeping openly.

"Actually, I don't suppose it's so bad," Renno said, "unless the grave is open, and you're looking up."

She punched him with her elbow. "You're horrid."

"So," he said, holding her close.

Sadness threatened to overwhelm him. By the time he reached the Cherokee Nation Toshabe could be dead; and, once again, he was going to leave the woman he loved for an indefinite period of time. It seemed that all of his life he was leaving behind the women he loved. He felt a surge of guilt—old guilt—as he thought of Emily, pale-haired Emily. He had left her to go journeying into the far west with William and Beth, and when he returned she was dead. He had left An-da to go scouting for Mad Anthony Wayne, and she had been killed.

"Renno?" Beth whispered, a bit shocked by the strength of his embrace.

He almost told her to pack a kit, but the thought of the hardships of winter travel made him reconsider. She was in a civilized town in the United States where law and order prevailed. Nothing would happen to her, and his mother was dying. He had no choice but to go.

Chapter Six

Renno, riding one horse and leading a spare, left Wilmington. At first he traveled light. He alternated the horses in order to maintain a fast pace. By riding hard he could cover ground faster than if he had been a passenger on the stagecoaches that bounced over rutted, sandy roads toward the growing Piedmont cities. He timed his travel to spend the nights at inns or boardinghouses.

The state had become much more thickly settled in the years since he had made his first trek from the coast to the Great Smoky Mountains. In fewer than a score of years villages and towns had sprung up, so that he was never more than a day's ride from a trade center. Fayetteville, on the upper Cape Fear, was a thriving town. The new capital in Raleigh was a handsome building and, as an example of the white man's advancement over the hunting and digging-stick cultivation culture of the Eastern Indian tribes, almost as awe-inspiring as the Capitol building in Washington.

In just a few years the white man had filled the land with his houses, his buildings, his farms, and his issue. He had stamped his culture on the land. His ambition, his desire to advance himself and make his own life more fruitful while building a better existence for his children, had changed the world forever. Almost every major town in the state had its bank. A great university had been established to teach young men the value of the freedoms that had been won on the field of battle and enumerated in the Constitution. A great network of trade connected farms and towns with the cities of the Northeast and, in normal times, the islands and the nations of the Old World. Courts of law had been established in each county to ensure the even application of law and justice.

In contrast to the changes that the white man had brought to the thirteen states and the frontier areas, the Indian wanted to live as he had lived since the dawn of time, abiding by the same traditions, fighting and killing his own brothers who happened to belong to a different tribe, keeping his numbers in equilibrium with the supply of fresh meat and the corn and vegetables hacked out of the earth by his women.

As Renno rode westward he was seldom far from signs of white vitality. Along the road he saw families of stair-step children playing in the smooth dirt yards of farmsteads. In the towns and cities was evidence of the breeding capacity of the former Europeans who were now Americans. Noisy herds of youngsters rushed from school-houses, where they were taught the magic of the white man's books—and, not incidentally, their own superiority over black slaves and dark-skinned savages—to whoop and run on the playgrounds.

Renno had plenty of time to think as he rode westward into colder temperatures. He endured a snow shower in the vicinity of Salem, then a hard freeze in the foothills of the mountains.

A few wise chiefs had realized early on that stone weapons, a small number of blades of iron, and even fewer muskets obtained in trade could not stand against the growing wave of Europeans. The great Ghonka, the

Seneca war chief who had taken as his own son the help-less white infant who became the first Renno, had allied himself with the British against the French. The white Indian's progeny fought on the side of the rebelling colonists. But many tribes still had not grasped the inevitable march of history, had not understood the vital messages embodied in the wide, fertile fields ripped open by the white man's plow, had not ridden past his barns and his pens and his pastures and his towns.

Before the landing of the Spaniards in the southeast, the land was all untamed, an ocean of trees, and all that lived in it was wild. Life for the Indian was easy. Game was plentiful. At first there were only a few of the white settlers, and the land was big. Understandably, only those tribes in direct confrontation with the expanding settlements cried out in alarm. Even as entire Indian nations disappeared, borne under by the white flood, others were confident that the same fate could not happen to them. They would fight. The white monster gobbling up land that had been intended for the perpetual and equal use of all would be stopped.

There were those, such as Tecumseh, who still preached the futile dream of halting the advance of white civilization; but, Renno thought as he watched smoke rising from six farmsteads within easy vision, if Tecumseh had ever seen the white man's cities, his plowed fields, his herds of cattle, he had missed their meaning. If every Indian who heeded Tecumseh's call to war could travel the width of North Carolina—and it was one of the less densely populated states among what the Shawnee called the "Thirteen Fires"—they would understand: To fight against the United States was to die. It was that simple.

Renno was not afraid of a fight. He had never held back when honor was at stake, but, on the other hand, he had never sought out a hopeless battle. To die in a futile cause was not honorable; it was foolish. The manitous had not given the gift of life to be thrown away. For Renno, to live and to continue his efforts to convince his own people and his cousins the Cherokee, with whom his clan was so closely intertwined, was the true honor. Feeling frustrated

and disappointed he had left off that noble cause; he had
been unsuccessful in persuading the Seneca and Cherokee in Rusog's land that he was correct in advising a gradual blending of Indian culture with that of the white man.
He would not be so weak again.

Snows clogged the mountain valleys and accumulated in gleaming white masses on the wooded slopes.
Renno had purchased camping gear in the small mountain
town of Asheville, but it was not necessary to spend every
night in the open. He was welcomed into the snug log
cabins of hospitable Cherokee families. Ice lined the edge
of the French Broad River as he pushed westward. In the
high passes the horses struggled through deep snow.

He rode into his home village in darkness. The
aroma of cooking food blended with woodsmoke. Dogs
announced his arrival. A few curious faces peered out to
see why there was so much frantic yelping. Formal Seneca
greetings were called out and returned.

Renno drew up in front of the longhouse occupied by
his mother and Roy Johnson. Roy stuck his head out the
door and yelled at the barking dogs before his eyes widened in gladness. He rushed out into the chill as Renno
dismounted and threw his arms around his son-by-marriage.

"You're a sight for sore eyes," Roy said in a choked
voice.

"You're faring well, my friend," Renno said.

"Tolerable," Roy said. "You must be half-froze."

"Maybe a little bit more than half," Renno said.
"How is she?"

Roy shook his head. "You'd best be prepared. She's
changed."

Toshabe was pitifully thin. Her cheeks were sunken.
She had aged heartbreakingly. She was sitting on a stool
beside the cook fire and stirring something in an iron pot.
"What were those fool animals carrying on about?" she
asked without looking up.

"Some feller with no sense, traveling in the dead of
winter," Roy said.

She dropped the ladle with which she'd been stirring a stew and struggled to her feet. Renno met her more than halfway and enfolded her in his arms. He felt wet tears on her cheeks.

"I thank thee that thou art well," she said in Seneca, then held him at arm's length. "There is more of your father in your face as you grow older."

"For that I am proud," he said. "But *you*. You have not been eating properly. Are you tired of your own cooking?"

She laughed. "This old man tries to cook now and then. That is why I am so skinny."

"Now *I* think I do pretty dag-gum well," Roy protested.

Toshabe sat down, took up her ladle, and tasted the stew. "You have timed your arrival perfectly. Wash up, and the food will be ready."

"I need to take my horses over to the stables at the Castle," Renno said. "Maybe I can send someone for Ta-na and have him do it. It will be good to see him."

Roy and Toshabe exchanged a quick glance. "Well," Roy drawled, "yes, it would be good to see him. Trouble is, he's his father's son. Gao and he have gone north to join up with William Henry Harrison as scouts."

"So," Renno said, hiding his disappointment.

"I'll take the horses to the house," Roy offered. "One of Aunt Sarah's boys can rub 'em down and feed 'em."

"No need for you to go out in the cold," Renno said.

"I want you to stay here and chat with your ma and warm your toes," Roy said as he pulled on a heavy bearskin cape.

Renno could not find words. He watched Toshabe stir the stew. She seemed unable to look him in the face. It was evident that she was very ill. When she stood, she swayed on her feet and reached out for an upright pole to steady herself.

"The others?" she asked.

"In Wilmington," Renno said. "You are the great-grandmother of twin boys."

Her face brightened. "Little Hawk's?"

"Yes. And Renna has a new boy."

"The manitous are kind."

"I will return for them in the spring," Renno said.

"It would be joyous to see them," she said, "but I will praise the spirits that I see my eldest son once more."

"You will see them, too," Renno said.

She doubled over suddenly, her face distorted into a mask of pain. He leaped to her side and took her arm. "Come, I'll help you to your bed."

"That will come soon enough," she said, straightening, breathing deeply.

"Mother—" Again he could find no words.

"Sing for me when the time comes," she said, touching his cheek with a cold, dry hand. "Sing the song of the dead for me, but don't color your life black with grief."

He started to speak. She put her hand over his mouth. "My life gives me no reason for regret. I have loved and been loved by three good men. I have borne two fine sons and a worthy daughter. There has been sadness, but it has been more than matched by much joy. My only regret is that my seed is so scattered. Ena's We-yo and Ho-ya are gone. Ta-na and Gao are gone as well. Little Hawk and Renna are so far away."

The door of the longhouse opened, and El-i-chi burst in with a whoop. He seized Renno in a bear hug and danced him around.

"Mind you don't fall in the fire," Toshabe said, and her voice was so normal, the injunction so familiar from years past when the brothers were boys roughhousing, as boys will, that Renno broke into relieved laughter.

El-i-chi went to bring Ah-wa-o and little Ah-wen-ga and while he was gone sent word to Ena and Rusog, so that by the time Roy returned, the house was crowded. The food and the talk was good, and for a time, at least, the stimulation of having the core of her family with her made Toshabe forget her weakness and her pain.

Beth had not mentioned her intention to attend the inaugural ceremonies in Washington before Renno left, lest he worry about her being at sea in the wintertime.

When she announced her imminent departure aboard the *Comtesse Renna* to Naomi and Renna, she was not surprised to hear both of her daughters-by-marriage express the enthusiastic wish to accompany her.

Beth wrote to Dolley Madison, accepting her invitation and informing her new friend that she would have family with her and, to avoid imposing, would take rooms in a hotel.

South of Cape Hatteras, the *Renna* sailed smack into a raging northeaster that threatened to drive her shoreward and onto the shoals that had earned the appellation Graveyard of the Atlantic. Adan took the ship seaward, heeled over to quarter away from the wind, and four days were added to what should have been a short, coastwise sail to the sheltered waters of Chesapeake Bay.

Beth hired carriages to transport her entourage into the city, then sent a messenger to the house on F Street to inform Dolley of her arrival. Within the hour, Dolley was at the hotel. She was full of enthusiasm and plans, her plump and pretty cheeks flushed with excitement and the cold. She said that she was sorely disappointed that Beth had not accepted her invitation to bring the whole family to the Madison house.

"Sweet infants would enliven the old place," Dolley said. "And it would make my darling little husband's blood flow more briskly to have these two lovely young ladies around. You and I could have ever so much more time together."

"That's wonderfully generous of you," Beth said, "but I know that you're going to be very busy. I hereby make myself available to help you. If you have errands to be run, notes to be written, whatever, please call on me."

"And on me," Renna said.

Naomi, awed by Dolley's statuesque handsomeness, her exalted position, and her assured air, merely nodded eagerly, more than willing to help and be a part of the group but not quite able to believe, frontier girl that she was, that she was in the company of the wife of the next president of the United States.

"Well, even if you are going to be stubborn," Dolley

said, taking Beth's hands in hers, "we're going to have a jolly time, aren't we?"

Across the Atlantic, Sir Arthur Wellesley was in Portugal again. This time, however, he had no superiors to compound the stupidity that had prevented him from destroying the French army on the Iberian Peninsula after his victory before Lisbon in August of 1808. Before resigning his civil office as Irish secretary and his seat in the Parliament, he had assured himself that all the decisions would be his own.

Initially there was only a small British presence in Lisbon itself, but reinforcements were arriving. Wellesley's first offensive was designed to retake Porto from the French. At the head of the first cavalry unit to approach the northern city to investigate French strength was a man who had served with Wellesley during his previous stint in Portugal, a young Scotch captain named Randall Farnsworth.

Farnsworth was a striking man of twenty-five years. He was red-haired, blue-eyed, and smoothly muscular; and he was a murderer at heart, for it was he who had shot Renna's husband, the comte de Beaujolais, in cold blood in the hope that he himself might win the heart of Beau's young widow.

Farnsworth had plans to establish his military reputation during Sir Arthur Wellesley's second campaign in Portugal. The former high command on the Iberian Peninsula had been thoroughly discredited. General Moore, chief of all British armies in the area, was dead in Spain, his troops shamefully defeated. With Napoleon himself now in charge of the French forces on the peninsula, there would be ample opportunity for action and, doubtlessly, many opportunities for an ambitious officer to distinguish himself. That hope was made more attainable, Farnsworth felt, by his having been given a small force of cavalry and orders to seek out the enemy positions around Porto.

When Farnsworth's unit closed on the northern city, the main force was not far behind. So eager was he to reach the city and begin the enhancement of his career that he neglected the fundamental rules of caution for an advance force. He pushed his troops hard, sticking to the road system. He decided not to put out flanking scouts because the terrain was rugged on both sides of the road, and he was in a hurry to locate the enemy.

The French commander at Porto had been notified, by more careful scouts, of the British advance. He had his main force lying in ambush on either side of the road leading up from the south. Seeing Farnsworth's troop for what it was, a patrol in force, the Frenchman kept his men in hiding and waited for Wellesley's army to march into the trap. French artillery would be firing down from high ground onto the road. When Wellesley's troops left the road seeking cover, as they undoubtedly would, they would run headlong into the French infantry that was dug in on the slopes.

The situation could have become serious for Wellesley had one teenage French soldier been able to control his nervousness. The boy, lying in a small depression near the road, was hidden behind low bushes through which he could see the advance of Farnsworth's unit of brazen British cavalry. As always the Englishmen were impressive. Armed with carbines and sabers, they came jingling and jangling their way up the road toward Porto. The young soldier's finger tightened on the trigger of his musket, and before he could control his tenseness and his desire to slay the hated Britisher in his sights, the piece fired. His aim was good. One of Farnsworth's sergeants toppled from his saddle with a hole in the side of his head.

At first Farnsworth did not know the source of the shot. He looked around with some alarm but saw only the steep, wooded, rocky slopes at the sides of the road. He guessed that a lone marksman had taken a cowardly opportunity to shoot from ambush. He gave orders to move on. Two lancers dismounted to check on the fallen man's condition. One of them saw a flash of movement in the brush and fired at it.

A fusillade of deadly fire burst out from both sides of the road. Behind Farnsworth, at the southern mouth of the narrow valley into which he had ridden so fecklessly, a group of infantry moved onto the road and took up defensive positions. His men were falling with dismaying rapidity. He had two choices. He could move on toward Porto and, quite possibly, ride into even more deadly fire, or he could wheel about and fight his way through the blockade of infantry on the road. He chose to do the latter. He kicked his horse into a lope through shallow water in a ditch beside the road to take his place at the rear of his troop. The rear became the fore as he gave orders, and with his hoarse and thrilling shouts of "Charge, charge," counterpointed with the blare of a bugle, he led his men through a hail of musketry toward the waiting infantry.

Cannon began to roar from the high ground, and just behind him two horsemen and their animals were riddled with shot. The horses sprawled on the road, their riders rolling and flopping loosely on the ground. Others rode on through the smoke, yelling their defiance. Farnsworth drew his saber, leaned down, and almost decapitated a French infantryman. Muskets were flaming at him from directly ahead. Men fell behind him, but the survivors came on, bellowing their high-pitched battle cries. His heart pounded with exaltation and pride, but even at the height of that supreme moment he found time to wonder why, in the heat of action, the shouts of men became shrill and quavering.

The remainder of his sorely punished troop burst clear of the French infantry and rode out of the ambush. Cannon fire chased them, and just when it seemed that they were in the clear, a musket ball took Farnsworth in the left shoulder, almost knocking him from his saddle. He dropped his saber, clutched the pommel, and hung on for his life. Then he was out of range, and the wild charge to the rear—he would never call it a retreat—slowed to a walk.

"Sir," Farnsworth told Sir Arthur, "I have located and punished the enemy."

"Well done, lad," Wellesley said as Farnsworth collapsed from pain and loss of blood.

Fortunately for the English forces, Wellesley was more cautious and sagacious in his military judgment than his wounded captain of cavalry had been. He carefully and patiently encircled the French positions, methodically reduced them, and sent the Frenchmen packing back toward Spain. Once again Porto was in the hands of Portugal and her ally, Great Britain.

To reward the gallant actions of Captain Randall Farnsworth, Wellesley wrote a commendation, hung a medal on the chest of the wounded hero, and sent him off to England to recover. As he had done once before, Farnsworth made straightway for Beaumont Manor, expecting to find there the woman for whom he had been willing to commit murder. He was given a cordial welcome by William, Lord Beaumont, and his wife, Estrella. To his great disappointment, however, Farnsworth learned that Renna, comtesse de Beaujolais, had gone off to America with her father and her brother.

As quickly as he could gracefully extricate himself from good British hospitality for a wounded hero, he made his way to London and, armed with a letter of high commendation from Sir Arthur, asked for and was given an assignment by the Foreign Office. He was to be a military adviser to the British minister in Washington. Technically he would be under the orders of Anthony Merry, but the papers he carried made him, in effect, an ambassador without portfolio and would allow him to travel with diplomatic rank wherever his duty as he saw it led him.

The man who held all of Europe by the throat was tiring of life in the field. He was finding the war in Spain to be dull, unrewarding, and infinitely frustrating. Wars, Napoleon believed, were to be fought by two opposing armies in uniform. Generals directed the movement of the armies, and when one army outmaneuvered or routed the other, the battle was over. A few battles won meant a war won. It was not so beautifully simple in Spain. Two armies in uniform had met, and one had defeated the other, the

French army killing a great many Englishmen, including their general; but there were thousands of provincial, unsophisticated Spaniards of the countryside who didn't truly understand war. They insisted on continuing the fight. They ran in small, ragtag groups, striking isolated French units, lying in ambush, and sabotaging French installations in the dark of night. Their sharpshooters made it hazardous for a man to leave ranks to relieve himself in the bushes or behind a hill.

The presence of Sir Arthur Wellesley's small force in Portugal didn't concern Napoleon. Wellesley could be handled by the French army already in place. Moreover, he felt that the frustrating nonwar against the Spanish partisans could be conducted by underlings.

The "little crop head," as he was called by some, summoned his aide. "My dear count," he said, "I have decided that my duty lies in Paris. You will, of course, accompany me."

Beau, the comte de Beaujolais, gave no argument. He, too, was glad to be leaving Spain, but for different reasons. Months previously he had sent a letter through neutral Switzerland to his wife in care of Beth's brother William at Beaumont Manor in England. He had not guessed at that time that he would be commandeered by Napoleon, who favored loyal members of the old aristocracy, to be his chief aide during the Spanish campaign. He had told Renna to write to him at their house in Paris. He felt sure that letters would be awaiting him. In fact, he harbored a secret hope that Renna herself, with their children, would be waiting for him at home. He had great confidence in the resourcefulness of his wife. It would be like her to have found some way to get across the Channel —something that Napoleon had never been able to do— and wait for him in Paris.

The emperor and his aides were escorted northward out of Spain by a crack unit of lancers, and in due time Beau was running up the stairs of his town house in Paris, only to find that no one was there but the staff Renna and he had left in charge before departing for Portugal via England so long before. There was, however, a letter. He picked it up eagerly, then was disappointed to see masculine handwriting. It was from Lord Beaumont.

William began the letter by expressing great joy for the knowledge that Beau was not dead.

Beau frowned and read on rapidly.

> I will send word immediately to Renna that you are alive, and I will pray that the current friction between my country and the United States will not delay or impede its arrival. I'm sure that Renna and her family will be overjoyed, as we are, at the news. I, for one, am still trying to understand how Captain—now Colonel—Farnsworth could have made such a mistake. I can only guess that you were wounded and that Colonel Farnsworth overestimated the extent of your injuries. At any rate, he himself might just learn of his mistake through Renna and her family, because he departed for America on diplomatic business shortly before the arrival of your welcome letter, which had been delayed en route from Spain to Switzerland.

An overwhelming sadness was an ache in Beau's breast. The pain was not for himself but for Renna. For months she had believed him to be dead. He could imagine her sorrow and the regret of his father-by-marriage. The situation was compounded by Renna's having taken the children to America.

At his first opportunity, Beau sought an audience with the emperor.

"Sir," he said, "I have just learned that I was reported dead to my wife and her family."

"Well, they will have a pleasant surprise, *non?*" Napoleon said without too much interest. He had problems of his own, namely some rather disturbing achievements by the English commander in Portugal and the continuing intransigence of the Spanish irregulars.

"I must go to America as quickly as possible, sir," Beau said.

Napoleon frowned. "Beaujolais, I need you here."

Beau sighed. He knew the emperor valued him because he was of the old aristocracy and, as such, gave a certain legitimacy to Napoleon's efforts to create a new elite, composed of members of his own family, patterned on the old. Moreover, he had come to depend on Beau's advice in diplomatic matters.

"Sir, my wife believes me to be dead."

"If she loves you, Comte, she will not remarry immediately," Napoleon said. "If that is your concern."

Beau was speechless. He would have said that the emperor was his friend and was genuinely fond of him. The man's callousness left him with a cold emptiness in his heart.

"I simply can't afford to risk losing you," Napoleon said. "It would be risky for you to undertake such an extensive journey."

"I can travel under a flag of diplomacy, as I did on the way to Portugal," Beau said.

"It's out of the question, Beaujolais," the emperor said. "Out of the question."

Beau left Paris that night dressed in the raiment of a man of the streets. The next day he purchased an old nag of a horse from a farmer and rode directly into a police roadblock. He did his best to sound like an illiterate countryman. He insisted on his rights as a man who had fought in the Revolution against the hated blue bloods and exchanged good-natured insults with the police, who were, mostly, illiterate countrymen in uniform. They allowed him to pass.

In Calais he boarded a small boat manned by professional smugglers and sailed away from his homeland once more.

A messenger came to Ho-ya and the group of self-exiled Seneca and Cherokee before the snow had melted completely in the snug little valley in the northern foothills of the mountains north of the Arkansas. Although there had been no formal ceremony to declare Ho-ya chief, it was evident that Young Elk, chief of the Osage, felt that his brother-by-marriage held that rank. The messenger spoke in lofty, diplomatic phrases, taking more than a few minutes to get across the simple fact that Ho-ya and the senior warriors of his clan were invited to sit in council with Young Elk's people to hear the words of a visitor from the east.

The people of the valley had spent the winter in some comfort. Hard work had resulted in several log cabins being erected, along with mud-chinked Seneca longhouses. True to the word that he had given upon his marriage to Ho-ya's sister, We-yo, the Osage chief ordered his warriors to allow the easterners to live in peace in their valley and to share the buffalo hunting grounds to the north with the Osage.

Ho-ya traveled to the village of the Osage, where he was greeted by his sister, his niece, little Summer Moon, and Jani, the Seneca boy whom We-yo had adopted at his instigation. Ho-ya leaped down from his horse and came forward. He was saddened, at first, to see his sister dressed not as a proper Cherokee but in the manner of the Osage. Doubt assailed him as he questioned the wisdom of his having led the group from their homes in Rusog's town and the adjoining Seneca village. He was witnessing just one of the results of that action, for his sister and his niece would be forever Osage, separated from the traditions of their people.

But We-yo's face was glowing with health and happiness as she embraced him, and little Summer Moon was radiant as she showed him a toy made by her "father." It was fashioned from the tail tassel of a buffalo. Jani was a sturdy little lad. He gave Ho-ya his arm in greeting and spoke in the language of his mother, who had died during the westward trek.

"There is food," We-yo said.

"It will be welcome," Ho-ya said.

"It is so good to see you," she said, holding on to his arm as they walked through the village. The expressionless faces of Osage women watched their progress to the house of Young Elk. The Osage chief greeted Ho-ya formally and invited him in. The evening meal was a time for exchanging news about the events of the winter.

The next morning Young Elk and Ho-ya walked to the men's house, the council room that was crowded with the senior warriors of the Osage and Ho-ya's delegation. A handsome, well-formed man did not wait for an introduction but greeted Ho-ya with a smile and a warrior's grip.

"It is good to see you, friend," the tall and impressive warrior said. "I am Tecumseh."

"I know you, Panther Passing Across," Ho-ya said.

"You are far from home, Cherokee."

"This country is now my home," Ho-ya said, "thanks to the generosity of my brother Young Elk."

"We Shawnee are not unfamiliar with such generosity," Tecumseh said. "It is a source of pride to be able to say that the Shawnee are welcome in the lands of others because they are willing to fight to defend the rights and the lands of their hosts."

Ho-ya nodded.

"Since you and your group have joined the Shawnee in their landless condition, I assume that you would fight against the enemies of your hosts."

"We would," Ho-ya said.

"And against the enemy of all Indians?" Tecumseh asked.

"We will eat," Young Elk interrupted, "then talk."

Women, including We-yo, served corn porridge and fresh buffalo roast. Tecumseh made no further attempt to speak of his purpose until, the meal finished, Young Elk passed the pipe.

"My brother Young Elk is to be praised," Tecumseh said, "as are all the senior warriors who give me the opportunity to plead the cause that has led me through many travels to the lands of many tribes."

For an hour the Shawnee spoke with the fire and eloquence that had impressed many tribes, from the sweet lakes of the north to the muggy lands of the Creek in the far south. Young Elk and the others listened with courtesy and patience. The Osage shared that common trait of all Indians, admiration for a fluent orator. Tecumseh urged the Osage to join the growing number of tribes that were uniting to push the white flood back across the Ohio. He listed the wrongs done to the Indian by the white man, naming dozens of tribes that had ceased to exist in the area dominated by the United States.

When Tecumseh had finished, Young Elk rose. "The Chief of the Beautiful River . . ." he began, using another name by which Tecumseh was known, then looked around and stared into the visitor's eyes, ". . . is not a chief—"

Tecumseh interrupted. "Not a chief but a warrior. Many of those who hold the title of chief bow before their white masters and agree to sell lands that belong to all."

"The Panther Passing Across," Young Elk continued, "speaks with great persuasion. His words generate a reply in my heart, to which I will give voice after my brother Ho-ya of the Cherokee shares his thoughts with us. I wish this because my brother, too, comes from the lands east of the Father of Waters."

Ho-ya was nervous at first. He was not accustomed to speaking in front of chiefs and senior warriors of several villages. His voice quavered as he said, "I am not an orator like my brothers Tecumseh and Young Elk, so I will give you my thoughts quickly. Tecumseh promises that all tribes will unite to fight as one, but I know of many who will not turn the muzzles of their rifles against the white man."

"Speak of them," a grizzled Osage warrior said.

"My father and my mother's brothers have fought the white man's wars," Ho-ya said. "From the days of the great Seneca chief Ghonka, my forefathers have cast their lot with the white man, and, indeed, my mother's brother, the Seneca sachem, Renno, teaches that the destiny of all Indians lies with the United States."

"I know your uncle," Tecumseh said. "At the Fallen Timbers, where the heart of the Ohio tribes was broken, I saw him at the side of the Chief Who Never Sleeps. The Seneca fought against his brothers."

"It is reported, Tecumseh," Young Elk said, "that you rode with our enemies the Sac."

"That is true," Tecumseh said. "I rode to the hunt. I will fight with any tribe as long as the face in the sights of my rifle is white. I will not ever turn my weapons to the killing of an Indian, regardless of his tribe."

"The Sac who raid our villages to kill our young men and take our horses and women do not have your sense of honor," Young Elk said.

"Will the Cherokee of your father's land join this confederation of tribes supported by Tecumseh?" an Osage asked Ho-ya.

"Perhaps a few of the young ones," Ho-ya said.

"You and those who came with you chose to retreat from the line of confrontation," Tecumseh said.

Ho-ya drew himself up. "You asked me if I would fight against the enemy of my hosts the Osage," he said. "I would. I will fight when it comes time to fight. I do not agree totally with my uncle Renno in his belief that we should buy plows, herd tame cattle, build log houses, and live as white men; but I do know that he is right in saying that war is not the answer. My blade will speak to any accusation that I acted in a cowardly manner by moving west to avoid confrontation with the whites, and there may come a time when it will meet the advance of the whites in these plains and hills. In the meantime I and mine will not leave our homes to participate in a suicidal war on the Ohio."

Young Elk held up his hand to prevent Tecumseh from speaking. "I drank wine and ate sweetmeats in the home of the man who will be the next great white father of the United States. I rode in the white man's wheeled houses. I saw the white man and his seed as thick as the leaves of grass in the beginning of the summer. I watched his long-knife soldiers perform feats of walking in unison in a city where the houses soar to the sky and blot out the sun." He turned to Ho-ya. "I broke bread and talked with your uncle, the Seneca sachem, Renno, and his words were straight, not wavering and bent like a crawling black snake."

He looked at Tecumseh. "You ask me, brother, to forget the blood that has been shed in our long battles with our enemies—the Sac, the Potawatomi, the Kickapoo, the Fox—and join arms with them. This I cannot do. There is too much blood."

Tecumseh sat in stoic silence as the others spoke, one by one, some of them using up half an hour to detail some past fight with the tribes to the north and east. Tecumseh was given the last word. He spoke quietly, his eyes down, his expression sad.

"When your forests have been cut down and your grasses burned and the land ripped open to its deep-beating heart by the plow, remember what I have said. When the white man's cattle graze where now there are buffalo, remember what I have said. When the hunting grounds of the Osage are dotted with the ugly log houses of the white man and there is no place for the Osage to hunt, you will remember, and then you will fall on your knees and put dirt in your hair and weep for what has been lost as you think on what I have said this day."

Ho-ya stayed on as guest in the house of his brother-by-marriage. The visiting chiefs and warriors had gone back to their homes. The Shawnee and his small entourage had ridden off into the distance in the direction of the great river to the east. Ho-ya put aside his concerns. The Osage house was warm and snug. Young Elk was his brother, and We-yo seemed happy as she performed her duties as a wife. Summer Moon sat in his lap and played with the beaded fringe of his tunic. The boy sat by the fire and watched the changing glow of the embers.

"Will you come with me to hunt?" Young Elk asked. "The buffalo have been seen not a day's ride to the north."

"With pleasure," Ho-ya said.

He knew that he and his had not escaped forever the westward push of the whites, but the confrontation would not come tomorrow. Tomorrow he would ride and shoot and thrust his hand into the opened belly of his kill to rip out the animal's hot, tangy, bloody liver. He would eat this symbol of the hunt with great pleasure. Tomorrow he would live as the spirits had intended the Indian to live. Tomorrow was all that mattered.

Chapter Seven

After months of cruising up and down the coast of the
United States from Savannah to a point just off the
entrance to Chesapeake Bay and southward again, HMS
Cormorant was now off the coast of Spanish Florida. Her
drinking water was old and soured, and her food supplies
were depleted. Jonathan Bowen gave orders to turn the
ship toward land. She tacked toward St. Augustine against
a westerly wind that brought the scent of vegetation, the
aroma of land, to all those aboard her.

The ship's Royal Marines, their small force aug-
mented by the noncommissioned officers, lined the rails
with weapons primed and ready to shoot any would-be
deserter. While the ship was being reprovisioned, Little
Hawk and Hensley stood together near the mainmast,
looked out at the bustling Spanish town, and deeply in-
haled the tantalizing perfumes of fruit trees.

"It would almost be worth getting shot just to put my feet on solid land," Hensley said.

Little Hawk nodded.

"But the gunner wouldn't let a man get that far, would 'e?" Hensley muttered. "If a chap decided to swim for it, I warrant Griffiths would let the bloke get, say, five or ten feet from the beach before giving the order to fire."

"This is not the time or the place," Little Hawk said.

"Will that time ever come?" Hensley grumbled.

"It will," Little Hawk said with such conviction that Hensley turned his head quickly to look at him, hungry for further talk of freedom.

Upon consultation with Hensley, who knew every member of the crew, Little Hawk had made a cautious approach to five men, all of whom expressed a willingness to make a break for it if and when there came an opportunity that provided even a chance of success.

Little Hawk did not speak of his plan to his cousin. On the rare occasions when Little Hawk and he were able to talk, James seemed reluctant to enter into conversation. Following his scourging while tied to the mast, James Ridley had become withdrawn. Little Hawk saw in his cousin's eyes a look of resignation and hopelessness. He wanted to tell James to buck up, but to offer hope was to hint that he had some design for ending the galling condition of slavery in which they were mired. He feared that James, in his misery, would act prematurely.

"Watch it," Hensley hissed as Gunner Griffiths approached.

"You," the gunner said, pointing at Little Hawk. "You speak the monkey talk of these bull-worshiping fops, don't you?"

"Yes, sir," Little Hawk said.

"Come with me."

Little Hawk followed the gunner down the gangplank onto the dock where two Spaniards in continental finery waited with imperious impatience. Captain Bowen stood nearby, his hands clasped behind his back.

"Tell these bast—these gentlemen," the gunner said, indicating the food dealers, "that we know feathers from macaroni and that if they think they're getting a hundred guineas for the rotting meat and overripe fruit they've sent us, they're as spare as ape shit."

Griffiths stood back while Little Hawk brought the negotiations to completion. He couldn't quite get a handle on the American. He had been quick to fight aboard his own ship, but he'd been as meek as a lamb since being taken aboard the *Cormorant*. The gunner wasn't a particularly honorable man, but he had his own code of behavior. He believed in strict discipline as the only means of keeping a crew under control on a warship where living conditions were miserable and discipline was harsh, but he approached his duty with a certain code of fairness. If a man toed the mark, obeyed orders, worked to the limit of his ability, and did not steal from the ship or his mates, he was safe from the gunner's lash. Where Little Hawk was concerned, Griffiths' code of fairness was a continual frustration, for the gunner would never forget having been sent sprawling by the Indian's hard fist. One day, sooner or later, the pretty boy who called himself a Seneca would be lashed to the mast with his hands over his head and his back exposed.

The *Cormorant* left the Spanish port, and for a while the crew awaited mealtime eagerly. There were potatoes, all a man could stuff into his mouth. Fresh fruit was handed out as long as the supply lasted. There were deliciously juicy oranges, bananas, and grapefruit with a sweet-tart tang. For two splendid meals there were turnips cooked with their greens, and there was even fresh beef for a few meals before the rations again were limited to bully beef, salt pork, and wormy biscuits.

Captain Jonathan Bowen savored the fresh vegetables and fruit and begrudged having to share them. He would almost have preferred to have the food rot rather than have it consumed by the crew, men who hadn't washed their hands in days, who ate without manners and gnawed on bones like dogs. He had, however, as much meat and fresh produce as the officers and he could consume before it spoiled or became tainted, so he allowed the crew its share not because of any humanitarian or health reason but simply because the food was aboard.

Time passed with excruciating slowness for Bowen.

His most frequent companion among the officers, Ensign Drake Mumsley, was so callow and uneducated that Bowen could tolerate his presence for only a short time. The captain had long since become disgusted with the coarse and common masculinity of Gunner Griffiths.

To pass the time, Captain Bowen had taken to walking on the deck during the pleasant parts of the morning and the evening. He could not have said when he first began to take notice of the tall, bronzed American with the Indian name, but as the days and weeks passed he found himself seeking any opportunity to observe Little Hawk. He had listened to him negotiate with the dealers in St. Augustine. The captain knew enough Spanish to understand that the American was being polite and diplomatic but firm. For long minutes he had watched, comparing the American with Griffiths. The Welshman came off second best.

He had heard the American speak in the cultured, upper-class accent of England. He had observed him acting as interpreter for Drake Mumsley, who was trying to give orders to two Spanish seamen who knew little English; and he had listened without looking when the American spoke French with a seaman from one of the Channel Islands.

Without knowing it—and if he had known he would not have acknowledged it—Bowen shared one habit with many men of the crew: He put himself to sleep each night fantasizing about the time when the *Cormorant* would be moored in an English port and he would be free to take a carriage up to London. It was at that point that his dreams began to differ radically from those of most of the men aboard. Women were not featured in his imaginings.

His libidinous fires had been damped from the age of twelve, when he had been exposed to the cloying affection and licentious desires of his nanny, sometimes to the point of literally fearing that he would be smothered by her soft, yeasty-smelling femininity. Nor did he share the unnatural urgings of the vices of Sodom. More than once he had ordered the lashing of men caught in acts condemned by the Bible.

What Bowen needed was food for the mind. He considered himself a gentleman of sensitivity. He hungered for civilized conversation. He had a longing that became an ache to discuss literature and the arts. His favorite fantasy was to find someone who was familiar with and truly understood, as he did, the writings of de Sade and the German who knew the true pleasure of giving and receiving pain.

The *Cormorant* sailed southeast from Spanish Florida into balmy, tropical nights. On one such evening Bowen called Gunner Griffiths to his cabin.

"The pressed American, the Indian," he said, "he has never given you any trouble?"

Griffiths rubbed his jaw. "Not since the day he was taken."

"You used him as an interpreter in St. Augustine," Bowen said.

"Yes, sir, I did."

"I listened. He reduced the asking price for our provisions by half."

"I told him what to say," the gunner muttered.

"Yes, of course. But he smoothed the rough edges off your undiplomatic language." Bowen yawned. "Perhaps we can find other uses for a man so educated."

"Give him half an opportunity and he'll be over the side," Griffiths warned.

"Quite right," Bowen said, "but that doesn't mean we can't use his abilities to our own best advantage, does it?"

"No, sir."

"I'll have a chat with him," Bowen said.

The crew was once more on biscuits and salt pork and grumbling about it. Little Hawk was finishing his evening ration when Griffiths came into the crowded quarters and pointed his lash.

"You," he said.

"Eh?" Hensley whispered. "Watch yourself."

Little Hawk nodded, stuffed the last bite of food into his mouth, then rose to follow the bosun out onto the deck and into officers' country. Griffiths didn't speak again. He knocked on the door of the captain's cabin with the butt of his lash. When Bowen called out, "Come," he opened the door, stepped back, and pushed Little Hawk in.

"That will be all for the moment, Mr. Griffiths," Bowen said. He looked at Little Hawk speculatively. "Close the door."

Little Hawk obeyed, then stood at rest with his hands behind his back.

"I have been watching you," Bowen said.

"Sir!"

Bowen spoke in French. "Apparently, you have been exposed to some education."

Little Hawk answered in the same language. "My grandmother spoke French, sir."

"Are you telling me that all of your education came from your grandmother?"

"No, sir."

Bowen's face darkened. "Don't exasperate me, boy. I have asked you a question."

"Were you inquiring about my education, sir?"

"I was," Bowen said dryly.

Little Hawk looked Bowen in the eyes, his blue eyes narrowed, their stare piercing. "I was tutored by my stepmother, who is Lady Beth Huntington, brother of Lord Beaumont, and wife of a chief of the Seneca Nation. I attended West Point."

Bowen let his eyes fall away from Little Hawk's defiant stare. "What is West Point?"

"It is the military college established by President Thomas Jefferson, sir," Little Hawk said, "to train officers for the United States military."

"Ah," Bowen said. "So that is why you claim to be an officer in the United States Marines." He rubbed his chin. "The stepson of the sister of a peer, son of a chief, an officer."

"Yes, sir."

"If those claims could be proven—"

"Your men also seized a ship's officer when they boarded the *Beth Huntington*," Little Hawk said. "James Ridley was and is first mate of an American merchantman and the son of a prominent North Carolina family, sir."

"I am not concerned with such things at the moment," Bowen said. "I want to hear more about you. Your name, for example. Is that typical of Indian names? How do you say it in your Indian language?"

"Os-sweh-ga-da-ah Ne-wa-ah."

"And that means Little Hawk?"

"Yes, sir. The Indian names his children for things in nature."

"Interesting," Bowen said. "Sit down, won't you?"

"If that is your wish, sir."

"It is, damn it."

Little Hawk sat in a hard wooden chair with his back straight.

"What studies did you pursue at West Point?" Bowen asked.

"Mainly subjects allied to the military arts," Little Hawk said.

"I suppose you were taught that it was rebel force of arms that won the nasty little war that pitted Englishman against Englishman," Bowen said. "And not that General Washington was able to prevail because of the stupidity of our officers in the field and politicians in England who didn't understand the situation."

"I studied the campaigns of the War for Independence, sir," Little Hawk said, not venturing to counter Bowen's implied contention that England had not really lost the war. He was familiar with that argument. He had heard it in England. The average Englishman was unwilling to accept the fact that an army of ragtag colonials could best British regulars and was certain that there would be another war sooner or later.

"And the finer things?" Bowen asked. "Were you exposed at all to literature? To art?"

"There wasn't much time for that, sir," Little Hawk

said. "My stepmother did twist my ear and make me read."

"She had to twist your ear?"

"Well, not really, sir. I found the tragedies of Shakespeare to be most interesting. Henry Fielding was rather heavy going, but I enjoyed Goldsmith's *Vicar of Wakefield*." Little Hawk was not truly interested in discussing his past readings with the man who had so enjoyed watching James being lashed. He answered the captain's questions and volunteered some information because he had not as yet ascertained what Bowen was really after.

"And the French classics?" Bowen asked. "Have you read them?"

"I speak French much better than I read it, sir."

"Too bad. You have not heard of the genius de Sade?"

"No, sir."

"Someday, when these endless wars are over and both you and I have returned to our own lives, you must remember the name and study his works."

"I'll remember," Little Hawk said.

"I understand that there is very little true art in the colonies," Bowen said.

"In the United States, sir?"

"Yes, yes."

"I really don't know."

Bowen frowned.

Little Hawk wanted to keep the conversation going. He would try to convince this man that he should not be pressed into living as an ordinary seaman, and if he succeeded, he might be able to help James.

"I visited the British Museum in Montague House when I was last in London," he said.

"Don't lie to me," Bowen said.

Little Hawk asked, in true surprise, "Why should I lie about that?"

But Bowen's attitude had undergone a sudden and drastic change. He waved his hand. "Go now. It is impossible, this trying to talk with an impressed seaman. I never should have asked the gunner to bring you here."

Little Hawk rose. "Sir, I would point out to you again that James Ridley and I were impressed illegally."

"Get out," Bowen said, rising from his own chair, his face flushing.

"You said, sir, that if my claims could be proven—"

"Leave."

"You have only to contact the Admiralty, sir, and inquire for William, Lord Beaumont, and ask him to vouch for—"

He didn't finish. Bowen moved swiftly, seized a lash from the top of his sea chest, and cut Little Hawk viciously across the shoulder.

Never before had any man laid the lash on Little Hawk. The blood of the white Indian was heated to incandescence, and his reaction was instantaneous. Little Hawk stepped forward as Bowen drew back to strike him with the lash again and slammed his fist into the captain's face. Bowen let out a startled cry as he fell. He crashed to the deck, taking his smoke stand with him. The piece of furniture shattered, and Bowen seized a separated leg as he scrambled to his feet. With a roar of anger and shock he leaped toward Little Hawk.

Little Hawk crouched and ducked under the captain's looping attack with the heavy piece of wood and buried his fist in Bowen's soft stomach. The captain's breath left him in a whoosh, and he bent over, his face red. He staggered back. Little Hawk followed, but not fast enough to prevent Bowen from drawing his saber from its sheath that hung beside his bed. The blade gleamed brightly in the light of the ship's lantern and made a hiss as it narrowly missed taking off the top of Little Hawk's head. Hawk fell to the floor as he evaded a thrust of the blade and came up with the broken pieces of the smoking stand in his hands.

A slashing attack cut wood and sent splinters scattering. Little Hawk was left holding a disjointed leg from the stand. He danced away from Bowen's lunge and jumped onto the captain's bunk, then used it as a springboard to fly to the other side of the cabin. Bowen whirled and sent his blade in a flashing arc; but Little Hawk ducked under

and slammed the heavy, round piece of wood upward
with all his strength. It smashed against the underside of
the captain's chin. The sound of the blow told Little Hawk
that he had done damage even before the sword fell from
Bowen's suddenly lax hand and the captain crumpled.

Bowen's eyes were wide and staring. They blinked
once, then began to dim as the light fades from the sky at
sunset. Little Hawk lifted the man's head. It turned
loosely in his hands. The force of his blow had broken
Bowen's neck.

The punishment for killing an officer aboard ship was
swift and sure. Unless he thought of something quickly,
he would hang by the neck from a yardarm until he was
dead. If he was to have even a slim chance of staying
alive, he had to find a way to leave the ship within the
next few minutes, before the body of the captain was discovered.

He bent over the chart table and saw that Bowen had
been a meticulous man in charting the ship's position.
The *Cormorant* was just west of the main grouping of the
Bahamas Islands. Within ten miles were small, outlying
islands, most of them waterless and, thus, uninhabited.

He lifted the sheath of the captain's saber from its
place, buckled it around his waist, and put the gleaming
weapon in its place. There were two pistols in the top
drawer of the captain's chest, along with powder and shot.
Thus armed, Little Hawk opened the door cautiously and
stepped out onto the deck.

Gunner Griffiths, consumed with curiosity as to why
the captain had wanted to talk in privacy with the American, had been waiting in the shadows. He stepped forward as Little Hawk emerged into the moonlight, and
when he saw that the American was armed, he reached
for the whistle that hung from a thong around his neck.

"Do you need help?" Little Hawk challenged, drawing the saber and stepping forward. "Are you afraid to
face one common seaman alone?"

Griffiths snarled denial, drew his blade, and surged
to the attack. Little Hawk was singing the song of death in
his mind, not because he feared dying on the gunner's

blade but because he was sure that the clash of steel on steel would rouse the ship and force him to face insurmountable odds. At the stern a steersman was at work, and the officer of the watch would be beside him.

Even though the ship was running before a moderate wind, her sails making soft thunder in accompaniment to the wet sloshing as the hull leaped crests and fell into troughs, the sound of saber on saber would be a clarion call of warning to unfriendly ears.

He would never be able to understand why the sound of the grim one-on-one battle was not heard by others. Perhaps it was because of the flapping of the sails, the moan of the wind in the rigging, or the rush of water past the hull. Perhaps the manitous dampened the sound and confined it to the bow in front of the captain's cabin, where Griffiths showed himself to be a swordsman who depended on strength rather than skill.

At first the gunner's fierce attack forced Little Hawk backward until he was against the rail. Griffiths snarled in satisfaction and pushed forward, the tip of his blade aimed for Little Hawk's stomach. A gut wound would be very painful for a long, long time. He got air instead as Little Hawk danced away along the rail and came at him from the side to drive his own blade into the soft flesh above Griffiths' hipbone. Griffiths was shocked into silence, his mouth agape. There was no doubt that tremendous pain had surged up in him, and Little Hawk guessed that the point of his saber had destroyed a kidney.

Griffiths cried out softly as the blade was withdrawn, then put all of his strength into a lunge that carried him directly onto Little Hawk's blade. It entered just below the vee of his ribs, thrust upward through the diaphragm and into the heart.

"For James," Little Hawk whispered as he twisted the blade and rammed it home.

He jerked the saber to him, letting Griffiths fall. He turned, expecting to meet a charge of officers and marines. He heard only the sound made by the sails and the wind and the water. He lifted Griffiths' body and let it fall over the rail. The splash was lost among the other sounds.

All was serene on deck. He went to the quarters for his watch, tiptoed to Hensley's bunk, then put his hand over Hensley's mouth.

The seaman's eyes flew open, and the man tensed until Little Hawk hissed for silence and whispered into his ear, "Get the others. Lower the boats."

Two boats would be taken because they would be able to move faster than one boat with eight men in it.

"Now?" Hensley asked.

"Now."

"But we're in midocean."

"Stay, then," Little Hawk whispered, "and I will go alone."

"Nay."

"Hurry. I will meet you at the boats."

He left the quarters silently and went to the hatch that led to the sleeping area for the men of James Ridley's watch. He took down a lantern and held it high, for it was dark in the belowdecks quarters. A man aroused and grumbled in protest at the light.

"Go back to sleep," Little Hawk whispered.

He found James and woke him by placing his hand over his cousin's mouth. He hissed for silence.

James's eyes were wide.

"Quickly," Little Hawk said. "Don't take time to dress. Bring your clothes."

James, dressed only in fraying, holed long underwear, rolled out of his hammock, gathered his clothing, and followed Little Hawk.

Hensley was directing the lowering of the second boat. Four men were already in the first boat. Another man was helping Hensley.

There was a half-moon to give some light. The sea was running in moderate, smooth-topped waves.

"Where away?" Hensley whispered as he took his place at an oar.

"Due east," Little Hawk said.

No one spoke again until the two longboats had put

enough distance between them and the ship to lower her running lights to the horizon.

"Hawk, do you know where we are?" James asked.

"We should see islands in the Bahamas with the morning's light," Little Hawk said.

"The cap'n'll know that, too," Hensley said. "Ought we to steer south, so's when 'e comes looking for us 'e'll find only empty ocean?"

"There'll be some confusion on board at the change of watch," Little Hawk said.

Hensley grunted. "When the gunner came for you, 'e took you to the captain, didn't 'e?"

"He did," Little Hawk said.

"Aye, God," Hensley said, "am I right in guessing that neither the cap'n nor the gunner will be in command when the sun comes up?"

"You are right."

"You killed that motherless son?" Ridley asked.

"It might take a while for the others to organize things and find out that we're missing," Little Hawk said. "I'm betting that we can reach the islands and lose ourselves before they come searching."

"You killed Griffiths?" James asked.

"Yes."

"I hope that it was not quick."

Little Hawk grunted. "Save your strength for the oars."

The sun rose from behind low, sandy spits. Beyond was a larger island, partially wooded. "With a will, then," Hensley called out. The men in the two boats increased the tempo of their rowing. Little Hawk was looking toward the west. As the light became better, he saw the *Cormorant* sweeping down on them under a full suit of sail. Someone among the officers had reacted swiftly.

A puff of smoke from the *Cormorant*'s bow told the men in the longboats that a cannon had been fired. The ball whistled overhead to splash into the sea ahead of them. Being fired upon put new strength into tired arms. The two boats leaped forward and, as another ball splashed down behind them, turned south toward the protection of a low, sandy point.

"We must reach the larger island," Little Hawk said.

"We'll be rowing across an open expanse," James protested.

"Can't stay 'ere, can we?" Hensley said.

"The longer we wait, the closer the ship will be," Little Hawk replied. "Let's go."

All of the men bent their backs with a will. As soon as they had left the partial protection of the low, treeless island that was nothing more than an exposed shoal, puffs of smoke began to come from the *Cormorant*'s cannon, and balls fell around them, one so close that it doused the men in Little Hawk's boat with foaming white water.

"She's turning away," James said.

"Getting too close to the shallows," Hensley said.

"We'll be out of range soon," James said.

Little Hawk's destination was the southernmost tip of the island. There, tall palm trees grew almost to the water, leaving a narrow, white, sandy beach. He estimated the island to be no more than a mile long and less than that in width. There would probably be no water, but there were milk-laden coconuts on the palm trees. Since the men had left the *Cormorant* in haste, there had been no time to think of water or food. Coconuts would give them liquid and prevent dehydration as the sun heated the day.

To Little Hawk's satisfaction, there was another, still larger island to the east. Coral heads in the channel between the two heavily palmed bits of land made dark shadows in the pure, turquoise waters. The ship would be unable to sail into the channel. The two boats landed, and the exhausted men began to gather coconuts. Little Hawk used the captain's saber to slice off the top of the green nuts. Everyone drank deeply, for the last sprint of rowing to reach shelter had been extremely strenuous, and there was already more than a hint of heat in the morning air.

"They'll come after us, 'awk," Hensley said.

"Let's have a look at that next island," Little Hawk decided.

*   *   *

It was midday before the longboats pushed their prows up on a sandy beach on the larger island.

"Gor," Hensley said, "I need a sit-down to catch my breath."

"We'll rest here until nightfall," Little Hawk said.

The boats were pulled up the beach and into a grove of palm trees and sea grapes, where they were covered by fallen fronds. The men quenched their thirst with coconut milk and sank down gratefully to fall asleep almost immediately.

"I'll take first watch," James said.

"Wake me if you get sleepy," Little Hawk told him.

"Don't worry. I have no intention of letting those Limey bastards sneak up on us," James said.

Little Hawk gave him one of the captain's pistols. He scooped out a hole in the sand for his hipbones, crossed his hands over his chest—the other pistol was held firmly in one of them—and was asleep within minutes. He awoke with James's hand on his shoulder.

"Boats," James whispered.

Little Hawk moved cautiously through the palm grove until he could see two longboats, each being rowed by four men. In one boat two Royal Marines sat with their muskets across their knees. In the other boat, in addition to the four oarsmen, were Drake Mumsley and another Royal Marine. Mumsley pointed toward the shore, and the boats turned sharply to make for landfall about two hundred yards north of the point.

"Too many muskets," James whispered as Mumsley's boat landed and the rowers took up rifles and waded onto the beach.

"We can use their weapons," Little Hawk said. "Stay here and watch them."

He ran silently back to the boats, roused the men, and told them of the situation. James came running, his feet throwing sand. "One party went north," he said, panting from the exertion. "The other is moving this way. Six men."

"Which group?" Little Hawk asked. "Mumsley's?"

"No, four seamen, two Royal Marines."

"You and I will take the marines," Little Hawk said. "Hensley, use the oars. As soon as James and I fire, you must silence the seamen before they can bring their muskets to bear."

"My pleasure," Hensley said, reaching for one of the heavy oaken oars.

Little Hawk positioned his force amid a dense clump of sea-grape bushes. The six men from the *Cormorant* came down the narrow beach, walking slowly, with difficulty, in the soft sand. The beach was strewn with debris —coconut husks, whole nuts, dried seaweed, and assorted bits of vegetative flotsam. Beside Little Hawk, James Ridley cocked his pistol. Little Hawk whispered, "Wait."

He let the two marines who were leading come even with the cluster of green that concealed him and his men, lifted his pistol, and nodded at James. The man was tense. Little Hawk prepared himself to leap to the attack with his saber if James missed his shot. He saw James tighten his finger on the trigger and yelled, "Now!"

Two shots sounded as one. The two marines went down. One of them, the one that had been in Little Hawk's sights, fell limply and heavily. The other man went to his knee and lifted his rifle, but in his shock and pain he could not immediately locate his target.

Little Hawk leaped to the attack, and his blade flashed. Behind him he heard Hensley yelling. The seamen from the *Cormorant* were raising their rifles. A shot found its target. The fourth man in Little Hawk's boat cried out and fell to the sand. Little Hawk's blade, wet with blood, flashed up and around, almost severing the arm of a seaman who was trying to bring his musket to bear. The other men were down. Hensley and the men from the second boat had wielded their oars well.

"That other group will be coming," Hensley said.

"Take the weapons," Little Hawk ordered. "If you don't know how to load and shoot, give the muskets to men who do."

"What about these?" Hensley asked, pointing toward

the seamen who had been felled by blows to the head from the heavy oars.

"Kill 'em," said one of the men.

"Belay that," Hensley said. "They're just blokes like us."

"Leave them," Little Hawk said.

He checked the load and prime of the six muskets that had been taken from the men of the *Cormorant,* then positioned the men to cover the beach to the north. He had not long to wait. The second group appeared, jogging through the sand with Drake Mumsley in the lead.

"Hold your fire," Little Hawk said. He stepped out of the greenery.

The ensign skidded to a halt while lifting his hand to stop the others. The marine at his side lifted his rifle.

"I have no desire to kill any more of you!" Little Hawk shouted.

"Give up your arms and surrender, then," Mumsley answered.

James stepped out beside Little Hawk, lifted his musket, and fired in the same motion. The ensign was knocked backward by the heavy-caliber ball as it impacted his chest. Little Hawk had to act quickly. He dropped the marine who had stood at the ensign's side even as the man was firing. The ball clipped leaves near Little Hawk's head.

"Don't shoot!" yelled one of the seamen, throwing his rifle to the sand and raising his arms. "Don't shoot!"

"That's old Marley," Hensley said. " 'e knows these islands like the back of his 'and."

The other seamen threw down their rifles. Little Hawk's men came out of concealment and surrounded the four survivors.

The man named Marley said, "I figure to join with a man who had the balls to kill Gunner Griffiths." He stepped forward and extended his hand. Little Hawk took it.

"May be that I can be of 'elp," Marley offered.

" 'e knows these islands," Hensley repeated.

"How about you other men?" Little Hawk asked. "Stay here, and you're deserters."

"Just give me 'alf a chance," said one man. The other two nodded eagerly.

"All right, Mr. Marley," Little Hawk said. "Where do we go that the *Cormorant* can't go?"

Chapter Eight

As if to compensate for the dark clouds of political threat that hung over Washington, spring weather greeted the coming of March and the date specified by the Constitution for the inauguration of a new president. The three ladies who were visiting from North Carolina left their suite in the hotel early, having been warned that the streets would be thronged and nigh onto impassable as the noon hour approached. For the occasion, Renna had abandoned the black of mourning.

The three women, dressed in the latest fashions, attracted no little male attention as they walked across the Capitol grounds. A navy band marched by on the avenue, drums sending deep-toned vibrations far into one's chest. Trumpets blared, and a tuba hooted like a foghorn. The three women paused to watch. Flame-haired Beth stood between the two younger women—Renna, with her pale hair and blue eyes, dressed in green, and Naomi, a bit more conservative, wearing light tan to complement her corn-silk tresses.

It was a good idea that they had heeded the advice to be in the gallery of the House of Representatives early. Many spectator seats were already filled. Beth led the way to three spaces together near the rail. With a swirl of skirts they took their places just as a distinguished man in black formal wear led two severe-looking ladies toward them.

"I'm sorry, ladies," he said, "but the front row is reserved."

From behind them, a female voice said, "Don't believe him. There are no reserved seats here."

"These ladies, you see," the man continued, "are the wives of members of Congress. I will have to ask you to move."

"And I," the woman behind them said, "am a citizen of the sovereign state of Virginia and, like these ladies you are trying to bully, have as much right to any seat here as you or the wife of whatever congressional nabob you might name."

Beth smiled up at the man, then nodded cordially to the two stern-faced women beside him. "It seems, sir, that we have a spokesman to protect us."

One of the women snorted through her nose and turned away.

"That's it, ladies!" the woman behind them said. "Stand by your guns."

A few minutes before noon Thomas Jefferson arrived. Twice he had walked through the streets of Washington to be sworn into the office that he was now abandoning with no regret. In contrast, James Madison came in a carriage escorted by the Washington and Georgetown Cavalry. He entered the Hall of Representatives with members of Jefferson's cabinet and a committee of Congressmen and was seated at the front of the chamber. Thomas Jefferson sat to the right of the central chair.

Dolley Madison's "darling little husband" began his inaugural address in a voice that quivered and was almost inaudible. His face was pale, and his hands trembled; but quickly he seemed to find his pace, and his voice rose as he spoke of the uneasy world situation. He concluded by paying tribute to his predecessor, saying that the citizens of the United States now would bid Jefferson a fond and grateful farewell.

A sour-faced Chief Justice John Marshall, chagrined at being forced to administer the oath of office to a political enemy, led Madison through the ritual. Outside, guns roared in salute. Bands of militia formed along the route to the Madisons' F Street home.

By the time Beth, Renna, and Naomi arrived for the festivities, the house was bedlam. They watched from the sidewalk for over half an hour before they could get in. The entry, the parlors, the dining room, and even the bedrooms were filled with people.

The new First Lady stood near the drawing room door. She wore a gown of elegant simplicity, a Paris creation in plain cambric with a long train. The neckline was cut low. Her hat was of purple velvet and white satin with white plumes.

"Forgive me, darlings," she said as Beth and her daughters made their way past. "Do be patient, and after the house has disgorged this mass of humanity we will talk."

Beth found herself standing next to Thomas Jefferson. Both the former president and the new one wore suits of black, American-made cloth ordered from the same factory in Connecticut as a demonstration of support for the embargo.

"I must apologize to you, Mrs. Harper," Jefferson said, "for taking your husband away from you again."

Beth explained that Toshabe's failing health, not Mr. Jefferson's request that he see Meriwether Lewis, was the reason for her being separated from Renno. Jefferson expressed his regrets.

James Madison was clearly not at ease as he stood by Dolley and extended greetings to the masses of people who filed past. Jefferson nodded toward the little man and said, "I am much happier at this moment than my friend."

"He has a rather impressive dignity about him," Beth said.

"Indeed," Jefferson agreed. "And his stint in the presidential penitentiary will be made more pleasant and less difficult by that lady who stands so proudly beside him."

There proved to be little opportunity, after all, to chat with Dolley. She invited Beth and the girls into her dressing room. She did not look at all tired, save for little lines at the corners of her eyes.

"While James is resting," Dolley said, "I'd like your advice, Beth, on the gown I'm planning to wear to the ball tonight."

She took down a pale, buff-colored dress in velvet and held it to her ample figure.

"I plan to accessorize this with a gaudy little bonnet and a pearl necklace. Is that too daring?"

"Not for you, Dolley," Beth said.

"*Très élégant,*" Renna said.

"Please, darling girl," Dolley moaned, rolling her eyes, "don't call attention to the fact that I defy my husband's policy and order my clothes from Paris."

"You will look like a queen," Naomi said. She was still a bit awed by the company in which she found herself.

"What I will enjoy most," Dolley said, "are the looks I will get not from the gentlemen present but from the Puritan ladies, such as Abigail Adams." She laughed. "She once said that my style of dress was really an outrage upon all decency."

"Not at all," Renna said, then added, "at least not when judged by European standards."

"I do envy you for having lived in Paris," Dolley said. She lifted a hand imploringly. "I know that you all have to get back to your hotel to get ready, but will you stay long enough for me to try on this dress? I want everything to be perfect."

"Of course," Beth said.

Dolley came out of the dressing room with her head high, radiant, her full bosom showcased. The dress she wore was cut so that it showed her ample form. Her arms were bared almost to the shoulders. There were no stays, no bodice. The pearls gleamed against her perfect skin.

"Is it too scant upon the body?" Dolley asked.

"Wickedly so," Renna said with a smile. "The finest artist could not make his art compete with you."

"You're kind," Dolley said. She frowned as she looked down at her bosom. "I don't want to look like a nursing mother. . . ."

Arrangements had been made to have two of Dolley's cousins—there seemed to be dozens of them around at various times—escort the North Carolina ladies to the inaugural ball at Long's Hotel. Both men were of mature age, grayed and dignified.

Jefferson had already arrived when Beth's party entered the ballroom. Smiling, he came over to greet her and stayed long enough to mention to her, with some satisfaction, that he was once more a plain, unassuming citizen. Dolley and James Madison were led into the hall to a martial air called "Madison's March," written especially for the new president.

"I pray," Beth said, "that such military pomp does not predict the future."

"Look at her," Renna said, smiling toward Dolley, who marched proudly on her husband's arm. "She disarms envy itself."

"If Mr. Madison is wise," Jefferson said, "he will allow Dolley to conciliate all of his enemies."

The members of Beth's party were far down the table from the Madisons at dinner. The places of priority were given to such international dignitaries as the French minister, who escorted Dolley to the crescent-shaped table. Beth saw that Jefferson seemed content watching and listening. And, she noticed, Madison's face was glum. Later, in a quiet moment, before the great crush in the ballroom, he confided to Beth that he would rather be at home in his bed.

* * *

The music began. The crowd elbowed around the President and the First Lady. People stood on chairs and benches in an effort to get a glimpse of Dolley. The two escorts she had appointed danced dutifully with their three charges. Renna, left alone while Beth and Naomi were on the floor, was musingly remembering similar affairs in Paris where she had danced in Beau's arms. When a familiar voice called her name, she was startled. Her heart leaped, and she looked up quickly . . . to see the face of Randall Farnsworth.

"Renna," he repeated.

Recovering her composure, she rose and managed to smile a greeting and extend her hands. She had once entertained mixed feelings about Farnsworth, since he was the one who had brought the news of Beau's death to her. In the end she had forgiven him for being the messenger, and now he was a friend, a familiar face in a strange place.

"I can't believe my luck," Farnsworth said, bowing over her hand, bringing his lips to within a fraction of an inch of her skin. "I feared that I would have to travel all the way to the far west to find you."

Farnsworth was dressed in regimental glory. Several medals gleamed against the red of his tunic.

"Please don't try to convince me, Randall, that you came all the way across the Atlantic in search of me," Renna said teasingly.

"Oddly enough," he said sincerely, "that is exactly what I did."

She smiled in spite of herself.

"It took a bit of doing," he said. "I had to convince not a few high officers and a few politicians that I would make a good military attaché."

"Ah," she said.

"But I sought out the office so that I could find you."

"You overwhelm me," she said.

"Since I have come so far, you must reward me with a dance," he said.

"That seems a reasonable request," she said.

It was pleasant to be on the floor with a handsome

man guiding her through the mincing steps of a minuet.
She was a practical woman. She had grown up in the
great wilderness among a people to whom death was familiar. She had lost two husbands, the first when she was
very young. She knew the intensity of the ultimate hurt,
the loss of someone she loved very much. Although she
called the God of her mother her own and attended
church when she could, she had been affected, too, by the
traditions of the Seneca. When death came to a Seneca
family, the sadness was intense and sincere, but the demands of day-to-day responsibilities prevented long periods of mourning. Life went on. There was a space in her
heart that was empty except for memories of Beau; but
she was young, and she had watched the installation of a
President and was the guest of the President's wife in an
exciting city at an exciting time. To meet a man whom she
knew and liked, a man her own age, a man who had dem-
onstrated his sensitivity in the matter of her husband's
death, was a pleasure she could accept without guilt. To
dance and to laugh were natural and agreeable activities
for an attractive widow of just twenty-three years.

Official Washington was, in effect, a small, closed
community where everyone of importance knew everyone
else of merit. There were those, however, who were curious about the three women who were special guests of the
President's wife, and especially the flame-haired beauty
who spoke with a cultured British accent. Several members of Congress wrangled introductions, for it was
rumored that Beth was the wife of a very important west-
erner who held President Madison's favor, as he had with
three presidents before Madison. Beth enjoyed seeing the
looks of shocked disbelief when she said, in answer to
diplomatically phrased but personal questions, that her
husband was a Seneca sachem. Since there were many
men who considered Indians to be nothing more than
ignorant savages, some of Beth's conversations ended
quickly.

The senator from Massachusetts was not one who

broke away immediately. "Ah, yes," said John Quincy Adams, son of the second president. "I have heard my father speak of your Renno."

"Really?" Beth asked.

"Oh, yes," Adams said. "The Seneca figured in one of his favorite stories about George Washington. He held to the belief, you see, that the general was rather kingly in his approach to government. For example, he gave his hand to no man, but my father saw him, more than once, join arms in a warrior's clasp with his friend Renno. And although the most powerful members of Congress often had difficulty obtaining an audience with the general, his door was always open to Renno."

"My husband thinks that General Washington was a great man," Beth said, "and that he was a friend of the Indian."

"Well, I would say that our noble red brothers are badly in need of friends now," Adams said.

"Indeed," Beth agreed. "There is constant pressure on the tribes to give up their lands."

"And where does your husband stand on this question?" Adams asked.

"My husband believes that the Indian must avail himself of education and then work to become a part of the United States."

"Bravo," Adams said, clapping his hands silently. "One day I would like to share the warrior's clasp with your husband myself."

"I'm sure he would be honored," Beth said.

"Mrs. Madison is looking after you well?"

"Quite well, thank you."

"My guess is that she'll put some life in this staid city," Adams said. He bowed. "Perhaps we'll meet again, Mrs. Harper."

"It will be a pleasure, sir."

"In the meantime, I am going to set a good example and go home," Adams said. "As pleasant as the company has been, I find the crowd to be excessive, the heat oppressive, and the entertainment bad."

"I agree with your assessment of the heat," Beth said, laughing.

"Good night, madam."

The heat was, indeed, onerous. A fine sheen of perspiration glistened on Renna's lip and brow when she and Farnsworth finished a dance and made their way to a refreshment table for a cup of punch. Farnsworth's linen was soaked with sweat.

Beth and Naomi had been amazed to see him, but the women soon accepted the coincidence of his being in Washington. He performed above and beyond the call of duty by dancing with all three beauties, trying hard not to make it obvious that he preferred to be with Renna.

"May I suggest that we go find a breath of fresh air?" he asked her now.

"I don't think that it would be a good idea for me to leave unescorted with a gentleman," Renna said.

"Yes, I imagine you're right," Farnsworth agreed. Behind him was a row of large windows. He tried to open one, without success.

"It is rather warm," Renna said.

Farnsworth picked up a chair, stepped up onto a bench, and used the chair to smash the glass in the upper panes of the window. The sound was, to Renna, terribly loud, but it was lost in the blare of music and the muted rumble of voices.

"There," Farnsworth said. "There's a tiny breath of air, at least."

Renna laughed nervously. "A British officer vandalizing Washington?" she teased.

"Only to prevent suffocation," he said, smiling. "One would never do serious damage to such a pleasant, if provincial, city."

Nearby, other men followed Farnsworth's example, and the sound of breaking glass traveled around the large room until cross ventilation began to dissipate the heat.

"See what you started?" Renna asked.

"All for your comfort, my dear Renna," Farnsworth said.

*   *   *

By rowing slowly and steadily, Little Hawk, James Ridley, and the men from the *Cormorant* brought their longboats around the point of a small island, then started across a wide channel. Little Hawk's attention was straight ahead as he called out directions to keep the boat away from the razor-sharp coral heads that bristled just below the surface of the water. A glassy swell rolled in over the shallows from the open sea.

The island where the battle with Drake Mumsley's force had occurred was a full day behind them. Since then they had been threading their way through areas of coral reef between close-lying isles and sand spits. According to Marley, the seaman who had knowledge of the waters around the group of uninhabited, waterless keys, three days of rowing would bring the men to a small fishing village on an outlying island. There they might be able to obtain a boat capable of sailing across the open sea to the United States.

The first indication of the presence of the British man-of-war came in the form of a cannonball that made a direct hit on the trailing boat. The ball traveled faster than the boom of sound that announced its firing. The boat disintegrated. Mangled bodies were thrown into the sea. Wood splinters flew through the air. One of them embedded itself in the soft flesh of the upper arm of the man at the back of Little Hawk's boat.

"Ship oars," Little Hawk ordered. He turned, searching frantically for the source of the destruction. The *Cormorant* was just coming into view around the tip of the island behind them. Even as Little Hawk turned his head, the sound of her first, incredibly lucky shot reverberated over the water. It was only by a wild chance of fate that her aim had been so accurate.

A man was crying out for help. Little Hawk gave orders to turn the boat. Shots from the *Cormorant* were splashing down within a few yards. Three men were gone, sunk in the crystalline green waters or lying broken on the coral heads nearby. The survivors, two of them severely wounded, were lifted as gently as possible into Little Hawk's boat. One of the men had a broken leg. White shards of bone protruded through his flesh. He was bleeding freely. The other man died even as he was placed on the floor of the boat. A long splinter of wood had pierced his throat, severing an artery. Blood mixed with salt water.

"Might as well put him over the side," a man said.

"We'll give 'im a decent burial," Hensley said harshly.

"Well, blimy, mate, 'e's in the way, you know," the man protested as he reached for his oar.

"Work around 'im," Hensley said.

"We'll go that way," Marley said to Little Hawk, pointing out a course that took them deeper among the reefs. "And quickly, sir, if I may suggest."

Little Hawk knelt at the front of the boat, leaning over to look down to spot the darker green that told of the presence of a lurking, razor-sharp mass of coral. He shouted out his directions.

"Sir," Marley said, "I didn't figure them officers on the *Cormorant* to be fools. They might well have taken the bottom out of 'er sailing amongst these islands."

"She's turning away now," James called out.

"The best thing that could happen from our point of view is for her to pile onto a reef," Little Hawk said.

"They's deep water off there to the south, where she's 'eaded," Marley said.

"And to the north?" Little Hawk asked.

"A deep channel."

"Splendid," Little Hawk said with rich sarcasm.

"But she'll 'ave to sail around the entire island group to get to it," Marley said. "If we keep up a smart pace we'll be across the channel and 'idden safe away in a snug little bay before she can come north."

"Back oars!" Little Hawk shouted as he spotted a sharp extension of the reef almost under the bow. He was too late. The boat was lifted on the slight swell that made its way into the channel from the sea. There was a scraping sound as the boat passed over the head. A quick glance told Little Hawk that the bottom was still intact.

He breathed a sigh of relief. If the swell had deposited the boat directly atop the head, they would all be swimming. "Hard port and pull straight ahead," he said, seeing the lighter green of a channel.

Two seamen were working with the wounded man. He gave one shrill, strained scream of agony when one man pulled on the leg until, with a grinding, popping sound, the broken bone was positioned end to end, at least as nearly as the self-appointed surgeons could tell. A man sacrificed his underwear as a binding.

"Gor," a young seaman said, "wouldn't want my wound done up wif' some bloke's skivvies."

"Rather bleed to death, eh?"

"We're out of 'er range now, 'awk," Hensley said.

"All right, rowers, ease off, steady on," Little Hawk said.

Beginning at dusk, they negotiated the deep channel between islands, even though the men were exhausted from taking turns at the oars. The body of the dead man had begun to swell from the heat of the afternoon sun. The wounded man drifted in and out of consciousness. The flesh around the lesions in his leg was red and angry. By the time the boat left the lift and fall of the open channel, he was talking deliriously of home, mother, and a dog named Nippy. A landing was negotiated in a darkness that was eased with the rise of the moon and by a million stars.

"We'd best put poor Tom to rest," Hensley said, referring to the dead man.

"Blood 'ell, 'ensley," a man protested.

"Otherwise 'e'll be making his presence known in a foul way by morning," Hensley said.

"I'll help," Little Hawk offered.

Using the wide ends of the oars as shovels, the two men dug a grave just deep enough to allow a covering of less than three feet of sand atop. Hensley bowed his head and said a prayer that had been taught to him by his mother. The men sang a hymn in low voices.

The last thing Little Hawk heard before he fell asleep was the groaning of the wounded man.

*   *   *

The hated embargo did not survive Thomas Jefferson's term in office, after all. It was rescinded by the Congress on March 1, 1809, just days before Madison took the oath of office on March 4. There was, however, little rejoicing among those who were involved in commerce by sea, for the embargo had been replaced with the Nonintercourse Act, which, although it allowed trade with some nations, forbade American ships from sailing to ports in France or England.

"But this does not help me or other southern shipowners," Beth protested politely to James Madison during a quiet dinner at the house on F Street. The Madisons were still in the house that had been their home for eight years because Thomas Jefferson was still collecting the belongings he had scattered around the Executive Mansion during the same term of occupancy.

"My dear Beth," Madison said, "let us count our blessings, because I fear there may be worse to come."

Both Renna and Naomi agreed quickly when Beth suggested that it might be a good plan to stay in Washington. Each had her own reasons. Beth was discovering anew the persuasive force that is an innate quality of a beautiful woman, and she planned to employ that force diligently in an effort to influence any powerful man she met to reinstate free trade. Adan had written that he would begin to seek out cargoes for South American ports, or perhaps even the Orient; but Beth feared that the fiery Spaniard would defy the Nonintercourse Act—as he had defied the embargo—and send her ships, carrying cargoes of cotton for England, into danger.

Naomi thought that it would be best to stay in Washington because it seemed logical that word of Little Hawk would reach the nation's capital before anywhere else, and she wanted to be among the first to know. Moreover, with both Beth and her keeping pressure on all those concerned, from the President to the British minister, something good was bound to happen.

Renna's reason for wanting to stay in Washington wore the uniform of a British colonel of cavalry. During the beautiful days of spring, she walked with Farnsworth along the Potomac and accepted with grace and pleasure his small gifts of flowers, lacy handkerchiefs, and candy.

"She acts much like a woman who is coming to favor the suit of a certain gentleman," Beth told Naomi.

"How do you feel about the colonel?" Naomi asked.

"He's of good family," Beth said. "But if Renna married him she wouldn't live the life of luxury that was hers with Beau in Paris. It is my guess that his only income is his military stipend."

"But how do you feel about him?" Naomi persisted.

Beth smiled. "I think, my dear, that you want to tell me how *you* feel about him, don't you?"

Naomi laughed. "You've caught me."

"What is your opinion of Colonel Farnsworth?"

Naomi pursed her lips. "It's nothing that I can define, not exactly."

"Ah."

"It's just that—well, there's something about him."

"Renna seemed to find something about him," Beth said. "Something she likes."

"I suppose he's an honorable man," Naomi said doubtfully.

"Just what is it about him that disturbs you?" Beth asked, now taking the conversation more seriously.

"Before my mother and father were killed, we had a big, black hound named Potlicker. He would go out and round up the cows for my father, but he couldn't catch or drive off the animal that was getting into the henhouse and breaking eggs. My father would sit up nights and keep watch, with faithful old Potlicker beside him, and nothing would bother the henhouse. Then, when my father slept, something would break all the eggs and lick up the goo inside. It was just by chance that my father woke up one night and discovered that it was old Potlicker who was sucking eggs. None of us had ever suspected that Potlicker was a suck-egg dog, but there was something about him—"

Beth laughed. "So the good colonel reminds you of a suck-egg hound?"

"I know it's silly."

"No. In fact, you worry me. Now and then I have those little flashes of intuition, and they're usually right. I pray for Renna's sake that your feelings are wrong."

"I, too. Randall is a personable man, and quite polite."

"What happened to old Potlicker?" Beth asked.

"My father had to shoot him. We depended on those eggs for a part of our own provender, and we needed them to have more fryers and broilers and to increase the laying flock. We couldn't allow a suck-egg dog to cause us to go hungry. I cried, and so did my mother—and when my father took him off, he was gone a long, long time after we heard the gunshot, so I suspect he might have cried a little bit, too."

Beth said, "Let's hope that our handsome colonel Farnsworth does not come to deserve such a sad end."

Dolley Madison moved into the Executive Mansion on March 11, 1809. She had drafted her three friends to help her get the household organized.

"It's going to be fun, Beth," Dolley said. "Congress has been very generous. They've appropriated twelve thousand dollars for repairs and improvements and fourteen thousand more for furnishing, decorations, and landscaping."

"That's wonderful," Beth said.

"The only problem is," Dolley said, "that the architect, Latrobe, is to be in charge of spending the money. When I heard that, I was flabbergasted. Do they not consider me capable of turning this great barn of a place into a proper home?"

"I'm sure you'll be able to guide Mr. Latrobe along the proper lines," Beth said.

The accuracy of her prediction was shown quickly when Latrobe approved the expenditure of $2,150 for three mirrors, $556.15 for china, and $220.90 for knives, forks, bottle stands, and andirons. Dolley's selection of imported yellow satin and damask upholstery in the drawing room caused a minor skirmish when Latrobe insisted that it would clash with the red velvet curtains; but after a rather heated exchange Latrobe muttered in his own language, as if it were a curse, "Your wish is my command."

When the new state vehicle was delivered from a carriage maker in Philadelphia, both Dolley and Latrobe were pleased with the reddish-brown exterior and the yellow lace trim of the interior.

Beth was a frequent guest, and she came to know Dolley's ward, Anna Cutts, and Anna's family, who occupied the southeast corner of the President's mansion while the Madisons lived in the southwest wing. There was a steady stream of visiting relatives, nephews and nieces, cousins, and friends from Virginia, Philadelphia, and Maryland.

Madison hired a maître d'hôtel and chef who had been left behind by the departure of the British minister, Anthony Merry, so the food was splendid, and the wine cellars were restocked with Madeira, port, and French champagne.

Where once pigs had rooted during the early days of the first Jefferson administration, Benjamin Henry Latrobe's men planted lines of native trees, shrubs for clumps and screens, and flowering plants for color. Soon Dolley felt that the house was presentable enough for her to begin to entertain. Renna was escorted to the first of Dolley's soon-to-be-famous Wednesday social affairs by Colonel Randall Farnsworth, who wore full dress uniform. There, with music filling the rooms, among congressmen, prominent business people, relatives, visiting belles such as the three ladies from North Carolina, and assorted foreign emissaries, Renna heard the first serious pledge of love from Farnsworth.

A military band was playing the "Madison March," so the atmosphere was not overly romantic. Around them what seemed like hordes of people helped themselves at buffet tables and sideboards laden with punch, cookies, ice cream, and fruit. Across the room the President, in black, his hair confined in an old-fashioned, powdered club, was standing beside Dolley, who was, of course, quite elegantly dressed.

"My dear Renna," Farnsworth said, "I have respected your grief, have I not?"

"For which I am grateful," she said.

"I will not be forceful, and I will try to curb my impatience," Farnsworth went on, "but sooner or later, my dear, I must speak. If you think that it is too early, you must tell me."

Renna was silent. A year had passed since Farnsworth had told her that Beau had been killed in Lisbon. *My God,* she thought. *A year?* The pain of missing him was still with her, but it was dulled. She was wise enough to know that everyone heals, except the dead. When she was very young and her first love, Philip Woods, was murdered by the villainous Frenchman, Othon Hugues, she felt for a long, long time that she, too, would be happier dead. She wished for death, but death did not come to her. She survived the sharpest pain she had ever experienced, only to have to live through the same torment again with Beau.

After mourning Philip had ceased to be a knife in her heart, she knew guilt and wondered if she were unnaturally cruel and selfish to be able to look forward to living while poor Philip was dead. The pain of losing Beau had been more punishing because she was older and understood better what she had lost. But now she knew that nothing she could do or say, no measure of tears and remorse, could bring Beau back to her.

She turned her face toward Farnsworth, let her large blue eyes play over his face. She had grown fond of the man. He was pleasant to look upon. He was a gentleman. He was considerate and kind. He was fond of her daughter and amusingly and masculinely unsure of himself when he was holding the infant Louis. It was not only her own future that she had to consider, but those of her two children as well. Children needed a father.

All this and more was flashing through her mind as she smiled into Farnsworth's face. She had planned to go back to the Cherokee Nation with her father and the others. What would she do there? Live in Beth's fine house, rear her children far from all the advantages of civilization, dry and shrivel with time and the weather like last year's corn husks? There was little possibility of her marrying again if she went back to Huntington Castle. Too many years and too much experience lay between her and her beginnings. A world of difference lay between her everyday life and that of the wife of a Seneca or Cherokee warrior.

She remembered someone saying once, "You never git too fancy fer your upbringing." In a way that was true. She would not scorn the people with whom she had grown up. The blood of the first Americans was in her, along with the bloodlines of old Europe, and she would never be ashamed of her Seneca heritage. But she could not see herself bending over a cook fire in a Seneca longhouse or a Cherokee log cabin.

For a moment she felt desolation, for it had come to her that she could never go home, could never be what she had been before Philip Woods came riding down from Pennsylvania in search of the blue-eyed girl who had skated with him on a winter day in the north.

It was as if Randall Farnsworth had read her mind. He took her hand and bent close. "You're too young, too beautiful, too appreciative of life to seclude yourself on the frontier," he said. "You are a creature of light and music. You must be displayed among the things of beauty that grace the cities—London, Athens, Paris when there is no longer war. I can give you that, Renna. Perhaps I'll never be rich, but one day I will wear the insignia of a general. The life of a wealthy man comes with the rank."

She was tempted. Although she wasn't thinking in exactly such terms, she would have said, if asked, that it is the bereaved marital partner whose marriage was happiest who is most likely to marry again. Both of her marriages had been love matches, and she had enjoyed every aspect of them to the end. She was an earthy wench, in some respects, she thought, for she liked being with a man—a man she loved. All that aside, she did not like being alone.

"You hesitate," Farnsworth said.

"Randall, I am fond of you," she said.

"Fond . . ." he whispered, letting his eyes fall.

"Perhaps more than fond," she said. "Bear with me. I am trying, but I think it must be too early to speak of love."

"Please do not say no, not just now."

She nodded.

"There is a new play at the theater," he said. "I've been told it's quite amusing. Tonight?"

"Since I have been away all afternoon, I think I should be with my children tonight."

"Tomorrow night, then?"

"Yes," she said.

When the small sloop carrying a cargo of smuggled brandy and a member of the old French nobility toward an English port ran into the worst storm to strike the French coast in years, Beau began to think that even nature was conspiring against his reunion with his wife and children. In the relatively shallow and confined Channel, gale winds piled the cold, dark water into steep-fronted waves that ran so close together that no sooner had the sloop survived the impact of one than it was diving down into a deep trough toward another onrushing wall of water.

The seasoned smuggler fell to his knees and gave thanks to the Virgin and a bevy of saints when, after long hours of fighting the storm, he steered into the calm of a small cove on the coast of Normandy, no closer to England than they had been before setting sail.

"My friend," the smuggler shouted to Beau, "if we are lucky, the soldiers have stayed in their warm barracks during such a storm. If they have not, and if they see us here, I will disappear very suddenly. You might want to do the same."

The young man nodded. Since he would be considered a deserter, he very definitely would not want to have to identify himself and explain his presence to any authorities.

The soldiers came while the brutal storm still howled over the dancing Channel, while sheets of rain rode the howling winds and the furled sails of the sloop slapped loudly against the mast. They were riding along the beach when Beau and the smuggler saw them. The smuggler tensed and muttered a curse.

"Easy," Beau said. "Maybe the rain will conceal us."

The smuggler stood by, ready to lower a small boat. Slowly the mounted patrol passed. When it could no longer be seen through the curtains of rain, Beau breathed again and said his own little prayer of thanks to the Virgin and a couple of saints.

The storm blew itself past before light. The ship's second attempt to cross the Channel was uneventful. Beau went ashore at Weymouth, made his way by coach through Southampton and Winchester to London, and from there by hired carriage to Beaumont Manor, where he was greeted with joy and fondness by William, Estrella, and the Beaumont brood of children. William was more than glad to be of help in obtaining a berth for Beau aboard a ship leaving for Jamaica. With the embargo lifted, it would be possible for him to get passage from Kingston on an American ship to an eastern port, perhaps even Wilmington.

Beau said his good-byes and was off once again. He had a private cabin aboard the merchantman, in which he could be alone with his thoughts. He dreamed happily of seeing Renna's face and of holding his children in his arms. He cursed the vastness of the world and its distances; and he feared that he would have to go all the way to Tennessee and on to the Cherokee Nation before he found his family.

Chapter Nine

It was cold. A piercing wind blew from a threatening
sky. Thomas Jefferson left Washington in a coach piled
high with the accumulation of papers and possessions
from his long years of service to the nation. At the age of
sixty-five he was, at last, going home. The wheels of the
coach cut through frozen ruts and sank to the axle into
the frigid mud. Jefferson transferred from the coach to the
horse that had been led by one of his servants. The wind
grew colder, and the small rain changed to snow.

Before he left Washington for Monticello, he had
been forced to borrow eight thousand dollars from an old
family friend in order to clear current indebtedness there,
and there were previous notes, one of which had been
cosigned by James Madison, that he hoped to satisfy by
selling land and through income from his farms.

At least temporarily all his concerns were left behind
when he rode through and around the outbuildings at
Monticello to find a blazing fire in the hearth and be
greeted by his daughter Martha, her gaggle of active chil-

dren, and by young Thomas Jefferson Randolph, son of his deceased youngest daughter, Maria.

He was eager to begin his participation in the management of his farms. "I've spent my life in occupations that kept me away from Monticello," he told his family. "Now there is an end to that."

As if to deny his desire to be just an ordinary farmer —with ten thousand acres of land divided into four plantations—mail began to pour in from men asking him to use his influence to help them obtain positions in the new administration. He printed a notice stating that he would not submit applications or make recommendations on behalf of anyone . . . but soon found that he had to break this rule for old friends.

In his new role as gentleman farmer he rose at dawn, lit a fire in his room, took a walk on the terrace, and by nine o'clock was riding out to oversee the work on his plantations. He sat ramrod straight in the saddle. He was thin and strong, his skin clear, his blue eyes undimmed. In those first heady days of freedom, reading and writing were activities reserved for a rainy day. When the weather was tolerable, he was out and about from early breakfast to a late dinner. To a friend he stated, "I shall give over reading newspapers. They are so false and so intemperate that they disturb tranquillity without giving information." He stopped all of them with the exception of the local sheets.

In spite of his efforts to keep the world at arm's length, he was motivated by events to send a steady stream of advice to his friend James Madison.

He saw the gathering war clouds and warned Madison that conflict had to be avoided at all costs. He stated that he knew of no government less capable of being efficient in war than that of the United States. He feared ". . . the lying and licentious character of our (news)papers; but much, also, the wonderful credulity of the members of Congress in the floating lies of the day." One of his worst nightmares, he intimated, was that Congress might use war as an excuse to remain in permanent session, with a potential for unlimited mischief.

*   *   *

Madison gave consideration to Jefferson's views, but he had ideas of his own. More often than not he failed to comment on the ex-president's letters, but Dolley observed him shaking his head in bemusement when the man from Monticello warned against war . . . and in the next sentence stated that at the first moment of war the United States should seize the Floridas from Spain, then Canada from England, in order to "have such an empire for liberty as she has never surveyed since the creation."

At the moment, war was not James Madison's chief problem. His efforts to establish a working administration were being stonewalled by a powerful group of Republicans allied with Federalists in the Senate. Specifically, Madison was being stymied in his desire to have Albert Gallatin approved as his secretary of state. While caught in this political snare and forced to work with a man in the State Department whom he considered to be incompetent, Madison had little thought for other matters large or small. He had completely forgotten, for example, that Jefferson had sent a private envoy to talk with Meriwether Lewis; and while routine reports continued to be forwarded from the governor of the Louisiana Territory, there had been no further mention in Lewis's correspondence of a matter so delicate that discussion of it could not be entrusted to the mails or a government courier.

In the end the Master of Life was kind. Although Toshabe grew weaker and more emaciated, her pain came only occasionally. Her greatest regret, when she was forced to take to her bed in the first warm days of spring, was that she was not able to join Ena, Ah-wa-o, and the other women in the gathering and preparation of tangy poke greens.

Renno spent many hours, day and night, sitting with his mother. Her mind was clear, her memory intact. She took pleasure in talking of times gone by. Renno had heard most of her stories but had forgotten many details. He smiled fondly as he listened to his mother speak of the time when she first saw dark-haired Ghonkaba, the first love of her life and the father of her children. He was musingly interested in her memories of his grandfather and grandmother, blue-eyed, blond Ja-gonh and his Seneca-Biloxi beauty, Ah-wen-ga. And when she spoke of her second husband, Ha-ace the Panther, he was vividly reminded of that brave warrior who had relighted his mother's passion in her middle years.

El-i-chi would encourage his mother to talk about Seneca traditions, for as both sachem and shaman it behooved him to store the oral history of the tribe in his own memory.

To have something to do, Renno evicted the squirrels from the thatched roof of the longhouse and did some minor repairs. Beth's Castle was more comfortable and was kept open by the staff under the direction of the old black woman, Aunt Sarah. Renno tried to convince Toshabe to let herself be moved to the large house, where there would be servants to care for her, well-heated rooms, and a soft, comfortable bed.

"It is too late in life to begin to pamper myself," Toshabe said.

Renno spent two nights in the Castle, but in the middle of the night he awoke and reached out to touch Beth, only to be reminded of how much he missed her. He moved back to the longhouse across the commons from his mother's home.

Thus it was that he was close at hand when Roy came in the middle of a clear-skied, gloriously starred night to summon him.

"The time has come?" Renno asked, pulling on clothes hurriedly.

" 'Fraid so," Roy said in a low, hoarse voice. "I've sent a boy for El-i-chi and Ena."

In the glow of an oil lamp Toshabe's face was pale.

"She comes and goes," Roy said.

It was as if she were conserving the last of her life's energy, for she waited until everyone was present before she opened her eyes.

"You are here," she whispered with obvious effort. "All of you?"

"We're here, Mother," Ena said, taking Toshabe's hand.

"Rusog?" Toshabe asked.

"I am here, Mother Toshabe," the stern-faced, stocky Cherokee said.

"We owe much to you, Great Chief, and to your grandfather, who accepted us and gave us land."

"You came as brothers and sisters, and we have faced our enemies as one people," Rusog said.

Toshabe's eyes blinked and looked into distances not visible to the others. She smiled and lifted her free hand. "Ah, my love," she said, and for long moments no one was sure to whom she spoke.

Renno felt a shiver of excitement. There was a charge in the air. For the first time in the presence of others he felt the aura of the manitous.

"Your hand, my love, give it to me," Toshabe said.

Ena looked at Renno questioningly, for she was holding her mother's hand tightly.

"No," he told his sister, "it is not you to whom she speaks."

A peaceful smile spread across Toshabe's wasted lips. "They are here, Husband," she said, "your children."

Roy looked stricken, for it was clear that Toshabe was thinking of Ghonkaba. Renno put his hand on Roy's shoulder.

"You can be proud of them," Toshabe said. Her eyes cleared. She lifted her head. "Renno."

"Mother."

"They await us."

"Yes," he said.

"El-i-chi, my sachem," Toshabe said.

El-i-chi took his mother's other hand.

"You are wise and good," Toshabe said, then slid her gaze toward Ena. "And my only daughter, you who are alone, with your own flesh and blood taken from you by distance."

"Yes, Mother?" Ena asked.

"Seize life and make it as sweet for you as it has been for me."

"I do," Ena said. "I will."

"Husband?"

This time she was looking at Roy. He moved closer, put his hand on her shoulder.

"They await us," Toshabe said.

Tears ran down Roy's cheeks.

A column of smoke rose from the fire and made its way out through the hole in the roof. Renno saw in the smoke the face of his father as a young man. Ghonkaba was smiling, and his arms were held out in welcome. With a long sigh Toshabe's spirit left her, and for a moment she and Ghonkaba were together in the smoke—a strong warrior and a shapely maiden, both young and vital. And then they were gone, drifting up and away through the smoke hole on the wings of Ena's song of mourning.

The chants of sadness continued into the night and past the dawn. The passing of the senior matron of the Senecas was mourned not only by her own people but by many from Rusog's town. The scholar Se-quo-i limped into the longhouse to pay his last respects and stayed to aid the shaman, El-i-chi, in preparing the spiritual atmosphere for the final ceremony.

Toshabe was buried dressed in bleached doeskin with Seneca accessories befitting a matron of her stature. The Master of Life decreed a perfect day of light breeze and warm sun.

Roy Johnson left the ceremony before it was finished. When it was over and the death songs were sung, Renno went in search of Roy and found him standing on a little rise outside the village. Roy's eyes were red, and he could not bring himself to look at Renno.

"My friend," Renno said, "you and I have buried too many of the women that we loved." He was thinking of Roy's daughter, Emily, who had been Renno's first wife; the sweet little Seneca girl, An-da, who had given Renno Ta-na, and Roy's own first wife, Nora.

Roy nodded.

"She said the same thing to you," Roy said. "They are waiting for us."

"Yes," Renno said.

Roy's voice was bitter. "She was thinking of your father there at the last, wasn't she?"

"Yes."

"And Ha-ace. He'll be waiting for her, too."

"Yes."

Roy's voice became angry. "Just how dag-gummed crowded can it get over there?"

"For the manitous, things are not as they are on this side of the river," Renno said.

"Well, they're not waiting for me," Roy said, " 'cause I'm not an Indian."

"Not even in your heart?" Renno asked.

Roy turned away to hide his tears. His voice shook when he spoke. "Guess an ornery old white feller like me will need a bucket of cold water more'n anything else." He looked up at the sky and sighed. "Or maybe, God willing, I'll be with Nora." He blew his nose between his fingers and coughed. A look of puzzlement squinted his eyes. "But we were all together in this life."

"Yes," Renno said. "I think we will be together in the Place Across the River."

Roy faced him. "Now you tell me how the Master of Life is going to justify white skin in Indian heaven after what whites have done to his people."

"I can't explain how," Renno said, "but I do know that it happens."

"How so?"

Renno considered the impact of his revelation on Roy before he spoke, then decided that it would give Roy comfort. "I have talked with the spirit of Emily," Renno said.

"The hell you have."

"She waits for me."

"She wasn't Indian."

"She was in her life and in her heart."

"Will she be waiting for you with An-da at her side?"

Roy asked. "And when it's Beth's time, will she make it a threesome?"

"I don't have the answers to your questions," Renno said. "I know only that I am never alone, that the manitous are there, that they come now and again to advise me, and that Emily is one of them. And I know that it gives me great pleasure to know that she is waiting for me." He shrugged. "Don't ask me to explain how it will be when I am with my fathers, when we are all together, because I do not have the wisdom to—" He paused.

"To know how the manitous will square things with you and three wives?"

Again Renno shrugged.

"Well, all that aside, let's consider what Toshabe said there at the last. Now me, I'm long in the tooth, but you're still a young man. I can understand why she would tell an old duffer like me that they are waiting for me, but you? Why would she say that to you and not to El-i-chi, for example?"

"I do not have the answer to that." It was his turn then to hide his emotions, because he felt a shiver—not of dread or fear, but of the anticipation of facing the unknown.

"Well, dag-gum it," Roy said, "don't worry me. You always have been too danged reckless, Renno. You're going to have to learn to take care of yourself and stop running around all over the world, looking to solve someone else's problems. Get Beth back here, and Little Hawk and Renna and Naomi and the kids, and settle down. Enjoy your grandkids while you can, because they'll run away from you and break your heart sooner or later."

"I have been waiting for the proper time to leave," Renno said.

"Good. The sooner the better. I've been thinking of going into Knoxville for a while. The old cabin's still there, probably full of varmints and spiders, but maybe I can make it livable. I just don't think I want to stay in the longhouse for a time."

"I understand," Renno said. "But I have decided that you should come with me."

"It's too far to Wilmington and back," Roy said.

"I'm not going there," Renno said. "Not just yet."

"Well, where in hell are you going, then? Don't you ever listen, boy? Didn't I just tell you to stop gallivanting around and get that red-haired woman?"

"I'm going to St. Louis, to see Meriwether Lewis," Renno said.

Roy scratched his chin, which was in need of a shave.

"St. Louis, huh? Any particular reason you want to see Meriwether Lewis?"

"I'm going at the request of Thomas Jefferson."

"Yes. Well, Jefferson was—is—a good man."

"Then you're with me?"

"No running . . ."

"We will ride two of Beth's fattest and slowest horses."

"And no fighting," Roy said.

"We will be men of peace."

"Well, all right, then," Roy said. "I guess traipsing off into the wild west ranks just a tad above getting hit in the eye with a sharp stick."

What was left of the family turned out to see them off. El-i-chi was looking wistful. His farewell was spoken in Seneca. He and his brother had been parted many times in the past, but saying good-bye never seemed to get any easier. He felt very much alone, although Ah-wa-o was at his side with little Ah-wen-ga's hand in hers. His mother had joined his father in the Place Across the River. His two sons, Ta-na and Gao, were far to the north, possibly facing danger. His niece and nephew, Ho-ya and We-yo, had passed out of his life and into the unknown. Now his brother was obeying that call of wanderlust to which he had been vulnerable all of his life, leaving him, El-i-chi, to be the stolid one, the dependable one, the one to whom the tribe could turn for leadership and guidance.

Rusog stated openly that he envied Renno and Roy, for it was a good time to travel. The spring weather was favorable, and there was plenty of young and tender game.

"We' re traveling in style these days, Rusog," Roy said. "Good horses, comfortable saddles, and enough food on that packhorse to feed a family. I recollect the days when we'd set out on foot for some oh-my-God place, with nothing but a couple of pieces of jerky in our pockets."

"Some of us are getting old," Renno said, winking at the others, "and have to be pampered."

Roy laughed good-naturedly. "You just keep up with me, sprout."

El-i-chi stood with his hand lifted in blessing as the two turned their horses and rode away.

There were times when El-i-chi felt much younger than his forty-two summers, times when he, too, had the urge to run toward the blue distance, to be responsible only for himself and his immediate family. In their youth, El-i-chi had been the impulsive, hot-blooded brother, and Renno had shouldered the weight of responsibility. How things had changed! he thought. Renno was Renno, and El-i-chi could not begrudge his brother the freedom that he now demanded as his own.

It was not a bad fate to be the leader of his small clan, to be trusted with the ancient secrets of a long line of Seneca shamans and sachems. And, as Ah-wa-o sensed his momentary melancholy and came to cling to his arm, it was all good to be with the little Rose and his sunny, smiling, beautiful little daughter. Someone had to be a symbol of stability. That someone was he.

Ta-na and Gao traveled as their fathers once traveled, without the benefit of horses, with only their weapons and packs containing sleep skins. They were soon out of Cherokee lands and into the farmlands of Tennessee. They walked along good roads, past crude log cabins no better and no worse than some of the houses in Rusog's town, past elaborate, tall houses built of milled lumber painted gleaming white. They were only a few days into their journey when they came face to face with something neither of them had experienced before.

They had trekked through two small towns without

incident when they entered a hamlet consisting of a livery
stable, a general store, a saloon, and a few log houses. On
the one street they found their way blocked by a group of
five men ranging in age from near their own to gray and
grizzled. A black-bearded farmer in homespun held his
rifle in front of him menacingly.

"Ain't you bucks a bit far north?" the man with the
black beard asked in a high-pitched whine.

"You lost, Injun?" one of the younger men asked.

Gao said, "We travel to Kentucky."

"I think you'd better travel back where you come
from," Black Beard said, swinging his rifle to point the
muzzle at Gao's belly.

"We seek no trouble," Ta-na said.

"Why you carrying weapons, then?" the young one
asked with a sneer.

"To hunt for our food," Ta-na answered.

"A farmer's calf now and then, huh?" Black Beard
asked.

"We mean no harm," Gao said. "We merely want to
pass through your town on the way to Kentucky."

"That so?" the young one asked. "Well, we don't like
red savages stinking up our air."

Ta-na's blood was running hot. His right hand
clenched his rifle hard enough to whiten his knuckles. He
sensed movement and glanced behind him to see three
more men approaching. He told himself to be calm, to
remember advice that had come from both El-i-chi and
Renno: Never run from a fight, but never enter into a
fight when there is no hope of winning. With odds of eight
to two, in the middle of a street in a white man's town,
there wasn't much hope of survival.

"We will go back the way we came," he said.

Black Beard laughed. "This un's got some horse
sense." He jabbed his rifle into Gao's stomach. "How
'bout you, Big Chief Chamber Pot?"

"We will go back the way we came," Gao said.

The young white man said, "Maybe we ought to let
'em go on through. Let them Kentucks shoot their red

asses off. They hate 'em up there in Kentuck even more'n we do here."

Ta-na turned slowly. Gao followed his example. With a great shout the black-bearded man kicked Gao in the rear. The young one tried to do the same to Ta-na but missed. Gao was jolted forward. His face was impassive, but in his eyes there was fury.

"Easy," Ta-na whispered as he and Gao walked down the street the way they had come.

The white men followed at a distance for almost a mile before turning back. The boys walked southward to a ridge, turned to the east on the southern slope, and made their way carefully around the small town.

"Do you still want to fight the white man's war?" Gao asked that night as they sat around their campfire. The meat was squirrel, hot and juicy.

"They are not all like those men," Ta-na said.

"Oh?" Gao asked sarcastically. "You are an expert on the character of the whites?"

"Our grandfather Roy is a good man."

"And the whites call him a squaw man."

"Not all of them. Andy Jackson is our grandfather's good friend. He doesn't call his friend a squaw man."

"Not to his face," Gao said.

"Say the word, Brother, and we will go home."

Gao grinned. "Tell me what the word is, and I might be tempted." He became serious. "What can we expect in Kentucky if here, where there has been peace between whites and Indians, they hate us?"

Ta-na shrugged. "Perhaps they will shoot on sight."

"You fill me with happiness," Gao said bitterly.

"We will have to travel carefully, not only in Kentucky but here in Tennessee," Ta-na said. "I don't care to have my ass shot off." He grinned. "Nor to have it kicked by a big, evil-smelling white farmer."

Gao grinned. "Uncle Renno tells us that we must be like the white man. Stand up and turn your back to me so that I can practice." He was grinning, but his eyes were cold. He would remember the indignity of being kicked down the dusty street of a small town for no greater offense than trying to walk through it.

It was several days before they dared travel developed roads again. Ahead of them was Nashville. To their surprise they were offered a ride in a farm wagon by a gray-haired, ragged old man traveling with a fat wife who sat silently by his side as the boys climbed gratefully into the vehicle.

"Seems like you speak English pretty good," the old man said. "Where y'all from?" He listened with interest as Ta-na answered, adding that he and his brother were going to Indiana Territory to scout for William Henry Harrison.

The farmer's name was Gus Trammel. As far as Ta-na and Gao could tell, the woman's name was The Wife.

"The Wife and I, we uns are goin' into Nashboro—"

"They call it Nashville now," The Wife said.

"—to see a new grand-young-un. Y'all best be keerful struttin' around dressed like wild Injuns. Someone's liable to take a shot at you."

"We have observed a tendency toward a certain amount of belligerence," Ta-na said.

"My, don't he talk pretty," The Wife said in admiration.

"I 'uz you, I'd git me some white man's clothes. Them old boys up in Kentuck, they see a Injun, they shoot first and ask questions in the hereafter."

"That sounds like an excellent idea," Ta-na said, "but we have no money."

"Poses a certain problem, don't it?" Gus asked with a snaggletoothed grin.

"We'll travel a lot by night," Gao said.

"Then you'd best be damned good at it," Gus said, "'cause someone sees a Injun lurking around at night, bang!"

Ta-na was thinking about Gus's suggestion. It made sense. He had heard his father speak of traveling as a white man. Neither his nor Gao's skin was as light as that of their fathers, but it was possible that they could pass casual inspection if they were dressed as white men.

"Mr. Trammel," Ta-na said, "do you know Andrew Jackson?"

"Colonel Jackson? Shore. Know him well."

"Is he in Nashville, do you know?"

"Got hisself a nice place out on the other side of town. Why do you ask?"

"He is a friend of our fathers and our grandfather. I'm sure he'd help us get some clothes."

"My, my," The Wife said. "We are riding with them that mixes in high society."

"Now, Wife," Gus said.

"If'n you can call that hussy what calls herself Miz Jackson any kind of society," The Wife added.

Andy Jackson had been devoting himself to developing his plantation near Nashville to solidify his financial position and expand his landholdings. After being forced to kill Charles Dickinson to erase an insult to his wife, Jackson had retreated from public life to build a square, two-story blockhouse of three rooms, one on the ground floor, two upstairs. Later, a smaller structure had been added about twenty feet away, connected to the main building by a covered passageway.

Andrew Jackson kept up his relationship with militia forces, just in case war came to give him another opportunity for the military glory he had always craved. But he was enjoying his life as a gentleman farmer. Moreover, he was prospering. He had harvested a series of bumper cotton crops, and he was successful in his horse-breeding and racing ventures.

Jackson was riding alone when he saw two Indians emerge from a copse of trees into a newly broken cotton field. He urged his horse into a trot, touched the butt of his pistol, and rode to intercept the two intruders.

"Trouble," Gao said when he saw the black horse. "Should we try to make it back into the woods?"

As far as he could determine from the directions

given to them by Gus Trammel, Ta-na guessed that they were on Andrew Jackson's land. "No. Stop," he said.

They stood perfectly still, rifles held in one hand at their sides. As the horseman neared, Ta-na lifted his right hand in peace.

"It's Colonel Jackson," Gao said.

Jackson reined in his stallion. The horse pranced. The rider was dressed well, and his hair was bushy under his hat. "You're trespassing," he said.

"We were coming to see you, Colonel," Ta-na said.

Jackson swung down from his horse, peered from under his bushy brows. "Well, I'll be hornswoggled," he said. "Is that you, Ta-na? And Gao?"

"Yes, sir," Ta-na said. He grinned. "And it's a pleasure to meet someone who isn't looking at us down a gun barrel."

"Small wonder," Jackson said. He stepped forward, exchanged the warrior's grip of greeting with both boys. "There's a tale here somewhere," he said, "but come along up to the house before you begin to tell it."

Rachel Jackson was a full-bodied, vivacious woman with smiling eyes and a friendly manner. "And what have we here?" she asked when Andrew entered the house with Ta-na and Gao in tow. She was never surprised by anything that Andy did. Showing up exactly at dinnertime with two wild Indians was just something that he would do.

"You've heard me speak of Roy Johnson," Andy said. "These are his grandsons."

"Well," Rachel said, "and handsome grandsons they are. Hungry, too, I'll bet."

"You're very kind, madam," Ta-na said with a little bow.

"Dog my cats," Rachel said. "Polite, too."

Ta-na and Gao told their story over a sumptuous meal. The Jacksons were childless, but they were always being asked by relatives and friends to act as guardians for fatherless children. One of these wards, son of a relative of Rachel's, sat at the table and listened with great interest.

"So you're going to join up with General Harrison?" Andy asked, nodding approvingly. "Following your fathers' footsteps. Good lads."

"We're having just a bit of trouble," Ta-na said. "We're discovering that Indians are, to say the least, looked upon with suspicion by the good citizens of Tennessee, and we are told to expect worse in Kentucky."

"What you should do," Rachel suggested, "is dress like those among whom you are traveling."

"We've thought of that," Ta-na said. "But . . ."

"I think I see the problem," Jackson said. "Do you think you can fix these young gentlemen up with some decent clothes, Rachel?"

Rachel allowed as how she could. And in the morning two bronzed young men in homespun breeches and proper shirts and coats told their benefactors good-bye, promised Andy that they would let him know the outcome of their adventure in Indiana Territory, and started northwestward. Thanks to the generosity of Andrew Jackson, they had a few coins in their pockets, enough to buy food and lodging now and then.

Spring came while they walked across Kentucky. The farther north they got, the more carefully they were scrutinized by men who were edgy from the old and bloody war that skipped back and forth across the Ohio River. Although the savage incursions from the north were not as frequent as they had been at times in the past, men still died when some young war chief decided that it was time to steal a few of the white man's horses or to strike just one more blow in the battle for hunting grounds south of the Ohio that had long since been lost.

Ta-na and Gao crossed the Ohio below the settlement called Louisville and were in virgin wilderness. The white man's clothes went into their packs. They were traveling through a disputed land where a white man's scalp was not safe. They thought that it would be safer to be Indian there, and events proved them to be right. Before they reached the East Fork of the White River, which would lead them eastward to the Wabash and Vincennes, they encountered sign of a large war party moving in the same direction. Among the imprints of Indian moccasins was the mark of a white man's boot.

The boys heard sounds from the encampment before they saw it. A hoarse scream reverberated among the tall, brooding trees, died, then rose again. They moved forward cautiously. The members of the war party were not very alert. Their attention was on the agony of a captive white man. He stood with his back against a tree. His hands were tied behind his back. A loop of rope around his neck restricted his movements to a small circle. His screams had been caused by the infliction of several gashes on his shoulders and chest.

"I think the best thing we can do is move on," Ta-na said.

"It's obvious that this is a raiding party," Gao said. "Won't it be our job to give information on Indian forces in the field? It would be to our advantage to have information for General Harrison when we arrive in Vincennes."

"I'm not sure I like what you have in mind," Ta-na said.

Gao stood and, hailing the camp, called out in Cherokee. A strong-looking warrior reached for his weapons and stood to face the boys as they approached. Others left off tormenting the white captive and watched as Ta-na lifted his hand in greeting.

"Brothers," Ta-na said.

"I know you not," said the warrior who faced them.

"We come from the south, from the lands of the Cherokee," Gao said. "We seek Panther Passing Across."

"You have found Red Horse," the warrior said.

"You are Shawnee?" Ta-na asked.

"I am of the clan of the great chief Catahecassa, who is a friend of Tecumseh. If you wish to join with Panther Passing Across, you may travel with us."

"We are grateful, Red Horse," Ta-na said. "For we have traveled far."

"Come, then. There is food, and there is entertainment," Red Horse said.

Gao cut a strip of meat from a roast of venison on a fire but quickly lost his appetite. The minor torture of the white captive was over. It was now time for him to die. Dry wood was piled in a circle around the tree to which the captive was tied. Great amounts of dry tinder were gathered and placed. When the pyre was ready, warriors started fires at several places at once so that the white man was quickly surrounded by a circle of searing flames.

Gao put aside his food when the captive began to jerk and writhe in pain from the heat. He circled the tree, free to move only so much because of the noose around his neck. With ribald comments and shouts of laughter the warriors used long poles to push the fire closer and closer until the white man's feet and legs reddened and peeled. With a puff the victim's pubic hair flamed, and the pain to his naked genitalia brought weeping screams of agony.

Gao turned away. Ta-na was swallowing hard to keep the meat he had eaten from coming up. He touched Gao's arm and nodded warningly, indicating that Gao should not show weakness; but he himself wanted to scream out. He had heard of such torture. There had been a time when the worst fate that an enemy could meet, be his skin red or white, was to be turned over to the women of the Seneca tribe. But such practices had been abandoned, at least by the clan led by the white Indians, before Ta-na and Gao were born. To encounter such cruelty unexpectedly was almost too much to bear without outcry.

Ta-na tried to dull his mind to the screams of the white man as, his noose severed, he fell to his knees and then onto his side. The warriors, those who were fighting to drive the white man back across the Ohio, shouted with enthusiasm and piled hot coals and pieces of dry wood atop the man until he was immersed in fire.

"Manitous," Ta-na whispered as, even then, the man's moans of agony did not cease. The body jerked, and the sounds would, Ta-na knew, haunt him for years. He fell back in exhaustion and disgust when, at last, after one long, shrill cry of total anguish, the white man was still.

Ta-na closed his eyes and muttered a prayer to the

Master of Life. "Is this, then, our enemy?" he whispered to Gao.

Gao shuddered. "At first I was thinking that I would like to have the man who kicked me in the butt in the same situation."

"Who is the enemy, then?" Ta-na asked. There was no answer either from Gao or from the manitous to whom the question was addressed. Around them the Shawnee warriors were quiet as they began to make preparations for the night.

Chapter Ten

Despite the work of Benjamin Latrobe's men in putting out native trees and dozens of varieties of shrubs and flowering plants, the grounds of the Executive Mansion still had a look of rawness in the spring of 1809. There were those among the visitors to the presidential "palace" who commented that the place was unkempt, that conditions were disgraceful. Old Washington hands pointed out that the landscaping, although skimpy, was an improvement over the pastures and woodlands of Jefferson's day.

In direct contrast to James Madison's workdays, which were filled with some frustration and much political opposition, Dolley's efforts to upgrade the mansion were highly successful. Her entertainments, which drew the cream of Washington society and distinguished visitors from around the nation and the world, helped Madison keep his spirits up.

Madison was a man who appreciated beauty—both

in the interior decor of the place that was to be his home for at least four years and in the women who swirled their colorful skirts to lively music at one of Dolley's drawing-room affairs. Among his favorites were the three ladies from North Carolina. Of late Dolley and he had been watching the blossoming of a genteel courtship between the pale-haired comtesse de Beaujolais and the distinguished and handsome English colonel Randall Farnsworth.

The President, the stately Dolley, and Beth Harper stood beside a buffet laden with refreshments and watched the colorfully uniformed Farnsworth guide Renna through a spirited reel.

"I will offer a wager," Dolley said, beaming a smile. "I contend that the gentleman will break down the lady's reserves in time for a June wedding."

"Name your stake, my dear," Madison said, "and I will meet your wager. She is, after all, still mourning the death of her husband."

"Tush," Dolley said. "This is the nineteenth century, and both of them are young and very beautiful. That is the combination that makes the sap rise in the spring."

Madison smiled at Dolley's daring double entendre. "Nevertheless . . ." he said.

"The stake shall be a Paris gown against a case of your favorite wine," Dolley said.

"Done," Madison agreed. "But in order for you to win, there must be a wedding before the end of June."

"Or the announcement of an impending wedding," Dolley said.

"That was not your first stipulation."

"You must have misunderstood."

"I did not."

"Beth," Dolley implored, "you heard what I said, didn't you?"

Beth laughed. "I will not let you draw me into a dispute between the President of the United States and the First Lady."

"Oh, hush!" Dolley scolded teasingly.

"And what is *your* opinion about the progress of the

red-coated Englishman with your daughter?" Madison asked Beth.

"I think she has become quite fond of him," Beth said.

"They make a handsome couple," Madison said, "but he is English, after all."

"That concerns me," Beth confessed. "Although I consider myself to be an American now, I know full well how one can experience mixed loyalties when one's adopted country is at odds with one's native land. If Renna should marry Randall and there is a war, she would have to make a difficult choice."

"She made that choice once," Dolley said, "by going to France with the count."

"Yes, but the United States was not at war with France," Madison said. "At least not officially." He frowned as he was reminded of the weight of his office. "Do you know what that scoundrel Napoleon has done?"

"I'm sure you're going to tell us," Dolley said.

"As you know, my dear, the Congress is considering an alternative to the Nonintercourse Act, which replaced the embargo."

"Oh, dear," Dolley said. "Must we talk of such dreary things?"

"I believe Beth will be interested," Madison said, "since the decision that is made by Congress and this office will affect her business."

"Very much so," Beth said.

"The bill before the Congress is called Macon's Bill Number Two," Madison said. "It states that should either England or France repeal the restrictions they have placed on United States maritime commerce, the United States would declare a state of nonintercourse on the other nation."

"I believe I anticipate you," Beth said.

Madison nodded grimly. "Through his minister, Napoleon has sent an unofficial message that he would cancel all restrictions on U.S. trade immediately should this bill be made into law."

"Once again he is making an attempt to have the

United States do something he has not the naval power to do himself," Beth said, "to impose a blockade on England. Is it not true, Mr. President, that France has seized more United States shipping than has England?"

"Quite true," Madison confirmed.

"Perhaps the war hawks are clamoring for hostilities against the wrong enemy," Beth suggested.

"Since the Senate refuses to let me have Mr. Gallatin as my secretary of state," Madison said, "I wonder if they would accept you, since you have such a grasp of the realities of international politics."

"You say that jokingly," Dolley said. "Because, as enlightened as you are, my darling little husband, not even you are aware of the wisdom of the suggestion."

"Hush, Dolley," Madison said with a smile, "lest you give my enemies more ammunition. Already they're saying that before I make any decision, I must consult my wife."

Renna's face, flushed with the exertion of the dance, was complemented by the rose of her gown. She agreed with enthusiasm when Farnsworth suggested that they follow other couples outside to get a breath of air. They walked in the rear garden, her hand on his arm. They could see the lamplight in the windows of the houses that had begun to encroach on the wide spaces around the mansion; but the brightest lights were in the sky—a full moon and a few stars brave enough to compete with the glow of the huge, silver disk that rode as proud as a galleon halfway up the sky. Neither of them spoke as they left behind the glow of light from the mansion windows behind and moved through a world bathed in soft moonlight. Nor did Farnsworth speak when he took Renna's hand and pulled her to a halt out of sight of the others.

She stood facing him, her hands in his, and looked up into his face with a smile. His eyes reflected moonlight. He smelled cleanly of soap and leather. When he put his hand under her chin and tilted her face upward, she made no effort to prevent the coming together of their lips.

She was fully aware of the objections that logic could raise against the fondness she felt for Farnsworth. He was the enemy of the people among whom she had lived with Beau, and his country was openly hostile to the United States. She had spent years away from her own family, and if she followed the leanings of her emotions she would be leaving them again, for Farnsworth had, once more, proposed marriage.

Her desire to remain with her own family was made stronger by the feeling of isolation that came with losing her husband, for in such times it is natural to turn to the comfort and security of the family. But if she chose that path, would it be fair to take Louis or Emily Elizabeth into the wilderness of the Cherokee Nation, to live among people who continued to struggle to keep from becoming a part of the nineteenth century?

There were other questions to be resolved. Her son, Louis, was heir to his father's title and to the considerable properties that had been restored to Beau by Napoleon, so her obligation to do the best thing for her son pulled her toward returning to France.

And what was fair to her? What would be the best course of action for a young woman who had lost two husbands, for a sensuous woman whose blood pounded in her veins as her lips parted to accept and return Farnsworth's kiss? She was a woman who needed to be loved, and Farnsworth's kisses stirred her sensuality. His arms around her, her body being pressed hard to his, gave fuel to the flames of youthful desire.

Stop, she told herself silently. *Stop worrying. Forget all the questions. Feel. Enjoy.* She pressed herself to Farnsworth and gave him her tongue in a deep, searching act of surrender.

"Oh, my darling," he whispered.

"Yes." She breathed the word into his kiss.

It was a long time before he spoke again, and when he did, his breathing was ragged, his voice trembling. "You will marry me, then?"

"Yes," she said, for where there was so much mutual need, love would blossom and bear fruit. At that moment everything seemed clear to her. Living in England with Randall would be an acceptable middle course between going back to France to allow Louis to take his rightful place and taking both children to Huntington Castle. When the war ended, as it must someday, she could take Louis to France and allow him to claim his inheritance.

She felt Farnsworth's hand at her breast. Warm fingers probed soft, heated roundness below the neckline of her gown. He bent, and she gasped with passion as he exposed one firm mound and engulfed a sensitive nipple with a kiss.

Beth had seen Renna leave the drawing room with Farnsworth. She began to be curious after a quarter of an hour, but the young couple did not reappear until a full half hour had passed. When they came into the room, Renna's face was flushed, and Farnsworth wore a smug smile. They came directly toward Beth and Naomi and, smiling with excitement, halted in front of them.

"Mrs. Harper," Farnsworth said, bowing, "it is my great pleasure to tell you that Renna has agreed to be my wife."

Beth nodded and looked quickly at Renna. Was there doubt in those blue eyes?

"In the absence of Renna's father, Mrs. Harper, I submit my suit to you," Farnsworth said, "and ask your permission to marry your daughter."

"Perhaps the decision should be postponed until your father has returned," Beth said to Renna.

"That would be good advice if we knew when my father is coming back," Renna said. "Randall's assignment to the United States is not an indefinite one. He'll be going back to England before the autumn storms."

"Well, that leaves us plenty of time to plan a wedding, doesn't it?" Beth asked. She reached out and took Renna's hands in hers. "You know, my dear girl, that I want happiness for you. If your decision is made, you have my blessings, of course."

"Thank you," Renna said. She kissed Beth on the cheek, embraced Naomi, and turned quickly to smile up into Farnsworth's face. "There, sir, you are committed. Now you must set a date."

"Since it is such a beautiful night, shall we talk about it as I walk you back to your lodgings?" Farnsworth asked.

"That would be lovely," Renna said.

"Are you leaving now?" Naomi asked. "It's early yet."

"I think they want to be alone," Beth said with a smile. "Go on, then. Naomi and I will be along later."

They walked slowly, hand in hand, enjoying the balmy evening. They talked as lovers will talk, with Farnsworth asking interested questions about Renna's childhood. They exchanged likes and dislikes. The conversation then turned to serious matters, such as where they would live in England.

"I guess I'm acting irresponsibly," Farnsworth said, "for I have no home to offer you, and God only knows how long my duty will keep me in the army."

"If you are called away, I can stay with Uncle William and Aunt Estrella at Beaumont Manor," Renna said. "I'll wait until you're free and can make a home for us."

"I *am* being selfish," Farnsworth said. Actually, he was feeling resentment toward the system that had thrust him penniless into the world, with his older brother getting the benefit of their father's not-too-abundant property and assets. "I'm asking you to keep your son from his rightful place in France."

"I don't think I'd like to go back to France as long as the war is going on," she said.

"For Louis's sake, would there be some way of bringing some of his assets out of France?" He asked the question lightly, trying to conceal his avid interest.

"I think it would be extremely difficult," she replied, "but that's something I could ask Uncle William about. He would know."

"Yes," he said. He was thinking that perhaps Beaumont would be willing to provide his niece with a proper home. "Renna, should we wait?"

"Are you trying to wriggle out of it?" she teased.

"Not at all. It's just that—with the war—with all of the uncertainty . . ."

Bits of her life flashed through her memory. She had been so happy with Philip, and there had been no premonition of his death, only the sudden finality of it. She and Beau had started for Lisbon, only to have their ship forced into Porto, where they were separated and imprisoned. Then he left for the war, and she never saw him again.

"There is always uncertainty," she said.

He pulled her to a halt in the shadows, turned her to face him. "You're sure of your feelings for me?"

"Yes," she said.

The kiss was long and deep, and the fires it kindled were still smoldering when the young couple reached the residential hotel where Beth had taken rooms. Farnsworth escorted her upstairs and waited while she slipped into the room where a nanny guarded all four of the children.

"They're all sleeping peacefully," she whispered as she came back out into the hallway.

"I want to kiss you just once more," Farnsworth said.

She shivered in pleasant anticipation. "Not here." She put her hand on his chest to hold him away.

"Where?"

"Come inside," she said.

She led him to her own room. There, in darkness broken only by the light of the moon coming in an open window, she felt his warm lips at her breasts once more, felt the heat of his hand as it explored tentatively and then with eagerness and assurance. Her youthful cravings welcomed his caresses, gave in return, and in the end, gasping in need, she took him to her as her right, for they would be married. She found that his body molded to hers perfectly, discovered that his passion, spent quickly, was easily rekindled and, once renewed, was more satisfyingly lasting.

He came to her for the last time over her whispered protests, for she had heard Beth enter the room next to her own and begin the routine of preparing for bed.

"Beth will hear."

"I'll be ever so quiet," he whispered.

She moaned softly as they became one again.

"Shush," he hissed at her, smothering a laugh.

She clung to him, and her explosion of passion was muted by closed lips to come out as rather unladylike snorts through her nose. When he made to leave her, she clung to him. "Now you must set the date," she said.

"Tomorrow."

"All right."

"You would? So quickly? What about preparations, all the woman's things that must be done before a wedding?"

"My dear," she whispered, "I have had two weddings for which there was much preparation. A simple civil ceremony will do nicely for me, if that's all right with you."

"'All right'?" He kissed her lightly. "It's perfect."

Ta-na and Gao traveled with Red Horse and his party up the Wabash River to Tecumseh's village just below the junction with the Tippecanoe. The site held the greatest number of Indians that either Seneca had ever seen. The smell of war was in the air and in the speech of those who had raided across the Ohio with Red Horse.

"Tecumseh is here?" Ta-na asked Red Horse.

"Perhaps, perhaps not," Red Horse said. "Here, however, is his brother."

Ta-na and Gao came to a startled halt as the Prophet came toward them. He was dressed in a welter of furs and feathers. His face was painted for war, and he had decorated the exposed skin of his arms with odd designs. Most strikingly, he had painted a glaring red eye on a white stone and inserted it into his empty socket.

"These two I know not," Tenskwatawa said.

"They come from the south, from the land of the Cherokee," Red Horse said.

With his head tilted, his one good eye glaring, the Prophet looked at the two boys. "Why are there not more of you?" he demanded.

"I speak only for myself and my brother," Ta-na said. "We would see the great warrior, Panther Passing Across."

"In time," the Prophet said pompously.

Others had begun to gather round to listen to the Prophet's words. He lifted his chin and spoke in a loud voice. "My brother has returned."

There was a stir among the crowd.

"He brings word that the Sac, the Fox, and the Kickapoo of the Illinois country will be with us, for now they know the truth. The Shemanese—the white men—have now built a fort, Fort Madison, on the western bank of the Mississippi. So now our western brothers believe what Tecumseh has told them."

"When will we see the great leader?" Gao asked.

"He is resting," the Prophet said. "Look around you, Cherokee. Look around you and see the bravest and best of all the tribes. See Ottawa, Chippewa, Potawatomi. See Seneca, Miami, Shawnee, Wyandot, and Mingo. Together we form an invincible army that will send the Shemanese fleeing to the eastern bank of the Ohio. Soon we will march on the stronghold of the intruders at Vincennes, and we will show them the wrath of the Great Spirit."

Around them, men turned their heads, shuffled their feet, divided their attention. Ta-na turned away from the mesmerizing presence of the Prophet to see Tecumseh, powerful and dignified, emerge from a hut. After he and Gao heard Tecumseh speak, it was evident why men followed the leader who was sometimes called by those who did not know him Chief of the Beautiful River, although he was not a sachem.

"No longer will we allow the weakness of the Indian and his tendency to fight among those of his own blood, to kill our brothers, to keep us from our purpose," Tecumseh said as hundreds of warriors from many tribes crowded close to hear his soaring voice. "Our strength is in unity. Together we will turn aside the flood of the white man's invasion. Together we will halt him in his tracks. Together we will push back the flood. We must do this, or we will drown."

Tecumseh took a paper from his clothing and held it high. "Here is a speech from our friends the British. They call us brothers, and they implore us to be ready." He smiled wolfishly. "The great English father who lives beyond the salt waters is again quarreling with the long-knife soldiers of the United States. Our English father will give us guns and powder and shot. And when the redcoat soldiers are ready to march with us against the long knives, we will be ready to fight the last battle and enjoy the final victory."

Ta-na looked around him at the faces of Tecumseh's followers. It saddened him to think that many of them would die in a war against the United States. A weight was on his conscience, for he was a traitor to his blood, a spy among those who called him brother.

"There is work to be done," Tecumseh said. "I will need help in sending the word to all tribes." He held up several carved, slender cedar slats just over a foot long. "This will be my means of communication. My brother has prepared them, and now we will name those who will carry them afar."

Ta-na and Gao were allowed to examine the carved slats. Tenskwatawa himself explained the markings.

"It is read from bottom to top," the Prophet said. "It tells all tribes from both sides of the Father of Waters to gather at the appointed place. The sign will be evident to all. The earth will shiver in dread, and this trembling of the solid ground will signal the coming end of the white man's intrusion beyond the Ohio."

Tecumseh showed his trust in his followers by telling the gathering about his recent travels. There were whoops of approval when Tecumseh announced that the Wyandot chief, Tarhe the Crane, had been forced by events to abandon his alliance with William Henry Harrison.

"As I foretold," Tecumseh said, "the greed of the Shemanese has brought many white settlers to the valley of the Sandusky. The log huts of the Shemanese in the heart of Wyandot hunting grounds have moved Tarhe to join us. The Wyandot will fight at our side." He smiled grimly. "Those who opposed Tarhe's decision are dead. They died with honor with the ceremonial application of four tomahawk blows to the head."

Again there were whoops of approval.

*   *   *

After a meal of stew dipped from a huge iron kettle tended by two plump, gregarious Miami women, Ta-na and Gao sat beside a small fire in front of a lean-to of brush on the banks of the river. From this place, where they would sleep, they watched as the beehive activity of the village slowed.

"There will be no moon tonight," Gao said. "They are so confident here in their stronghold that they mount no sentinels."

"Are you saying that it is time for us to go?" Ta-na asked.

"We have information that will be useful to General Harrison," Gao said. "If we leave as soon as the village is quiet, we will be miles away before morning."

"There is a better way," Ta-na said.

"Yes, if we take wings and fly."

Ta-na shivered, remembering the tales that Renno and El-i-chi had told about the evil shaman Hodano, who soared with the spirits. "We do not need the powers of the evil ones to keep from wearing out our moccasins," he said, and pointed toward the river. In the glow of campfires a row of canoes lay on the muddy bank.

"Sometimes I have hopes that you will be wise some-day," Gao said, grinning.

Ta-na dozed. He was awakened by Gao's hand on his shoulder. He opened his eyes to darkness broken only by the glow of dying fires. The stars lit the sky, each of them blazing brilliantly as if to outshine all others. On the far side of the village a dog barked without alarm, regularly, monotonously.

Ta-na gathered his weapons and pack, then followed Gao quietly down the bank to the fleet of grounded canoes. To prevent making any sound, they lifted one of the vessels. The water was cold on their feet as they carried the canoe into shallow water. Ta-na boarded while Gao held the boat in balance, then vaulted in with one movement. Ta-na pushed the canoe away from the bank and turned it while Gao readied his paddle. It was so quiet that they could hear the rippling sounds of the current against the side of the canoe. With each of them stroking evenly and strongly but being careful not to let the paddles splash, they quickly left the village behind.

The two young men from the land of the Cherokee were around a bend in the river when Red Horse and five warriors pushed three canoes into the current and paddled swiftly in their wake. Tecumseh was in the canoe with Red Horse.

"You were wise, brother, in suspecting them," the Panther said.

"They must be spies for Harrison," Red Horse said. "They will deny it, of course, but we will see how long it takes for their tongues to loosen when they feel the fire." For the moment, in his anger, he had forgotten that Tecumseh was opposed to the torture of captives.

Once they were safely around the river bend, Ta-na and Gao slowed their rowing and settled into a slow but steady rhythm. They kept to the center of the stream, for near the banks were dark, deceptive shadows, making it difficult to tell where the water ended and land began. Now and then Gao looked over his shoulder to see nothing more than the stars reflected in the expanse of water. He relaxed his vigil and concentrated on the effort of rowing. It seemed that they had left the village unobserved.

The first indication that they were being followed came in the form of a rifle ball that made a thumping, concussive sound as it passed Gao's ear. He looked behind quickly to see the shadowy outline of at least three canoes bearing down on them with the rowers stroking fast and hard. Even as the sound of the shot came to them, another ball splashed water at the side of the canoe.

Ta-na set the tempo, and they bent to it with a will. The paddles dug into the dark water. The canoe picked up speed, but it was quickly evident that their inexperienced efforts would not outdistance the pursuers.

"Steer for the western shore," Ta-na said, gasping.

He backed oar, and Gao pulled, turning the canoe toward the shadowed bank.

The canoes behind them were closing quickly. Two things happened simultaneously. The prow of the canoe ran up onto a mud bank, throwing Ta-na forward over the bow and into the mud. The sudden stop caused Gao to come to his feet in an effort to keep from being pitched onto his face. As he stood, a large-caliber ball slammed into the meaty muscle of his thigh. Inertia and the force of the ball sent him sprawling over the side, into shallow water.

Ta-na heard the sound that the ball made as it struck. He pushed himself up. He could not see his brother. "Gao," he called out.

Hearing a moan, he ran around the beached canoe, the mud tugging at his moccasins, to lift Gao's head from the water. Rifle balls were singing their high-pitched whines of death around him. He dragged Gao across the mud flat and toward the high bank of the river. The pursuers were close now. He could hear their breathing.

He heard Tecumseh say, "Hold your fire. One of them is down."

The bank was almost vertical. Ta-na assessed his chances. Gao was trying to help him, hopping along on one leg, but the ground was slippery.

"Into the woods," Ta-na said.

"Too late." Gao gasped. "Go! Leave me my rifle, and I will delay them."

"Cherokee!" Red Horse called out. "Cherokee!"

Ta-na lifted his rifle, not knowing whether it would fire after his plunge into the mud. He shot without aiming, pointing the long rifle as if it were an extension of his finger. With a startled bellow of pain one of the men in the first canoe lunged to his feet and toppled, overturning the canoe. Ta-na seized Gao's rifle. It did not fire. He looked around in desperation as he unslung his bow.

He had been trained well by his father and by Beth, both experts with the weapon that had stopped sixteen successive charges of heavily armored French knights at Crécy. His bow was designed after the longbows that

Renna and Beth had used with equal success against the light armor of Spain in the far west, although it was not a full six feet long. Se-quo-i had helped him fashion the bow of unblemished ash. In practice he could hit a man-sized target at two hundred yards. He had never killed a man with one of the slim, wooden arrows he carried at his shoulder—not until he drew the string back near his ear and loosed a shaft to drive deeply into the chest of another rower. Even as the man slumped, Ta-na was drawing again.

He heard Tecumseh's voice but didn't catch the words. The overturned canoe was drifting down the river. One man was in the water, swimming with the current, being carried downstream. The other two vessels turned sharply away from the bank. The rowers, including Tecumseh and Red Horse, bent low. An arrow from Ta-na's bow sang its way directly over Red Horse's head.

"They are coming to the bank below us," Ta-na told Gao. "There are five of them."

"Leave me," Gao urged.

Ta-na had been evaluating his position. Just up the river a large tree was in danger of falling. Its root system was partially exposed, creating a dark cave under the bank.

"How badly are you bleeding?" he asked.

"I have no feeling in my leg," Gao said.

Ta-na tried to answer his own question by running his hand over Gao's thigh. He felt hot, sticky blood on the deerskin legging, but the amount did not seem excessive.

"Do you think you can load and fire?" Ta-na asked.

"I think so."

"I'm going to move you."

Gao let one moan escape his lips as Ta-na dragged him to the dark opening under the exposed roots of the tree.

"Make yourself as comfortable as you can," Ta-na said. "I'm going to make sure the bleeding stops." He used his knife to rip open the legging, took goose down from the medicine kit that Gao carried at his belt, found the entry hole and the ragged exit wound, and stuffed them with the feathers. He bound the two wounds with a strip of deerskin ripped from the legging.

Gao sat with his head back against the dirt bank.

"Are you awake?" Ta-na asked.

Gao moaned.

Ta-na loaded his own rifle, then removed the wet powder and charge from Gao's, cleaned it as best he could, and loaded it.

"If they come this way, use my rifle first," Ta-na ordered. "Sit quietly. If all goes well, you will not have to shoot at all, and I'll be back for you."

"May the spirits be with you," Gao said.

Ta-na climbed to the top of the bank and moved silently toward the south, then halted to listen. He heard only the nearby ripple of the current, the faraway hoot of a hunting owl. Moving slowly, he stayed close to the riverbank and watched for movement in the shadows. He was motionless behind a large tree when he saw a warrior emerge from one shadow, only to blend silently and quickly with another. Ta-na waited. The man was coming directly toward him, and he seemed to be alone. Ta-na removed his tomahawk from its sheath at his sash. The blade was cold as he touched it. He waited until the Shawnee was even with him before he swung the sharp iron. The blade met resistance as it sliced into the throat of the man. Ta-na caught the warrior before he fell, then lowered him to earth without sound, save for the helpless gurgling of attempted breathing. He felt the death tremors. One leg kicked one, two, three times . . . and then all was still. A stench filled his nostrils as the dead man's bowels were evacuated. Acid burst upward into Ta-na's throat as his stomach rebelled. He swallowed hard. He had never killed a man before that night, and now, on the banks of the Wabash River, far from home, three men were dead by his hand.

There was little time for him to contemplate what had happened. He heard a sound and rolled away as a sharp blade hissed past his ear and thudded into the earth. He swung his tomahawk in sheer panic, and a sharp cry came as his blade cut the tendons at the back of his attacker's knee. The enemy fell heavily, then rolled, and his knife left a shallow line of fire on Ta-na's forearm before Ta-na's backswing with his tomahawk buried the blade in the Shawnee's temple.

There were two more of them, and now they had been alerted by the Shawnee's yelp. Ta-na moved swiftly back toward Gao's hiding place as a shot rang out in the blackness of the night.

The pain came like a bolt of lightning with the first dim light of dawn. Gao sucked air between his teeth and told himself to be quiet. The wound began to throb as if evil spirits were pounding on drums of torture inside his body. He was so engrossed with his own agony that he almost missed seeing the approach of the two warriors. He was alerted by the sound of sucking mud as they came slowly toward him, walking at the edge of the water on the muddy bank. Alarm sent a surge of alertness into his gut. He lifted Ta-na's rifle slowly. The two warriors halted. In the gray, dim light he saw their silhouettes but could not distinguish their faces.

"There," said a voice that Gao recognized as Red Horse's. "There is the canoe." He moved slowly, making sucking sounds with each step. "They came out of the water here." He bent, looking at the sign. "We know that one of you is hurt," he said loudly as he straightened. "Yield, and I promise you that your death will be swift and merciful."

Gao tried to steady the muzzle of the rifle, but his arms were weak. The point of the weapon made a wavering circle. He squeezed the trigger when the muzzle pointed at the chest of his target, and the charge exploded. The rifle fell from his weak hands even as Red Horse's heart was smashed by the ball. Gao fumbled for the other rifle.

Tecumseh, having seen the flash of the shot, charged up the mud bank as he shrilled a war cry. Harrison's young spy was lifting another rifle when Tecumseh knocked it from his weak hands with a powerful slash of his tomahawk. The Panther lifted his blade, poised for the kill. But his young enemy's arms fell weakly to his sides, and his head slumped.

Tecumseh put out his free hand and lifted the Cherokee's head by his hair. Dawning light told him that the boy's eyes were closed. He released his hold, and the head lolled limply. For a moment Tecumseh stood motionless; then he walked to check on the fallen Red Horse. The warrior's heart was stilled. Tecumseh lifted his head and hooted three times quickly, cocked his ear waiting for an answer.

Ta-na stood on the bank and looked down on the Panther. He notched an arrow, drew the string, then hesitated. He stepped into the open as Tecumseh repeated the signal hoots.

"There will be no answer," Ta-na said.

Tecumseh, jerking his head upward, started to lift his tomahawk.

"Don't," Ta-na said. "I have heard your words. You said that brother must not kill brother."

"Nor should brother spy on brother for the Shemanese," Tecumseh said with controlled fury. "If you are going to release your arrow, do so."

"That I will not do unless you force me to," Ta-na said. "I have smelled the blood of men with red skin. I did not like it."

"Your bow is not that of an Indian," Tecumseh said.

"No."

"I knew a man who carried an English longbow. I saw him at the side of the Chief Who Does Not Sleep at the Fallen Timbers. He, too, was a traitor to his people."

"You speak of my father, Renno, sachem of the Seneca."

"Ah," Tecumseh said.

He saw the Panther shift his stance subtly, preparing to throw his tomahawk and fall to one side, away from the path of Ta-na's arrow. In response, Ta-na moved the point of his arrow to aim directly at Tecumseh's chest. "Don't make me kill you, warrior."

The Shawnee let his shoulders sag. "No," he said. "It is not time for me to die, nor am I fated to die at the hands of a mere boy." He sighed. "All the others are dead?"

"Yes."

"You are your father's son."

"Will you go now?"

"I will go."

Tecumseh turned and, heading downstream toward the canoes, walked past the body of Red Horse. Ta-na relaxed his pull on the bowstring and leaped down into the mud. Gao groaned as Ta-na put his hand on his shoulder.

"I'm going to carry you to the canoe," Ta-na said.

He lifted his brother and staggered through the mud, sinking to his ankles, losing both moccasins in the process. He lost his grip as he lowered Gao, and Gao's landing was rough. After he had recovered his moccasins and washed the mud off them, he took enough time to reload his own rifle and to check the charge in Gao's before pushing the canoe into the current and leaping in.

Tecumseh was standing beside a beached canoe as Ta-na's craft floated downstream. Ta-na kept his rifle at the ready, but the Shawnee made no show of belligerence.

"We will meet again," Tecumseh called as Ta-na's canoe drifted past.

"May the manitous will that it be in peace," Ta-na called back.

"There can be no peace with traitors," Tecumseh replied.

Chapter Eleven

It was not pleasant to watch a man die slowly, knowing that nothing could be done. Although Little Hawk and James were eager to move on toward an inhabited Bahamas island where, Seaman Marley assured them, there would be boats, they delayed leaving the secluded spot where they were hidden. That much they could do, for moving the man with the broken bone and mangled leg was extremely painful for him. Tropical heat had accelerated the development of infection and blood poisoning. The rank odor emanating from the suppurating wound was a clear indication that the man was doomed.

"Sir," Hensley said, "without a sawbones to whack off that leg, 'e's going to meet 'is Maker."

Within two days the wounded seaman was delirious. On the third morning he was dead, and his rotted leg was so rank that those who dug his shallow grave and placed him in it turned their heads from the stench.

Marley set course across an expanse of open water. It

was a risk. The *Cormorant* had had time to sail around the low islands with their adjacent coral shallows, and if she had guessed the intent of those who had fled her, she could very well come down on them in open waters. The experienced sailors rigged the boat's small, triangular sail, and favorable winds allowed the rowers a rest. Despite the use of the sail, by the time the men sighted land, Little Hawk's hands were blistered from holding the shafts of the oars. His hands, neck, and face were red and painful with sunburn.

"I figure that'll be 'er," Marley said as a green island rose slowly from the sea. "She's off from the main group, so if we're lucky, there'll be no navy about. They's a couple of big plantations with white overseers. Rest of the island's made up of blacks and Creoles. They's a few fishing boats, and now and again a ship will call."

They had to row eastward along a green shore densely grown with palms to the entrance of a small harbor. Half a dozen ragtag fishing boats were in the shelter. The loading docks were idle. A score of thatched huts sprawled in rowdy disorder away from the U-shaped bay. Dusky, naked children swam in the blue shallows along one section of the bay. The one sandy street was noisy with children and dogs.

"Where are the plantations you mentioned, Marley?" Little Hawk asked.

"One lies west along the coast, and the other is inland," Marley said.

"There's no British presence in the village?" Little Hawk asked. "No police?"

"Nay," Marley said. "And no more'n half a dozen white men at each plantation. The main thing we have to worry about is a man-of-war like the *Cormorant* dropping by."

"I think it would be advisable to get away from here as soon as possible," James said, then looked toward the moored fishing vessels. "But as boats go, that's a sorry lot."

"I agree," Little Hawk said. "I don't fancy trying to

cross the open ocean in any one of them. I would as lief try to row to an American port in the longboat."

"Deliver me from that," James said, looking ruefully at his blistered hands.

"At least we can have a drink," Marley said. "The black fellers here make a potent batch of poison out of coconut juice." He laughed and slapped a rower on the back. "That'll make you pull 'arder, eh?"

They were met at the shore by a crowd of silent, wide-eyed, dark-skinned urchins, some of them still naked from their swim. The longboat was pulled up onto the sand. A group of ragged men came out of a ramshackle building and advanced toward them. One fellow lifted his hand and with enthusiasm and a rather charming singsong accent said, "I say, Mr. Marley."

"I know this bloke," Marley said, stepping forward and raising a hand in greeting.

"So, you have deserted again, Mr. Marley."

"'is name's Brutus," Marley said in an aside to Little Hawk. "Ex-slave. Freedman. 'e's a big man in the town." He took the black man's hand. "'ow's it been, Mr. Brutus?"

"Tolerable, Mr. Marley. Just tolerable," Brutus said.

"Me and my friends need a way to get to the United States," Marley told him. "Any chance of an American ship coming in 'ere in defiance of the embargo?"

"Ah, but you are not in the know," Brutus said. "The embargo is finished." He shrugged. "But what has come after the embargo is, for us, as bad. The Americans still prohibit trade with any British port, which, such as it is, we are."

Marley turned to Little Hawk. "Well, you 'eard 'im."

"Mr. Brutus," Little Hawk asked, "is there a boat on this island that would make it to an American port? When I get to Wilmington, North Carolina, I can make it worthwhile for the man who gets me there."

"Well, you see what we have," Brutus said, showing a wide expanse of white teeth as he nodded toward the fishing boats riding at anchor or pulled up onto the beach. "But perhaps you are the adventurous type, eh?"

"I'm not sure I'm quite that adventurous," Little Hawk said with a laugh.

Brutus looked with piercing brown eyes at him. "My guess is, sir, that you would not want to encounter a representative of His Majesty's Navy."

"Your guess is good," Little Hawk said.

Brutus nodded. He was a thick-chested man who stood at least two inches taller than Little Hawk. It was evident from his well-formed nose and full but not Negroid lips that his mother had been closely involved with an Englishman.

"You want to say something, Mr. Brutus?" Marley asked.

"There is a boat. . . ."

"Now you're talking," Marley said with a grin.

"Two miles along the beach there is a cove where the English boss keeps a trim little sloop for his own pleasure," Brutus said. "It is possible that one or two men without honor, men who are willing to steal from our generous and kindhearted benefactors, the English, just might be able to slip her out of the cove in the dead of night." His straight-faced sarcasm brought snickers from his fellow islanders.

Marley winked at Little Hawk. " 'awk, do we know a couple of men without honor?"

"When it comes to the bloody British, who don't know the meaning of the word, I think I'll qualify," James said, lifting his hand without realizing what he was doing to rub a welted scar on the top of his shoulder.

"I think that I can rationalize seizing a boat from citizens of the nation that orders her warships to kidnap American citizens," Little Hawk said, looking at Marley.

"I am not a greedy man, Mr. Marley," Brutus said, "but if I am to lead you to this trim little sloop that is fully capable of taking a group of deserters from the Royal Navy to an American port, it would improve my outlook on what can be a rather difficult life if I could look forward to some compensation."

Marley spread his hands. "Wot you sees is wot we got."

Brutus rubbed his chin. Little Hawk could hear the scrape of beard stubble. "I see some fine rifles. I see a British officer's saber. I see a perfectly good longboat."

Little Hawk quickly unbelted the saber and handed it over. "We'll keep two rifles," he said. "The boat is yours, but I would think that it would not be wise to let an Englishman see it. It's too easily recognized as a boat from a British warship."

"That can be remedied," Brutus said, and again his voice was rich with sarcasm. "You know how we darkies are incapable of taking care of things. I'll have some of my young ones scour off that pretty, fresh paint and scar up the smooth wood with sticks and rocks. In a day no respectable British gentleman would claim it."

"Mr. Brutus, you're an out-and-out reprobate," Marley said admiringly.

"Thank you very much," Brutus said. "I do try my best, you know."

Six men in the longboat pushed off from the beach when the moon was high in the sky and the village was settled in for the night. Hensley, who was more knowledgeable about sailing small boats, would board the sloop with Little Hawk, James, and Brutus. The islander insisted that he would not be deprived of the fun and satisfaction of stealing the English boss's sloop. Marley and a seaman would stand by in the longboat. If things went smoothly, they would take the boat back to the village, where Brutus's young ones would begin immediately to make it invisible to British eyes.

The great house of the plantation sat back from the beach about a hundred yards, amid a grove of coconut palms. There were no lights in the windows when the longboat moved slowly toward a pretty little sloop about thirty feet long that was lolling at her mooring posts just offshore from a neatly built dock. Little Hawk whispered an order, and the seamen stopped rowing until they were all satisfied that nothing was moving on shore and that there were no watchmen.

The longboat edged up alongside the sloop, and the

hulls made contact with an almost inaudible bump. Little Hawk leaped on board. His only weapon was a long cane-cutting knife that he had borrowed from Brutus. James had the same type of blade. Brutus carried the late Captain Bowen's saber.

"It has come to my attention, 'awk," Hensley said, "that there ain't no bloomin' breeze."

That possibility had been anticipated. Hensley ran forward and took a line from Marley, in the longboat, while James and Brutus began to pull the sloop toward the forward mooring post to detach one line. Little Hawk was keeping an eye on the plantation house. A dog had started barking. Hensley loosed the stern mooring line, and with little groans of wooden protest the sloop took on headway as Marley and the seaman bent to the oars. Slowly the two boats crept away from the beach and moved toward the entrance of the cove.

"Tell Marley to slack off," Little Hawk said to Hensley. "We'll give him two more men for the oars."

Hensley went to the bow and hissed out the message. The sloop slowed, then came to a stop just as the door to the cabin burst open and a man clad in nightclothes demanded, "What in bloody hell is going on here?"

James was nearest to the hatch. He swung his long, sharp blade with all of his strength. The Englishman fell, his head dangling by nothing more than a layer of skin at the back of his neck. Blood pooled darkly on the polished, moonlit mahogany.

"Ugh," Hensley said. "Get 'im overboard."

"Not here," Little Hawk said. "Wait."

"'e's bleedin' all over the bloody deck," Hensley protested.

"Find something to soak it up," Little Hawk said. He himself moved cautiously down into the cabin to make sure that there would be no more surprises.

Once out of the cove and the lee of the land, there was a breeze to send the sloop, with the longboat in tow, sliding smoothly toward Brutus's village. It was still dark when they arrived.

"Mr. Brutus," Little Hawk asked, "have you ever thought of coming to the United States? You'd be a good man to have along on this voyage."

"The slaves there have black skins, too," Brutus said.

"There are freedmen," Little Hawk said. "And there would be work for you and your family in Wilmington."

"I think it best that I deal with the devil I know," Brutus said. "But thank you, Mr. Hawk, for your invitation."

"We're grateful to you."

"Be grateful as you sail west," Brutus said. "I hope before the English boss discovers that he is missing a sloop and a man."

"You're right," Little Hawk said. "Hensley, get the men aboard."

"Wot about the dead un?" Hensley asked.

"Perhaps Mr. Brutus can supply us with something compact but heavy so that we can give the man a proper burial at sea."

"Ballast rocks," Hensley said, nodding. "I'll gather a couple."

Along the shore, as in many American and island ports, heaps of English stones, rounded and smoothed by the friction of movement in the holds of sailing ships, gave mute testimony to the inequality of early trade between the old country and her colonies. Ships came out from England with short loads that required weight in the hull as ballast. The stones were dumped, unneeded, since the ships sailed east toward English ports fully laden with the produce of the western lands. Hensley picked up four round stones to weight each corner of a canvas sheath that would be sewn together and serve as the dead man's shroud.

Before the sky reddened with dawn, the sloop was loping westward on the wings of a soft, cool morning breeze, heading for the open sea between the Bahamas group and the Florida coast.

"Far as I'm concerned," Hensley said as he pushed a big sail needle through the canvas to close the end of the sack at the dead man's head, "we could just toss 'im over for the sharks."

When the weighted sack was ready, Hensley called for assistance and was about to push it overboard when James stopped him.

"I think I'd like to say a few words," James said.

"Well, 'urry it up, lad," Hensley said. "'e's 'eavy, you know."

James did not bow his head, but looked up toward a sky that was beginning to be decorated with spun-cotton clouds that beamed gleaming white in the brilliant sunshine. "He was one of your sons, Lord, and we commit him to you, as we consign him to the deep. Have mercy on his soul."

"That should do it," Hensley said, nodding to the seaman who was helping him. The sack hit with a splash.

James could see it for a long time as it sank into the clear, green depths. And then the sloop was past the spot, and the breeze was freshening.

James joined Little Hawk at the tiller while Hensley and Marley went below to catch a nap. The other seamen made minor adjustments to the sail and watched the bow wave of the sloop with satisfaction. She was making good time. Already Brutus's island was receding into the distance. The course was northwest.

"Hawk," James said, "I didn't have to kill that Englishman."

"So," Little Hawk said in unconscious imitation of his father.

"I guess I was striking out at Gunner Griffiths and Captain Bowen. I heard the English accent, and all of the inhumanity that I'd seen and helplessness I'd felt aboard the *Cormorant* flashed through my mind. I struck out against them. He might have been a good man. Maybe he had a wife and children."

"I know how you feel," Little Hawk said. "It would be easy to think of all Englishmen as cruel and evil. I know that I would die fighting before I'd ever let myself be impressed again. I told myself, back there aboard the *Cormorant*, that I understood, at last, why my great-grandfather decided to join the Americans in their fight against the British." He shook his head. "But it's not as simple as that. In that war they were all English—or at least most of them were. It was Englishman against Englishman. So I am forced to accept the concept that not all Englishmen are like Griffiths and Bowen." He smiled. "After all, my Harper ancestors were English. My stepmother is English."

"I didn't have to kill him," James said miserably. "I never knew that a man could have so much blood in him."

"You have never killed before?"

"And I pray never again."

Little Hawk was silent. He looked ahead into the watery distance. He refrained from telling James that, unfortunately, there came a time when killing was necessary, that there were things worth killing for. Freedom was worth killing for if the slain were those who opposed it or threatened it. He would not tell James, either, that his own blade had been poised to slice the Englishman's throat, only to have James do the job before him.

James, Little Hawk knew, would have to silence his own demons, and, God willing, he would do so before the next time he was forced to choose between protecting his own life and liberty or causing the death of a man who would deprive him of one or both. The world could be sweet and good, but it could also be cruel.

Hensley and Marley were navigating by dead reckoning with nothing more than a compass to guide them. "Don't worry, 'awk," Hensley said, grinning. "North America is a big continent, and the only way we could miss it is to discover for ourselves the Northwest Passage —which, I might point out, ain't been found by them wot tried."

Oddly, the winds failed them after the sloop had sailed into the vast ocean river that flowed northward along the coast of the United States. By the sun and the stars Hensley figured that they were being carried north by the current.

"My guess is, 'awk, that we're directly abeam of Savannah and movin'. Alls we need is a bloomin' wind, and we can sail into Charleston with no problem a'tall."

When it came, the wind was a surplus of plenty. The brunt of it could be seen as it moved toward the sloop from the southeast with the speed of a stampeding bull buffalo. It slammed into the vessel with a force that almost sent Little Hawk tumbling. The sloop heeled, and the wheel was almost wrenched from his hands. The seamen leaped to reduce the area of sail exposed to the gale, but their efforts came too late. With a splintering crash the mast broke at the deck line and fell over the port side, carrying sail and rigging with it. Water poured over the scuppers.

"Cut 'er away!" Marley yelled, seizing an ax and attacking the lines that held the deadweight of mast and sail that threatened to capsize the sloop. Men rushed to obey his orders, and the boat lurched upright as sail, mast, and rigging were freed to float away.

"We're in for it now," Marley said grimly. "Grab something and 'ang on, 'awk."

Several times during the night Little Hawk thought that the end had come. Waves that seemed as high as Beth's house towered over the sloop as the forces of nature conspired to capsize the sailless vessel and throw all of the men into the sea. He lashed himself to the stem of the wheel. Chill salt water drenched him as waves broke over the boat, keeping him cold and wet. He chose to stay on deck instead of joining James and one or two of the others in the cabin. If he were going to drown, he wanted to die fighting the sea in the open, not trapped inside the hull.

A dim, dingy light allowed him to see the top of the waves that tossed the sloop. An hour after dawn the light was not much better than at night, but it was enough to show that the sloop had taken a terrible beating. The rail was torn away on the port side, and when Marley and Hensley took a census it was discovered that one of the seamen from the *Cormorant* was gone.

By midday the waves were less mountainous. Little Hawk dozed. He awoke with a feeling that something was terribly wrong, but it was only that the sloop was riding smoothly up and down on a humpbacked swell. The waves no longer showed angry white teeth.

The ship's biscuits, which were all that remained of the little stock of food that Brutus had been able to give them, were soaked with seawater. There was little fresh water left to drink. Hensley rationed out a draft to all, then shook his head.

"Where are we?" Little Hawk asked.

"Might as well be in the Chiner Sea," Marley said.

"Maybe we'll be in 'ell 'fore nightfall," Hensley said, pointing.

There, at close hand, dauntingly close, were the sails of a full-rigged ship.

Little Hawk's hand closed on the haft of the cane-cutting knife. In the cabin there were two rifles. With one of them in hand he could take a few Englishmen with him before the sloop could be boarded . . . unless the enemy decided to use cannon at the first show of defiance. If the English tried to board, it would be his cane knife against sabers.

"I'm not going to let them take me again, Hawk," James said in a low voice.

" 'ere, lads!" yelled a seaman. "She's flying the Stars and Stripes!"

James ran to the stern to get a better view. He lifted his arm and waved. He yelled something that was not words, and then he turned, eyes bright with tears, to Little Hawk. "She's a Yankee! She's one of ours!"

The captain of the clipper out of New Bedford, on his way home from Recife, Brazil, was sympathetic to men who had escaped impressment in the British navy. He altered course and four days later was taking on a pilot to guide the ship up Cape Fear.

The port at Wilmington was no longer a forest of bare masts. Two ships passed them, heading south down the river, and Little Hawk and James could see a great deal of activity around the dock area. The *Beth Huntington* was at wharf side, off-loading. Those who had escaped from the

Cormorant were gathered in the bow with Little Hawk and James.

"Some of the lads are going to stay on board," Hensley said. "The cap'n is short'anded. Says 'e can fix 'em up with citizenship papers and all—for the good it'll do if they get stopped by the likes of the *Cormorant*."

"Tell them," James said, "that there'll be places for them on board either a Ridley or a Huntington ship if they want to sign on with us."

"We 'ppreciate that, guv'nor," Marley said. "Hensley and I, we intend to take you up on that."

"Good, good," James said, then pointed. "There's a Huntington ship now."

"A yar craft," Hensley said. "Who be the skipper?"

"A wild Spaniard, most of the time," James said. "But I suspect, now that the embargo is off and we're at least able to sail to non-European or non-British ports, that old Adan might be staying ashore to take care of business, leaving the *Beth* to a certain handsome young captain named James."

"Gor," Hensley said. "I reckon I might be willing to sail with that lad."

It was Adan himself who first saw two familiar faces on the bow of the incoming Baltimore clipper. At first he couldn't believe it; then he whooped with joy and almost fell into the muddy waters of the river in his eagerness to leap on board before the ship was secured at dockside. First he seized Little Hawk, then held James in a bear hug, speaking a mile a minute in his native language.

"Speak English, hoss," James said.

The word spread. Men from all over town gathered to give Little Hawk and James a hero's welcome. Nathan, James's father, seized Little Hawk's hand after hugging his son tightly.

"We knew you'd make it, Hawk," he said. "But we thought your release would come as a result of the efforts that Beth and the girls are making on your behalf in Washington."

Little Hawk's soaring spirits faltered. "Naomi is in Washington, too?"

"All three of them," Nathan said. "And Renno went west. Your grandmother was ill."

" 'Was'?" Little Hawk asked.

Nathan shook his head. "Haven't heard anything since the letter telling Renno that your grandmother was very sick." He took each of them by an arm. "Well, come along. You both look as if you could use a good meal."

"Excuse me," Little Hawk said. "I want to speak to the captain."

He did so immediately, and he was told that he was welcome to stay aboard until the ship docked in Baltimore Harbor. In fact, the captain said, it would be no trouble to drop him off at Annapolis, so that he'd be nearer to Washington.

The ship stayed in Wilmington overnight. Little Hawk had that good meal at the Ridley home. Adan was there. He was entering all of the Huntington fleet into the South American trade, with, he hinted, a little side trip now and then to the islands.

"I hope you fellows don't fault me for not sailing back here immediately to let your folks know what had happened to you," Adan said.

"You did exactly right," James said. "By completing the bonded voyage, you saved a Huntington ship from seizure for having defied the embargo."

"Of course you did right, Adan," Little Hawk said.

"I've had letters from Beth in Washington," Adan said.

Little Hawk looked at him expectantly, eyebrows raised. "She says that Naomi and the twins are just fine," Adan said. "Says that Renna has a beau." He grinned. "Whoops, didn't mean to make a pun in bad taste, considering that her husband was called Beau. She's got a suitor. He's an Englishman."

For a moment Little Hawk felt bristly, but the feeling passed quickly. "Good for Renna," he said. "By any chance, might this Englishman's name be Farnsworth?"

"Why, yes. Do you know him?"

"He brought word of the count's death to Renna in England," Little Hawk said.

"What sort of fellow is he?" Adan asked.

"He's a Scot. Seems to be a decent sort. Good family, as the English would say, but according to William a penniless second or third son. He was with the English armies in Portugal. Fought rather well, apparently."

"You sound doubtful about him," Adan observed.

"As I said, he seemed to be a good man, but for some reason I could never cotton to him. He had a way of looking through you when he spoke."

"I'm not sure I'd like to see Renna married to a professional British soldier," Adan said.

Hawk grinned. "Scot or whatever," he said, "a Britisher would not be my first choice as a new brother."

"This fellow has followed Renna all the way to the United States?"

"Sounds like it," Little Hawk said. "If so, you can't fault his persistence, can you?"

The voyage north along the coast to the Chesapeake was uneventful and swift due to favoring winds. Little Hawk occupied a cabin with one of the junior officers. He was freshly outfitted with clothing he had left behind at Beth's Wilmington house when he shipped with Adan aboard the *Beth Huntington*. He looked every inch the young American gentleman when he shook the captain's hand at the docks in Annapolis and left the clipper. He watched the crew making preparations to sail immediately, since the ship's only business at Annapolis was to allow Little Hawk to disembark. He waved and shouted a farewell to the young officer whose cabin he had shared.

Even as the ship that had brought him north edged away from the pier, a British warship was coming in. The sight of the Union Jack fluttering at the masthead caused Little Hawk's face to freeze into impassivity. His hand reached reflexively for a weapon, but he was carrying none. He was near the civilized heart of the United States, where a man did not carry his rifle or walk around with a marine saber at his side.

Because the Britisher was a warship, Little Hawk thought it curious that it was allowed to dock peacefully in an American port while what could only be called a state of belligerency existed on the open seas. He watched in fascination as sailors scurried about, reefing sails, shouting back and forth to the longboats that were pulling the ship to dockside. He saw the uniformed officers standing in a group, saw arrogant faces that reminded him of the *Cormorant*'s captain. At that moment, if he had had the power, he would have declared war on England and would have begun it himself with a belaying pin, if that were the only weapon at hand.

Standing with the officers as the ship's crew eased her to the dock and whipped out and attached mooring lines was a man in continental morning dress with ruffled cuffs and gleaming white linen at the throat. At first his face did not register with Little Hawk. It was only when the gangplank was lowered and the nattily dressed man was the first off the ship that Little Hawk looked at him closely. Startled, he walked toward the gangplank, where the man whose face was hauntingly familiar was making his farewells to two ship's officers. In profile the nose, the smiling mouth, the erect stance were unmistakable.

"Beau?" Little Hawk called out from a distance of ten paces. "Beau, is it you?"

Beau, the comte de Beaujolais, turned his head, looked inquiringly at Little Hawk. "Sir?" he said.

Little Hawk halted, his smile fading. "You are the comte de Beaujolais?"

"I am." Recognition lit Beau's face. He leaped to throw his arms around Little Hawk and, as Frenchmen were wont to do, to kiss him lightly on both cheeks. "Hawk!" he shouted. "Little Hawk. *Mon frère*."

"It *is* you, then! You are not dead."

"At one time, almost," Beau said. "At this moment the only thing that will make me feel any better is my wife in my arms."

"She's in Washington," Little Hawk said.

"Delightful!" Beau cried. "I had expected to have to

travel either to Wilmington or to the Cherokee Nation to find her and my children."

Seamen carrying Beau's trunk came down the gangplank. For the next few minutes he was occupied in the hiring of a carriage and in directing the loading of his baggage. Little Hawk was traveling light, with only one small carpetbag. When, at last, they were seated side by side in the carriage, Beau sighed wearily and said, "So you yourself have just arrived?"

"On the ship that was departing as you came ashore," Little Hawk said. "I am eager to hear your story. Renna was told by an English officer that you had been killed in Lisbon by Portuguese partisans."

"I was shot by an English officer," Beau said. "He sought me out in the French offices where I had lingered too long in an effort to destroy documents. He asked me if I were Beaujolais. When I said that I was, he fired without further comment."

Little Hawk felt a chill of intuition. "You didn't know the man?"

"No."

"He didn't give you his name?"

"He didn't take time to do even that before he shot me in the chest."

"Can you describe him?"

"I'll never forget him. His accent was Scottish. He was tall, well formed, and he had red hair."

"So," Little Hawk said.

"How did Renna take the false news of my death?" Beau asked.

"With bravery," Little Hawk said.

"Yes, she would."

Beau fell silent. Little Hawk's mind was in turmoil. As he had told Adan, he had never fully been able to accept Randall Farnsworth by his surface values. There'd been something odd about the man, something intangible but bothersome. He tried to piece it all together. He remembered very well how they had met Farnsworth for the first time, in the field in Portugal. Renna had remarked more than once on how helpful Farnsworth had been to her in Wellesley's camp when she and little Louis were left alone there. In retrospect it seemed decidedly odd that Farnsworth had been the one to learn of Beau's death, odder still that a man who answered Farnsworth's description had asked Beau's name in a Scottish accent before shooting him.

Throughout the centuries, many things had been excused in the name of love, and love had been the rationale for many odd actions throughout the history of man. Was Farnsworth so villainous that he would deliberately seek out Renna's husband to kill him in order to give himself a chance to win the hand of the woman he loved? Could a man capable of such a deed also be capable of feeling true love? Unreasoning fear for Renna made Little Hawk shiver.

"What do you think of my son?" Beau asked, breaking into Little Hawk's mood of uneasiness. "Estrella said that he was a beautiful baby."

"As babies go," Little Hawk said, grinning. He patted Beau on the shoulder. "A fine little lad. Strong and sturdy."

"And my Emily Elizabeth?"

"She'll be as beautiful as her mother."

"God is good."

Sometimes, Little Hawk thought.

The carriage was moving at a steady pace, with the horses trotting easily. He had the address of the residential hotel were Beth, Renna, and Naomi were staying. Soon he and Beau would be in Washington. How could he tell Beau that the man who had, in all probability, tried to kill him in Lisbon was courting Renna? *How do you eat a whole buffalo? One bite at a time.*

"Beau—" It was difficult.

The Frenchman was smiling to himself, obviously enjoying the anticipation of seeing Renna and his children. "What is it, *mon ami?*"

"The man who brought word of your death to us in England is named Randall Farnsworth. He was an officer with Wellesley's army."

"Yes?"

"He's Scot. Rather handsome. Tall. Red-haired."

"What are you saying?" Beau asked, stiffening, his smile fading.

"He's in Washington. He has taken a fancy to Renna."

Beau flushed. "Renna would not—"

"No," Little Hawk said.

"This Barnsworth—"

"Farnsworth."

"How did he know who I was?"

"We met him after you rode south toward Lisbon. He looked after Renna and Louis for a time after my father and I left the encampment to do some scouting for Sir Arthur. I'm sure that she would have told Farnsworth all about you. Later, he spent considerable time at Beaumont Manor during the time that Renna was recovering from the news of your death."

Beau's face was grim.

"Perhaps he is not the one who shot you. . . ." Little Hawk did not place much weight on his own words.

"Perhaps."

"Renna will be overjoyed to see you," Little Hawk said. "We must talk about how the news is to be broken to her." He chuckled. "I thought I had seen a ghost. It was quite a shock to me, and I'm not a woman in love with you."

"Good news is never too great a shock," Beau said tensely.

"Yes, I suppose you're right."

"You know where she is?"

"Yes. The three of them have rooms together."

"We will go there directly?"

"Yes."

Beau made a face. "I have not even asked why you are not with your wife and children."

"That's a long story, too," Little Hawk said.

Beau laughed. "A story for the campfire, yes?"

"Yes, and like all good stories told by the light of a campfire, it will grow with time." He looked in Beau's eyes. "Let me say only that my experiences of the past few months have done nothing to make me love the men of jolly old England. If Farnsworth is the one who shot you, I will handle the matter."

"Not on your life," Beau said.

Chapter Twelve

Pierre Laclède Liguest, one of the French traders who were called "the ragged men of the woods," had established the city of St. Louis on a waterfront shelf under a bluff on the western bank of the Mississippi. The site was just south of the mouth of the Missouri and was almost fifty years old by the time Renno and Roy Johnson arrived to seek out Governor Meriwether Lewis. The town had spread to the edge of the vast prairie to the west under French and Spanish rule before Captain Amos Stoddard of the United States Army took possession in 1804 and made St. Louis the district headquarters of the newly acquired vastness known as Louisiana.

By 1809 a new spurt of growth was under way, fueled by those who were following Lewis and Clark's earlier example of using St. Louis as the jumping-off place into the still largely unexplored west.

"Must be a thousand or more folks living here," Roy said as they rode slowly along a muddy street crowded with heavy wagons. Around them were hairy, buckskinned frontiersmen and Indians in a mixture of native and European dress. From the doorway of a public house a woman in a faded but well-ruffled red dress gave Renno a big smile laden with not-so-subtle invitation.

"All the benefits of civilization," Roy said, grinning at Renno. "Whiskey shops and whores. The white man's blessings for the wilderness."

They found the territorial headquarters without having to ask. The wooden building was marked by a huge flag that rippled in the constant prairie wind and by a company of uniformed militia at drill in a dusty field nearby. Roy led the way up a wooden walk and onto a stoop. He shuffled his feet to get off some of the mud before opening the door to step into a room lit dimly by glassed windows. A desk and several chairs were grouped against the back wall. An oaken hat tree was beside the door.

"Anybody home?" Roy called out.

The man who came into the room from the rear was dressed in black. His high collar cupped a rectangular face of pleasant proportions capped by a mass of dark hair arranged in a pompadour that was, for Roy's taste, just a bit too pretty. One lock of hair fell down on a broad, pale forehead. His lips were Cupid's bows framing a half-smirk, half-smile. His eyes would have been the pride of many ladies.

"Gentlemen," the newcomer said.

"We're looking for Governor Lewis," Renno said.

"So are many of his creditors," the man replied.

Renno quickly reappraised the man, for his remark showed that he was no friend to Meriwether Lewis.

"Know him, then, do you?" Roy asked.

"Indeed."

Roy looked at Renno, and he had to work hard to hold back a grin at the impassive set of his face. Renno's distrust of the pale-faced gentleman was obvious to Roy.

"Well, sir," Roy said, "since we've traveled quite a spell 'specially to see Governor Lewis, and since you seem not only to know him but to know a lot about his

financial affairs, maybe you could tell us where to find
him."

"I suspect, sir," the pale man said, "that by this time
he is well on his way to take ship at New Orleans."

"The devil you say," Roy grumped, joining his aching
joints in begrudging the long trip Renno and he had taken
for nothing.

Renno shifted his rifle to his left hand. The pale man,
seeing the look in Renno's ice-blue eyes, turned the half-
smirk into more of a smile. "Please excuse my levity,
gentlemen. I'm sorry that you've missed the governor.
Perhaps I can help you. I am Frederick Bates, secretary
for the Upper Louisiana Territory. I am in charge in Governor Lewis's absence."

"How long has Mr. Lewis been gone?" Renno asked.

"A fortnight," Bates said.

"And his destination?" Renno asked.

"Washington City by water, via New Orleans," Bates
said.

"Well," Roy said to Renno, "I don't fancy hanging
around here until he gets back."

"That might be a long wait," Bates said smugly. "It is
doubtful, with his record, that he will retain his office."

Roy waited for Renno's reaction. He grinned inwardly again as he saw his son-by-marriage change facial
expression once more. The smile that came to Renno's
face was one reserved for people he didn't much like but
wanted to string along.

"We have heard rumors," Renno said. "They're true,
then?"

Roy cleared his throat. The Indian in Renno was at
work, making lying to a white man easy. The Seneca had
given Bates the impression that he knew something about
Governor Lewis's affairs.

"We never had any financial problems while General
Wilkinson was governor," Bates said.

The mention of one of the slyest scoundrels in the
country interested Roy. "You a friend of the general's?" he
asked.

"I have served with him, each in our own official capacity," Bates said.

"Knew him myself," Roy said. "Me and my son here, we scouted for Anthony Wayne whilst Wilkinson was his second-in-command. You with him then?"

"No," Bates said with a laugh. "I was a little young, I guess."

"Wilkinson ran a tight shop," Roy said, winking at Renno. They both knew just how skillfully Wilkinson had looted the supplies of Anthony Wayne's American Legion.

"He would never have spent government money without permission," Bates said.

"And Lewis did, huh?" Roy asked.

Bates nodded. "Not only that, but there is the possibility that he used government money in his frenzy of land speculation."

"Do tell," Roy said. "That why he went to Washington?"

"He went to Washington, I imagine, to try to convince President Madison that he was justified in spending hundreds of dollars of the government's money to convey a Mandan chief back to his home on the Missouri River." Bates snorted. "Washington had authorized seven thousand dollars to ensure that Mr. Lewis's friend got back to his village, but that wasn't enough for the governor. He advanced even more money to the adventurers who were to do the job, although the military escort authorized by Washington was ample."

"Governor Lewis got in trouble with Washington, huh?" Roy asked.

"With Washington and with anyone in the territory who would lend him money," Bates said.

"Well, Renno," Roy said, "I reckon we have enough time for me to have a little taste of something before we start home."

"Your business here was with Mr. Lewis personally, and not in his capacity as governor?" Bates asked.

"More or less," Roy said. "We 'ppreciate the information, Mr. Bates."

"Good day, sirs," Bates said, turning to stalk back into the inner office.

Roy had his little taste of something at the public house from which the woman in the red dress had smiled at Renno. She was not in evidence when they first entered. Roy downed a glass of good trade whiskey and extended his hand for a refill. Renno smelled the aroma of cooking meat, inquired about food, and was soon seated with Roy at a crude table. Two huge buffalo steaks, red and juicy, lay on plates in front of them. The whiskey had given Roy an appetite, so he was concentrating on his meat when a tall, distinguished man entered and stood at the bar. Roy looked up only when Renno touched his arm.

"Is that who I think it is?" Roy asked.

Renno rose and walked to the bar. "Do I address Captain Clark?" he asked.

"You do," said William Clark, looking closely at Renno's face. He appeared puzzled for a moment, then a wide smile came to his face. "Renno!" he said. "It's been a coon's age."

"It's good to see you, Captain," Renno said. "You remember my father-in-law, Roy Johnson."

Roy had come forward, wiping his mouth on his sleeve. "Lot of water under the bridge since Fallen Timbers," he said as he clasped Clark's hand.

"You're holding up well," Clark said to Roy.

"Hell, everybody was young back then," Roy said.

"Especially me," Clark said with a laugh. "And Meriwether. I met him while we were both serving with Anthony Wayne in the Ohio country, you know."

"Listen, Cap'n," Roy said, "how 'bout you coming on over to the table, where I got me a two-pound buffalo steak getting cold."

Clark picked up his drink and joined them at the table, where the talk was good and the memories were sharp. Clark told a couple of anecdotes about Little Hawk's deeds during the trip back from the Far West.

"Yep," Roy said with a wink at Renno, "Tom Jefferson spent a lot of government money sending you and

Meriwether out west, just to find my grandson already there waiting for you to show you the way back."

"Is that why your eyes are brown, Roy?" Clark asked, grinning.

"What?"

"Because you're full of it right up to the eyeballs?"

"My Little Hawk told y'all about some land you didn't get to, didn't he?" Roy asked.

"That he did," Clark said. "I've been sorry ever since that we didn't take a look at the country north of the Columbia." He turned to Renno. "What brings you two to St. Louis?"

"Mr. Jefferson wanted me to come to speak with the governor," Renno said.

"About what?" Clark asked. He lifted one hand quickly. "I don't mean to pry. Meriwether left me in charge of his personal affairs while he's away."

"He had written to Mr. Jefferson stating that he had information too delicate to entrust to a courier or to the mails," Renno said.

Clark made a wry mouth, thought for a moment, then shook his head.

"You don't have any idea what was bothering him?" Renno asked.

"He had some gripes against the officials in Washington because they were not honoring his chits," Clark said. He spread his hands. "Other than that . . ."

"Bates at headquarters intimated that Lewis was involved in wild land speculation and that he might have spent government money for private purposes."

"That's bull balls," Clark said angrily. "Land speculation? Hell. If Meriwether is a speculator, then so are we all. Any man who can't see that St. Louis will grow is either blind or stupid. Meriwether has purchased a few lots and some acreage. He may even have borrowed some money from friends, but I'd bet my right arm that he would not misuse government funds."

"Bates said that he gave money to someone who was taking a Mandan chief back up the Missouri," Renno said.

"Damned right he did," Clark said. "We brought that

chief down with us so that the government could talk treaty with him. We had specific authority from Jefferson himself to use our best judgment in dealing with the Indians, and we thought that it would be good policy to have a solid and peaceful treaty with the Mandans. We promised the chief that we'd get him safely back to his village. Things developed so that it was more difficult than we'd envisioned to keep that promise, and the money that Washington authorized wasn't enough. The Cheyenne and the Arikara got straws up their asses about something and wouldn't let boats through their territory. Meriwether advanced about seven hundred dollars of his own money for tobacco and powder to be used as gifts and bribes for the hostiles upriver. When Washington wouldn't honor his chit, leaving him stuck with the loss, it just about ruined him."

"Bates doesn't like Lewis very much," Roy said.

"Bates was acting governor for over a year before Meriwether was appointed. He wants to be governor again," Clark said. "Or, failing that, he wants his good friend Judge Coburn to have the job."

"Tell me more about Bates," Renno said.

"He's a contradiction in a lot of ways," Clark said. "When he was acting governor, I cooperated with him to reorganize the militia, and he was not bad to work with at all. He and Meriwether just didn't hit it off—mostly, I suspect, because Bates was jealous. Bates was also superintendent of Indian Affairs for a while, and he and Meriwether often locked horns about relations with the Indians."

"What was the relationship between Bates and General Wilkinson?" Roy asked.

"He had dealings with Wilkinson, of course. Had to. Wilkinson's in command down at New Orleans and in the lower part of the territory. The major part of communications and most of the supplies come through New Orleans."

"Are Bates and Wilkinson particularly close?" Renno asked.

"You're making me curious," Clark said. "I don't

know all of what went on up in the Ohio country between you two and Wilkinson."

"Wilkinson was stealing guns and ammunition intended for Anthony Wayne and selling them to the Spanish," Roy said.

Clark nodded grimly. "It was all kept pretty quiet, wasn't it?"

"I still can't figure out why Wilkinson wasn't hanged," Roy said. "He's a traitor two or three times over. They almost got him after the Burr trial, when it was obvious that he was lying, but he seems to lead a charmed life."

"And you think that Bates might have Wilkinson as an ally in his ongoing battle with Meriwether?" Clark asked.

Renno shrugged.

Roy said, "Bates mentioned Wilkinson in comparison with Lewis as an administrator. It just made us wonder."

"By God, it had never occurred to me," Clark said. "I appreciate your bringing it to my attention. As soon as Meriwether gets back, he and I will do some talking, and maybe we can just get Mr. Bates off his back once and for all."

The talk turned general, with Clark asking questions about the state of things back east. Roy finished his steak and expressed his satisfaction with a lusty burp. Clark offered the hospitality of his home for the night and was accepted. There they met Clark's wife of fewer than two years, who served a hearty supper and, after she found that Renno had been in the East recently, asked questions about what the ladies were wearing. Neither Roy nor Renno could offer descriptions that satisfied her curiosity.

The travelers took their leave of Clark the next day. A flatboat was casting off for New Orleans and just happened to have space for two men and four horses.

"I don't imagine you're going to chase Meriwether all the way to Washington," Clark said.

"We'll leave the flatboat at Chickasaw Bluffs and then ride cross-country to the Cherokee Nation," Renno said.

"I'll give you a letter to the officer in command at Fort Pickering," Clark said.

"That won't be necessary," Renno said.

"Speak for yourself," Roy said. "I'll take that letter, Cap'n, if it means getting a bed to sleep in and some good army food."

As the crew of the flatboat began to loosen lines to cast off, Clark shook hands with Roy, then exchanged the warrior's clasp with Renno. "If there's another war, gentlemen, and you care to become a part of it, I'd be more than happy to have you scout for my militia."

"We'll keep that in mind," Renno said.

"Me, I doubt if I've got another war in me," Roy told him.

"Well, Godspeed," Clark said.

The leisurely trip to Fort Pickering, the army post at Chickasaw Bluffs, allowed Roy to rest and regain his energy. Renno made no objections when Roy presented William Clark's letter of introduction to Captain Gilbert Russell. The officer read the letter and put out his hand with a smile.

"I have heard of you, of course, Colonel Johnson," Russell said. "And of you, Sachem."

Renno nodded.

"We'll bed you down in the officers' quarters. It ain't sheer luxury, but it's better'n sleeping in the stables," Russell said. "You will, of course, be my guests for dinner."

"Much obliged," Roy said.

"You're the second set of visitors we've had from St. Louis in the past two weeks," Russell said. "I recently had the honor of playing host to Governor Lewis. As a matter of fact, he left only a week ago."

"Stopped here on the way to New Orleans, did he?" Roy asked.

Russell nodded. "But we convinced him not to continue on to New Orleans."

"How's that?" Roy asked.

"Well, you know how it is," Russell said, "what with

the British acting up. War could come at any minute. Governor Lewis had all of his papers with him, including the journals of the expedition to the Pacific, and he didn't want to risk losing them in a fight at sea or to have them seized by some Royal Navy officer."

"Struck out overland, did he?" Roy asked.

"Yes, after I tried to convince him to stay longer," Russell said. "He was not yet fully recovered from his illness when he left. He was a very sick man when he got here, burning up with fever and talking out of his head. We put him to bed and had our sawbones treat him. Nothing would do but for him to leave just as soon as he could stay on his feet."

"Did he tell you his route?" Renno asked.

"He was planning to hit the Natchez Trace and follow it to Nashville," Russell said.

"Well, we might just run into him, after all," Roy said.

"How is he traveling?" Renno asked.

"Horseback," Russell answered. "He and his man, a Creole fellow, were going to leave alone. I knew that he was carrying a bit of money. A prosperous-looking man is always a choice target for the bandits that work the trace, so I warned him. He said he figured that he could take care of himself and his man all right; but as it happened the Indian agent to the Chickasaw Nation, James Neely, was planning to go to Nashville. When he realized Governor Lewis wasn't in the best of health, he decided to leave early so he could sort of look after the governor. He even loaned Lewis a couple of horses to carry his gear and papers."

"There are three of them, then," Renno said.

"Four. Mr. Neely also has a servant—a slave," Russell said.

Dinner was a formal affair with the fort's officers in dress uniform. Fort Pickering was a frontier post, and the routine was dull and repetitive, so the arrival of visitors, especially two men presented by such personages as the militia general and famous explorer William Clark, was an excuse for a ceremonial meal at which each man's cup was kept filled.

Roy Johnson lifted his glass to the latest toast and winked at Renno. "Looks like I'm going to have to give these whippersnappers a lesson in serious drinking," he said out of the corner of his mouth.

Renno raised his cup and touched his lips to it in toasts to the United States, to President Madison, to President Madison's lovely wife, to Governor Lewis, to Captain Russell, to one another, etc.

A young lieutenant sitting to Renno's left was becoming bleary-eyed. "That old man can hold his liquor," he said to Renno, wobbling his head toward Roy. "'Most as good as Governor Lewis."

"So," Renno said.

"Wouldn't have thought it of Lewis," the young man said. "Came here in a state of mental derangement so's the cap'n almost had to force him to stay and rest up. But 'fore he left, he drank us all under the table."

"Why do you say that he was mentally deranged when he arrived?" Renno asked.

"Well, you know."

"No, I'm afraid I don't."

"Unsteady on his feet, talking out of his head."

"But wasn't that from fever?" Renno asked.

"Well, that's what *they'd* like you to believe," the young man said. He drew himself up, tugged at his tunic, tried to focus his eyes. "I talked with the crew of the flatboat that brung him to the fort. Said he tried to do himself in twice on the way downriver."

"How?"

"Tried to jump overboard."

"Tried to jump—or perhaps almost fell from the weakness of the fever?" Renno asked.

"That's what *they'd* like you to believe," the lieutenant said again, putting his finger to his lips and winking.

Roy moaned in protest when Renno woke him the next morning. Renno persisted and shortly after dawn they left Chickasaw Bluffs and headed eastward. Meriwether Lewis had stayed at Fort Pickering for six days. The two travelers were over a week behind him.

"Renno, durn it, what's the hurry?" Roy protested when Renno set a fast pace that would cover more than fifty miles a day. "If you're thinking of catching up with Lewis, we've got two chances—slim and none."

"Unless he is slowed by his fever," Renno said.

"What's the all-fired need to catch him?"

"There isn't one, really," Renno said.

"Conscience hurting you because you didn't rush right on out to St. Louis after Mr. Jefferson asked you to?"

Renno laughed. "Perhaps."

"You oughta know that family comes first."

"I know."

"But you still feel guilty."

"Not so much guilty as curious," Renno said. "I keep wondering what was so delicate that Lewis wanted to communicate directly with Jefferson."

"Well, he'll do it in person now," Roy said. "Maybe not to Mr. Jefferson but to Mr. Madison."

"Yes, you're right," Renno said, but he did not slow the pace.

"Here's about where we turn east," Roy said two days later.

"So," Renno said.

"Do I get the idea that we're going to take the long way home, through Nashville?" Roy asked.

"Perhaps we will turn southeast later."

"If we don't catch up with Lewis pretty soon?"

Renno did the Indian act and grunted.

"Couple of days? And don't grunt at me again."

"A couple of days." Renno could not explain why he felt compelled to travel to the north of the direct line homeward, but that desire seemed to have been implanted in him.

Renno and Roy had traveled through the lands of the Chickasaw on previous occasions, and Renno in particular was familiar with the Natchez Trace. On his previous trips, there had been no travel accommodations, but in recent years persistent pressure from their white neighbors had persuaded the Chickasaw to allow three settlements north of the Tennessee River. The Indians had balked at white requests to operate inns in Chickasaw lands, but since travel on the trace continued to increase, a few enterprising Indians, most of them half-breeds, built crude shelters not quite comfortable enough to be called inns. These Indian-operated establishments came to be called stands.

The first stand that Roy and Renno encountered was nothing more than a hut with small saplings for walls. The thatched ceiling was just high enough to allow them to stand with their hair brushing the roof poles. Bedding was a moth-eaten bearskin that smelled as if its previous owner had left a legacy. The floor was packed earth. Renno took one look and decided to sleep in the open. Roy sat down on the bearskin, allowed that he wouldn't mind having a roof over his head, but joined Renno beside a campfire at a distance from the stand still scratching flea bites.

Moving northeastward at the rate of fifty miles a day, they reached the Duck River, where, to Roy's relief, a man named John Gordon had established a ferry.

Gordon said yes, he'd ferried a party of three white men and a Negro across the river just three days past.

"Distinguished feller," Gordon said. "The same what went to the Pacific Ocean."

"Was he in good health?" Renno asked.

"Seemed a mite irritable," Gordon said. "Camped right over there t'other side of the river. Talked to himself, he did."

"Seem like he was out of his head with fever?" Roy asked.

"No, sir," Gordon said. "More like speechifying. Walked around making motions with his hands. Talkin' in a big voice."

"Did you hear what he was saying?" Renno asked.

"It was like he was trying to explain something. Something about vouchers on the guvment and the like."

Renno and Roy camped at the same site and were

traveling again with the sun. Gordon had told them that the next stand on the trace was kept by a Chickasaw named Factor's Son and the next after that was Grinder's Stand.

Renno continued to push the pace. Roy had long since given up complaining, for he, too, was beginning to look forward to meeting the man about whom he'd heard so much from Little Hawk.

To call the Natchez Trace a road was to diminish the definition. The word *trace* was more accurate. The easiest route between the Tennessee River and that point on the Mississippi that later came to be called Natchez was felt out by generations of Indians who blazed their paths through the unbroken wilderness before the coming of the white man. The white man's use of the trace had come about when an old enemy, Spain, tried to close off the watery highway that was the Mississippi. Hunger for some of the richest land on the continent pushed western pioneers down the old Indian trail, seeking a route to the Mississippi Territory and the Southwest.

By the time of Renno and Roy's passage, the traffic had become so heavy that in places the road was worn deeply into the earth, similar to the buffalo trails Renno had encountered on his trip toward the Apache lands of the far Southwest. In spite of the traffic, however, there was still danger. Bandits robbed and killed. Once the Harp brothers, Wiley and Macajah, had plied their criminal trade on the trace.

As if to bring home the fact that they were two men alone in the wilderness on a track that had seen much violence in the past, Renno and Roy saw a bleached, grinning skull hanging by a spike driven into a tree trunk. Bandit or victim, the weathered skull kept its secret.

Once they met a post rider, for a mail route had been established to cover the five hundred and fifty miles between Nashville and Natchez, ten days of hard riding; and more than once they met other travelers who looked at them warily, nodded a greeting, and hurried on their way. When they reached the place called Grinder's Stand, they had ridden about two hundred miles on the trace itself.

Grinder's Stand consisted of two log cabins connected by a covered walkway. Smoke was issuing from the chimney of one of the cabins when Renno and Roy approached.

"I wouldn't want the man who built them cabins to build me one," Roy said.

The cracks between the logs were as wide as four inches and were only partially chinked with wooden lengths held in place by clay.

Renno reined in his horse at a short distance from the cabins and called out, "Hello, the stand."

A door formed of rough-hewn oaken planks opened a crack, then farther. A woman in a soiled calico dress hanging loosely from bony shoulders stood in the doorway. Her hair was lank and pulled back Indian-style, although her skin was pale, showing that she was at least half-white. Her face was grooved with wrinkles and hardened by the elements.

"Afternoon," she said.

"Afternoon," Roy said. "Are you Mrs. Grinder?"

"I am," the woman said in a flat voice. "You want beds, they's in that other cabin. You want food, it'll be ready 'bout sundown. You pays in advance."

"Thank you," Renno said. "We will sleep in the open, but it is with pleasure that we accept your offer of food."

"I ain't offering," Mrs. Grinder said. "I'm providing. For a fee."

"Of course," Renno said.

"You want feed for your horses, that's extra."

Renno nodded.

"I'll send out my girl to take keer of the animals," Mrs. Grinder said. "You'll hear the bell for supper. You can pay me then."

A young Negro girl came hurrying out of the cabin. She walked with her head down and did not meet Renno's gaze as she took the reins of his horse.

"They's jest hay," the girl said.

"Give 'em all they can eat," Roy said.

"Yes, sir." For the first time the girl looked up. "Y'all come a long ways, sir?"

"A fur piece," Roy said. "Been up to St. Louis."

"T'other gentleman, the one that kilt hisself, he was from St. Louis," the girl said.

"Malinda, you git on 'bout taking care of them animals!" Mrs. Grinder yelled from the doorway.

The young girl led the horses away toward the stables after Roy and Renno removed their packs from the spare horses.

"Looks like a likely place over there," Roy said. He didn't move. "Sure you don't want to try the cabin?"

Renno laughed. "I like to sleep alone," he said. "At least without the company of various biting insects."

"Yeah, reckon you're right." Roy spat. "You didn't ask questions about what that slave girl said."

"There'll be time for that," Renno said.

Roy led the way across the trace toward a grove of trees. He halted and nodded toward a mound of fresh earth. "New grave," he remarked.

"So," Renno said.

Leaving Roy to start a fire, Renno walked once around the fresh grave. It had not rained since the earth was disturbed. He saw the tracks of four different men, those of a woman, and signs of one or two children, perhaps the prints of the Negro girl, who was still in the stable tending the horses. He walked across the trace. He deliberately made noise as he entered the stable. He didn't want to startle the child. She was in the hayloft, tossing down forkfuls of feed for the four animals. The horses had been unsaddled.

"That's hard work for a girl," Renno said with a smile.

"I don't mind," Malinda said. "I'll curry 'em after they eats a little."

"Yes, that will be fine," Renno told her.

"Supper'll be ready soon."

"You said that another party had come here from St. Louis?" Renno asked.

"Yes, sir. The gentleman that kilt hisself."

"Do you remember his name?"

"Yes, sir. It was Mr. Lewis."

Renno started. "Can you tell me how it happened?"

"Miz Grinder, she could tell hit better," the little slave said. "I hearn the shots, and I seen him laying there, poor man."

"Where?"

"In the cabin. The guest sleeping cabin."

"He shot himself?"

"Twicest."

"Two times?"

The girl tossed down one last forkful of hay. The horses were standing side by side, munching steadily. She came down the ladder with a flash of skinny black legs.

"Miz Grinder, she say he missed first time. Jest knocked a chunk outten his head."

"Does it bother you to talk about it?" Renno asked.

"No, sir. I seen folks scalped afore."

"He shot a chunk out of his head?"

"Right here," the girl said, touching her forehead. "And then he shot hisself in the side, here." She touched her side above her hipbone. "They was so much blood it took me the better part of the morning to clean it up, and I still didn't git all the stain outten the floorboards."

"Where were the men who were with Mr. Lewis when it happened?" Renno asked.

"Mr. Lewis's man and the Negro slave, they was sleeping here in the stable."

"And Mr. Neely?"

"He de other white man?"

"Yes."

"He come next morning."

"He didn't arrive with Mr. Lewis?"

"No, sir. Mr. Lewis, he come by hisself, and Miz Grinder she say, 'My husband he not home. But if you want a bed, they's the sleeping cabin.'"

"Where were Mr. Lewis's man and the Negro servant?"

"He say his servants they come later. They come after a while, and Miz Grinder she puts 'em in the stable."

"So Mr. Lewis was alone in the sleeping cabin when he shot himself?"

"Yes, sir. I hearn the shots."

"Did you go out to see what was happening?"

"No, sir. I was skeered."

"You said you saw Mr. Lewis lying in his own blood."

"That was next morning. Miz Grinder she wouldn't go out to the sleeping cabin until daylight. When we go in, he laying on he bed. Miz Grinder she say, 'You run down to the barn and get them fellers.' I run and get 'em, and Mr. Lewis's man, he name Pernier, he wearing fancy clothes like a gentleman wear. Then the other white gentleman he come, and they bury Mr. Lewis."

"What happened to Mr. Lewis's effects?"

"This Mr. Neely, he say he take Mr. Lewis's things to Nashville."

"Thank you, Malinda," Renno said. "You've been very helpful."

"Please, sir?"

"Yes?"

"I'd 'ppreciate it if'n you don't tell Miz Grinder I tole you this stuff."

Renno nodded. The girl moved toward the stable door.

"By the way," Renno said, "where was Mr. Grinder the night it happened?"

"He gone," Melinda said. "He got a farm down on the creek a few miles, and he was off there working."

"He didn't come home to help the others bury Mr. Lewis?"

"He didn't come home for a couple of days," the girl said.

As Renno returned to the campsite, where Roy had spread his blankets on the upwind side of the fire, a cowbell clattered from the cabins.

"You look like you got something to say," Roy ventured.

"The girl said that Lewis shot himself."

"Lordy, Lordy," Roy said, shaking his head.

"Twice."

Roy's eyebrows rose.

"First shot just knocked a chunk out of his forehead," Renno said.

"The hell you say."

"Second one was in the side, here."

"Determined feller, wasn't he?" Roy asked.

The cowbell clattered again.

"Grub's ready," Roy said. " 'Bout time, too."

The long days and weeks in Washington had begun to lose their excitement for Beth. For a time she had enjoyed the whirl of social activity that centered around Dolley Madison, but now the year was past its midpoint, and she found herself waking in the night, disturbed, because when she reached out her hand in her sleep to touch Renno, he was not there. She told herself that her reasons for staying in Washington were sound. She had received letters from her husband that told of Toshabe's death and of his and Roy's departure for St. Louis. It would be months before Renno could come for her, so it seemed logical that she should stay where she could pursue two goals: having the trade restrictions lifted from her ships and obtaining the repatriation of Little Hawk and James Ridley. With the help of the President's wife and Mr. Madison himself she was keeping steady pressure on the British representatives in Washington to move more swiftly in locating her illegally impressed stepson and his cousin. To her pleasure, Randall Farnsworth was doing his best to be helpful as well.

The date for Renna's marriage to Farnsworth had been set, and seamstresses were busy making a simple but elegant wedding gown for Renna and new dresses for Beth and Naomi. The worst of the summer's heat was past. The fevers that came with hot weather were slacking off, and there was less complaining about George Washington's having chosen a swamp for the site of the capital city.

Beth made her decision to go home several days before the scheduled wedding. She picked an evening free of social activity to announce her plans to Renna and Naomi.

"I imagine, Renna, that you will be accompanying your husband to England soon after the ceremony," Beth said, to open the subject.

"I hate to think of leaving you," Renna said.

"We'll miss the little ones," Beth said. "And you, too, of course."

Renna pouted prettily. "But not as much as you'll miss your grandchildren."

"I've decided to go overland through Virginia and Kentucky to Huntington Castle," Beth said.

"Oh, dear," Naomi said. "When?"

"Shortly after the wedding."

"Then I must go with you, I suppose," Naomi said.

"I want you to, but if you feel that you should stay here . . ."

"I want to see Hawk as soon as possible when he comes back to the United States."

"He may go to Wilmington first," Beth said. "He may even go to New Orleans and come up the river and the Natchez Trace to Rusog's town in the belief that Renno would have taken all of us home."

"Yes, I have thought of that. I'll go with you," Naomi said.

"Won't it be good to have your reunion with him at home?" Beth asked. She tried to submerge a recurring fear that Little Hawk might be dead. If that were the case, however, it would be best to have Naomi at home in Huntington Castle.

"Yes," Naomi agreed.

A Negro servant entered the room. "Miss Beth, they's a young gentleman here axing for Miss Naomi. He's—"

The servant did not get to finish. Little Hawk burst into the room. His blond hair had been allowed to grow long. He was bronzed by the sun, and to Naomi he was the most beautiful sight she'd ever seen. She leaped to her feet with a glad cry and rushed into his arms.

Renna's initial burst of thankfulness at the safe return of her brother was smothered in shock when she looked past the embracing couple and into the smiling eyes of the husband she had given up for dead. She felt the blood rush from her head, and the world went dim for a moment in giddy happiness; but then a horror of realization came over her, devouring her soul.

Beau was alive, and she was scheduled to marry Randall Farnsworth in two days. Her husband was alive and had come back to her, and only hours before, in the warm night, she had lain brazenly and sated in the arms of another man.

"Renna?" Beau asked, moving toward her swiftly. "You're not going to faint, are you?"

"No," she quavered, rising to meet him. But as his lips sought hers in gladness and love, she wanted the oblivion that she had flirted with, wanted the lightness in her head to take her and give her at least temporary escape from her bitter regret.

Chapter Thirteen

Ta-na was very tired. He had been paddling steadily for eighteen hours. Gao slept in the bottom of the canoe, not moving even when Ta-na shifted the paddle from one side to the other and dripped water onto his face. The day was coming to an end, and Ta-na began to look for a likely place to beach the canoe and make camp. He decided to go just a bit farther, to keep moving until the sun was almost touching the earth in the west. As it happened, it was a good decision, for he saw the log palisade of a fort just before the long shadows began to turn into darkness.

He steered toward a landing, ran the prow of the canoe up onto the shore, and stepped out to face two uniformed men. They held their rifles at the ready and looked at him with suspicion.

"I am Ta-na-wun-da of the Seneca," he said, holding up his right hand in peace. "My brother is wounded. I'd be very grateful if you would help me get him to a doctor."

"Speaks English right good fer an Injun, don't he?" said one of the soldiers.

"I have information for Governor Harrison as well," Ta-na said.

"That so?" drawled the other soldier.

"How come you comin' downriver from up-country?" asked the first man.

"My information is for Governor Harrison," Ta-na said.

"We don't need no smart-assed Injuns 'round here," said the taller of the two soldiers. "Best you git back in your little canoe and go back where you come from."

"Perhaps you would like to refer the matter to your officer before you make such a decision." Ta-na's blood felt like fire in his veins. Fury boiled just behind his impassive mask.

"I told you to git," the tall soldier said, starting to lift his rifle.

Ta-na's hand moved with snakelike quickness. His pistol appeared as if by magic, and the sound of the cocking of the hammer was loud in the quiet of the evening.

"Point your rifle at me, and you're a dead man," Ta-na hissed.

"You can't get both of us with one pistol," the man said, licking his lips nervously.

"But I'll get you," Ta-na said. "Now, if you don't mind, will you please summon an officer."

"Do it," the tall man said, unable to take his eyes off the dark muzzle of Ta-na's pistol.

"Officer of the guard!" the other man bellowed.

A young lieutenant emerged from a sally port, buttoning his tunic. When he saw the pistol in Ta-na's hand, he halted, then moved forward cautiously, his hand on his own pistol. "What's going on here?" he demanded as he drew near.

"This Injun threatened us," said the man under the muzzle of Ta-na's weapon.

"I have information for Governor Harrison," Ta-na repeated, forcing himself to be patient and calm. "My brother is wounded and needs medical attention."

"Put the gun away," the lieutenant said.

Ta-na slipped the weapon back into his belt.

The lieutenant stepped toward the canoe. Gao was awake, but his face was burning with fever. "Fetch a stretcher detail," the officer ordered. "Ask the surgeon to report to the medical shack."

The tall soldier gave Ta-na a hard look, then moved away.

"And you," the officer asked, "who are you?"

"I am Ta-na-wun-da of the Seneca."

"You're a long way from Seneca country."

"We come from the south, from the land of the Cherokee."

The young lieutenant looked puzzled. "Seneca in the south?"

"Governor Harrison will know," Ta-na said. "Tell him that I am the son of the sachem Renno, grandson of Colonel Roy Johnson."

"That will mean something to the governor?"

"It will," Ta-na said.

Two men came carrying a litter, and Gao was placed on it carefully while Ta-na watched tensely. Gao chewed on his lower lip to keep from crying out with pain. Ta-na walked by his side.

The surgeon was a short, stout, middle-aged man who smelled of rum; but his eyes were alert, and his voice was firm as he ordered the men to put Gao on a treatment table. His hands were sure as he finished cutting away the leg of Gao's breeches.

"What's this?" the doctor asked, pulling at the down with which Ta-na had stuffed the wound. He answered his own question. "Not buzzard down."

"No. It's from a goose," Ta-na said.

"Well, it stopped the bleeding all right, but—" He fingered the swollen red flesh around the entry wound. A grunt escaped Gao's lips.

"Speak English, son?" the doctor asked.

"Does a bear shit in the woods?" Gao asked through tight lips.

"Guess that means yes," the doctor said, and chuckled. He took forceps and began to pull the feathers from the wound. "It doesn't look as if it's gone septic. Your friend here—"

"My brother," Gao said.

"—did a pretty good job, and the ball didn't hit bone, so I reckon you'll be doing rain dances in a couple of weeks."

"I don't like rain," Gao said.

"Come to think of it, neither do I," the doctor said. He picked up a bottle. "This is going to hurt a bit, so if you feel like yelling, have at it."

Gao hissed through his teeth as the doctor poured whiskey over the wound. There was more pain as both the entry and exit holes were cleansed and subjected to more of the fiery alcohol. Then Gao was lying back, at ease, with a clean bandage on his thigh.

The doctor turned to Ta-na and the lieutenant. "I'll put him to bed and have him fed when he gets hungry." He put his hand on Ta-na's shoulder. "Don't look so worried. He'll be fine. He's young and strong, and it's a clean wound."

After Ta-na was satisfied that Gao was in good hands, he was asked, not too politely, to accompany a sergeant. They walked out of the fort, through the little village that had grown up along the Wabash, and into the walnut grove that formed a setting for Grouseland. A servant answered the door of the governor's impressive brick home, and soon Ta-na was in a handsomely furnished study facing William Henry Harrison and the young lieutenant. The sergeant who had been Ta-na's guide clicked his heels and withdrew.

"General, this is the man who said you would know him and that you'd want to see him," the lieutenant said.

"Do I know you?" Harrison asked, cocking his heavily maned head toward Ta-na.

"You know my father, sir, and my grandfather," Ta-na said. "I am the son of the Seneca sachem Renno. My grandfather is Colonel Roy Johnson."

"I know them indeed!" Harrison stepped forward

and with expert knowledge exchanged the Seneca warrior's grip with Ta-na. "Your name?" he asked.

"Ta-na-wun-da."

"What can I do for the son of an old friend?"

"You recently sent a message to my grandfather and my father," Ta-na said. Suddenly he felt terribly young and inadequate. He spread his hands, speechless for the moment.

"Do I get the impression that you are the answer to my request?" Harrison asked.

"With my brother," Ta-na said. He straightened his shoulders. "My grandfather was unable to answer your summons because of the illness of my grandmother. My father was away. We have come in their place."

Harrison's long face was softened by a smile. "It is not that I am unappreciative, my boy—"

Ta-na interrupted, cutting off what he anticipated to be a negative response from the governor. "Tecumseh has made his peace with Tarhe the Crane. The Wyandot will fight with Tecumseh's alliance."

Harrison's smile faded. "How do you know this?"

"We came here from the village at Tippecanoe," Ta-na said.

"I think you'd better sit down, young man," Harrison said. "Can I offer you something? Food? Something to drink?"

"Nothing, sir," Ta-na said. He took the chair indicated by Harrison. "Tecumseh is hopeful that the Sac and the Fox will join with him because of the building of the new fort on the west bank of the Mississippi."

"I am not surprised," Harrison said grimly. "How many warriors at Tippecanoe?"

"A thousand, no more."

"Tribes?"

"Shawnee, of course," Ta-na said. "Kickapoo, a few Wyandot—"

"With more coming, if what you say is true."

"Yes, sir. Ottawa, Chippewa, Potawatomi, Miami, a handful of Delaware, and sprinklings of others from the Iroquois country and from west and south."

"Tecumseh was there?"

"He was there," Ta-na said.

"Did you talk to him?"

"Briefly." Ta-na smiled wryly as he remembered the confrontation with the Shawnee on the riverbank. "Mostly we listened."

"Yes, he is a great orator," Harrison conceded. "Last time I listened to him, he almost convinced me that I should pull back across the Ohio."

"Just almost," Ta-na said, grinning. His grin faded quickly as he realized his temerity.

"Whose side are you on, son?" Harrison asked, raising a bushy eyebrow.

"My brother and I offer our services as scouts," Ta-na responded.

Harrison rubbed his chin. "Who shot your brother in the thigh?"

"We were not careful enough when we decided to leave Tecumseh's town. It was necessary for me to kill one of Tecumseh's war chiefs."

Harrison released a loud, half-strangled cough. When he recovered, he asked, "Who was this chief whose death became necessary?"

"He was called Red Horse."

"I'll be damned," Harrison said. "If that's the case, it wouldn't be a good idea for either of you to show your face up around Tippecanoe again."

"No, sir."

"If Tecumseh's people know you, it would be dangerous for you to work for me. I need scouts who can penetrate Indian country and keep me informed about what the Panther is up to."

"There are ways to gain information without being overt about it," Ta-na said.

"I reckon you're right," Harrison said. "As I recall, when your father was scouting for Anthony Wayne, he was known to just about every war chief in Little Turtle's crowd." He rose and paced. "Well, Thomas, if you want it, you've got a job."

"Thank you, sir, but why do you call me Thomas?"

"Good name," Harrison said. "A good American name. I had a talk with your father once, boy, and he made it clear to me that he felt the Indian's only choice was to join the United States, to give up the old way of life. Seems to me you've made the same choice."

"That does not mean that I will take a white man's name," Ta-na said.

"Suit yourself," Harrison said. "But I hope you agree with your father's teachings. My sole purpose for being here in this territory is to push the tribes all the way across the Mississippi River. After that there'll be someone else coming along to push them farther to the west. The world's too small, Thomas, to allow one man, one Indian, to roam freely over thousands of acres of virgin wilderness. Big as this country is, there's not enough space for a few thousand Indians to live by the hunt, using up millions of acres, while white men who can produce enough food to feed a family from a few acres of good ground and have some left over for trade to nonfarmers are hungry for land." He looked closely at Ta-na. "Does that make you uneasy?"

Ta-na did not answer immediately. Finally he nodded and said, "My friend, a very wise Cherokee called Se-quo-i, broke his leg trying to use a white man's plow. To this day he walks with a limp. In my village many of the women still use sharp sticks to plant beans and squash and corn. The men hunt. But many of the Cherokee have built log cabins in the style of the white man, and no lodge or longhouse is complete without the metal cook pot of the white man. No warrior is well armed without a blade made of the white man's metal and a white man's gun. One day, I fear, others will have to drive the point of the metal plow into the earth, as Se-quo-i tried to do."

"We understand each other, then?" Harrison asked.

"Yes, sir. I think so."

"You will want to work with your brother?"

"The doctor said that he will be able to walk in about two weeks."

"Good, good. Take care of him. I'll have quarters assigned to you. You will report directly to me. I have scouts out, of course, on a regular schedule. If you get restless and decide to take a walk in the woods up along the Wabash, I won't try to stop you. But if you do, be careful."

Emily Elizabeth, awakened from her nap, rubbed her eyes sleepily and squinted them to stare at the smiling male face that was bending over her.

"*Papa!*" she cried in French, lifting her arms. "*Papa.*"

Beau took his daughter into his arms. Tears ran down his cheeks. She smelled of clean soap and sleep.

"I knew you'd come back," Emily said. She trilled the words in French. "Have you seen Louis?"

"No, my darling, I haven't."

"He's still asleep," she said, disengaging from Beau's arms and pointing to the crib near her own bed. "He's still a baby, you know."

Beau, with Emily sitting on one arm, looked down at the sleeping face of his son and saw his own dark hair combined with Renna's nose and mouth. When the boy stirred and opened his eyes, they were startlingly blue, like his mother's.

"Louis doesn't know you, Papa," Emily said.

"It will be my pleasure to get to know him," Beau said, "and to kiss you until you giggle." He nuzzled her neck, and she obliged his request with a peal of laughter.

Renna stood just inside the door of the children's room, and her heart was a leaden weight inside her.

In the next room another father was being reintroduced to his children. Little Hawk hefted first one of the twins and then the other.

"You two have grown," he said.

"Yes, children do," Naomi said with a happy smile.

"You're Michael," Little Hawk said to one of the boys.

"Me So-wing Hawk," the boy said.

"Soaring Hawk," Little Hawk said. "Yes. In your own language—" He paused, looked at Naomi. "I guess they haven't had a chance to learn any Seneca."

"You can teach them," she said.

The other twin, slightly smaller, lifted his arms and

made claws with his hands. "Me 'tandin' Bear," he growled.

"Yes," Little Hawk said. "Michael Soaring Hawk and you—" He hugged the child closer. "You are Joseph Standing Bear."

"Why?" Michael asked.

"Why not?" Little Hawk countered.

"Why?" Joseph echoed.

"Where?" Little Hawk teased, looking around.

"Who?" Michael asked, expecting to see someone.

"When?" Little Hawk asked.

"What?" Michael asked, puzzled.

"Why?" Joseph said.

"A most intelligent conversation," Naomi said, rolling her eyes.

Beth was thinking, *Now I can go home. Now we can all go home.* When a knock came at the door, she walked slowly to answer it, deep in pleasant anticipation.

"Randall," she said, and a chill passed down her spine. "It's you."

"I was going to stay away, Mrs. Harper, to give you ladies a chance to get your chores done, but it's terribly lonely out there."

"Come in, Randall," Beth said.

"If I'm intruding—"

"No," she said. "In fact, your timing is good." She waited until the Englishman entered the room and turned, hat in hand, to face her. "We have had wonderful news," she said.

"About your son?"

"He's here," Beth said.

"We must thank God," Farnsworth said. "I trust he is well."

"He is well."

Farnsworth studied her face. "I would think, my dear Mrs. Harper, that events would have you all smiles. Is there something wrong?"

"Only for you," Beth said.

"Something is wrong for me?"

Naomi came into the drawing room, with Little Hawk close behind. "Well, Farnsworth," Little Hawk said, extending his hand.

"It is so very good to see you," Farnsworth said. "I thank God that you're safe and that you've returned in time for the wedding."

"Congratulations," Little Hawk said. "Who is the lucky lady?"

"I'm sorry," Farnsworth said. "You had no way of knowing, did you? Your sister has kindly consented to be my wife."

Little Hawk was momentarily stunned.

In the children's room Beau fell silent and put a finger to Emily Elizabeth's lips. "I know that voice," he said.

Renna knew it all too well, and the guilt of her betrayal paralyzed her with indecisiveness and remorse. Beau put Emily down on her bed and reached reflexively for his sword. His hand touched only his hip. He stepped from the room and stood in the entrance to the parlor to see Randall Farnsworth smiling, smiling, smiling at Beth and Little Hawk. He looked around quickly, seeking a weapon. There were only women's things, decorative pieces, items of furniture. Beth caught his eyes. She looked stricken.

"Here's Beau," Beth said.

Farnsworth turned. His face went pale, and as Beau had done in the children's room, he reached for a weapon that was not there. Gentlemen did not go armed while calling on a lady in the capital city of the United States.

Every iota of his manhood urged Beau to the attack; but the blood of kings ran in his veins, and he was in the parlor of a hotel in the presence of ladies and children. At great cost he contained himself. While Farnsworth swayed indecisively on his feet, Beau stepped forward slowly, shoulders back, hands at his side, head held high. His hand lashed out, and the impact of his palm on Farnsworth's cheek was ringingly loud.

Renna entered the room in time to see the blow. Farnsworth took a quick step backward.

"I will give you another chance, Englishman," Beau grated, his voice heated with his fury. "Today. No later. Since you chose the pistol when we met in Lisbon—although you did not do me the courtesy of allowing the same weapon to me—pistols it will be. My brother Little Hawk will inform you of the time and place if you will be so kind as to tell him where you can be reached."

Little Hawk nodded.

"Your servant, sir," Farnsworth said, bowing quickly. "The ladies know my address."

"Stop playing the gentleman with me," Beau snarled. "Leave, before I forget myself."

Farnsworth's exit was made with some poise and with no evidence of haste.

"Beau?" Beth asked.

"He is the man who shot me in Lisbon," Beau said. "He asked me if I were the comte de Beaujolais, and then he shot me."

"Beau, are you sure?" Beth asked.

"How could I forget?" Beau asked. "I felt sure that his was the last face I'd see on this earth."

"But that means—" Beth could not go on.

"That means," Little Hawk said, "that he deliberately looked for Beau in Lisbon and shot him so that he would be free to pay court to Renna."

Beau's jaw dropped, and his face flamed with emotion. He whirled to face Renna. "He dared approach you?"

Renna, trembling violently, could not speak. Beth, seeing her distress, rushed to her stepdaughter's side and put her arm around Renna's shoulders. "It's all right," she whispered. "It's all right. He's back."

"Renna?" Beau asked, anguish in his voice. "Renna, don't worry. I'll kill the blackguard, and then it will be over."

Renna's torso shook with her sobs. Beth turned to Beau. "Excuse us for a few minutes, please. I'm afraid this has been a bit much for all of us." She led Renna through the doorway.

"Hawk, you will make the arrangements?" Beau asked when they were alone.

"Dueling has been against the law in the United States for a long time," Hawk said.

"How can that be so when Aaron Burr killed Alexander Hamilton only a few years ago?" Beau demanded.

"Burr had to go into hiding," Little Hawk said.

"It is, I think, a law to be ignored. How else can a man protect his honor?"

"This isn't France," Little Hawk said. "The United States likes to think of itself as a civilized Christian nation. I'm afraid the authorities would take a dim view of your going around killing your enemies on the streets of Washington."

"If you will not help me, I will arrange it myself," Beau said.

"No." Little Hawk shook his head. "I will be your second."

Beth led Renna into her own room and sat her on the bed. "You can't be blamed," she said. "You did nothing wrong. You thought Beau was dead. You were deceived shamefully by Randall, but there's no real harm done. Beau will not hold it against you. Of that I am sure."

"Oh, God," Renna said, and it was both a moan of distress and a prayer.

"Go to him," Beth said.

"No. Not now."

A pain of understanding began to grow inside Beth. She had not allowed herself to speculate about the relationship between Renna and Randall because they were both adults, both responsible people; but Renna's extreme reaction spoke volumes.

"Renna?"

"I can't face him, not after—"

"Listen to me," Beth said. "Whatever happened, you did it as a woman in love, a woman alone, a woman who had lost her husband. What you did or did not do is known only by you, and perhaps it would be best if it stayed that way."

She felt a surge of an old sadness in her own breast, for once, long before, she had said good-bye to Renno and had found herself in the arms of another man. To his great credit, Renno had never asked a single question about the time she'd spent in England while he was in Africa, and afterward, he had never questioned her about her social activities at the court in London.

"I could not deceive him further," Renna said. "I cannot lie to him."

"Then tell him now, before he fights Farnsworth. It will bring accuracy to his eyes and quickness to his hand."

"Oh, my God," Renna whispered. She pulled away and flung herself facedown onto the bed.

"Stay, then, and be a coward," Beth said angrily. "Hide yourself away and let him face Farnsworth, believing that you no longer love him." She waited for a moment to see if her words would shock Renna into action, but her stepdaughter was still lying on her face, sobbing wildly, when Beth closed the door behind her.

She met Beau in the hallway.

"What's wrong?" he asked, moving toward the door.

Beth took his arm and stopped him. "Give her a few minutes, Beau."

"Yes," he said, then swallowed. "This Farnsworth—" He couldn't go on. "She—"

"She mourned you," Beth said. "We all mourned you. She was a woman without her husband. She couldn't bring herself to go back to France, where she would be even more alone, separated from her family. Randall was persistent, and he gave us all the impression that he was a gentleman."

Beau swallowed again, and it seemed to hurt his throat. "I understand." He pulled against Beth's arm. "I must go to her."

"Perhaps that would be best," Beth agreed.

Beau stood beside the bed and looked down on Renna's back. She was no longer weeping. When he spoke, his voice was soft. "My poor little Seneca maiden," he said.

Renna gave no indication of having heard.

"So much guilt for such a small girl," Beau said. He sat on the edge of the bed and put his hand on her shoulder. "I want you to turn over, my love. I want you to look at me."

She turned her head. Her eyes were red with weeping. He lifted her gently and placed her on her back. She turned her head away. He put his fingers on her chin and made her face him.

"Do you think that anything you could do would make me stop loving you?" he asked.

She snuffled.

He laughed fondly, brought out a handkerchief, and wiped her nose. "We are shameless, we men," Beau said. "Be we English or French or American, we use any means, fair or foul, to gain our desires with a beautiful woman. Not that you are weak, my dear. I, too, know the scourge of loneliness. I was alone. But *I* knew that you were alive, and I had every reason to hope that I would see you again. I can only imagine the devastation I would have felt had I been told that you were dead. And if that had happened, my dear, perhaps I, too, would have accepted a pair of sweet arms to help me forget my pain."

"Beau, you don't understand," Renna said in a low voice.

"If I do not hold you to blame, why must you blame yourself?"

"You don't know—"

"Nor do I want to know or need to know," he said softly, bending to brush his lips lightly over her forehead. "It doesn't matter." He chuckled. "After all, I was dead. What you think you did to me, you were doing to a dead man, and nothing can hurt the dead, can it?"

He was alive, his body warm against hers. His weight was a familiar dearness on her. His lips knew every nuance of her kiss. He had been dead, and now he was alive again. *Oh, manitous,* she wondered, *how could I have ever surrendered to Randall Farnsworth that which was Beau's?*

She was furious, furious with the fates that had led Farnsworth into her life in the first place, furious with being cheated, tricked into thinking that there was nothing left in life for her but marriage to Farnsworth. But most of all, she was furious with herself. Her anger boiled over into momentary irrationality, and there was the cold hatred of the mountain lioness for the slayer of her mate as she said, "Kill him, Beau. Kill him quickly."

He pushed her to arm's length. Her eyes were ice blue and bright. "He tried to take you from me," she said. "I want you to kill him."

"That's my little Seneca," Beau said. "And as it happens, killing him is exactly what I intend to do."

She accepted his lips, and for the first time since she had seen his face, her heart stopped aching. A deluge of passion and gladness filled her. She could see herself in his eyes, and she knew that he meant exactly what he had said, that nothing mattered but their being together again.

"Forgive me," she whispered.

"Oh, my love," Beau whispered as he held her close. "There is nothing to forgive."

As Randall Farnsworth left Beth Harper's hotel suite, he had no eyes for the beautiful autumn day, the stretch of green in front of the Capitol Building, the expanse leading down toward the Potomac. The sky was clear and blue not for Farnsworth but for others, for he had been robbed of the object of his desire.

A one-legged beggar approached him on a street corner. "Help a poor feller, sir?"

Farnsworth snarled and gave the cripple a nasty shove, sending him to land on his posterior in the gutter. A passerby, outraged, shouted, "See here, sir!"

His lips set in a snarl, Farnsworth glared at the meddlesome intruder. The man turned away quickly.

At the British ministry a red-coated guard who was merely observing standard procedure asked Farnsworth for his identification.

"Get out of my way, fool," Farnsworth hissed.

In his quarters he paced, rage and disappointment

boiling in him. He cursed himself for not having made sure that the Frenchman was dead in Lisbon. Another pistol ball to the head or a clean thrust of a knife to his heart would have done it. He had been so close to having Renna as his own. He had possessed her, and the heat of their lovemaking would be in his blood always. The wedding had been only days away, and then, by some freak of fate, he was out of the race forever. It would make no difference now if he killed the Frenchman; there would be no hope of winning Renna. She knew that he had tried to kill her husband.

He whirled at a knock on the door. A servant said, "Mr. Hawk Harper to see you, Colonel."

Farnsworth stood with his hands behind his back as Little Hawk entered the room.

"You know why I'm here," Little Hawk said.

"You may dispense with the formalities," Farnsworth said.

"There is a small meadow on the riverbank beside a hidden cove two miles west of the city," Little Hawk said. "I will be seconding the count. You may bring no more than two seconds."

"And the weapons?"

"Pistols. Two per man. Do you have weapons?"

"I do."

"The count desires satisfaction as quickly as possible."

"He does not wait on me."

"One hour before sundown. Today," Little Hawk said. "I will arrange transportation for you. The driver will know the site."

"Kind of you," Farnsworth said coldly.

"He will be waiting for you in front of the ministry at three o'clock." Little Hawk bowed. "Until then."

"Yes, yes," Farnsworth said impatiently, and turned away.

"Oh, there's one more thing," Hawk said.

Farnsworth looked back just in time to meet a round-house punch that sent him staggering.

"Sorry, old man. Not very sporting of me," Little

Hawk conceded. "But I *am* her brother." The door closed behind him.

Once again Farnsworth paced. Historically, dueling had never been as prevalent in England as it had been in France and Germany, but it was not unknown. In the modern days of the new nineteenth century, there were occasional affairs of honor in England. In fact, it had only been in recent years that the age-old concept of judicial dueling, the practice of determining guilt or innocence through a fight to the death, had been abandoned.

Since he would not be breaking any law of his own country, Farnsworth came to look upon the scheduled meeting with Beaujolais as a welcome opportunity to finish the job he had bungled in Lisbon. He would not have the woman, but he would at least have the satisfaction of knowing that the Frenchman would never again taste her charms. He opened a drawer, took out a brace of pistols, and busied himself with cleaning them, oiling them carefully, and recharging them with powder and shot.

The pistol balls were heavy in his hand. The weight of them reminded him of the impact of the ball that had smashed into his shoulder in Portugal. He lifted a pistol, sighted along the barrel, put it down, walked to the door, and summoned a servant.

"Find out for me when the next ship sails for a British port either in the home country or the islands," he said.

The man returned to report that a warship acting as diplomatic courier was sailing on the evening tide from Annapolis. It took Farnsworth only a half hour to pack.

He arrived at the wharf minutes before the ship's crew began to cast off lines to ease her away into the river. It was one hour before sundown.

Farnsworth stood at the rail and watched the Annapolis docks fade into the dusk. The night was starry and balmy. It was pleasant to walk the deck of a warship again, to feel the swell of the sea under him, to be going back to England. He had lost a woman; but he had position, and he was young. His life was before him.

He did not have to be present in a meadow on the banks of the Potomac as the sun set to know what was being said about him by the Frenchman and the white Indian, but that did not really matter. He was sailing back to the wars and to his destiny. He was a professional soldier, and as such, he was confident that he could have killed Beaujolais easily. It was just that he had found himself in a situation where even if he won the fight, he had already lost the war. He saw no real risk in dueling the Frenchman, but neither did he see any gain.

He was confident that sooner or later England and her allies would smash Napoleon and, in defeated France, perhaps he would meet the comte de Beaujolais again, with more satisfying results.

"The blackguard is a coward," Beau fumed. "He was brave enough in Lisbon with a pistol in his hands against an unarmed man, but where is he now?"

"I imagine we will discover that tomorrow," Little Hawk said, as he boxed the set of dueling pistols that Beth had borrowed from a retired army officer who lived in the same hotel.

"Someday I will see him again," Beau vowed.

"Perhaps," Little Hawk agreed. He was berating himself for not having kept an eye on Farnsworth so that when it became necessary, he could have shamed the Englishman into keeping his engagement of honor or, that failing, delivered him by force to the meadow. He was not surprised, in retrospect, that Farnsworth had run. After all, the man was a cold-blooded murderer, and quite often those who administered death so casually knew paralyzing fear when they faced the same fate.

Dolley Madison, all atwitter with the excitement of knowing that her friends were happy again with their men at home, planned a special dinner party in honor of the count and the gallant young former marine officer. James Madison remembered Little Hawk well as the young man who had acted as Jefferson's agent in North Africa. He saw to it that Little Hawk and Naomi were seated to his right. Old French royalty and his beautiful young wife had to take a lesser position, by Dolley's side.

"I want to hear how you were impressed," Madison said as the meal was being served.

The President listened with interest as Little Hawk described the incident and briefly recounted the method of his escape.

"It's undeclared war, isn't it?" Madison asked. "Men are killing and being killed."

"In a small way and in many different places, yes, sir, it is war," Little Hawk said.

"No war is inconsequential to the men who die fighting it," Madison said. "I hope that you did not feel abandoned by your country. I assure you that we were using all the means at our disposal, short of a declaration of war, to have you and your cousin returned."

"I never doubted it," Little Hawk said.

Madison sighed. "Significant numbers of our countrymen are crying out for war against the old enemy, you know."

"Yes, sir."

"The war sentiment is especially prevalent in the west, in your part of the nation. There are men there who want us not only to declare war on England but to invade Canada and the Spanish Floridas as well."

"Sounds like some of the frontiersmen I know," Little Hawk said with a chuckle.

"Men like Andy Jackson?" Madison asked.

"I think Mr. Jackson would jump at the chance to take a militia army into the Floridas."

"He may have his opportunity," Madison said. "How about you, young Hawk? If you're ready to resume your military career, I have a job for you. I need someone in the White House who speaks the language of our sterling warriors of the army and the navy. The position carries the rank of captain. I assume you would want your uniform to be that of your original branch of the service?"

"You make me feel very proud, Mr. President," Little Hawk said. "May I presume to ask you to hold that offer open for a few months?"

"That's a reasonable request," Madison said, "in view of your forced separation from your family."

"I do want to go home," Little Hawk confirmed. "My grandmother is dead, and I want to see my grandfather and father and the other members of the family."

"Shall we plan a fresh start in the new year, then?" Madison asked.

"Thank you, sir."

The President smiled at Naomi. "Dolley will be very disappointed if you don't bring your charming wife back to Washington with you."

"I would like that very much, sir," Naomi responded, blushing with pleasure.

"Dolley can help you find suitable accommodations."

"Mrs. Madison has been so gracious to my family in my absence that I would hesitate to impose on her further."

"Nonsense," Madison said. "Dolley likes nothing better than arranging things." He sipped his wine thoughtfully. "You know, Hawk, the time is swiftly coming when this nation will need all of its young men of courage and ability. I am quite serious in saying that there will be a place for you when you return."

Chapter Fourteen

The evening meal at Grinder's Stand was a simple one —corn and venison stew served with slabs of coarse pone baked with water. If one wanted to pay extra, there was whiskey, but both Roy and Renno settled for water served in thick-sided, fire-baked pots of Chickasaw design. The table was made from three rough-hewn planks. The chairs were homemade constructions of bent-willow branches. Mrs. Grinder sat at the head of the table, with her daughter, Bethenia, beside her. Tin plates were set at the far end of the table for the men, who were served by the little Negro slave girl who had cared for the horses. The Grinder daughter appeared to be younger than the black girl. Renno guessed her age at more than ten.

Coins passed from Renno's hand to Mrs. Grinder's before any food appeared. The woman lowered her head to lessen the distance between her mouth and the plate and began to eat by stuffing huge spoonfuls between her tight, parched lips. Roy sampled the stew, nodded, and crumbled corn pone into it.

Renno respected the woman's silence until the meal was over, but when she rose and began to brush pone crumbs off her skirt, he said, "Mrs. Grinder, may we please have a word with you?"

She looked at him through narrowed eyes and nodded.

"If you'll have a seat," Renno said.

"Malinda," Mrs. Grinder said harshly, "git this here table cleared."

"Mrs. Grinder," Renno said, "Governor Lewis was a friend of mine. I'd be interested to hear from you just exactly what happened the night he came here."

"Told the other gentleman all about it," Mrs. Grinder said in a low voice.

"What gentleman was that?"

"Mr. Lewis's traveling companion, Mr. Neely."

"Would you mind very much telling it again?" Renno asked. He took a silver coin from his pocket and let it ring against the rough wood of the tabletop.

"Well, I reckon it won't hurt nothing to tell it again," the woman said. She cleared her throat and spat on the floor. "He come up jest at sundown and asked if'n he could stay the night. I 'uz all by myself here, 'cept for the young un and my girl, and I 'uz jest a little techy about him 'cause he had a kind of wild look in his eye."

"Go on," Renno said encouragingly.

"He had on a long blue-and-white-striped riding gown to keep the dust offen his clothes. I asked him if he was alone, and he said he had two servants who'd come on later, so I told him if'n he wanted a bed to go to the sleeping cabin. He asked me if'n I had any spirits, so I had the girl bring him some, and he took no more'n a couple of swigs. He went off to the sleeping cabin, and his two servants come up—one of them a nigger like my Malinda, the t'other some kind of furriner. His name was Pernier. I hearn Mr. Lewis ask the furriner where was his powder."

"His gunpowder?" Roy asked.

"I took him to mean that," Mrs. Grinder said. "I didn't hear what this here Pernier said. I went off to see to supper. Mr. Lewis, he was walking back and forth, back and forth, out there by the sleeping cabin. I warn't trying to pry, mind you, but I hearn him talking to hisself like he was outten his head."

"Was he raving?" Renno asked. "Or did what he say make sense?"

She shook her head. "Hit didn't make no sense to me. All about honorable sirs and Mr. Presidents and stuff like that. And he kept saying he'd vouch for something. The two servants, they'd gone off to the barn, and I tole 'em I'd have Malinda bring them their grub, so we 'uz more or less alone with Mr. Lewis, jest me and my girl and the nigger. It got right techy here, what with him stomping around and talking high and mighty to hisself. He didn't eat but a mouthful, and then he went off and smoked his pipe and allowed it was a right pretty evening, just as normal as you please before he started walking around in the yard agin.

"I had the girl make his bed, but he said he would sleep on the floor, since he was used to it, and he had his own buffaler robe and all. I said well and good if'n that was his wish and went off to see that Malinda did the kitchen proper. I hearn him through the kitchen winder making speeches like a judge or something, and it give me the cold shivers, the way he 'uz carrying on. I didn't sleep much, I tell you. I 'uz 'bout half-awake when I hearn the first shot, and then I hearn the t'other one. I hearn something fall in the sleeping cabin, and I hearn someone say 'Oh, Lord.' "

"Is that when you went out to find him dead?" Renno asked.

"Not on your life," the woman said, widening her eyes and shaking her head. "I warn't about to go out there in the dark. No, sir. First thing I knowed I hearn someone sorta scratching and pounding at the door, and I peeped through the logs. It 'uz him. He said, 'Madam, give me some water.' He said, 'Help me with my wounds.' I saw him stagger off and stumble agin a stump my husband ain't dug outten the yard yet, and then he crawled off and sat down agin a tree trunk."

"You knew the man was wounded, and you wouldn't help?" Roy asked.

"Mister, I 'uz a woman alone, and they's some bad people on this trace, let me tell you. I had my little girl and my propity to think about, too. I kept my door locked. Later on I hearn someone on the porch at the water bucket, and I figured maybe he 'uz all right and gitting hisself a little drink. When it come light, me and the girl and the nigger we went out to the sleeping cabin, and there he was on his robe, all blood. They 'uz a chunk tore outten his head right here." She touched her forehead. "And they 'uz another bullet hole in his side."

"An' they 'uz knife cuts on his arms and laigs," said Bethenia Grinder in a solemn, little girl's voice.

"You hesh," her mother said.

"Knife cuts?" Roy asked.

"I cain't rightly say. They 'uz so much blood."

Roy looked at Renno with his eyebrows raised.

Mrs. Grinder continued. "He said, 'Madam, take my rifle and put me out of my pain.'"

"He was still alive?" Renno asked, incredulous.

"Offered me all the money he had in his trunk. He said, 'Dying is so hard 'cause I am so strong.'"

"What did you do?" Renno asked.

"Nothing I could do."

"How long did it take him to die?" Roy asked.

"'Bout two hours, I guess. I didn't have no clock to put on it, but it warn't long after sunup."

"And the money in the trunk?" Renno asked.

The woman's face became sullen. "Ain't nobody can accuse me of stealing."

"That was not my intention," Renno said quickly.

"Mr. Neely, he taken them trunks. If'n they 'uz money in 'em, he taken that, too."

"Where was your husband all this time, Mrs. Grinder?"

"Off working the farm."

"Did he come home the day after Mr. Lewis died?"

"Nobody come but Mr. Neely. He took keer of Mr. Lewis's necessaries and buried him out there near by the trace, saying that Mr. Lewis was a great man and that his grave should be put where folks could see it and remember him. He left me some money, telling me to have my husband put a fence around it to keep the hogs from digging him up."

"There's no fence that I saw," Roy said.

"My husband been too busy what with his own farming," she said. "Out here a man has to think of feeding his family first." She rose and brushed again at her dingy skirts. "Well, I don't know 'bout you gentlemen, but I'm a working woman, and I need my rest. You need some grub 'fore you start off in the morning, Malinda will give you something."

"Thank you," Renno said.

Renno lay on his back, his hands under his head. The fires in the sky were dancing. One of them died, racing across the spangled blackness in a trace of flame before disappearing.

"Some good man's spirit just went west," Roy said.

"I'm surprised you're still awake."

"Can't sleep for trying to figure out how a man like Lewis, who lived with guns, faced up to bears, fought Injuns, and got shot in the ass once, could try to shoot himself in the head and miss."

"It does pose some interesting questions," Renno said.

"And that woman. Hell, she's half-Chickasaw. She was born and bred in these woods. Scared to go out to see what was going on? My bet is she wouldn't be skeered of a pack of wolves with the foaming fits. Something don't ring true, Renno."

"I wonder how much money Lewis was carrying."

"Couldn't have been much, if he was as broke as they said in St. Louis."

"It wouldn't take much money to make some men commit murder," Renno said.

"Grinder?"

"Isn't it odd that he's not around?"

"Lewis told Mrs. Grinder that he had servants coming and that his traveling companion would be along. I doubt if even a Chickasaw half-breed would risk murder under those circumstances. Me, I'd like to talk with Neely and the two men with Lewis. You remember the black girl saying that Lewis's man was all dressed up the morning after Lewis died?"

"Makes one wonder, doesn't it?" Renno said.

"It does, indeed," Roy agreed. "Well, we'd best get to sleep, since my guess is that we're going to be riding hard toward Nashville in the morning."

They rode into Nashville in the middle of the afternoon of the second day after leaving Grinder's Stand.

"Place keeps growing," Roy grumbled. "Never could figure out what it is about a town that makes folks want to live in it."

They had decided during the ride that the best place to begin their search for James Neely was the sheriff's office. It seemed logical that Neely would have taken the first opportunity to report Lewis's death to the authorities. They were wrong.

A sheriff's deputy didn't take his feet off the desk behind which he was sitting. "Nope," he said, "I cain't tell you where this feller Neely is. Fact is, we ain't seen hide nor hair of him. First we heard of Governor Lewis shooting himself was in the newspaper. Neely told Guy Potter all about it, and Guy wrote it up in the paper. Happened in Chickasaw lands, so it was none of our affair."

"You wouldn't happen to have a copy of that paper around?" Roy asked.

The deputy laughed. "Nope. We put newspapers to good use around here. We give one sheet each to the prisoners, and they tear it up into strips and—"

"Thank you kindly," Roy said. "We get the idea."

Guy Potter was a round-nosed, massive blob of a man with bloodshot eyes and the trembling hands of a heavy drinker. They found him in the print shop where the daily newspaper was produced, and an unsatisfactory conversation ensued between Roy and Potter at the top of their voices with half the words being drowned in the clatter of the hand-operated press. Finally the fat man motioned them to follow him.

With two doors closed between them and the printing press, Potter indicated chairs and took his place behind a desk.

"You want to know about the death of Governor Lewis," Potter said. "Perhaps it would be best if I give you a copy of the paper in which I printed James Neely's account of the tragic affair."

"We'd appreciate that," Renno said.

"Skeeter!" Potter roared, startling Roy. A door opened quickly, and a boy of about twelve years stuck his head in. "Get a copy of the edition that headlined Governor Lewis's suicide."

"Neely was convinced that it was suicide?" Roy asked.

"He was very sure. He said that Lewis had been acting irrationally all the way from Fort Pickering, that he had been drinking heavily."

The boy burst into the room and extended a newspaper toward Potter, who nodded toward Renno and Roy. Roy took the folded sheets and glanced at the black headlines.

"Take your time, gentlemen," Potter said. "If you have any more questions after you've read it, I will do my best to answer them."

First of all, there was an explanation for Neely's late arrival at Grinder's Stand. According to the story he told Potter, two horses had strayed, and because Lewis was not feeling well, Neely stayed behind to search for them while Lewis rode on toward Grinder's Stand.

"There's just one thing wrong with this," Roy said, after reading for a while.

"He's basing his entire story on what he was told by Mrs. Grinder," Renno said.

"Exactly. Neely didn't know any more about it than we do."

"Except that he buried Lewis, so he saw the body."

"Yep," Roy said.

Potter's account also included a report Mr. Neely had written to be sent to Thomas Jefferson. The letter to Jefferson began:

> It is with extreme pain I have to inform you of the death of His Excellency Meriwether Lewis, Governor of Upper Louisiana who died on the morning of the 11th instant and I am Sorry to Say by Suicide.

Neely's story began with his arrival at Chickasaw Bluffs, where he met Lewis, who was "in very bad health." He confirmed that Lewis had intended to go down the river to New Orleans and take ship for the east coast of the United States but that the governor was "induced to Change his route and to come through the Chickasaw Nation by land" lest his papers and journals fall into the hands of the British through a hostile act at sea.

Neely recounted the incident of the missing horses and went on to write:

> He (Lewis) reached the house of a Mr Grinder about Sun Set, the man of the house being from home, and no person there but a woman discovering the governor to be deranged. gave him up the house & slept herself in one near it, his servant and mine slept in the stabel loft some distance from the other houses, the woman reports that about three oClock She heard two pistols fire off in the Governors Room; the servants being awakined by her, came in but too late to save him, he had shot himself in the head with one pistol, & a little below the Breast with the other—when his Servant came in he says, I have done the business my good Servant give me some water. he gave him water.

"Not exactly what Miz Grinder told us," Roy said. Renno read on.

> I have got in possession his two trunks of papers (amongst which is said to be his travels to the pacific Ocean) and probably some Vouchers for expenditures of Public Money for a Bill which had been protested by the Secy of War, and of which act to his death he repeatedly complained. I have also in my care his Rifle, Silver Watch, Brace of Pistols, dirk & tomahawk; one of the Governors horses was lost in the wilderness which I will endeavour to regain, the other I have Sent on by his servant who expressed a desire to go to the governors mother & to Monticello: I have furnished him with fifteen Dollars to Defray his expenses to Charlottesville; Some days previous to the Governors death he requested of me in Case of accident happened to him, to send his trunks and papers therein to the President, but I think it Very probably he meant you . . . the Governor left two of his trunks at Chickasaw Bluffs in the Care of Capt Gilbert C. Russell, Commanding officer, & I was to write to him from Nashville what to do with them.

"Ain't it odd that it was Lewis's horse that was lost?" Roy asked.

"And no mention of money, save for the fifteen dollars that Neely says he gave to Pernier," Renno said. He looked at Potter, who was leaning back in his chair with his eyes closed. "Mr. Potter."

Potter snorted and came awake.

"Is Neely still in town?" Renno asked.

"I don't know," Potter said.

"Did he send Mr. Lewis's effects on to Mr. Jefferson?"

"I believe he did."

"And the horse?"

"I don't know." Potter rubbed one eye with the back of his hand. "Since you ask, it does seem coincidental that it was one of Lewis's horses that was lost. Also, Mr. Neely told me that he had loaned money to Mr. Lewis and would have to file a claim against the estate to have any hope of being reimbursed."

"What about Lewis's weapons and his watch?" Renno asked. "Were they sent on with the trunks to Monticello?"

"You're making me very curious," Potter said. He rose. "I tell you what. Let's just walk over to the stage depot and ask some questions."

Questions produced answers that caused Roy to look at Renno and nod in grim confirmation of his suspicions. Two trunks had been freighted toward the east. The stageline agent had inspected the trunks for breakables and to be sure that the value stated by Neely, who had arranged for the shipping, was accurate.

"Nope, there were no guns in the trunks," the agent said. "They were not large enough, of course, to hold a rifle, and there were no pistols. Nor did the list of contents include a silver watch." He buried his fingers in his beard and scratched as if trying to root out unwelcome guests. "Noticed, now that you mention it, that Mr. Neely was wearing a fine brace of pistols."

Renno had one more question for the newspaperman. "Mr. Potter, when Neely was giving you his story, did he mention that there were cuts on Lewis's arms and legs?"

"No, he did not," Potter said. His eyes brightened. "Are you saying there were?"

"Just asking," Renno said.

"Look, I had no choice but to accept Neely's story," Potter said. "He is a man of position, after all, a government man. If there's more to this than what Neely said, I think we owe it to Mr. Lewis to tell the public. It hurt me a lot to think that a man like that, the man who had traveled all the way to the Pacific Ocean, would go mad and kill himself."

"Mr. Potter, we wouldn't want to start any rumors," Renno said.

"You already have taken a great interest in the affair."

"Lewis was a friend," Renno said.

"If you find Neely and get any new information, I'd sure appreciate it if you'd let me in on it."

"We'll keep it in mind," Renno said.

Nashville was still near enough to the wilderness to attract long hunters and frontiersmen. In the street Roy and Renno attracted little attention in spite of the fact that each was carrying a long rifle. In addition to his shot pouch, powder horn, tomahawk, Spanish stiletto at his belt, and travel pack, Renno carried his longbow and a quiver. At a hotel the clerk wanted to see the color of their money before he gave them a room with two beds. They ate a solid meal in the dining room. Roy sampled a taste of store-bought whiskey.

"What that little Grinder girl said about knife wounds keeps going around in my head," Roy said.

"With wounds in his head and in his side, there would have been a lot of blood," Renno said. "She could have been mistaken. Mrs. Grinder denied it."

"I'd have trouble believing that woman if she were sitting on a stack of Bibles ten feet high," Roy said. "Even wild drunk or out of his head with fever, a man like Lewis wouldn't shoot a chunk out of his forehead, then shoot himself in the side. If Lewis wanted to take himself off to Paradise, he'd be able to do it with one shot. I flat-out refuse to believe that he tried twice and then tried to finish the job by cutting off his own arms and legs."

"Mrs. Grinder said that he complained about its being so hard to die," Renno said. "If there were cuts on his arms and thighs, perhaps he was trying to open a vein and bring death quicker."

"Now can you really believe that?" Roy demanded impatiently.

"Not for a second," Renno admitted.

"You know what we've got to do, don't you?"

Knowing what Roy meant, Renno shivered. He was a

man of two worlds; but the lore of his Seneca ancestors
was ingrained deeply within him, and the Indian in him
protested, because to disturb the dead was to commit a
deed of great shame.

"We'll talk with Neely first," he said.

But James Neely was nowhere to be found. The clerk
at the hotel where he had been staying said that he had
checked out without mentioning his intentions, taking his
slave with him. Lewis's man, Pernier, had ridden east on
Lewis's horse, dressed, according to the clerk, in the
clothes of a gentleman.

"So what do we do?" Roy asked. "I'd like to talk with
Pernier, but I don't fancy chasing him all the way to Vir-
ginia. You reckon Neely went on back to the Chickasaw
Nation? He's still the agent, after all."

"Perhaps we will find the answer to that question at
Grinder's Stand," Renno said.

Naomi clung to Renna, and tears dampened the
shoulder of her gown. Beth patted Naomi on the back.
Renna's eyes were damp as well.

"I hate good-byes," Beth said.

"We've come to love you so," Naomi said. "And little
Emily and Louis."

"You're making me feel like a heartless monster,"
Beau said.

"Well, you are taking them away from us again,"
Beth said with a wan smile.

"I must return to my country," Beau said.

"Your country," Beth said with sudden anger. "Damn
your country and all the other countries that make war.
Haven't you done enough for France? You were almost
killed!"

"You're making this very difficult for me," Beau said
uneasily.

"That is my intent," Beth said. "Come with us to
Huntington Castle. Renno will be there by the time we
arrive. We can be a family, at least for a little while."

"Nothing would please me more," Beau said. "But

France is my home. There I am a man of substance. Here I am a penniless curiosity, a member of the old royalty living on your generosity. My property in France will belong to my son one day. I owe it to him to return. That is a powerful incentive, in addition to my duty to the emperor."

"Napoleon will probably have you shot," Beth said, "for disobeying his orders."

Beau laughed. "Oh, let us hope not. He might be angry, but he will recover. He finds me both amusing and useful."

"Men are so stubborn," Beth fumed.

"Please," Renna said to her stepmother. "Have mercy on poor Beau."

"Oh, all right," Beth said. "I have to agree that there is merit to your arguments, Beau. Our hearts will go with you."

And so it was that distance would separate the members of Renno's family once more. Beau, Renna, and the two children sailed for England aboard a British man-of-war, for man was a curious creature to whom an enemy ceased being an enemy, at least temporarily, if he called himself a diplomat.

There had been no word from Renno since the letter telling Beth that Toshabe was dead and that he and Roy were going to St. Louis. Both Beth and Little Hawk were concerned, but each tried to hide that worry from the other.

There were more good-byes shortly after Beau and Renna sailed away. Beth assured Dolley Madison that she and Renno would do their best to visit Washington again. Little Hawk would, of course, return with Naomi and the children to take up his new position for the President. He said only half jokingly that he was reluctant to venture out to sea again, what with the British still halting American ships seeking deserters from their navy; but he boarded the *Comtesse Renna* in good cheer with Beth and his family when James Ridley brought the ship into the Chesapeake on a coastal run.

*   *   *

The voyage to Wilmington was made without event. Huntington Shipping was not exactly thriving, for trading with British and French ports was still forbidden. Adan's entry into the South American trade was keeping most of the sailors and shore employees at work. The company was, in fact, showing a small profit.

Little Hawk began organizing the trip across the length of North Carolina. There was just time to reach Knoxville by coach and by horseback through the mountains before winter's snows made travel difficult.

Within a week of arriving at Fort Harrison, Gao was walking, after a fashion, leaning on a crutch formed by lacing a crosspiece to a freshly cut staff and padding it with leather. His wound was healing well, but it was obvious that it was going to take time before he could hold the warrior's pace for fifty miles. Ta-na would be taking to the road with Harrison, however, and Gao accepted the news with studied indifference, although inside he was chafing.

The governor's party consisted of Harrison himself; his secretary, Captain Peter Jones; interpreter Joseph Barron; a Negro servant; Ta-na; plus two friendly Indians. They traveled along a newly cut trace to North Bend and on to the metropolis of Cincinnati, with its two thousand inhabitants. The final destination, Fort Wayne, was reached by travel through closely spaced farms.

"Look at it, Thomas," Harrison said to Ta-na as they passed one homestead, only to see the smoke of another not far ahead. "We're conquering this wilderness. They came here, these people, even when there was a chance that they'd lose their hair; and now look at them. Two thousand folks in Cincinnati, and soon there'll be towns all over this territory, with churches and schools and law and order."

Ta-na had given up asking Harrison not to call him Thomas.

"But they're hemmed in," Harrison continued. "They're fenced away from rich lands by the Greenville Treaty line drawn by Anthony Wayne after Fallen Timbers. We can't abide that. We can't have the yearnings of the many be submerged by the selfish and thoughtless traditions of the few."

Ta-na knew that Harrison was again voicing one of his favorite themes—that it was not right to allow the continuous use of vast lands by relatively few Indians in a manner that Harrison and other white men thought wasteful.

"We'll see what can be done," Harrison said.

Ta-na was soon to understand the governor's meaning. His purpose at Fort Wayne was the negotiation of still another treaty, which, translated, meant another cession of lands by the Indians.

As they rode, they were joined by a handful of Delaware and their interpreter, a man named John Connor. A minor Potawatomi chief, Winamac, awaited them. The council was joined by the Miami chiefs Peccon, The Owl, and Silver Heels. The Shawnee were represented not by either of the two men who were recognized by the majority of the clans of the tribe as their leaders—not by either Tecumseh or the Prophet—but by a minor chief named Blackhood.

Harrison visited each separate Indian camp in turn. Expansive and affable, he showered the various chiefs with gifts. It became quickly evident to Ta-na that the treaty talks would be mere formalities, that the decision to cede more land had already been made by the Delaware and the Potawatomi chiefs who had not aligned themselves with Tecumseh.

As the talks began, a company of United States regular soldiers leaned on their rifles and observed the proceedings. Harrison spoke first. He emphasized the security involved in getting money and aid from the United States. "I do not have to tell you," he said in a loud, ringing voice, "that there is little game left. I do not have to remind you that the price you are paid for your pelts has fallen. You know. You can look around you and see hunger. You can see that your people are poor and that the promises of those who profess to be your friends, the British, have no more substance than the evening breezes."

He talked for well over an hour. He reminded the Indians of Thomas Jefferson's advice to them. "To raise hogs and cattle requires little work," he told them, "but offers sure returns. Do not allow your people to become like the Wea tribe that dwells along the Wabash, for they are poor and miserable and spend all the money they earn by hunting pelts on whiskey. Let the wise chiefs among you convince you that all the branches of the tribes would become a formidable and respectable unit when assembled in the western areas."

What Harrison was asking for was a vast expanse of land along the Wabash north of Vincennes, plus a long, twelve-mile-wide strip west of the present Greenville Treaty line. By the third day of the conference, only the Miami held out against Harrison's blandishments.

"Look at your women and children," Harrison told them. "See them exposed to the winds and the rain and the snows of the winter. You need not suffer. Some of you say that you will turn once again to the British. What have the British done for you other than to urge you into war? If the United States goes to war once more with England, will those false friends again try to position Indian bodies between themselves and the strong armies of the United States? The British have always encouraged you to fight the Americans. We, on the other hand, have asked only that you be neutral in the white man's wars, to remain at peace. And consider this: The United States pays you for your land. The French, Spanish, and the British appropriated it for their own use."

In the end those chiefs eager for the white man's annuities carried the day, although there were some concessions on Harrison's part. History would record that the Treaty of Fort Wayne decreed the transfer of three million acres of Indian land to the United States in exchange for annuities of $1,750, plus $5,200 worth of goods and $1,500 worth of hogs, horses, and cattle.

After it became clear that Harrison was going to have his cession of land, Ta-na talked with an elderly Mohican, a sad-eyed man who spoke of the days when his tribe roamed free in the lands of the east. The old man, having nothing to barter, was only a spectator at the negotiations.

"So once more it happens," the Mohican said to Ta-na. "And now we move ever closer to war."

"How so, old father?" Ta-na asked.

"Tecumseh," the Mohican said. "And the British, for their agents from Malden even now are traveling among the tribes and warning them not to sell any more land, reminding them what has happened in those lands ceded by the tribes at Greenville. This time more of the tribes will fight beside the British."

Remembering the old Mohican's warning, Ta-na decided not to return with the governor's party to Vincennes. He told Harrison that he was going to detour into the Wabash lands and learn what he could about Tecumseh's reaction to the new treaty.

"Watch your hair, Thomas," Harrison said.

It would be dangerous to go back to the village near Tippecanoe, but something seemed to draw Ta-na in that direction. He seized upon an opportunity to take ragged clothing from an abandoned Shawnee lodge, then caked mud in his hair and splotched his face with various colors of paint. The object was to disguise himself as one blessed by the spirits with dim wits. As he neared the village of the Prophet, he affected a limping, awkward walk. No one looked at him twice.

He waited until darkness came. There was a full moon. Slowly he crept through the brush until he found a little mound from which he could look directly down into the common area at the center of Tecumseh's town. The Prophet was holding audience. With a resigned sigh, Ta-na decided that it was the will of the manitous that he be subjected to much oratory. He had just endured several days of it at Fort Wayne, and now he was to hear more.

What might have been a thousand people were gathered around a wagon in which Tecumseh's brother stood. The white pebble with its fierce, painted eye gleamed in its socket. His voice soared toward the sky. Ta-na could hear him well.

"I *am* Tenskwatawa, and my people have chosen me as their prophet," he said. "I am a true prophet, for I have no need of the paraphernalia of the shamans. I scorn their bits of bone and their pretty little rocks. I have no need to draw sand pictures on skins, for that is nothing more than witchcraft, nothing more than the work of Match-emenetoo, who is the enemy of the Great Spirit, Moneto.

"This I tell you: Hear me. I lead you from evil. Once I poisoned my soul with the white man's whiskey. No more. And I tell you to shun liquor. I tell you to give up staggering and vomiting from the white man's poison.

"Brothers all, we are all Indians. We must forbid the marriage of our women to white men. Never again shall the blood of our people be mixed with that of the Shemanese. We must become what we truly are, one people. The property of one Indian, the land, is the property of all. We must dress as our fathers dressed, in the skins and feathers meant for us by Moneto, and not in the cloth of the white man.

"And above all, brothers, we must believe—for it is true as I swear it by Moneto—that we, not just this tribe or that clan, *we*, we *Indians*, are a most excellent people. We Indians are inferior to none and superior to all Shemanese. We have the power given to us by Moneto, and we do not need the help of anyone outside our Indian race."

The Prophet paused, as if to let his words sink in. When he continued, his voice was softer, as if he were imparting a confidence.

"I rose into the clouds, my brothers, and was with my personal good spirit, Naanteena. Hear what she revealed to me." He lifted his arms to the sky, his fingers spread and pointing to the stars. "She showed me the pale-face warrior destroying our trees and fouling our clear streams. She showed me rivers of red blood, the blood of the Indian. She said, 'Awaken! Rouse yourselves. Take yourselves to council. Hear your Prophet. Listen to him, brothers, and soon the rivers of blood will no longer be the blood of slaughtered Indians. It will be the juices from the veins of the Shemanese.' Know this to be true, for I am the Prophet."

In spite of himself, Ta-na was moved. He had studied the white man's history books with his stepmother, Beth. He had heard the old ones talk in quiet tones in front of the fire. He knew that what the Prophet said was true, that the history of the Indian since the coming of the white man was one written in blood and illustrated with lost hunting grounds. He was young. He was alone in enemy territory, risking his life for the cause of the white man, who had just convinced weak chiefs to give up land that, in all honesty, was not even theirs to sell. As a matter of fact, the village of Tecumseh and the Prophet lay within the strip of land along the Wabash that had been ceded to William Henry Harrison by the chiefs at Fort Wayne. Obviously the Panther, who stood in shadows near the wagon from whose bed his brother was orating, had not heard. Ta-na wondered what would happen after he did.

From near the river an owl hooted. It was time for Ta-na to leave. He would not risk penetration of his disguise by entering the village. He had seen enough: The number of warriors in Tecumseh's village had grown since he and Gao were there, and it was obvious that Tecumseh, through his spokesman the Prophet, was fomenting war.

Chapter Fifteen

Renno led the way, riding into a towering southwestern sky that boded a change in the weather. Rows of clouds reminiscent of the tilled furrows of a settler's field climbed from the horizon. The lowering sun was a gleaming gold coin that metamorphosed into sprawling widths of golds and flaming reds as Renno selected a campsite and began to gather deadwood for the fire. Roy, grunting with effort, unsaddled his horse. They had ridden a full fifty miles from Nashville, then spread their blankets on the ground beside a creek. After a good night's sleep, they would reach the vicinity of Grinder's Stand by midday unless the weather became violent.

The evening meal was consumed in a comfortable silence. It was evident to Roy that Renno was troubled. He respected the white Indian's mood.

Just before the red glow in the west was muted by growing darkness, a vee of geese flew over them toward the south. One distantly voiced honk waffled down to them. It was a lonely sound that seemed to challenge a whippoorwill who, in response, began his mournful wailing from the trees along the creek's bank.

"It will be an early winter," Renno said.

"You becoming a shaman, reading weather signs?" Roy asked idly.

Renno shrugged.

"Renno, we're going in the wrong direction," Roy said. "We should be following the trail to Rusog's town." When he thought of the Seneca village and the longhouse he had shared with Toshabe, a core of pain throbbed deep inside him; but even without Toshabe, the village and the house were home, a place were he would find ease for his aching joints.

Renno laughed. "We share the same thought."

"No help for it, though, is there?"

"No."

"I wouldn't rest easy, thinking that the honor of a brave man like Lewis was tainted forever by lies," Roy said. He had finished eating and was whittling a twig to a sharp point to be used as a toothpick. "And then I ask myself, 'Self, who do Renno and I think we are, the law west of the Smokies? Where is it written that we have to be frontier avengers?'"

"And what does Self answer?"

"He says, 'Well, Roy, since there ain't no law in the Indian lands 'cept that which the chiefs and the tribal councils apply to their own people, someone's got to get the answers to a few questions, if only for the sake of his own curiosity.'"

Renno nodded. The flickering fire lit his face, making shadows of his chiseled features. "Why is it that others are so quick to try to bring a great man down to their own level?"

"I know what you mean. Already they're yapping and biting and tugging on Lewis's reputation like a pack of wolves after a gut-slashed deer. He stuck his head above the level of the crowd, and they're trying to pull him back down among 'em. Calling him crazy because he was out of his head with fever and almost fell overboard from the flatboat? Because he talked to himself?" He leaned back, put his head on his saddle. "Ever talk to yourself, Renno?"

"I plead guilty."

"Since, judging from what Miz Grinder said, he was talking about vouchers and addressing the President, he might have been rehearsing the speech he was planning to make in Washington. The man was in financial trouble. The meetings he had scheduled in Washington meant solvency or poverty. I can understand why he'd want to be sure he was ready to say the right things. Man does what Lewis did—work at the right hand of a president, blaze trails where no white man had ever gone, be named governor of a U.S. territory—I can see where he'd get right agitated facing the prospect and the shame of bankruptcy."

"The worry drove him so hard he was traveling sick, maybe with the fever coming and going," Renno said. "And carrying a sum of money."

"I keep thinking about the money, and I reckon we'd better have a conversation with Mr. Grinder about it," Roy said. "There are a lot of things about Mrs. Grinder's account that don't set right with me. If Grinder killed Lewis for the money, his wife might cook up a cock-and-bull story. You know, when some people tell a lie, they think that the more detail they put into the lie, the more believable it is."

Soon Roy was snoring. Renno watched the fire die down. The whippoorwill had moved closer to the water, and his mournful call was loud and penetrating. The milky sky of the afternoon had become dark clouds that blocked all light from moon and stars. Renno pulled his blanket up to his chin and closed his eyes, but sleep was somewhere far away. When the nightbird suddenly ceased his calling, a silence deep and black caused Renno's eyes to pop open. The fire was flickering low, with small flames consuming the last of the unburned wood on a bed of glowing embers. From the embers arose a smoke, a vision that jerked Renno into a sitting position.

Words formed in silence, passing from the spirit

world into Renno's consciousness in traditional Seneca greeting. "Sachem, I thank thee that thou art well."

"Mother," Renno whispered, for the image that grew with clarity in the dim glow of the dying fire was Toshabe's, the Toshabe of his childhood, beautiful of face, dark of hair. The fresh grief that lived strongly in his heart caused a deep ache in his chest.

"You have traveled far," the manitou said, her voice soft and loving. "It is not good that you are alone."

He understood that she was referring to Beth.

"Mother, this trail that we ride—guide me, advise me."

"Some long trails lead nowhere," the manitou said. "But often even those must be followed."

"I understand," Renno said. The manitou was smiling. "You are content, Mother?"

"As you will be."

A chill shivered down Renno's shoulders. The weather was worsening. Along the creek the treetops bent and shook their heads in mild protest against the presumption of the wind.

"To right an injustice is orenda," the manitou said. "Failing that, to strive is honor."

With that the vision faded, and the wind gusted, rustling through the trees. Roy slept on. The whippoorwill called from farther away, and his song lulled Renno to sleep.

The rain didn't begin until after they had been riding for two hours. It came as a fine mist that dampened them, then turned into a veil of small and delicate drops falling straight down in a cocoonlike silence. Beads of crystal adorned every leaf and every blade of grass.

The farmland that was being worked by Robert Grinder lay east of the trace and north of the stand. Renno and Roy left the horses in a thicket of wild plums and approached the cultivated field in the hushed quiet of the small rain. Water ran down Renno's nose. He slung moisture off his forehead with a curved forefinger and squinted to see.

Grinder had constructed a lean-to of sticks and mud at the end of a cornfield. The crop had been partially harvested. Two sacks of unshelled corn were stacked under the overhang of the lean-to. Smoke emerged from a hole in the roof. On the other side of the shack, under a brush arbor, two black mules chewed steadily on cornstalk fodder. A paint-faded farm wagon sat in the rain, metal wheel rims rusted.

Renno had long since learned the value of intimidation. He left the cover to dash to the back of the lean-to. The slanting roof merged with the sod from which it was made. Hearing a man snoring, Renno edged his way to the door and peered around the log frame. Grinder was lying on skins on a platform of saplings. He was dressed except for his moccasins. His bare feet protruded over the end of the sleep platform.

A pistol in one hand, stiletto in the other, Renno moved silently to the foot of the bed. He pressed the needle-sharp point of Toledo steel against the bare instep of Grinder's foot. The Chickasaw snorted and rolled his head from side to side. Renno pressed harder without penetrating the skin. Grinder's eyes flew open. He saw the black muzzle of a pistol and, behind it, a bronzed face set in an impassive stare.

"Be calm," Renno said in Chickasaw.

"Who are you?" Grinder asked. His eyes were wide.

"Where is the money?" Renno asked in a soft voice.

"What money?" Grinder asked, his brows coming together. "Do I look like a man who'd have money?"

Renno let the stiletto taste blood, the point breaking the skin below the arch of Grinder's foot. Grinder's lips set against the sharp pain, but he did not move, not even to try to jerk the foot away from the knife. Renno made sure the man saw death in the icy blue eyes behind the black muzzle of the pistol.

"I have little time," Renno said. "Where is the money?"

"By the spirits," Grinder said, "you have chosen the wrong man."

Roy stuck his head in the door. He was not as fluent

in Chickasaw as Renno, but he knew enough of the dialect to get the gist of Grinder's statement. "He don't look like the wrong man to me."

Renno cocked the pistol. The metallic click seemed to fill the space inside the lean-to. "If you have no money, then you are of no use to us."

"Wait!" Grinder said as he saw Renno's finger tense on the trigger.

"For a moment only," Renno said.

"I have some money. Not much."

"You are wise to remember."

"It's at the house with my old woman."

"The money you took from the man you killed?"

Grinder's eyes widened again. "You wrong me," he said. "The money I have was given to me by Mr. Neely to build a fence around the dead man's grave."

Renno put pressure on the knife. Blood coated the tip of the blade. Grinder grunted. "By the spirits of my fathers," he said, "I speak true."

"The dead man carried much money," Renno said. "Do you value it more than your life and perhaps the lives of your wife and daughter?"

"My old woman looked for money," Grinder said. "She went through his pockets. She took a quick look through his necessaries. There was none."

Just as he knew that sudden fear can loosen a man's tongue, Renno also knew that an Indian had difficulty lying to another Indian. "What happened to the money?"

"I don't know," Grinder said, reverting to English as if to emphasize his statement. "Maybe them that was with him got it."

"Were there cuts on the dead man as well as gunshot wounds?"

"I don't know. I didn't see the body. Me and the old woman have a rough time making a living out here. I had to get this crop in so's we'd have something to eat this winter. I been here keeping the deer and the 'coon outten the corn ever since it started to form ears."

There was a smell of truth to what Grinder was say-

ing. Renno wiped his knife on the leg of Grinder's buckskins, then put the blade in its sheath.

"I was going to use that money the Neely feller give
me to build a fence around the grave."

"So," Renno said. "Gather your corn."

"You won't hurt my old woman and my kid?"

Renno didn't answer. He led Roy to the edge of the
woods and waited until Grinder emerged from the lean-to
with a deerskin poncho over his shoulders.

"He'll be going to his family now," Roy said. "You
convinced that he didn't rob Lewis?"

"No," Renno said.

Grinder set out toward the stand at a pace that left
Roy panting far behind as Renno ran to keep within hearing distance. Grinder did not slow until he was in the
front yard of the stand. He started calling out to his wife,
and the door opened.

Renno waited, keeping out of sight. Within minutes
Grinder burst out of the door with Mrs. Grinder and the
daughter behind him. The females were swaddled in
skins. Grinder steered them into the woods. They carried
nothing.

Roy came up at a slow trot, panting and grunting.
"Still in there?" he asked.

"He took his wife and his daughter and left," Renno
said, pointing.

"What about the little Negro gal?"

"I haven't seen her," Renno said.

As if in answer to Roy's question, the front door
opened, and Malinda, the young slave, peered out with
wide, frightened eyes. She looked around the clearing for
a moment, then slammed the door.

"I don't think she'll come out," Roy said. He was
beginning to breathe easier.

The grave was just beside the trace. Even with the
small rain falling, there was a possibility that someone
might come, pushing hard to reach the shelter of
Grinder's Stand for the night. Not wasting time in the
lengthening day, Roy rummaged quietly in the barn and
came out with a pick and a shovel and material with

which to make torches. Renno, meanwhile, had found a dry spot and some soft hay and was sleeping. He awoke immediately when Roy touched his shoulder.

"It's dark," Roy said.

The rain had stopped at last. The ground was wet, and moisture dripped from the eaves of the barn. Light gleamed from the cabin windows.

"We'd best wait for the girl to go to sleep," Roy said. He busied himself wrapping and tying gunnysack material around sticks. He saturated the porous material with axle grease from a large can. "These should give us enough light, and I reckon if anyone was going to come up or down the trace, they'd have done it before now."

The light went out in the cabin no more than an hour after dark. Renno and Roy crossed the trace to the fresh grave. The rain had eroded the mound. The dirt was sodden and heavy. The smell of decay began to seep up through the damp earth when Renno had dug down no more than two feet. Roy coughed and turned away. Renno steeled himself and kept on digging. The stench became heavy and cloying.

"Give me some light," Renno said.

Roy lit the torches.

Neely and the others had buried Lewis only three feet deep. The body was wrapped in his bearskin sleeping robe. Renno, gasping, trying not to breathe, scraped earth away, gagged, then leaped from the grave to run a few feet away and bend, retching. When he came back, Roy said, "Let me help."

"You would not make a good Choctaw," Renno said.

"How come?"

"Choctaw bone pickers let their fingernails grow long so that they can pick the rotted flesh from the bones of their dead."

"Reckon I wouldn't," Roy agreed. "Why would they want to do that?"

"I guess Choctaws just like clean bones," Renno said.

"Helluva time to joke."

"No joke. They do clean the bones before burying them."

"With their fingernails?"

"Yes."

"Things would have to be pretty ripe before they could do that," Roy said. "Let's get on with this before Mr. Lewis gets that way."

They stood in the grave at each end of the body with barely enough room for their feet.

"Now or never," Roy said.

They unrolled the bearskin. A great blast of putrefaction caused both of them to gag. The body lay on its back. Renno seized a torch and held it low. The bloat that precedes decay had come and gone. The resulting juices had soaked the bearskin. The torch guttered as a breeze swept past, bringing a merciful puff of breathable air.

Renno held the torch close. Bone showed through at the wound in the forehead. Roy held his breath and pulled up Lewis's shirt. The wound in Lewis's side was blackened and dry. Renno handed the torch to Roy, took his knife in hand, slit the material of the sleeves of Lewis's shirt. The knife wounds were shallow at both wrists. Quickly, with his stomach heaving, Renno cut open the dead man's trouser legs. The slashes were on Lewis's inner thighs, on both sides, deep. They would have bled freely.

Roy was heaving, sucking air into his lungs. Renno boosted him out of the shallow gave. "Go on," he said. He covered the body with the bearskin, then bowed his head. "Forgive us for disturbing your rest," he whispered. "Father of Life, give this good man peace and give me the wisdom to do what should be done."

The stench was on them even after they shoveled the twice-disturbed earth back into the grave and packed the mound anew. There was a feel of midnight in the air as they walked by unspoken agreement to the creek, removed their clothing, and scoured the deerskin with sand, then punished their own hides with handfuls of white sand from the bottom. Even then the smell seemed to be lodged in their nostrils. They put their clothes to dry beside a fire, wrapped themselves in blankets, and, at last, slept.

It was Roy who opened the discussion just after sunup. "Renno, you remember when I got shot in the head by soldiers down in Mississippi?"

Renno nodded. He remembered it only too well, and thinking about it reminded him of the sadness he had known when he saw Roy fall with all muscular tension, all animation gone from his body.

"That shot didn't even touch my skull bone, just carved a crease in the scalp, but it put me out for a long time. That wound on Lewis's head actually took out a chip of bone. Now, he may have been a stud hoss, but I don't think there's a man alive who can function very well after being hit on the forehead with a pistol bullet hard enough to chip bone."

"Grinder didn't do it," Renno said. "He's half-Chickasaw. If he had been trying to kill Lewis, he wouldn't have been so inefficient, especially with the knife."

"The woman?" Roy asked.

"She's half-Chickasaw," Renno said. "It would be my guess that she's seen men wounded in war or hurt at work. I would think that she'd know what it takes to kill a man."

"On the same grounds, you'd have to discount the possibility that he was killed by bandits," Roy said, " 'less it was a beginner on his first job. And that brings us back to a certain servant who showed up wearing Lewis's clothes the next morning." He shook his head. "But dang it, would even a Frenchman be stupid enough to kill his master, steal his clothes, and start wearing them right away?"

"I don't know," Renno said, "but suspicion does seem to fall on the Creole and the Negro."

"And Neely?"

"He didn't show up until the next morning."

"Maybe he was showing up *again* the next morning. Maybe he'd already been there during the night. After all, he, more than any of them, would have known if Lewis was carrying money."

"But would he be as likely as the servants to kill for a relatively small amount of money?"

"Depends on what kind of man he is."

Renno nodded. "Come," he said.

Roy followed him to the stand. A hail brought Malinda to the door. "You remember us, don't you, child?" Roy asked.

"I do," she said. "But y'all better not come in. Miz Grinder ain't here."

"We'll talk here on the porch," Renno said, sitting down on the edge. "We want to know about the night Mr. Lewis died."

"Oh, Lawdy," she said. "Miz Grinder she tole me not to talk 'bout that."

"But you'd like to, wouldn't you?" Renno asked. "After all, Mr. Lewis was a nice man."

"He was," she said. "What you want to know?"

"Just start at the beginning," Renno said.

"Well, he rid up late in the day and ax if he can stay fer the night. Miz Grinder she say yes, but that they's no man in the house to take keer of his hosses."

"Why couldn't you take care of Mr. Lewis's horse?" Renno said.

"I donno," Melinda said. "Maybe 'cause I 'uz gittin' supper. Mr. Lewis he say that's all right, 'cause he got his two servants comin'. They come with one or two packhosses. Mr. Lewis he walked up and down the yard movin' he hands and mutterin' to heself so that Miz Grinder she got skeered and shooed me and Bethenia in the house. Me and Miz Grinder we go out later to fix up Mr. Lewis bed, but he say he gone sleep on his buffaler robe on the floor. His servants, they 'uz sleepin' in the barn.

"We goes on back to the house, and Mr. Lewis he walks in the yard wavin' he hands and talkin'. I hearn him say that someone has tole lies on him and ruint him. I goes to sleep, but then I woke up when I hearn two shots. The white feller, this Pernier, he come running, and Mr.

Lewis he crawl out of the sleeping cabin and ax for water. We goes in, and he moaning and rolling around on the floor, and Miz Grinder she ax him why he done it, all that blood and all. He drink a lot of water and puke it up real quick, and then he die."

"He didn't come to the door of the house and ask Mrs. Grinder to give him water and help him?" Renno asked.

"No, sir, 'less he done it while I wuz asleep."

"Did you see the cuts on his arms and legs?"

"Yes, sir."

"Malinda," Roy asked, "was Mr. Grinder home that night?"

"No, sir."

"When did he come home?"

"Three days, maybe."

"And did you see Mr. Neely that night?" Roy asked.

"No, sir, not till mornin'." She brightened. "I seen him again, just two days ago," she said. "He come through and stopped jest fer a drink of water."

"Going south on the trace," Roy said.

"Yes, sir."

"Oh, Lord," Roy said wearily. "Here we go again."

Renno set a leisurely pace. The weather system that had brought rain was followed by pure, northern air. In the mornings their breath made clouds of vapor, and the horses were frisky in their efforts to dispel the chill of the night.

The weather had warmed by the time they reached Fort Pickering. Captain Russell was surprised to see them. "You fellows get lost?" he asked.

"I'm beginning to wonder myself," Roy grumbled.

"You've heard about Governor Lewis's death, I assume," Renno said.

"Yes. Shame, isn't it? Neely told me about it, and I have written a report to Washington," Russell said.

"Is Neely still here?" Renno asked.

"No, he's gone back to the agency," Russell said.

"What did he tell you?" Renno asked.

"That Lewis was deranged and committed suicide. That Lewis had been drinking heavily." He paused, squinting, and examined Renno's face closely as if considering his next statement. "I drank with Governor Lewis here at the fort. He could hold his liquor. It didn't sound right that he'd been skunk drunk on the trip, so I asked Neely's man a few questions. He said that Neely kept pressing Lewis to drink. I'd guess that if a man took too much hard spirits while the fever was on him, he might get a little wild."

"Was Neely carrying a brace of fine pistols?" Roy asked.

"Matter of fact, he was. I noticed them immediately," Russell said. "He said he'd reported to Mr. Jefferson that he was holding Mr. Lewis's weapons."

"By what right?" Roy asked.

Russell shrugged.

"What did you write in your report to Washington?" Renno asked.

"I could only report what I'd been told by Neely," Russell said. "It grated on me to say that Governor Lewis committed suicide, but I had only the word of Neely and his slave to go on."

As Renno and Roy rode into the village that had grown up around the Chickasaw Agency, it was evident from the smell that the sanitary habits of the tribe hadn't improved. In matters of cleanliness the Chickasaw were true cousins to the Choctaw. The agency was a slant-roofed building built of rough-hewn planks and logs. A couple of horses were tied at the hitching rail, and Indian women were clustered here and there in the street. Pigs rooted in mud puddles. A goat had climbed to the top of a thatched hut and was eating the roof with evident enjoyment. A tumble of small boys playing at war rolled across in front of the horses, causing Renno to rein in.

"I'm not sure what we're doing here," Roy said as they rode toward the agency.

Renno threw his leg over the pommel of the saddle

and slid off to land lightly on his feet. Roy made a more sedate dismount, grunting with effort.

A Chickasaw woman dressed in calico was alone in the agent's office.

"Mr. Neely, please," Renno said in English.

"He is not here," the woman replied in her own language.

"We have come far to see the agent, Mr. Neely," Renno said.

"Only today he left," the woman said, persisting in speaking Chickasaw.

"Where was he going?" Renno asked, switching to the woman's language.

"On business," she said.

"Perhaps we could catch up with him, for our business is of some interest," Renno said.

"He is on his business," the woman said, making it evident that she would reveal no more.

Outside, Renno gave the sign of peace to a pair of Chickasaw senior warriors who were, it seemed, having a contest to see who could spit tobacco juice farther. They did not share the woman's reluctance to speak.

"Only this morning he left for the big river and the city at its mouth," one of the old men said, pointing to the southwest. By casual questioning, Renno learned that the agent was traveling with three Chickasaws and two packhorses.

"Lord have mercy," Roy moaned. He waited until they were mounted and could not be heard by the old men. "Tell me that we're not going to follow Neely to New Orleans."

"You have a voice in the decision," Renno said.

"Will you leave me here to crawl under the nearest tree and sleep until you come back?"

"Winter's coming. You'd freeze."

"Dag-nab it—"

"It *is* a long trail," Renno said, remembering the words of the manitou. "I do not know if it is a trail we should follow."

"Well, what the hell," Roy said. "We've followed it

this far. Maybe if we skedaddle, we can catch him 'fore he gets to Natchez."

Neely had only a half-day's head start. By switching horses often, the pursuers were able to keep up a pace that brought them to the scent of a campfire just before sundown. The trace was a twisting trail searching out high ground between marshy areas. The smoke from the campfire came from a hummock near a sluggish stream. Renno left Roy to keep the horses quiet. He abandoned the beaten track and picked his way slowly through dense brush until he heard voices.

Neely and his three Chickasaw companions had chosen their campsite well. It was a protected bank, high and dry, with the stream below and dense brush and trees behind. A coffeepot boiled over the fire, sending out a pleasing aroma. Neely was seated with his back against a tree as he ate a chunk of venison roast held in his hands. The three Chickasaws showed no particular indication of alertness. They were in their own nation, only one day's ride from home. They had no reason to be wary.

Renno backed away, returned to the point where he'd left Roy, and announced his coming with the coo of a dove.

"How many?" Roy asked.

"As we were told."

"Neely and three bucks."

Renno nodded.

"So what do we do?"

"It would be simpler if we merely observed old custom," Renno said musingly.

"Know what you mean. Count a little coup. Kill the Chickasaw, and the sight of their blood would make Neely *want* to talk like a gossip-starved woman."

"Do you want to do it that way?"

"This isn't war, I reckon. And we don't know that Neely killed Lewis."

Renno nodded in agreement.

"So what do we do?"

"Disarm them."

"Easy to say."

"Do you suppose you remember enough woodcraft to get close without their hearing you?"

Roy snorted.

"You take the trace. They're camped less than a hundred feet from the trail. You'll smell the fire before you see it through the trees. I'll go down the creek bank, and when I'm in place I'll coo three times. We'll step into the clearing simultaneously."

Roy stood behind a big cypress tree and watched the three Chickasaw eating. The roasted meat smelled good. It made his mouth water. The meat was the reason Renno and he had been able to catch up with Neely's party. It had taken time to kill a deer, skin it, and cook the venison roast. He figured that Neely wasn't in too much of a hurry to waste time like that less than a day's ride from the agency. He was about ready to step out and invite himself to dinner when he heard the call of a dove, once, twice, three times. He saw a flash of movement, then leaped from behind the tree and into the clearing.

"No move," Renno said in Chickasaw. The three Indians froze, one of them with a mouthful of meat.

"Goes for you, too, Neely," Roy said, leveling his rifle as Neely started to reach for a pair of handsome pistols lying on a blanket beside him.

Neely drew back his hand. He licked his lips, looking first at Roy, then at Renno.

"Throw your weapons toward me," Renno told the Chickasaw. "Throw them gently. Make no quick moves."

The Indians obeyed. They had nothing to lose except their weapons, so they would not resist what was, they felt, no more than another robbery on the trace. If the bandits took money from the agent, it was not their loss.

"Mr. Neely," Roy said, "I want you to put your hands behind your head."

Neely obeyed. "You know me?"

"Yes and no," Roy said.

"Walk toward the south," Renno told the Chickasaw,

urging them to their feet by waving his rifle. "Don't come back before morning. If you come back, I will kill you."

Roy bent and removed the pistols from Neely's reach. Renno listened as the sounds of movement faded. He threw more wood on the fire to create light, then stood in front of Neely. The man was clearly nervous.

"Look, I have a little money. It's there, in my saddle-bags."

"How much money did you take from Meriwether Lewis's trunks?" Renno asked.

"My God, man, is that why you're here? Are you one of those fools who think that Lewis was a rich man?"

Roy, while listening with great interest, was slicing off a chunk of roast from a spit over the fire. He gnawed at it and grunted with pleasure.

"Why did you send Lewis ahead of you, alone?" Renno asked.

"What is your interest in Mr. Lewis?" Neely asked. "The poor fellow was demented. He killed himself."

"Why did you send him alone to Grinder's Stand?"

The evenness of Renno's voice and the look in his eyes told Neely that Renno's was no idle curiosity. Neely felt instinctively that his very survival might depend on what he said during the next few minutes.

"He was sick," Neely said. "But even sick he was concerned about the loss of the two horses. I stayed behind to look for the horses to ease his mind. He'd paid four hundred dollars for one of them."

"Was that the one you didn't find? His horse that was lost?"

"Yes. Besides, I figured the servants could take care of him."

"But Mrs. Grinder said that he arrived at the stand alone. The servants came later. Why?"

"I don't know," Neely said.

"Why didn't you arrive at the stand before morning?"

"It was a dark night. I couldn't keep to the trace in the dark. I made camp."

"You told Potter in Nashville that Lewis shot himself

twice," Renno said. "You said nothing about the fact that there were serious knife cuts on his arms and legs."

"That's news to me," Neely said.

Renno sighed elaborately. His rifle shifted so that the muzzle was aligned with Neely's right eye.

"Before God," Neely said. "I saw no cuts!"

"Any man with eyes could have seen them."

"I asked the woman to tidy him up a bit before I buried him," Neely said. "I didn't look at his arms and legs. When I saw him, he was lying on the bed, and there was a lot of blood. There were two bullet wounds. I guess I thought that was enough to cause all the blood."

"Among my people," Renno said, "it is believed that a man who dies with a lie on his lips does not make it across the river to the place of his ancestors. Do white men who die pouring lies from their mouths burn in your God's hell?"

"You've got to listen to me," Neely said desperately. "Who are you? Are you a friend of Mr. Lewis?"

Renno nodded slowly.

"His death disturbed me as much as anyone," Neely said. "He was a great man. Besides, I'd sort of committed myself to looking after him. He'd been ill. It made me miserable to think that I'd failed him. If I'd been there, I could have stopped him from shooting himself."

"He was ill?"

"Yes."

"But not demented," Renno said.

"I don't know. Fever, maybe. Out of his head with fever."

"And yet you wrote that he shot himself twice, once in the head, once in the side. You wrote that he crawled out of the cabin and begged Mrs. Grinder to help him, to give him water and treat his wounds."

"I wrote down just what she told me," Neely said. "She said he did it. She said he told her so, said he did it to keep his enemies from having the pleasure of killing him. That sounded to me sort of like the ravings of a demented man."

"Where's your slave?"

"I sold him in Chickasaw Bluffs."

"Sold him down the river so that he wouldn't have an opportunity to tell anyone what happened at Grinder's Stand?"

"I sold him because I needed the money more than I needed a slave. They drag you down, slaves, always depending on you. Just like children."

"Why are you going to New Orleans?"

"I'm not," Neely said.

"Where, then?"

"Just on a tour through the Chickasaw lands," Neely said. "I am the Indian agent, you know."

"You're not headed for Natchez?"

"We'll stop there eventually for a good bed and a decent meal."

"How much money are you carrying?"

"Fifty dollars."

"You have Lewis's pistols. What happened to his rifle and other things? His dirk and tomahawk, his watch?"

"I let his man, Pernier, take the rifle for his own protection. He took the watch, too. He said he was going to go see Mr. Lewis's mother to see if he could get her to pay him what Mr. Lewis owed him in back wages, and he'd give the watch to her. I guess the dirk and the tomahawk went into one of the trunks."

"Did you also give Pernier Mr. Lewis's clothes?"

"I did," Neely said. "The poor fellow was all in rags. The clothes weren't going to do Lewis any good anymore."

Neely moved his hands slowly, taking them from behind his head and letting them fall to his side. "Look, if you're a good friend of Mr. Lewis, why don't you take the pistols? I was just going to hang on to them until I could get them into the hands of whoever was handling his estate. Same way with the horse."

"What horse?"

"I found the one that was lost."

"Why are you going to New Orleans? To see General Wilkinson?"

Neely's eyes twitched. Renno placed the big, hard,

cold tip of his rifle on the tip of Neely's nose. "No more
lies. You were going to New Orleans. You were going to
see Wilkinson. Why?"

"All right," Neely said. "All right." He lifted one
hand and with shaking fingers pushed the muzzle of the
rifle away. "I know that General Wilkinson would want to
hear firsthand about the death of his good friend, Governor Lewis. I thought it was my duty to go to New Orleans
and tell him."

"How much did Wilkinson pay you to kill Lewis?"
Renno asked coldly, moving the muzzle of the rifle back
to Neely's nose.

"On my oath," Neely said, his voice shaking, "I have
not seen or corresponded with General Wilkinson for over
two years, although we are old friends. I swear before
God that is the truth. How could I kill Lewis? I wasn't
even there when he died."

"On that we have only your word," Renno said. "Was
it Secretary Frederick Bates who paid you?"

"I've never seen the man."

As he'd felt that Grinder was telling the truth, now
Renno sensed truth in Neely's fear. He felt as if he had
come to the end of a long trail that dead-ended against an
unscalable bluff. At one stage in his life, the admitted
connection between Neely and General James Wilkinson
would have been excuse enough to kill the agent quickly
and painlessly, just in case Neely was lying; but Renno
was not the man he once was. Life no longer seemed to be
a cheap commodity. Life was too precious to be snuffed
out on mere suspicion.

"What happened to Meriwether Lewis's money?" he
asked, but even Neely sensed that all menace had gone
out of his voice.

"I swear that I don't know. I know only that he borrowed money from me and that it is unlikely I will be
reimbursed from his estate."

Now Renno could see the lie in the white man's
eyes, smell it in his fear, sense it in his tone of voice just
as he'd sensed the truth in Neely's denials.

"Renno," Roy said, tossing aside the hunk of venison,

"let's get the hell out of here. I've suddenly lost my appetite."

"You intimated that a friend of the governor's should have these pistols," Renno said, picking up the weapons along with their accompanying powder horn and shot bag.

"Yes, yes," Neely said. "Take them."

Chapter Sixteen

The long trail that Roy and Renno had been following turned once more to the northeast. Roy grumbled that the trace between the border of the Chickasaw Nation and Nashville was becoming "too durned familiar" and that it was taking them once more in the wrong direction. Rusog's town and the Seneca village lay to the southeast. He agreed that it was necessary to return to Nashville in order to report what they had seen and heard at Grinder's Stand, particularly the nature of Lewis's wounds; but he maintained that his age gave him the right to grumble about it.

Since it had previously been made clear to them that the county sheriff had no jurisdiction over events in Chickasaw Territory and wanted none, they made their way to the newspaper office, where they found Guy Potter's nose to be a bit redder and his eyes a bit more bloodshot.

"You exhumed him?" Potter asked incredulously. "You dug him up?" He listened carefully, his hand jerking as he made rapid notes. "Hold it, hold it," he said, looking up. "Are you trying to tell me that the man shot himself in the head, then in the side, and then tried to cut himself up with a blade?"

Potter had more questions. After the journalist was satisfied, Renno and Roy took their leave. There were still hours of daylight, and the road to Knoxville was a good one. Potter would print their description of Meriwether Lewis's wounds and mail a copy of the paper containing his story to Huntington Castle.

"Well, Renno," Roy said that night after they'd made camp twenty miles south of Nashville, "short of chasing Pernier all the way to Virginia, I reckon we've done all we can do. Leastwise we've cast more'n a little doubt on that suicide story."

The manitous, however, had decreed that there was more to be done.

Balmy days saw them through the low hills and into the thriving little city of Knoxville. They chased a few mice out of Roy's cabin, brushed away the spiders, swept out the worst of the accumulated dust, threw their blankets onto two beds, and slept like hibernating bears for twelve solid hours. They awoke to two mutually shared urges, one of which was quickly satisfied by a trip to the little house outside the big house. The other, hunger, sent them into the town to find an eatery. Roy saw mostly strange faces. Like all of the towns west of the mountains, Knoxville was growing. At the inn, where they each consumed four eggs along with a slab of salt-cured ham and chewy biscuits moistened by liberal applications of fresh-churned butter and topped with black sorghum, Roy was greeted by the chubby, smiling wife of the proprietor.

"Roy Johnson, you old grizzly bear, where in tarnation you been?"

"Off to see the big, wide world, Bertha," Roy said. "How you been?"

"Tolerable," big Bertha said. "Tolerable. Too bad 'bout that explorer feller, Lewis, ain't it?"

"Sure is," Roy agreed.

"Poor feller," Bertha said. "Out of his head. Killed himself so's that his enemies wouldn't have the pleasure."

Roy felt as if his ears were pointing. He glanced to his left to see that Renno was giving Bertha his full attention.

"That what the newspapers say?" Roy asked.

"You know the papers," Bertha said. "They don't say much that a blubbering two-year-old wouldn't say. No, I heard this from the horse's mouth, from a feller that was there."

"What was his name?" Roy asked.

"He was Mr. Lewis's man," Bertha said. "Name of Pernier." She nodded her head, pleased to be the center of attention. "Told me all about it, how Mr. Lewis said, 'Well, I have done the deed,' and all that. All the blood and all."

"Pernier was here?" Renno asked, his voice low but penetrating.

"Yep. Stayed right here in our place. Left no more'n an hour ago," Bertha said. "Said he had to get through the passes into North Carolina afore winter."

"How long did he stay here?" Renno asked.

"Ten, eleven days," Bertha said. "Spent most of his time in his room. Just him and a bottle of whiskey. Whooooeee! That man could drink."

"Spend a lot of money, did he?"

"Good whiskey don't come cheap," she said. "And Ida Red, she don't come cheap, either."

Roy raised an eyebrow in question.

"Girl from back East. Wears red all the time. Name's Ida, so's everybody calls her Ida Red."

"Working girl, huh?" Roy asked.

"Ordinarily we don't 'low goings-on like that," Bertha explained, "but my husband says that man Pernier's been through enough, what with having his master kill himself, owing him so much. We sorta looked the other way when Ida Red went up to his room."

"He said he was heading for North Carolina through the passes?" Roy asked.

"My husband asked him why he didn't go up through

Kentucky and the Cumberland Gap," Bertha said. "He said he'd always wanted to see the high mountains, and besides, he might not go all the way to Virginia."

They caught up with Pernier while the sun was no more than two hours past the zenith. The trail to the east was wide, rutted, rocky, and well traveled that near Knoxville. Pernier was riding at a walk, leading a packhorse. He wore a coonskin hat with the ringed tail of the late animal hanging down behind. His clothing was that of a gentleman, and he held a handsome rifle.

Renno, in the lead, was overtaking him at a trot. He motioned Roy to come alongside. "I'll ride past him and turn. You stay behind."

"At your service," Roy said, nodding.

Pernier turned when he heard the sound of hoof-beats.

"Afternoon," Renno called out.

Pernier nodded without speaking. His hand tightened on the rifle as Renno drew near and passed him on the left. Pernier reined in, thinking to let the other horseman pass, also. Instead, Roy pulled his horse to a stop just as Renno jerked his mount to a halt and whirled him around. A pistol was in his hand.

"Don't," Renno said coldly as Pernier started to lift his rifle.

"If you've picked me to rob," Pernier said with an accent that made it sound as if he said *peeked*, "you are going to be greatly disappointed."

"We have not come to rob you," Renno said in Spanish.

"What can I do for you, then?" Pernier answered in the same language.

"That is a handsome rifle," Renno said. He maneuvered his horse closer and took the weapon from Pernier's hand. The initials *M. L.* were engraved on a beautifully crafted silver plate on the stock.

"Governor Lewis's rifle?" Renno asked.

Pernier started visibly. "Who are you?"

"You didn't answer my question," Renno said.

"I have a few questions I'd like to ask him myself," Roy said. "How about we move off the road so that we won't be interrupted?"

Pernier rode between them as they moved into the trees and down a steep slope to the bank of a creek.

"I asked you if this is Meriwether Lewis's rifle."

"It is."

"Then you're his servant, Pernier."

"Yes." Pernier's eyes were shifting around quickly, furtively, as if he sought a source of help or hope. "Why do you ask?"

"How do you happen to have it?" Renno asked.

"When he killed himself, he owed me over three hundred dollars in back wages," Pernier said. "The man who was with us—"

"Neely?"

Pernier swallowed nervously and looked at them one at a time as if to memorize their faces. "Mr. Neely, yes. He said that I deserved something."

"You took Lewis's watch, too," Roy said.

"Yes."

"Where is it?"

"I sold it. I needed money."

"Neely gave you money."

"Fifteen dollars," Pernier said contemptuously.

"You sold Lewis's watch to pay for booze and a woman?" Roy asked.

"Why are you asking me these questions?" Pernier demanded with a show of bravado. But his hand holding the reins of his horse was shaking.

"Because we think you killed Lewis for the money he was carrying," Renno said.

"No! I—" He paused. "Is that what Neely told you?"

"What do you think he told us?" Renno asked.

"If he said I killed Mr. Lewis, then he lied," Pernier said. "He killed himself."

"How much money did you steal from him?" Roy asked.

"He had no money. He was broke. That was why we were going to Washington."

"Captain Russell said that he was carrying over a hundred dollars," Roy said. He turned to Renno. "Reckon we better turn out his pack and his pockets?"

Renno nodded.

"Wait!" Pernier said. "Wait! I'll show you."

"Easy," Renno warned as Pernier turned and put his hand into a rolled-up blanket behind the saddle.

"I'm just going to show you that I have only a few dollars left," Pernier said. His face was turned away from Renno. He jerked his hand out of the blanket roll and bent his head down to meet it so quickly that Renno had time only to tighten his finger on the trigger before a pistol blasted. Pernier's head jerked. Something damp and sticky spattered Renno's face. Pernier toppled from the saddle. The ball had entered his right temple and exited through the left.

There was nothing in Pernier's gear to give them any further inkling of his role in the death of Meriwether Lewis. They left him beside the creek and turned his horses loose on the trail. The animals began to walk slowly back toward Knoxville. Someone would find the corpse sooner or later. Neither Roy nor Renno could muster sympathy for the dead man, for to them his own suicide belied the claim that Meriwether Lewis had taken his own life.

Pernier had shot himself in the head in the state of Tennessee. Neither Renno nor Roy wanted to have to stay around and explain how it had happened. The white Indian took Meriwether Lewis's rifle, thinking at first that he would turn it over to either Lewis's mother or the administrator of the estate. He realized quickly, however, that to admit possession of Lewis's rifle and his pistols would require more explanation than he cared to make.

Winter swooped down from the northwest as they rode the familiar trail from Knoxville into the Cherokee Nation. Cold rain made traveling miserable, and after the rain stopped, the temperature dropped. In the still night the rain puddles became ice.

The pecan trees that Beth had had planted along the

lane that led to Huntington Castle were stark against a
slate sky. Fat cattle stood with their rumps turned to the
chill north wind.

But from the chimneys of the house rose separate
columns of smoke. There was smoke from the kitchen,
from the great room, from two upstairs bedrooms, and
from the small, cozy room where Renno had spent quiet
evenings with Beth. His heart pounded. He kicked his
horse into a trot, and the iron shoes clattered on the frozen ground.

One of the black workers, a former slave freed by
Beth, came running up from the quarters.

"Hidee, Mr. Renno," he said, beaming. "I takes de
hosses."

"Thank you," Renno said, throwing himself off. He
ran up the steps, and then Beth was there, her flame hair
hanging loosely past her shoulders to cascade down behind and in front. She was wearing a woolen overdress in
winter wine to complement her hair. She met him at the
top of the steps.

"I was afraid I'd get here only to find that you were
still in North Carolina," he whispered, with his lips brushing hers.

"I'm here, darling," she said. "And I thank thee that
thou art well."

With a fire blazing in the big fireplace in the great
room, stories were exchanged. Rusog and Ena were there.
Rusog was the one-hundred-percent stoic. Renno felt that
Ena looked lonely with all of her chicks flown. He knew
how she felt. He was pleased that Beau was alive but
disappointed that Renna, Emily Elizabeth, and little
Louis had already accompanied the comte back to France.
Ena was not alone in missing her children, for El-i-chi
and Ah-wa-o were without their eldest son, Gao, and
Renno's second son, Ta-na, was away as well. Three-and-
a-half-year-old Ah-wen-ga, El-i-chi's only daughter, was
there to take bossy charge of Little Hawk and Naomi's
twins, Michael Soaring Hawk and Joseph Standing Bear.

Renno insisted on hearing an account of Little

Hawk's adventures first. He agreed with Little Hawk's heated statement that sooner or later the English would have to be taught a lesson. Renno and Roy alternated in telling of their trip to St. Louis, Chickasaw Bluffs, and Grinder's Stand. Beth and Naomi shuddered when Roy described in graphic detail the unique experience of digging up a dead man. With great interest El-i-chi and Rusog examined Lewis's beautifully crafted pistols and his fine rifle, while Renno and Roy ended their narrative with an account of what they interpreted to be Pernier's terminal admission of guilt.

"So you see," Renno concluded, "we are not in a position to return the weapons either to Mr. Lewis's family or to his executors. Neely said to me that he felt the pistols should be with someone who had been a friend of Mr. Lewis's. I think the same could be said of the rifle. I know one man who was with Lewis during the return portion of his great exploration. You, Os-sweh-ga-da-ah Ne-wa-ah, shall have them."

"So," Little Hawk said, taking the pistols to hold them almost reverently in his hands.

"We can never be sure that Pernier did actually kill Lewis," Roy said. "But I think we can prove to the world that he didn't shoot himself twice and then try to cut himself up. When the Nashville paper prints what we told Guy Potter about the knife wounds on Lewis's body, nobody will be able to believe it was suicide."

Roy accepted the offer of two rooms on the second floor. Each had a fireplace. One had comfortable chairs and a desk, the other a big, soft, warm bed. Roy said he'd see everyone again as soon as he was caught up on his sleep, but he was up and about shortly after sunrise, puttering around the house, coaxing snacks out of the tyrannical old black cook, Aunt Sarah, and wandering over to the village to talk with the senior warriors about the old days. He cleaned up Toshabe's longhouse and told El-i-chi that he should give it to a Seneca family; but no family needed a house badly enough to move into an old-fashioned longhouse with its drafts and chills and smoke.

More and more the Seneca were joining their Cherokee
neighbors in building log cabins in the manner of the
white man.

Renno was content. He was with the woman he
loved. He had his most excellent son with him, a beautiful
and gracious daughter-by-marriage, and two splendid
grandsons. The house was big and warm, and the smoke-
houses were full of hams and sides of beef. And a man
could still find deer sign within a day's hunt.

A Cherokee fur trader returning from Knoxville
brought mail a week before Christmas. There was a letter
from Renna. She and Beau had spent two weeks with
William and Estrella at Beaumont Manor before sailing
for France. A letter from Adan, in Wilmington, consisted
mostly of a financial report for Beth. The Huntington
Shipping Company was doing all right, considering the
restrictions on trade.

And there were several newspapers from Nashville.
Roy opened the package and began scanning pages while
Renno was listening to Beth read Renna's letter aloud.
Roy waited until she was finished.

"You might be mildly interested in this," Roy said,
handing Renno a note that had been attached to one of
the newspapers. The note was from Guy Potter. It said:

> My Friends, Renno and Roy,
>   When you read the story on page two you'll
> understand why I didn't print what you told me.
> I think that you, especially, Sachem, will agree
> with me that to do so would put a great man in a
> bad light.

Renno looked over Roy's shoulder to read the story.
Thomas Jefferson was quoted as saying that Meriwether
Lewis had shown signs of being unbalanced in certain
ways from the time of his youth. It was evident that Jefferson had accepted the suicide theory in its totality. His
statements gave the impression that he had personal
knowledge that Lewis was mentally disturbed even before
he left St. Lewis.

"Since when was Guy Potter appointed to worry so much about Thomas Jefferson's reputation that he's willing to ignore the truth?" Roy growled.

There was nothing in the papers about a body being found on the road east of Knoxville. There were editorials urging Washington to go to war against England. One editorial writer predicted that the war hawks would win big in the midyear congressional elections in the coming year. Aside from the article quoting Jefferson's opinion of Lewis's mental condition at the time of his death, there was no other mention of the tragedy. Death was a familiar visitor on the frontier, and in spite of Tennessee's progress, it was not far removed from the days when scalps were being taken by both sides in the old war between red and white.

"Maybe you ought to write to Jefferson," Roy said to Renno.

Renno shrugged.

"Just a little bit disappointed in him?" Roy asked.

"Perhaps it is best to let the matter die with Lewis," Renno said. "We know, you and I, that the man most likely to have killed him is dead. It's true that we don't know whether or not Pernier did it, or if he was alone in it if he was the murderer; but if he did act on orders from someone else, only God or the manitous could prove it."

"Maybe someday Potter will find the guts to print what we told him," Roy said.

"Perhaps," Renno said.

Naomi came in from the kitchen, bringing the smell of gingerbread with her.

"Anyone care for hot cake and coffee?" she asked.

"Don't stand betwixt me and the kitchen, girl," Roy said, coming to his feet. "You might get trampled."

Author's Note

On the evening of October 10, 1809, Meriwether
Lewis arrived at a crude travelers' rest on the
Natchez Trace known as Grinder's Stand, about seventy
miles southwest of Nashville. By morning he was dead.
With no admitted eyewitnesses, accounts of his death
are based largely on hearsay repetitions of the statements
of one person, Mrs. Robert Grinder, and to a lesser ex-
tent on the memory of a Negro slave who might not
have been present at all. Although Lewis was shot twice,
once in the forehead and once in the abdomen, and
according to some reports bore knife wounds on his
arms and legs, it was accepted without question for
decades that the great explorer had pursued his own death.

By involving Renno and Roy Johnson in a fictional
investigation of Lewis's death, this writer has sought to
point out inconsistencies in the original reports of what
occurred. Let it be noted that some liberty has been
taken with chronology in weaving the mystery of Gov-

ernor Lewis's death into a fictional story. Let it also be stated that no historical evidence implicates either General James Wilkinson or Territorial Secretary Frederick Bates in any real or imagined conspiracy to murder Lewis.

Those who perpetrated the theory that Lewis, in a fit of derangement and despondency, blew a chunk of bone out of his forehead with one shot, missed his heart with another, and then possibly tried to cut his veins with a razor or a knife include Thomas Jefferson himself. It was probably Jefferson's public pronouncement, more than anything else, that convinced the nation that Lewis's death was suicide.

Thomas Jefferson appointed Lewis governor of the Upper Louisiana Territory in March 1808. To the problems one could expect in the administration of such a vast frontier was added the enmity of the territory's secretary, Frederick Bates, who had been acting governor for two years before Lewis's appointment. Bates did not hide his contempt for Lewis and campaigned to have him removed from his position.

In the years following Lewis's death much was made of his financial troubles. However, while it is true that he borrowed money, upon his death his remaining estate was ample to satisfy all his obligations.

Some historians cite Lewis's correspondence during this period to substantiate the claim that he was unbalanced, basing their theory on first-draft copies in which Lewis crossed out phrases, left thoughts uncompleted, and, as did many men of his time, misspelled words. (Thomas Jefferson himself once stated that he had no respect for a man who could spell a word only one way.) But a careful examination of Lewis's preparations for the long, hazardous trip to Washington shows a man who was very much aware of his responsibilities. He made provisions for the handling of his financial affairs during his absence and in the event of his death and left his estate solvent.

In the final analysis there is but one source of contemporary, firsthand information about the events at Grinder's Stand: the letters of James Neely, who was not a witness to Lewis's death and was not even on the scene at the time. He was simply the only man to talk with Mrs. Grinder immediately afterward. With no formal investigation of the tragedy, the newspapers in Nashville and ultimately the country as a whole accepted Neely's hearsay account of Mrs. Grinder's tale of suicide without examining obvious contradictions in either her story or his.

Mrs. Grinder's version was recorded by others on four different occasions. Each version differs significantly from the rest. She told Neely—or so he said—that when she heard the shots she had Lewis's servants awakened and that he died a short time later. She told the next man who questioned her that Lewis came to the kitchen door begging for water and that she kept the door barred until morning. Years later she related that she opened the door to give him water.

We can never know whether Mrs. Grinder was a liar or just a simple, frightened woman, but we must question some of her statements. A year after Lewis's death she said that after the first shot she heard him fall to the floor and call out, "Oh Lord!"—from a cabin fifteen feet away and through two log walls. Later she added that he cried out, "Congress, sustain me!", a curious utterance from a wounded man.

She said variously that Lewis died quickly, that he lived until after sunup, that he died before she could get a doctor—the nearest doctor was in Nashville, seventy miles away—and, in her last reported version, that the servants found him in the woods and brought him to the cabin.

The claims that Lewis was mentally disturbed—made by the crew of a flatboat aboard which Lewis traveled and by Mrs. Grinder, among others—are contradictory. But for decades no one questioned the qualifications of riverboatmen and an unschooled frontier woman to diagnose mental illness.

It was left to Thomas Jefferson, who had not seen Lewis since September 1807, to make it semiofficial doctrine that the governor had killed himself in a fit of madness. In 1813 Jefferson wrote: "Governor Lewis had, from early life, been subject to hypochondriac affections. . . . During his Western expedition, the constant exertion, which required all the faculties of his body and mind, suspended those distressing affections; but after his establishment at St. Louis in sedentary occupations, they returned to him with redoubled vigor, and began seriously to alarm his friends. He was in a paroxysm of one of these, when his affairs rendered it necessary for him to go to Washington."

Contrast the above with Jefferson's earlier assessment of Lewis: "Of courage undaunted; possessing a firmness and perseverance of purpose which nothing but impossibilities could divert . . . careful . . . yet steady . . . honest . . . of sound understanding."

Among the inconsistencies in the Lewis story is the exact number of people who were present at Grinder's Stand. Also, Mrs. Grinder's statements differ markedly from those allegedly taken from the slave girl at a later date: One said Lewis was on the floor; the other said he was in his bed.

The purpose here is to show that there is considerable doubt regarding the generally accepted verdict of suicide. Those who want to delve deeper into the mystery will find that there is little easily available material and that most of it is mere speculation. Perhaps the most complete compendium of facts and opinions can be found in a privately published book by Vardis Fisher entitled *Suicide or Murder? The Strange Death of Governor Meriwether Lewis* (Denver: Alan Swallow, 1962).

This writer agrees with Dr. John Bakeless, who wrote in his account of the Lewis and Clark expedition: "He [Lewis] was certainly ill. He had had difficulties with Bates, a singularly irritating individual. His personal finances were in a bad way. He had been drinking. His reappointment was in doubt. His accounts were disputed by Washington auditors. But though the government's financial methods drive men to distraction, they rarely drive them to suicide. If they did, the streets of Washington would be littered with corpses."

From this great distance in time it must be concluded, it seems to this writer, that Meriwether Lewis was murdered for the money he was carrying. We agree with some who have written on the subject that Lewis's man, John Pernier, is the prime suspect. There are other possible explanations; Neely did, indeed, profit from Lewis's death, and Bates did become governor again for two years.

Meriwether Lewis's family, including his mother, never accepted the theory that his death was suicide. Pernier was considered the murderer by family members as late as 1933.

One melancholy aspect of the aftermath of Lewis's death was that even Thomas Jefferson laid a claim on his estate, for around one hundred dollars. In 1815 the estate was settled with a balance of $9.43.

THE WHITE INDIAN—BOOK XXVI
RED STICK
by Donald Clayton Porter

On November 16, 1811, the panther passes across the sky at midnight, exactly as foretold by Tecumseh. The great meteor is seen all the way from southern Canada to Florida, from New York to Missouri. The chiefs who have been entrusted with the prophecy anxiously await the next sign that will tell them to rise up in unison against the white enemy.

But before that sign comes, brother will turn against brother, cousin against cousin.

Tecumseh, furious at Governor William Henry Harrison for buying three million acres of Indian land, promises war if President Madison does not return it to the Indians.

Gao, son of El-i-chi and nephew of Renno, learns to hate the white man when he is unjustly accused of molesting a brutal soldier's Indian stepdaughter. Although his cousin Ta-na gets him released from jail, his desire for revenge is undiminished.

Meanwhile, Little Hawk is called into active duty by President Madison, but while he is away, his old enemy Calling Owl kidnaps his beloved wife, Naomi, and their twin sons. Eager to inflict a pain worse than death on Little Hawk, the demented Indian makes them suffer unbearable agony.

Everyone caught up in this period of violent change is astonished when, on December 16, 1811, forty thousand square miles of earth dance to the culmination of Tecumseh's prophecy. But it is too late—the dismantling of the Creek Nation is at hand.

Coming in late 1994 wherever Bantam Domain books are sold.

FROM THE PRODUCER OF WAGONS WEST
AND THE KENT FAMILY CHRONICLES COMES
A SWEEPING SAGA OF WAR AND HEROISM
AT THE BIRTH OF A NATION

THE WHITE INDIAN SERIES

The compelling story of America's birth and
the equally exciting adventures of an
English child raised as a Seneca.